Keep the Faith Pure

This is a work of fiction. Names, characters, and incidents are either the product of the author's imagination or used fictitiously. Any other resemblances to actual persons, either living or dead, business establishments, events or locales is entirely coincidental.

Cover based on design by

www.rrhaestudios.com

FIRST EDITION
ISBN-13: 978-0-9797036-2-1

Available at www.amazon.com

Also available in electronic Kindle format

Keep the Faith Pure

A Short Novel

By:

W. H. Short

2019

Dedication

To the Enemy

Without enemies to fight there would be no heroes. The only enemy powerful enough to challenge humans is another human. War and enemies brings out the worst and the best of what we are. No other creature can be so brutal yet be so compassionate – that seems to be one of the ironies of our existence. Maybe there is hope that someday we as a species can live without war, because when we live without war we become so productive and produce great wonders of art, music, and literature.

Acknowledgments

Each person in my family has affected some part of this book - thanks for putting up with my madness. Thanks to my mother for her support and encouragement. A special thanks to my wife Lorraine and daughters, Arlene & D.D., for extensive proof reading and editing this project; a very time consuming and enveloping effort. Also, thanks to Colonel Charles (Skip) Ryder III, USA (Ret) for his editing help. Each of them now owns a piece of this novel.

Thanks to all the sailors, divers, and submariners I have known and have sailed with. They have provided me with a treasure trove of sea stories and other lies to relate to my readers.

Thanks to Rene Rhae for the book cover concepts and space ship designs.

Table of Contents

Introduction to Keep the Faith Pure:

You are entering into a future or one scenario of possibility. In this story humans now have reached out and explored the planets of our solar system and some along with moons and asteroids are home to human settlements.

This is the 2nd story in the 'Keep' series. Book 'One', *Keep the Union Safe* begins with the surprise attack against the Solar Union forces on Freedom Settlement, Earth's Moon Luna, and the Union military forces, by the Pan Crimbian Empire who dominate Earth the third planet in the solar system. This story begins at the end of 2227 just before the Christmas - New Year's holiday season.

The people who now populate the Solar System of the star we call Sol are at war – an all-out war which started in May of 2227, when the Crimbian military launched a surprise and devastating attack against the Solar Union military. The losses by both military and civilians were immense. The Union settlements on Earth's moon Luna and the settlement in orbit known as Freedom were captured and occupied by the Crimbian military forces.

The Earth is still a home for humans, but the population of Earth's humans has been reduced to a number far less than that of the early 21st century. Most humans on Earth now live in the Southern Hemisphere. War, disease, religion, and human stupidity have contributed to this situation on Earth itself. World War III resulted in a vast nuclear exchange which made most of the Norther-Hemispheres of Earth uninhabitable. Then diseases raged, further reducing the Earth's population.

Meanwhile the people who went into space were left to fend for themselves without direct support from Earth. These people became independent in space to survive. This resulted in settlements scattered throughout the solar system. The spacers settled most of the planets and moons that can be lived on. Obviously, planets like Mercury, Venus, Jupiter, and Saturn are so inhospitable that they cannot be lived on; but any other rock is fair game.

At first all were small but some grew. The settlement on Mars split and grew larger, as did the settlement on Earth's moon now called Luna. Finally, came a time when all these settlements came together to form a Union. The Solar Union is a loose government of common purpose for all of the people settled in the solar system. By 2227 the population of humans has once again exceeded 7 billion about half of whom live on Earth. The rest are scattered throughout the solar system.

On Earth the nature of government changed. Concurrently, out of the ashes of many disasters rose a new religion called Crimbian. Over time the Pan Crimbian Empire became the dominant ruling government on Earth. Now the Solar Union in space and the Pan Crimbian Empire have grown apart and have little in common. One of the goals of the Pan Crimbian Empire is to convert all humans to one Faith. This has set the stage for a new struggle - control of the people who live in the solar system.

In this future there are no space aliens of another race of intelligent non-humans. Life beyond the planet Earth has never been discovered. The only life in the solar system is that which has been brought there by humans from Earth. Ships travel between planets in months and sometimes years to the outer planets. Ships built for long space voyages must spin on an axis to provide artificial gravity. These interplanetary space ships are huge by today's standards - some are several miles long. Looking at the space ships from a distance they resemble an oversized cigar. If you need to get from one ship to another you must get into a shuttle and make the trip through open space.

Many of the Union citizens came from the old United States and they never adopted the metric system which was later was termed as the SI system or International System of Units. They kept the old English system of inches, feet, and miles. They also kept the old method of time keeping on a twenty-four hour clock and calendar of 12 months, even though other planets have different rotational periods. Thus all times and dates in this narration are in keeping with official Solar Union times and dates as recorded in the Journal of Solar history. Times are listed in standard 24 hours military style on Greenwich Mean Time and on the Gregorian calendar. There is a future history time line listed as Appendix A. Other Appendixes list some of the details on ships, military ranks of the various Union armed forces and a list of characters in order of appearance.

In this world technology has evolved however people are still people. Humans are still the worst enemy of other humans. This is a story of war and the people who are forced by circumstances to be part of this war.

So, with these facts in mind please read on and enjoy this story.

W. H. Short

"Only two things are infinite the universe and human stupidity, and I'm not sure about the former." – *Albert Einstein*

Part 1 - Insurgency

On Sunday 6th of May 2227 the holy forces of the Pan Crimbian Empire launched an attack on the Solar Union. After years of raids and looting of the Planet Earth by the barbarian forces of the Solar Union, the Pan Crimbian Empire forced to defend their faith and strike out against oppression and domination. Carrying the banner of God, the faithful holy troops were able to occupy the massive Solar Union space station Freedom and Earth's moon, Luna. These initial attacks captured and destroyed many Union ships, but the Union was still strong. Union forces were able to decimate the great fleet that was sent on the holy mission - to strike at Mars and end Union domination for good. The Union forces were able to actually bomb Earth and inflict damage to the heart of the Crimbian Empire. Now the holly war goes into a new phase where the chosen must strike back to keep the faith pure.

Holy History of Pan Crimbian Empire, Vol XVII

Chapter 1-1
0415 Friday 21 December 2227
Luna Farside,
Pan Crimbian Empire Moon Fortress 4

Earney MacLean looked over the sights of the big gun. Everything was in place. He turned on his command communications network and gave the command, "Commence firing at will."

Immediately firing started from eight different directions. The guards in the enclosed sentry posts were killed immediately. Then the big guns were turned on the antenna arrays; in less than a minute the communications uplinks were destroyed. One fire team had been assigned to the bunker door. The suited figures could already be seen in front of the door. Suddenly an explosion fanned out from where the massive security doors use to be. The main assault force was up and running. The explosion caused immediate massive decompression of the entire complex - anyone not in a pressure suit would be dead in moments.

First squad went through the doors to the command and communications center. Second squad went to the berthing bunkers, while the third squad swept through the common areas; lounge, shops, labs and galley. This was a bloody business; the watch standers in suits were shot down and killed immediately.

Most of the Crimbian troopers were

caught in their bunks. They were in space bunks, which have a standard cocoon system installed that is designed to protect sleeping men from explosive decompression, however this protective system trapped most of the troopers for the first critical minutes of the battle. When the complex decompressed by the sudden loss of pressure the bunk cocoons automatically pressurized and contained the sleeping troopers. This design saves them from normal accidents, but in a surprise attack like this, it trapped them in their bunks out of reach of their weapons. When the second squad arrived the first of the Pan Crimbian troopers were breaking out of the bunk cocoons and were trying to get into their combat P-suits. The squad opened fire and killed everyone in the compartment.

Third squad had a hunt and seek job, shooting stragglers as they found them. Anyone that appeared to be alive was shot. Enemy Crimbian troopers who were out of P-suites were already lying on the deck dead or in pain from the decompression of the complex, already freezing, or suffocating in the lunar vacuum. But, orders were orders - there were to be no survivors. One man was found in the galley refrigerator praying; the seals on the refrigerator had protected him- a chattergun cut him in half. A suited Pan Crimbian trooper came out of a side room and shot one of the attackers, three others shot him.

It took less than five minutes from the first shot fired until the battle was over.

Earney MacLean walked in the front door and looked around. He was pleased, all he saw were bodies of enemy troops and a couple of Crimbian civilians. He was pleased to see that none of his Union fighters were lying there, although he already knew that one man was wounded. In fact, this operation was going too smoothly - this worried him. He looked back through the doors and the little mining hover carts were there. Earney stepped aside to let them come in.

The raiders already had their hands full of loot and as the carts pulled in they started dumping plunder on the carts. Earney went to the communications and command center. One of the specialists was already sweeping instruments over the equipment looking for bugs and hidden explosives that could be triggered by handling the equipment.

Earney looked at the young boy Alexander Savage. "What have we got?"

The freckle-faced boy of fifteen was beaming. "There's just a standard charge on the decoder. Everything else here is clean - no evidence of any other devices. You were right, a small base with no real military presence, so we have a trophy. This should be no real problem"

"Just be careful," Earney replied. He watched as the boy attached the plastic leads to several components on the back of the instrument. Earney had seen this method demonstrated in the lab but now an actual field application of the procedure sent chills up his spine. He knew it would take a few minutes for the boy to be ready.

Earney pitched in with the others working feverishly unplugging and removing all of the equipment from the room. Soon everything was gone except for the bodies, tables, chairs and the decoder bolted to the bulkhead. Earney motioned for everyone else to leave. If anything went wrong both Earney and the boy would be dead because the explosion of the detonation would take out the entire room.

"Go ahead, Alex," Earney encouraged while patting the boy on the shoulder.

He watched as the boy attached one final lead to a board on the back of the panel. He spoke softly to his computer. Earney couldn't hear what he was saying through the P-suits, but he could watch the display as the numbers spun around.

This was a typical Crimbian method of protecting this piece of vital equipment. If a service specialist wanted to work on the decoder then he would have to place the code into the machine to keep from blowing himself up. It was a built-in protection which Earney and his small band of fighters had found out the hard way - three others had already died trying to steal one of these decoder boxes.

One of the numbers stayed illuminated. A long minute passed as the others in the sequence clicked on one at a time. They were running out of time. Suddenly his command circuit comms came on as a familiar voice reported, "Skipper we are all loaded. Time's up in thirty seconds."

Earney made his decision instantly. "Move out!"

"But Earney..."

"But nothing!" Earney snapped back. This was no time for discussions. "Leave the last cart - we'll be right behind you."

"Yes Sir" came the reply of a voice that was not happy. Earney shook his head grimly. This group was composed of survivors and refugees. Only a few of them had any real military training. They were thinkers, but in times like this, thinking too much could get them killed. Right now discipline was needed. If things went wrong he wanted to get most of the group clear – and as soon as possible. Another number - they were making progress breaking the cypher code.

Earney turned his head in the helmet looking out through the door. They were moving out, following his order. He wondered, *how long before the enemy showed up.* He had figured that as soon as the attack began the defenders here would have hit their attack panic button. The nearest military strike force was over fifty miles away in this sector. He had calculated ten minutes to scramble the troops onto the response craft, then another ten minutes to fly to the base. So they had twenty minutes. He had cut the time off at fifteen minutes. He sneaked a look at his watch, it had already been eighteen minutes. They had four numbers and still four to go.

The long minutes passed as they stood there. He could see the boy sweating through his visor. The life support fan on his suit kicked on - so he was sweating too. The comm circuit crackled again. "We are at the cave. Leaving one squad here to cover your approach."

"Very well," Earney replied in a crisp, non-emotional voice.

Earney was no Marine, although recent events had thrust him into that role. By trade, up until recent months, he had been a Warrant Bos'n on a fleet combat exploration ship. An occupation he found both satisfying and rewarding. As a Chief Warrant in the Fleet he was assigned as the Senior Enlisted person aboard a ship. It was a good job. He worked directly for the Captain and First Officer and he basically ran the ship as far as routine matters were concerned. He made the watch lists, decided who did what and selected and led boarding parties and exploration teams. Yes, that had been a good job.

Then the war had come and he had been given a field promotion to Lieutenant and sent to school as a Cadet. Someone went through the records and discovered that they had a man available who had been on Luna before and was familiar with the Apollo Project. He had been pulled out of school - voluntarily, of course - and sent to the moon. Initially his assignment had been to collect intelligence, but when he had discovered there was a secret base and an almost complete project in place to develop a new weapon, he had been ordered to take action. Since he had been so successful in blowing up the base, Earney was now a brevet Major in the Marines and in command of the Lunar resistance forces.

Voila, the last number illumined and the face panel popped open. Earney looked at his watch - twenty-one minutes. The boy started to reach in but Earney stopped him, he didn't know why just a hunch. He eased the boy aside then peered into the box. The decoder was there but sitting beside it was a package of explosives. There was another timer on the package. The little clock showed elapsed time from the moment the front panel had been opened. There was a red button and a green button - 50 - 50 chance. Earney depressed the green button and the counter stopped.

"Okay kid, it's all yours."

The boy didn't even reply but went right to work pulling the decoder from the unit. As soon as the boy stepped away, Earney placed another charge into the box. It would take them a while to figure out if the box has been compromised. Out through the door and into the cart. Alex was cradling the decoder in his arms. Earney could see the

Pan Crimbian Viking assault craft settling down in the yard. *Time to go the other way.*

Earney drove the little mine cart like a mad man thorough the maze of corridors and passageways. The cart had originally been a mining cart used to carry ore or people out of the mines – now outfitted with a new engine the cart was capable of high speeds on the low gravity of the moon. He didn't have to watch the Viking to know what was happening. Troops armed with assault rifles were pouring from the ship and as soon as they saw the carnage left by Earney's team they would be out for blood. He looked quickly at the boy, just to be sure he was still there. Alex had grabbed the rail with one hand and still held the decoder with the other - there was a look of terrified determination on his face. Earney had been driving through the passageways at better than sixty miles per hour. He had been dodging and turning like steering like a fighter through asteroids. Yes, no doubt Earney was a skilled pilot.

As they came to the end of the passageway, they could see the big Mylar 4.5 reinforced plastic window pane at the end of the long hall. Alex was startled but kept quiet as Earney advance the throttle to full - Alex knew they couldn't break through. They would wreck and be killed. Earney pulled up the big chatter gun and started shooting as they flew down the passageway. Just as the cart reached the window the effects of the shooting splintered the window and the little cart sailed through. They were out in the open on the vast surface of Luna. There was a smaller Crimbian Recon Beta craft just sitting there. Not nearly as big a threat as the Viking, but as far as Earney and Alex were concerned it was bad enough. One man was out with a side panel open apparently working on the little Beta. Three suited figures tried to jump out. They didn't have their guns ready. That was all Earney needed.

He turned his little cart to the right and started shooting at the Beta troopers. The four troopers saw the threat too late as Earney slipped by and turned. He shot three as he passed then the chattergun went dry. The fourth man slipped behind the Beta, but was between the Beta and the wall of the tunnel - he was crushed when Earney smashed the side of the broken Beta with the cart into the wall of the tunnel.

Earney backed off, swung the little craft around and gunned the throttles full. They went flying up a canyon. Weaving around corners and into the deep canyons the little base was soon out of sight - there was no sign of pursuit. Earney grounded the little craft. "You okay Alex?"

"Yes, I'm fine. Why did we stop?"

"Listen Alex, this was a long gamble at best. Actually, I never really thought we would pull off getting the actual decoder." Earney reached behind into the cart and grabbed a duffel bag. He shook it open.

"Stick that thing in here, it too dangerous to leave in plain sight. Stand up." When the boy stood up Earney stood up too. He then stuffed the bag under the seat. "Listen to me carefully Alex - this thing is dangerous. It's like sleeping with a bomb under your bed and holding your finger on the switch - one sneeze or movement the wrong way and you're dead. The only chance for either of us to stay alive is if no one knows we have it."

"Okay," the Alex replied softly. It did not really make sense but he would go along for now. They sat back down and Earney lifted back off, within moments they were away flashing down the canyon.

Major Von Gibbons third order of the Royal Imperial Faithful walked through the door and was immediately nauseated at the carnage. Here was even more evidence of the barbaric nature of these spacers. They talk endlessly about freedom, yet they demonstrated no responsibility or duty to the rest of humanity. Not only had they looted the entire compound they had desecrated the dead, by leaving them where they had fallen. Not only that, someone had mocked the holy symbols of divinity hanging on the bulkhead. The picture of Ruffus hanging on the wall had been painted with a beard and glasses then the words '*drop dead Ruffo*' were printed below. *Such arrogance. The Major was wishing that he could get his hands on the perpetrator just for a few minutes.*

The Major was still angry as he walked

through the compound to the command center. The decoder box was still bolted to the bulkhead. Good he thought, they were learning. He had investigated the last such raid and had seen the results when the decoder box exploded after being tampered with. As he got closer he could see something was wrong; the front panel was loose. He opened it carefully and looked inside. He only had a moment to register surprise – the container that once held the decoder box exploded - vaporizing the Major, the entire room and then out through the front doors and engulfed the Viking. It was only a very little nuclear bomb - very crude, *but it did the job.*

Earney and Alex reached the mouth of the cave, where familiar faces greeted them. “Did you get it?” someone asked.

“No, we ran out of time, and the bad guys arrived - so we left them our present,” Earney responded.

The flash of light told them all what had just happened. *God, he thought – Having this decoder is bigger than the nuclear bomb we left. I only hope this thing is worth all the people who died getting it and all those who will die keeping it.*

****

Chapter 1-2
1940 Monday 24 December 2227
Royal Palace Pan Crimbian Empire
Africa, Earth

The attendants carried in Ruffus: Holy

Leader of the Crimbian Faith, Successor to the Oracle, Holder of the Holy Scepter, Proclaimed Ruler of Earth and the Solar System, and Supreme Commander of all Pan Crimbian Military. Ruffus was not a well man at the present time, so he was carried on a litter to the Pallets of Judgment. Even though Ruffus was not particularly a big man, it took four men to place him comfortably on the grand pillows in the middle of the pallet. Everyone worked carefully together as a team. Each of the big men working with Ruffus was a trained and skilled nurse. One - two -three -then they moved in professional unison until their leader was positioned carefully and not in any pain.

Ruffus had been injured two months ago when the barbaric Union forces had bombed Africa. There had never been any real thought that the wounds would be fatal, but they got infected in the beautiful tropical climate and the man had been sick and debilitated with fever. The real problem was that he had suffered injury to the spinal cord down low, so now his legs were numb and he was unable to walk. Further complicating the situation was the fact that the Royal surgeons had operated and now he had strange pains when he forced himself into certain positions. Needless to say Ruffus had become somewhat unpleasant to be around. Many of his closest advisors now came up with excuses whenever possible to stay away from him.

The attendants continued to fuss with him carefully until everything was just right. He was positioned carefully then draped to conceal the injuries and braces. Juice and water were by his hand along with his favorite sweets. Then the final touch - the lighting was adjusted so that Ruffus was bathed in royal radiance. This was how the faithful would see him, in all of the regal trappings - Ruffus would never allow himself to be seen in a power chair or on a litter. The people were not allowed to know of his injuries.

This room was the Grand Reception Room for conducting the business of state and for holy ceremonies. The room was over three hundred feet long, about fifty feet wide and opened up to a height of more than three stories. The walls were adorned with curtains and gold fixtures depicting the glory of Crimbian religion, and the floors were covered with thick, plush violet carpet. Columns lined the room supporting a balcony where more of the faithful could watch. Chairs were lined up in front of the columns - this is where the Crimbian Holy Priests would sit in formal ceremony. However, for tonight's use the room would be empty. Cameras would record the events for the people.

Once everything was set he was ready for the women. These were the Crimbian Holy Order of the Daughters. There were over three hundred in the Order. Their sole duty was to provide for the Holy Leader of the

Faith. Women of the faith were kept in their place, unlike the barbarians who actually took orders from women and treated them as equals. The Union even allowed women to command ships. That's why they were barbarians. They didn't understand the holy role of women in God's plan. In all formal ceremonies such as this Ruffus was surrounded with ten of the Daughters.

To be a Daughter of the order the woman had to be genetically pure and extremely beautiful. Complexions ranged from very dark to very fair - there were redheads, blondes and brunettes. One thing Ruffus insisted on was that they all had very prominent breasts. Most of the women were young, probably ranging in age from fifteen to twenty-five. Some of the women stayed in the order for years while others were gone within a couple of months. The reason for most losses was that women had a habit of becoming pregnant. Once that occurred a suitable marriage was arranged for the Daughter and the new royal child. Ruffus had long ago lost count of the number of descendants he has sired, but as the Holy Leader of the Faith it was his chosen duty by God to leave a progeny to perform God's work. This was another thing that angered him; in his present condition he was unable to perform his holy duties. However, he still slept with a woman for his nap and two in his bed each night.

As they came in, he looked each of them over carefully. As each one approached him he checked to be sure their make-up was just right. This had become a private ceremony between him and the women. Each of the women would come forward opening her robe so he could inspect her worthiness. He would then caress each to give a holy blessing - finally the royal kiss of approval - then the woman would pull the robe back up to the appropriate level and take her seat. When he was finished viewing the women, each took her proper position seated in a ring around him. Ruffus then depressed the call button to begin the evening's agenda. Now the priest technicians would begin recording the proceedings.

The formal announcer stepped forward into the view and announced, "Sky Marshal Custus sends his prayers and requests an audience with Ruffus Holder of the Holy Scepter."

Ruffus motioned with a sweep of his hand.

Grand General Holy Sky Marshall of Crimbian Abaama J. Custus entered wearing the full dress blue uniform of the Holy Space Force. Since they were on camera for the record Custus knelt and went through the formal prayer of acknowledgement. While this was going on Ruffus was thinking. "*Custus had been a disappointment to Ruffus, by allowing the bombing attack that had caused his injures. Of course on the other hand he had planned and executed the successful battles that had resulted in the acquisition of Earth's Moon Luna and the Giant Space Station, which had been called Freedom by the Spacers. Most of all after years of knowing the man. Ruffus knew that Custus was loyal only to the holy mission of Crimbian Empire.*

Custus then stood and offered a scroll to Ruffus. Naturally, in formal ceremonies there was no direct contact so this was the method for public consumption. The scroll was handed to the nearest Daughter who then crawled on her hands and knees to Ruffus and handed him the scroll. The document was carefully prepared and written in a gothic lettering that was almost unreadable. It was thick with many pages. But that didn't bother Ruffus, since he had been given the document to read that morning. He scanned it quickly in a pretense for the cameras.

"Very Well, Sky Marshal - You are given holy permission to begin this operation. Pray to God for guidance, so you can be successful in this venture."

"Thank you for your blessing," Custus replied bowing. "I am sure your approval is all that is needed for success."

That was that. Custus backed away from the pallet, came to attention, and saluted in the Pan Crimbian method of a clenched fist across the chest. He then turned and snapped his heels together in a loud clicking noise and paced to the double doors, which opened automatically to allow him to pass.

This endless procession of formal ceremony continued for the next hour and a half. Finally, the last visitor was gone. The royal clerk came forward so Ruffus could sign his approval of all matters that had been attended to. Ruffus motioned for the women to gather around and he gave each a royal hug and kissed them good night. Once the women were gone, he pressed the button for the royal nurses. They placed him in a power chair and he went directly to the Holy Mission Prayer Room. Again he was transferred to a pillow chair that had controls for Ruffus to operate all of the monitors and displays. Once the nurses were gone he was ready.

General Custus came in and knelt before Ruffus. "I have offered a prayer for your continued wisdom to lead us on this holy mission."

"Thank you for the blessing. However I am most displeased with the continued disturbances on the Moon from these barbarians. I have decided that it is time for the final phase to begin. All inhabitants of the Moon must be assimilated into the faith. You will direct your forces to crush all resistance so the holy ones can take up their work. I have directed the Grand Inquisitor to assign a team to this purpose. We must have order on the Moon."

"As you wish, but I will still need a couple of weeks to finish the military operations."

"Very well. Do not take too long, my

patience grows thin." Ruffus changed the subject, "Are we ready with the barbarian woman?"

"Yes, Holy One."

Custus left momentarily and returned with a woman. The woman was wearing the green uniform of the Solar Union Army. Ruffus noted that she had an officer's crest over her breast. He had been told she was a Colonel. He knew already that she was in her late thirties but she looked to be in the mid-twenties. She was not beautiful by Ruffus' standards, her build was athletic. She appeared to be in good physical condition considering what she had been through to find faith. She immediately dropped to her knees and crawled up to Ruffus. *Even though she was a barbarian, she had been instructed properly.*

He placed his hand on the back of her head and pronounced, "You have my blessing, daughter arise and speak your heart to your confessor and link to God. Now it is your duty to keep the faith pure."

"I have lived impure and without the word of God."

"Now you have purity of the blessings of God and the word of God. Do you understand what your holy mission is?"

"Oh yes, I am to return to the barbarians and report. So the Holy quest of Crimbian can continue until all throughout the Solar System have the word and blessings."

"You understand perfectly. Do you understand what will happen if you fail in your holy duties?"

"Yes, Holy One. I have been implanted with an explosive device which will go off if I fail God."

"That is correct. But what is important for you to understand is that no person actually controls your destiny, it is only between you and God. If you fail, God will know what is in your mind and heart and your life will end. Then your soul will wander endlessly because you will not be worthy of being in the presence of God."

She fell back to her knees crying, "Oh please, Holy One, pray that I will have the strength to carry out this holy mission."

Ruffus closed his eyes and drew the woman into his lap; he hugged her and silently prayed for her success. He then released her and she fell to the floor unconscious with emotion and awe of the supreme prayer. *Yes this one was ready - Ruffus knew.*

"Stand up Daughter," he commanded. Custus had to help her up - she was wobbly but finally she stood before him.

"What is your barbaric name, Daughter?"

She could not look him in the face; she looked down - *Ruffus approved.* She spoke softly, "Sara Lynn Samuels."

***

*****

Chapter 1-3
1820 Saturday 29 December 2227
CE-46 Galileo
Admiral's Quarters

When the door to the admiral's quarters opened, Warrant Arnold B. Jones stepped in. Jonesy was the only name used to refer to the man who was the admirals aide. He was a huge bull of a man who by his size alone dominated a room. He was six foot, six inches, massing more than 250 pounds of muscle, big boned yet graceful, and had wide blue eyes. His body was covered with freckles and flaming red hair.

The other impressive fact about the man was that he was the most decorated fleet spacer serving aboard *Galileo*. He had seen almost thirty years of rugged fleet service, authorized to wear two Golden Crosses of Valor, the Distinguished Service Cross, two Silver Valor Medals, three Bronze Commendation Medals, five Copper Achievement Medals, two Purple Hearts (for being wounded in the line of duty), four Exploration Mission medals; and the highest military honor possible in the Solar Union - the Medal of Honor.

Seated at the desk was Admiral Lorraine E. Wilson Commander of Fleet Task War Exploration Mission C (Charlie). She was a stark contrast to the big man. She had short hair, a dark complexion and gleaming green eyes from which shone extreme intelligence. The Admiral had an athletic body and was in excellent physical condition. She worked out daily at least one hour with Jonesy; and at least twice a week they worked out for over two and a half hours. Jonesy knew she was in good shape because he was exhausted at the end of a two hour session, while she was barely out of breath.

"Message from Headquarters," Jonesy remarked as he handed Lorraine the vellum. "I am sure you want to see this right away."

BEGIN TRANSMISSION

FROM: FLEET HEADQUARTERS MARS

TO: COMMANDER TASK FORCE CHARLIE

SUBJECT: FLEET PRIORITY ORDERS

IMMEDIATE PRIORITY TOP SECRET BLUE

INFO TO: COMMANDER CE-46 GALILEO

COMMANDER SECOND MARINE DIVISION

COMMANDER ST-19 GUARDIANT

ADMIRAL LORRAINE E. WILSON YOU HAVE BEEN OFFICIALLY APPROVED BY THE FIRST CITIZEN AS COMMANDER IN CHIEF, AS COMMANDING ADMIRAL OF THE WAR EXPLORATION TASK FORCE DESIGNATED CHARLIE. YOU WILL ASSEMBLE TWO SQUADRONS ONE OF FLEET COMBAT SHIPS AND ONE OF TRANSPORTS AND SUPPORT SHIPS.

YOU WILL EMBARK THE SECOND MARINE DIVISION UNDER THE COMMAND OF BRIGADIER STEVEN B. RIDGEWAY. COMMODORE ROBERT M. DOYLE WILL COMMAND THE EXPLORER CE-46 GALILEO AND SERVE AS FLAG CAPTAIN AND SECOND IN COMMAND. BRIGADIER RIDGEWAY WILL COMMAND THE INVASION FORCES. CAPTAIN DAVID S. SNICKER COMMANDING ST-19 GUARDIANT WILL COMMAND THE SUPPORT SQUADRON.

TASK FORCE CHARLIE MISSION IS TO INVADE AND CAPTURE THE UNION OUTPOST OF EROS NOW HELD BY THE PAN CRIMBIAN FORCES. EROS IS HIGHLY FORTIFIED. YOU CAN EXPECT HEAVY RESISTANCE. INTELLIGENCE REPORTS BELIEVE AN ENEMY FLEET OF THIRTY PLUS WARSHIPS ARE IN THE AREA, PREPARED TO RESIST INVASION AND ENGAGE YOUR FORCES.

THIS OPERATION IS NOW ON THE TIMETABLE PRESENTED AT CHIEF OF STAFF ADMIRAL WATSON'S CHARLIE BRIEFING. THE FIRST CITIZEN HAS MADE NO CHANGES TO THE BASIC PLAN. POUCH COURIER WILL BRING THE APPROVED DETAIL PLANS.

KEEP THE UNION SAFE

MARGARET G. O'BRIAN

FLEET ADMIRAL

END TRANSMISSION

Jonesy watched the Admiral as she read the orders. This was official - she was now the commander of the forces and would lead the invasion. This was quite a change. Only a few months ago they had been prisoners of war down on Earth, subjected to the cruelty of torture and inquisition. But that was nothing compared to what awaited her at home. She had been in command of the Explorer Magellan when the ship had been lost in battle. She had lived all the time in captivity knowing all that awaited her here at home was a general court martial. She had survived all that to be advanced to Admiral and now had been given the most prestigious command available in the Union Fleet.

He could still see the scars on her neck that would be with her for the rest of her live. He had the scars too - they had been shackled together for months. Jonesy was pleased that she had been selected for this job - this was a job that needed a warrior. Jonesy knew she was a warrior. He had served with her for many long months and had been in battles with her at his side. He could think of only one other that would be as good to have at your side in a fight – that was his friend Mike O'Brian. Admiral Lorraine Wilson was a superb fighter pilot with deadly skills proven in battle. The one thing about skills proved in battle was that those were the best - the ones not good enough died.

Lorraine looked up at Jonesy. "Well, I

guess this makes it official. When the courier gets here with the detailed plans bring them up."

"Yes, Ma'am," Jonesy replied. "One other thing. Commodore Doyle isn't aboard. Apparently he's still dirtside. I believe he intends to attend a New Year's party before returning. He wanted to be sure that you knew that he was taking a few days leave and does not intend to take command until next Friday."

"Oh, I think we can live for a week without Mr. Doyle- don't you? I would say that he certainly deserves some leave. In fact you should have taken some leave yourself."

Jonesy laughed. "Admiral, if I needed or wanted any leave you would already know about it. I'm where I belong, right here on a ship. Anyway, we both know why Commodore Doyle took a couple days off. It's plain as day when you see him and Commodore Norris together. Although, I don't think they realize it yet - it's coming. If I had someone like that I'd be dirtside too."

"Have you ever had someone, Jonesy?" she asked.

He suddenly realized if they had a normal aide to admiral relationship she would never have asked such a personal question of a subordinate, particularly someone of the other sex. But he realized it was different between him and her.

"You know, Ma'am, if you're going to ask questions like that on a Saturday night after working hours - the least you could do is offer me some of that good whiskey you keep and one of those nice cigars."

"Help yourself and you can fix me a drink too." She replied with a wave of her hand. "I'm sorry if I asked a sensitive question about your personal life. I certainly didn't mean to offend you."

"No offense taken. Anyway after everything we've been through together, you have more right than anyone to ask." Jonesy handed her the drink and took a sip of his own, then took a seat in the overstuffed chair next to her desk. She sipped her drink, kicked off her shoes and leaned back with her feet on the desk. She watched as he went through the procedure of cutting the end just right and then lighting the cigar. After a couple of puffs he started talking. "I was born somewhere in the asteroids - I certainly don't know on which one nor is it important. My father was a miner and we moved from strike to strike - that's just how miners lived. When I was seven my mother got sick and died – leaving Dad with five kids. We got along fine for a few years until Dad was killed in a mining accident. All of my brother and sisters went into an orphanage. One by one each of them were adopted out - guess I was too big. So at fifteen I went to work in the mines too."

Lorraine was watching the big man carefully. This was his life and if he had ever told anyone else this story, it had been a lot of years ago. He puffed some more before continuing.

"After four years of working in the mines, one of the old timers came up to me and said simply that I was wasting my life in there. I don't know why, but I knew he was right. There was a war going on then. Actually the Union was not even really involved - you know the Argentine conflict." Lorraine nodded her head yes not wanting to break the story line. "I drew my pay and hitched a ride all the way to Phobos where I enlisted. I didn't have the schooling to be a fleet specialist so I ended up in the Marines as a private. I went through basic training and was assigned to the First Marine Division being shipping out for duty on Luna. We made the crossing on one of the old Yankee class transports. Then I met a young girl on board; her name was Natasha Yacovich, from a fine old Russian family. It took over ninety days to make the crossing. We met every chance we could and finally we told her parents we wanted to get married. They seemed fine with the idea, but they knew I was heading into combat so they asked us to wait - we agreed."

He gulped another drink. "We landed unopposed on Luna in the Argentine sector on near side. They waited until we were all down and then attacked. It was a brutal night; I've read reports and books that call it a tactical victory. But I was there - we got our butts kicked."

"That's when you won the Medal of Honor?" Lorraine asked.

"Been peeking at my service record, Admiral?" He flipped off the ashes. "Well, of course you have. In your position you have to know what kind of baggage you're hauling around. I'll tell you the truth this one and only time about the Medal. But you got to promise to keep it between us."

"Okay," Lorraine agreed.

"It was day three after we fought out of a box. By now I'd come to realize what a mistake I made becoming a Marine, but I figured that I had to stay alive long enough to quit. We were planning to attack an enemy fortification. It was almost like in the vid shows. The Lieutenant had us set our watches. The plan was to attack at nineteen hundred hours. So I sat there with a big gun waiting - I was on the point. Meanwhile, the word had come down from the Commanding Admiral that we were about to attack a fortification of regiment strength with only one battalion. Well, that would have been crazy, so they told everyone except me that the attack was off. At nineteen hundred I jumped up and charged up the hill and slapped a haversack of L7 explosives on the front gate and I blew the place open. I was so juiced up that I still didn't realize that I was alone. The only thing I can figure is the sentries must have thought I was crazy and couldn't do any real damage. They did not shoot, so I did. I rushed through the gate to find a meeting or briefing going on in the middle of the area. The enemy Colonel had been showing slides and had all of his officer's right there. I was carrying one of the big over under scorpion guns - I just cut loose."

"It was about that time I realized I was all alone. I crapped in my suit. I shot at anything that moved until I ran out of energy pellets, and then I emptied all of the launchers. I didn't know what else to do so I kept running all the way across the compound, tossing grenades as I went. The fortress was built over an old mining complex - I kept running until I was lost in the mines."

"When the others saw me blow open the gate, everyone else followed me up the hill. Since, I had killed all of the senior officers just by sheer, stupid luck, the enemy was thrown into a panic. We won the battle. They found me the next morning and I got the Medal."

"What about your girl?" Lorraine prompted.

"While I was down being a dumb hero, that old *Yankee* was attacked and was lost with all hands."

****

Chapter 1-4
0910 Monday 31 December
Fleet Headquarters
Mars

General Nathan P. Graham stepped off

the elevator into the oversized hallway of the Fleet Admiral's office. He was dressed in the familiar red coat of a Fleet Marine. However, this Marine was special; Nathan was the Commandant of the Fleet Marine Force and General of all Marines in the Solar Union. He stepped out with a bold and forceful almost marching gait, his boots clicked on the hard marble floors. There was no slouch in his form even though his silver white hair showed his age. Officially he was listed as sixty-six but he knew his actual age was somewhere in the late seventies. He was a short man only about five-five, but he masse every bit of 210 at one-G. There might be a little of it that could be called fat - but it would be very little.

Nathan Graham had been a Marine since he was sixteen. No one had ever served as long. He wore every decoration possible on his uniform except the Medal of Honor - which was one he had never earned, nor did he have any desire to have one - since most Medals of Honor were given posthumously to the next of kin. People passing rendered salutes crisply then wondered what a Marine General was doing wondering around fleet headquarters without an aide. Nathan Graham had better things for his aide to do than follow him around all over the place.

Everything here was clean and gleaming. He knew that much of that was due to automation. These corridors were alive at night with little cleaning drones working away at the dirt and polishing everything in

can't carry you off today."

She chuckled. "I am sure Carol would still have something to say about that. Coffee? I presume that she is well?"

"Yes, she is well and sends her regards." Nathan motioned towards the coffee, "Please, if you don't mind."

Maggie was ready and quickly drew two cups. He sipped the coffee; she had programmed her coffee pot to put sugar in, exactly the way he liked it.

She had been a hard-nosed lieutenant and he had been the major commanding the onboard Marine Detachment. Yes, he remembered that voyage - *that was the first time Mike had saved his life.* Nathan had led a boarding party onto a transport suspected of smuggling. When the smugglers resisted - they overran the small team of Marines pinning Nathan in a corner. Mike had piloted them over and had been waiting on the shuttle. It looked like all was lost when Mike showed up and outflanked the smugglers.

Maggie had backed up Nathan then and had helped when he had been accused of having too few marines to control the situation. It was nice to be around old friends that he had served with, but he knew that behind the charm was a deadly purpose. He was curious to find out what it was. She motioned for him to take a seat.

"Nathan, we've been friends for a long

time and I've been going over your plans for the upcoming invasions. Overall I like them. Tactically they're sound. I have no complaints, nor do I intend to make any changes except some very minor ones."

"That's good to hear." Now he was lost and really wondering where she was going. She could've told him this with just a call or message.

"I noticed on the time table that you plan to command the Marines when we invade Luna."

Now he was really confused. "Yes, I thought it would be appropriate since all three divisions will be going in at the same time."

"I understand how you feel, but I have other concerns. If you were not in command who would you select?"

"Maggie, if you're going to relieve me as Commandant of the Marines I want to know on what grounds"?

"Relax, Nathan, you aren't going to be relieved, but I'm not going to allow you to command your forces in combat."

"For heaven sake - I've waited my whole life for something like this. We both know a military action of such magnitude will be a moment in history. Never before will all the Marines in the force ever been asked to make a single assault such as this one and it may never happen again. It's too important of an operation. It's certainly worthy of being commanded by the Commandant."

"Don't you think I know that? It will be more important for you to remain here with me. I brought you here today to brief you on a secret that is the most important secret of this war. Keeping this secret will make the difference between winning and losing this war. Don't you think that when we put together this armada that I will want to command it? But I won't."

"It's that important?"

"Yes. I believe that if you have this information you can save thousands of Marine lives."

Nathan shook his head and rubbed his eyes. He leaned forward with his head in his hands. *He had been trained his entire life to make these monumental decisions, never had one so affected his personal pride and honor. Any choice between himself and the well-being of his Marines was simple - the Marines always won.*

"George Evans," he replied.

"Who - what"- she was taken off guard by his reply. Now she realized what he meant. General George Evans was being recommended to lead the three divisions of Marine's in the upcoming offensive. "Thank you, Nathan."

She got up and reached over to her desk and took out a velum. Maggie handed it to Nathan. "Would you please sign this?"

SECURITY BRIEF ACKNOWLEDGMENT

I, GENERAL NATHAN P GRAHM, HAVING BEEN BRIEFED ON TOP SECRET VOODOO INFORMATION DO SWEAR THAT I WILL PROTECT ALL INFORMATION AND EQUIPMENT ASSOCIATED WITH THIS PROGRAM WITH MY LIFE. ANY BREACH OR VIOLATION OF THIS OATH CAN AND WILL RESULT IN PROSECUTION UNDER FLEET ADMIRALTY JUSTICE LAWS. MAXIMUM PENALTIES MAY INCLUDE LIFE IN SOLITARY CONFINEMENT OR EXECUTION.

__________ __________________ __________

SERV NUM SIGNATURE DATE

He signed and handed the sheet back to her. “Okay, what’s Voodoo?

“We’ve broken the Pan Crimbian codes at the first and second level, and there is a team working on the other levels as well. This information was the difference in both of the successful fleet battles we’ve had so far. Both Admirals Watson and Walker had the benefit of intelligence from this source. Between myself and the First Citizen we made the decision that anyone who knows about this will not be placed in harm’s way. If you are killed the secret is still safe, but if you are captured the knowledge can be extracted. I would rather that you make your decisions based on the knowledge of where the information comes from - I think you understand the total ramifications of this."

He nodded his head in agreement. "How many know about this?"

She was glad for a question such as this - he was now thinking about how important this was. "You are the twentieth on the list or twenty-two. There are now thirteen in the code breaking section, Mike, myself, Tom Watson and Samantha Norris here in headquarters; the First Citizen and his military aide Admiral Price. I've also been authorized to brief the Chief of Secret Service and the Chief of the Federal Police."

"Okay, I understand your situation now you have my full support."

"Thanks, Nathan. One other thing General Evans will not be in command of all of the Marines, you will. Tomorrow you will receive a message authorizing the formation of a fourth and fifth divisions. The Corps is going to double in size during the next six months." Maggie smiled in her little gremlin-like expression that Nathan had come to know so well over the years.

****

Chapter 1-5
2115 Monday 31 December 2227
Capital City
Mars

The doorman was ready; he had seen the two senior officers get out of the luxury auto-pilot ground vehicle. Both were

Commodores. He motioned for the headwaiter.

"Commodore Doyle, Commodore Norris your table is ready." The headwaiter greeted them with a big grin of welcome. "The rest of your party has already been seated."

The Commodore couple followed the waiter to the table. They were certainly a conspicuous pair even in a room full of service personnel. When they arrived at the table it was ringed with familiar faces. Doyle shook the man's hand and Samantha hugged and kissed the younger woman on the cheek before taking their seats facing the other couple.

The couple was Officer Cadet Charles and Lieutenant Dolores Mako. They were newlyweds and Dolores was already expecting. She was just now starting to show and it was apparent that she had modified her uniform, but she wouldn't be able to wear it much longer. They certainly made an unusual looking couple. He had a middle-aged professor look and she looked much younger than her age early twenties – more like father and daughter than a couple. At the present time Charlie was in Officer Candidate School and Dolores in her delicate condition was detached from regular duty and assigned as an instructor, but most of her time was spent working on her advanced studies.

Charlie started the conversation. "Skipper, when are you going to take over the *Galileo*?"

"Probably Friday or Saturday. There are still a couple of weeks' worth of work to do before she'll be ready for a shakedown cruise. Admiral Wilson is already aboard; she assures me she can handle any real problems until I get there."

Charlie was a Science Specialist and as far as Doyle was concerned, one of the best in the fleet. Charlie had served under Doyle for more than ten years making several long voyages. He knew that Charlie was going to make a great officer. In fact, he had recommended Charlie for OCS.

The waiter arrived bringing water and took their drink orders. Beer for Doyle, whisky for Samantha and Charlie and fruit punch for Dolores. Then he was gone.

"Charlie, I want you to know that I placed a request for you after you complete school, but I was told that you had already requested a new assignment," Doyle commented as a matter of fact.

Everyone was quiet around the table. Rob Doyle was the one person at the table without the special Voodoo clearance. It certainly was not something to be discussed casually at a social dinner, but Doyle did not know that Charlie and Dolores had actually met and fell in love while breaking one of Pan Crimbian codes. Charlie had discovered the key buried in a pile of trash and had brought it back to fleet headquarters where Samantha as the head of Intelligence Section had placed Charlie on the team.

Dolores was another story. She was a mathematical genius and supplied the part that Charlie lacked, the ability to decipher the endless mathematical possibilities. They were a natural team. He had an instinctive conceptual science view and she had the in-depth math aptitude. They were so opposite that they complemented one another perfectly. The Fleet Admiral had already grounded Charlie for the duration. *Charlie couldn't tell Doyle about this.*

"Skipper, you know how I feel about serving with you, but when I made that decision, you were off on the *Pegasus*. I had no idea that you would come back and get the *Galileo*."

"That's okay, I understand. Relax, I wasn't trying to recruit you."

Actually, that was somewhat of a little white lie -everyone at the table knew it. In the Union armed forces everyone was a volunteer. Assignments were offered and taken by the people who served. Orders for assignments could be refused, of course usually to the detriment of one's career. This made the Commanding Officers of any ship a recruiter; it was always an effort to fill out the manning of a vessel about to go out. The good commanders like Rob Doyle had no problems, but if the word got out that a captain was not a leader or endangered people unnecessarily then that captain would have a hard time finding a crew. This method served well to weed out the bad captains. All Commanding Officers were always looking for good people, especially someone who had just been given the command of an Explorer.

They were interrupted by the arrival of the drinks and ordering of meals. They were trying to get the orders in before the show started. The music was playing and there were couples dancing.

Charlie looked at Dolores. "Shall we dance before you get any fatter?"

Dolores looked at the other couple. "Oh, he's such a charmer," she mocked his comment concerning her condition. "Okay, let's go and find out if you really have two left feet." Off they went flowing with the music.

Doyle looked over at Samantha and patted her hand. "You know we have to talk before I leave."

"I know, let's just enjoy the evening."

Doyle couldn't explain why he enjoyed her company. It was just that he felt so relaxed around her. Since the war had started, everything had been on a tempo of go-go-go. Doyle had been in command of a small ship, a frigate named *Carthage*, on a voyage near Luna when the attacks began. *Carthage* came straggling back to Mars with other ships that had escaped from the initial attacks. On the way they found the wreckage of an ore freighter. Charlie figured out that a fleet of ships had been in the area and devised a method to follow the ion trails. Carthage followed the trail to Flora Industrial Complex. A Pan Crimbian squadron had already been there and had killed all of the defenders - another terrible loss for the Union. By the time Doyle and his ship *Carthage* arrived he enemy squadron had already departed. The enemy, however, had left a cruiser behind to finish off *Carthage*, or any Union ship that coming to check on Flora. Doyle and Charlie were here now, so needless to say no one in the enemy cruiser went home.

After that, Doyle was advanced to Commodore and was assigned to Fleet Headquarters. It was there that he met Samantha. He didn't stay long because he had come up with a hair-brained idea to bomb the Pan Crimbian homeland. So off he went. Now he was going out again. They had spent the last week together, going to museums, plays and visiting historical places. They both enjoyed the same things, but both were Commodores with command responsibilities.

Charlie and Dolores returned from the dance floor at the same time the meal arrived. As soon as everyone was served the lights dimmed and the show started. It was a running ballad of tunes and dancing which continued throughout the meal.

The show went on for over an hour. At the intermission both women got up and went to the ladies' room. A big advertising board was now displaying a countdown to the New Year.

"Charlie, could I ask a personal question?" Doyle asked.

"Sure, Skipper."

"What's it like being married after all the years we spent in deep space alone?"

"I don't really know how to explain it. I really enjoyed the life we had out there and I never knew that I was missing something. Now I can say I'm complete, because there is something more than just me. I guess the word might be fulfilled."

"Charlie, that must explain it well, because I understand perfectly."

The ladies came back and the dance music started again. Dolores grabbed Charlie's hand. "I want to dance some more. I'm getting fatter."

As they went off he chortled, "Yeah, you are fatter, but more beautiful all the time."

"Dance?" Doyle asked Samantha. He stood and motioned towards the dance floor.

"That's what we came for," she responded. Hand in hand away they went.

"You know I really enjoy your company," he murmured as she laid her head on his shoulder. "When this crazy war is over maybe we should get married."

Samantha kissed Doyle fiercely on the lips. They entered their own world as the countdown to the New Year boomed in the background.

****

Chapter 1-6
0335 Tuesday 1 January 2228
Aboard Raider Callie I
Underway Deep Space

Chief Exploration Specialist Jake Sutter was awake. He was having trouble sleeping, so he got up and wandered down to the galley. Coffee was always ready so he drew a cup and walked into the recreation lounge - he needed to find a good book. He was surprised to see Marine Fleet Sergeant Major Gus Collins seated in the lounge this early in the morning. They had been outbound on this ship for over a week. Gus waved to Jake so he went over and sat down with him.

"Acey - Deucy?" Jake though about it for a moment. *A game - why not?*

"Sure."

Gus reached into the locker behind him and pulled out a box. The checkers were just tossed into the box so he started fishing out fifteen of two different colors. Acey-Deucy is an old game that evolved into space from the old wet Navies on earth. It is a lot like backgammon, however, instead of starting with the stones in a pre-set position in Acey -Deucy you bring the stones on the board by the roll of the dice. The other difference is that whenever a one - two combination (ace - deuce) is rolled, the player gets a bonus of being able to take any combination of doubles he or she wants.

The tables had backgammon and checkerboards already imprinted into the pattern of the metal tabletops. The two men sat down and gathered their checkers. The checkers were slightly magnetized so they stuck lightly to the table. Rolling dice on a space ship was a different problem. Depending on the various conditions it was possible they could be trying to play in a no weight condition. So the dice were contained in a roller. This was a clear plastic box that also would stick to the table. The dice were magnetic also and clung to the bottom of the box. When the box was depressed a grid came up and tossed the dice around in the box, once released the grid went back down and the dice were attracted back to the bottom. Around the game went; the only sounds were the normal creaking of the ship and the popping of the dice roller.

Gus asked, “You going to give me some word on what we are going to be doing?”

“What have you been told?”

“Not much. Just that we are going to Luna, there will be guerrilla fighting and you’re in charge.”

“Well, I haven’t been told much more than that. Actually I’m not going to be in charge. There is already a fleet officer there named MacLean who is now officially a major in the Marines - he is in charge. The six fleet Specialists with me are mostly communications guys. You have the fighters. You're going to train the resistance volunteer fighters and lead them in battle."

"Well," Gus said with a shake of his head. "I figured it had to be something crappy. They spread it on thick before we left. Fighting with a bunch of amateurs - that's a good way to get killed."

****

Chapter 1-7
1805 Saturday 5 January 2228
Marine Barracks

Sergeant Donald P. Thompson stepped down from the transport bus stopped at a gate. The driver came back and opened up the storage area of the bus and took out his three bags and dropped them in the dust by the road. Quickly he closed up the back doors went back aboard and the bus was gone, leaving the Thompson standing in the road. He picked up his bags and walked over to the gate. There was a large sign hanging over the gate:

CAMP SIDNEY MARS

HOME OF FLEET 2ND MARINE DIVISION - THE FIGHTING DEVIL DOGS

THE DECENT INTO HADES IS MUCH THE SAME FROM WHEREVER WE START

- ANAXAGORAS (6 B.C.)

Don walked up the gate and read directions posted at the gate:

1. All Marines and some Fleet personnel Welcome.

2. You must be in proper uniform when entering.
3. If you do not have any official business keep going down the road.
4. Pick up the handset and speak with the sentry. Be prepared to give your name, service number, rank, date of birth, and state your business.
5. If your answers are satisfactory someone will come for you. If you are denied access and attempt to enter, be advised the perimeter wire is electrified, mines are set in the first 100 yards, roving sentries carry live ammunition and patrol dogs are out roaming. Any trespasser's family will be billed for the funeral.

He lifted the handset and the voice on the other end answered immediately. "Corporal of the Guard."

Don provided the requested information and inserted his orders chip in the slot. The corporal on the other end responded, "Sit tight, Sergeant, someone will be right there."

True to his word in less than two minutes a dust cloud could be seen coming towards the gate. It was a large Marine triphibian armored car; over thirty feet long designed to carry a full squad and all their gear. The car rolled up to the gate. Don was a little surprised to see there was a driver, a private. Most vehicles were controlled by a master computer. The private got out and unlocked the gate from the other side. By the time the private had returned, Don had already hoisted up his backpack and one of his bags; the private came up and grabbed his other bag before Don could.

"Got to get going. Major Markel wants to see you right away."

"Major Markel is?"

"Company Commander for Aster. Eleventh Infantry."

All of Don's bags were in the car. Both men got in the front, and the private accelerated immediately to over a hundred and fifty. The nice thing about these triphibians was that they had a smooth ride. There were no wheels the car rode on an energy wave. Don thought about it briefly trying to remember a presentation given to him a long time ago. The car sensed the type of matter all around it. Matter was like magnetism it could be attracted and repelled depending on the ion energy put out. The car's computer adjusted the output to repel the matter from the dirt of the planet, this lifted the car off the surface, another set of sensors sensed the dirt at one foot in height, the other set attracted to hold the distance at a foot. Then it sensed the atmosphere from behind and above the car and the dirt at an angle behind the car; these sensors pushed the car forward across the plains. There was no road and it was not needed because the car never actually came in contact with the ground unless it was stopped. Friction was reduced to almost zero in the atmosphere because the sensors reached out and pushed the atmosphere back in a very aerodynamic shape. Of course the private driving the car scarcely knew that - all he cared about was it steered where he wanted to go, went forward when he accelerated, and stopped when he hit the brakes.

Once the private got the car settled down and in the groove, Don asked, "How come I'm not checking in with the duty officer?"

"You already did. You've been assigned to Aster Company."

Don was surprised, usually anyone arriving at a new station checked into the duty officer and then to personnel the next day. Then the Marine had time to see what billets was available and speak with others then decide what company to apply for. *Guess the war tended to change things*.

A range of rolling hills popped up on the horizon, the private changed course and headed for a specific landmark. As they got closer it was obvious that the hills were camouflage covering the communications network and temporary surface buildings. He slowed down, picked an opening and drove into the interior of the area. Now he barely crawled less than twenty. He pulled up to a gray tent structure.

"End of the line," he declared simply.

Don jumped out and grabbed his bags.

He tossed them beside the stairs at the entrance. The private was gone right away without a word. He knocked and found the Major seated inside working on a computer simulation battle.

Don was already somewhat irritated at the arrogance of this man. For some reason he had taken it on himself to decide where Don was to serve - of course that could be good or bad.

"Sergeant, good to see you. I trust you had a good trip." He extended his hand and Don shook it.

The two looked each other over. Both were in their late twenties and in excellent physical shape with regulation close cropped haircuts. But that's where the resemblance ended. Don was tall and thin, six four at about 190 (at 1 G weight); blond hair, blue eyes, and fair skin - Viking ancestry. The major was shorter and heavier five eleven, 210 (at 1 G), black curly hair, brown eyes and dark skin - his speech indicated American southern ancestry.

"I'll get right to it. We have been tasked with a major operation and we are short on sergeants with combat experience. Most of the Marines in the company are raw right out of boot training. It's going to take a lot of work and effort to get the men up and ready for a landing. The Colonel owes me a favor so I talked him into letting me have first go at you. You will have your pick of units; every unit is short and more than half the sergeants are breveted so you can go anywhere. I looked your record over and I like what I see. I want you to join 'A' company."

Don changed his mind a little, the man was not trying to capture him - he was just a go-getter trying to get a leg up on the other company commanders. "What are you working on?" Don asked looking at the game.

The Major stood aside and showed him the game. "I'm just about set up, this is the Battle of Saratoga - American Revolution. These are fun to run and figure out what events can happen to change the outcomes of the battles. This was a battle that the Americans should have never won, but they did and it became the turning point of the American Revolutionary War. It's kind of my hobby."

Don thought quickly - *a major who studies old battles and history as a hobby and on the ball enough to get him here first. Maybe this guy has something going for him.* He really did not want to be in the infantry. Don had always been a Ship Marine. But right now there were no openings so this had been his only option. 'Volunteer' was a loose term in the Marines; sure everyone was a volunteer, but once assigned you obeyed without question, the last order given. The Major seemed to have a good way about him. It didn't look so bad right now.

"Major, why don't you assign me a billet

for the night and let me get to know the guys, if things work out I'll make it final in a day or so – Okay?"

"Agreed." Major Markel was beaming.

****

Chapter 1-8
2225 Tuesday 8 January 2228
Tranquility Base
Far Side, Luna

Earney and his little team were watching as the little ship settled onto the surface of the moon and cut its power. There were some burn marks on the little ship but it really looked good to Earney. Although it looked from the outside like an old yacht or maybe a mining survey ship, *Geosearch* was actually outfitted with the most up-to-date equipment available. The crew was Ben and Freda Papers; a husband and wife team retired from fleet service.

They had brought Earney to Luna on this very ship only a few months ago. He had been a lone passenger and had come to know and really like them. The outer lock cycled open and a suited figure was in the lock. Earney stood up and started forward towards the ship. He could see the sensors extend from the ship and track his approach. He looked back to be sure the smaller suited figure was coming after him. Alex caught up and was alongside Earney by the time they reached the lock. He recognized the outline of Freda's familiar shape inside the suit helmet.

The lock was small so the three had to huddle together to get inside. Freda operated the controls and soon the inner hatch opened spilling them into the interior of the little ship. Forward they went into the main lounge.

“This had better be important to have me set down on this crummy rock,” Ben started out in his typical gruff greeting. He smiled when Earney lifted his visor and extended his hand. “Good to see you again, Bos’n.”

Earney popped his helmet off. Alex already had his off by now. Freda came over and hugged Earney. “We came to meet a Marine Major, didn’t think it was you,” she smiled.

Ben reached down and pulled up a plastic self-venting bottle of Tennessee Black Label whiskey which was currently produced on a little rock in the asteroids called Lynchburg, for whatever reason. Ben popped open the snap top and took a drink and passed the bottle to Earney. Earney took the bottle and had a sip. He started to hand the bottle back and Ben motioned for him to keep it. “Better tuck that away and hang on to it. I can always steal more, in fact I have a whole case. Take it and keep it for those cold and lonely nights.”

Earney grinned. This man was a scalawag; he would steal anything for the right price. But he was loyal to the Union without question.

“Guys, I have a job here that’s so

important that I cannot tell you how important it is."

"Oh, come on Earney, it's your old shipmates; you know we would never give up the ghost."

"Of course, I know that," Earney shot back. "That goes without saying. This is for your own safety. If anything goes wrong, if anyone suspects what you know, they would kill you for the information or to silence you."

"Damn," Ben commented. "You're real cheerful. Okay let's deal the cards."

"I need you to transport this boy and the package he is carrying to the Fleet Admiral. No one is to know you have him or the package. The boy is important but the package is even more important. If the boy is killed I expect you to deliver the package."

Earney handed Ben a vellum.

BEGIN TRANSMISSION

FROM: COMMANDER LUNA RESISTANCE FORCES

TO: FLEET ADMIRAL

SUBJECT: AUTHORIZATION OF PAYMENT

TOP SECRET RED

THIS IS AUTHORITY FOR BEN AND FREDA PAPERS CREW OF Y/S GEOSEARCH TO TRANSPORT UNION CITIZEN ALEXANDER D. SAVAGE TO FLEET HEADQUARTERS. PAYMENT

AUTHORIZED AS FOLLOWS:

ONE MILLION DOLLARS.

FULL TITLE OF VESSEL GEOSEARCH.

RELEASE FROM ALL PREVIOUS AGREEMENTS WITH FLEET AUTHORITIES.

HONORABLE RETIREMENT AT HALF PAY AND BENEFITS.

EARNEST K. MACLEAN

MAJOR FMF BREVETED

END TRANSMISSION

Ben looked up and handed the message to Freda. "You don't have the authority to authorize anything like this."

"If I don't, the Fleet Admiral does. And she'll honor this once she finds out what the boy has to say, and sees what he is carrying."

"Earney, I'm getting a bad feeling about this. If it were anyone else, I would throw you and that snot-nosed kid right off this ship. I have other assignments. How do you propose to get me past them?"

Earney persisted, "Show them this!"

BEGIN TRANSMISSION

FROM	COMMANDER LUNA RESISTANCE FORCES
TO	FLEET ADMIRAL
SUBJECT	AUTHORITY

TOP SECRET RED

THIS IS AUTHORITY FOR BEN AND FREDA PAPERS CREW OF Y/S GEOSEARCH TO TRANSPORT UNION CITIZEN ALEXANDER D. SAVAGE TO FLEET HEADQUARTERS. THIS IS A FLEET AAAA PRIORITY OPERATION AS AUTHORIZED BY FLEET DIRECTIVE 22AU27-11107TS.

EARNEST MACLEAN

MAJOR FMF BREVETED

END TRANSMISION

Ben sighed, and then accepted the second vellum. "I got a lot of equipment for you," he said. "In fact it's 20 crates."

"Good. Just drop it down. I've got two mine carts ready to take it with me."

Fifteen minutes later Earney dropped from the lock. He would miss the boy. But this was more important than himself, the boy or those wonderful people flying that ship. He walked back over the cave mouth and watched as the ship lifted then launched smoothly upward from the lunar surface. Earney repeated the little fleet prayer: '*God please don't let them screw this up.*'

Monty his civilian explorer and friend had already had loaded all the crates on the carts and was ready to go. They only had a hundred feet or so to get inside the tunnel opening they had come out of.

Earney turned to see Monty standing

there by the cart he was planning to drive. Monty plugged into Earney's suit directly. They were on radio silence routine. "Major, we've got big problems."

Earney turned up his volume to make sure he had heard right. "I've just lost the link to Apollo Base. Before the link dropped they reported that they were under attack by the Pannies. It's real bad, they told me that Doc Parks is dead."

Earney sat down on his cart as the full weight of the news hit him. Doc Parks had been his friend for more than twenty-five years - not only that, Earney was engaged to be married to Jill, Doc's granddaughter. *The loss of Apollo base would be devastating to the resistance. If Doc was dead what happened to Jill?*

****

"Those who can win a war well can rarely make a good peace and those who could make a good peace would never have won the war." *Winston Churchill*

Part 2 - Saipan

With the destruction of Flora Industrial Complex and damage to Castillo Complex by the Pan Crimbian Fleet forces, Ganymede settlement and base now became the principal industrial center in the Solar Union. Ship builder Harvey Salem has sworn to the First Citizen, his old school friend that he can build a new ship in two months in addition to refitting all damaged ships. The hiring of technicians presses entire families into the fury of this activity. Refugees from the Lunar Colonies and other displaced Union citizens find useful employment and safety in this remote outpost of the Union. Before the war there were only about thirty thousand in this settlement – now the population has swelled to more than a hundred and fifty thousand with more arriving every day. Admiral Juan V. Gonzales is the fleet procurement officer in charge of overseeing this massive undertaking.

Journal of Solar History

Chapter 2-1
0900 Saturday 12 January 2228
In Orbit around Ganymede
CC-144 Arial

Captain Jacqueline P. Thomas stood and looked out of the view port; as the little shuttle came around the edge of Ganymede she got her first glimpse of *Arial.* The ship was held by a series of cables extended to the work cradle. *Arial* is a fleet cruiser. She's a large cylinder over six thousand feet long with a diameter of over fifteen hundred feet containing over fifty decks or levels. Suited figures were still welding on the outer hull. There was a mess of cables and attachments stringing off the ship providing various services. However, to Jackie it was one of the most beautiful sights she had ever seen.

This was her ship. She looked it over with the keen eye of a professional spacer. A young female specialist was flying the shuttle. Jackie motioned to her. She leaned over so she could hear what Jackie had to say.

"Take a pass around the ship. I want a close look from the outside."

"I don't have clearance to go around."

"Get Clearance."

"Yes, Ma'am."

The specialist was speaking on the comms and then changed course and slowed down making a slow pass down one side and back up the other. Jackie looked carefully at the multiple arrays of missile tubes and row after row of turrets. This was the third of a new class of cruiser; it was not supposed to be space ready for at least two more years. They had pushed hard on the building. Jackie could look down the row, in orbit there were at least ten other ships started. Last night she had passed warehouse after warehouse where production was in full swing. Sub-assemblies were being constructed wherever there was space.

Arial is a warship with forty missile tubes forward, sixty aft and almost four hundred amidships. Almost two thousand cannons defended the hull. These were the new type of cannons where twenty could be controlled by a single team. She would carry a squadron of Fighter Shuttles and an additional squadron of Recon and Survey Shuttles. Over five hundred and eighty in the crew and fifty-seven officers, with an additional complement of over two hundred Marines commanded by a Colonel; the ship was an splendid war machine. Excitement jumped in her veins with just the thoughts of commanding this awesome fighting machine.

The last ship Jackie commanded was a little survey ship with only two missile tubes and four turrets. Jackie had brought little *Pigeon* back to Mars shot to pieces. Her thought crystallized, *by God they would have to have some serious crap to shoot this one to pieces.*

"Okay you can go ahead with your approach," Jackie informed the specialist.

"Yes, Ma'am."

The young woman maneuvered going around the bow. She spoke softly into the mic then she released the controls. A mooring umbilical came snaking out from the docking bay. Jackie did not have to see what was happening - she knew. The launch bay had taken over control of the approach. The little shuttle was vectoring on the launch bay's transponder beacon, just barely making headway.

A light came on, indicating that the combined umbilical and cable was connected - the pilot shut down all systems as directed by the shuttle bay. Now the shuttle was drawn into the bay. As the shuttle entered, a capture basket came up from the deck and down from the overhead, in one smooth motion the shuttle was moored in the big hangar. No one in their right mind would ever consider flying a shuttle into the hangar of a big ship under any normal conditions. This method of snagging with a cable and in-hauling with a winch had proven to be the only safe way to recover a shuttle.

A few mild bumps and the shuttle settled into the cradle. The specialist was up and at the door. A pressure seal extended and pressed firmly against the door. The green light came on indicating that there was now a breathable atmosphere of at least 14.65 PSI. When the door opened Jackie could see the familiar sight of her friend, Major Jane Polanski *Arial's* First Officer.

The two shook hands solemnly. It had been less than a month since they had seen each other. The two looked as different as night and day. Jane was very tall over six-foot and skinny. She had a fair complexion with black hair and brown eyes. Jackie was the older of the two by at least ten years; she had the beginning of age lines in her face. Jackie was much shorter - about five-five and some girth in the hips. Jackie had children who were now grown, but she had never regained her girlish figure. Her husband had been a fleet officer too; he had been lost on an exploration mission more than fifteen years ago. Jackie had reddish hair and very blue eyes, which had a tendency to become green when she was upset.

"Welcome aboard, Captain."

"Remember I'm still Jackie when we are alone. Where's Captain Porter?" Jackie asked referring to the Port Captain who she would relieve when she took command of Arial.

"In the Captain's quarters. He sends his respects and asks for a meeting at your earliest convince."

"Let's go!" Jackie replied, motioning for Jane to lead the way.

Jackie followed Jane through the winding passageways to the elevator, then down several decks to the proper level then out and across. Since the ship was in a no weight condition they had to hand-over-hand themselves down the passageways using the traveler line. Jackie could not help but think they needed to get some spin on the ship to build up some artificial gravity using centrifugal force. There were two reasons to build a ship in the shape of a cylinder - first it made the structure stronger than any other shape other than a complete sphere, and most importantly was to allow the ship to spin on its axis. Humans needed gravity - long term exposure to zero gravity caused health problems. Even though humans had adapted to living in space they still needed some gravity. Gravity provided body shape and resistance to muscles. Even people who work in zero gravity have houses that spin to give them the needed gravity.

"How long before we can spin the ship?" Jackie asked as they crawled along using fingers and boot toes to propel themselves forward.

"Hopefully, by tomorrow or the next day. Crews have been shifting all service connections to the bow or stern. Everybody is being centrifuged daily for at least an hour and I have implemented 3 hours of daily exercise."

They stopped. Jane knocked on the door with the word 'CAPTAIN' affixed to it then entered. This was the Captain's outer office; this room alone was larger than the entire bridge on her last ship. The captain's desk was at one end of the room, a conference table stuck out from the desk. The room was covered with plans and charts, boxes were clipped down all around - Captain Porter was packing. Captain Trevor Porter was seated in a power chair at the conference table going over some plans of the ship. He swung out and she could see that he had no legs and much of his body had atrophied from years of sitting in the chair. His skin was as dark as Jackie's was fair, and his hair was snow white. He offered his hand to Jackie.

"Glad to meet you Captain Thomas. I've heard a lot of good things about you. I'll be moving later today into the Captain's cabin behind the bridge, with your permission." He was referring to smaller cabin that allowed the captain on a large ship to sleep near the bridge control room. This was a carryover from the old navy tradition of the captains sea cabin.

Jackie took his hand and was surprised at the strength she felt. "Likewise, why don't you stay here until you're ready to move? I'll camp in the little cabin, most of my things won't be here until tomorrow anyway."

"Thanks," the man said looking somewhat relieved.

Jackie already knew a little about the man. He had been severely injured in a collision between two ships over twenty years ago. His spine had been severed so there was no possibility of grafting new legs on. He was an engineer by trade and a good fleet Captain so they had found a job he could do with his physical limitations. As a Port Captain he was paid three-fourths of a Captain's full salary and most of all he got to command ships in a limited fashion. A Port Captain was assigned to a ship to oversee and manage her construction or repair for the fleet. He had to deal with the hundreds of primary contractors and thousands of sub-contractors that were needed to assemble such a giant project. He coordinated the efforts of the primary ship superintendents from the various prime contractors.

"Have a seat, Captain." He dialed up a program on his computer and the opposing wall illuminated with a chart. Jackie belted herself in the seat and motioned for Jane to take a seat also. "This is the overall master schedule. As you can see we are two weeks behind on the latest revision and three years ahead on the original plan. I have good news; by tomorrow morning we will be spinning. The techs have solved the generator problems and they're closing the outer hull in that section right now."

He brought up an overlay schematic of the entire ship and pointed to the section. "I intend to have you relieve me in three days and then we'll commence the first space trials."

When the Commodore briefed her he was under the impression that it might be at least two or three weeks. Already this was going better than planned.

****

Chapter 2-2
0530 Sunday 13 January 2228
War Room Fleet Headquarters
Mars

Mike was seated at the Fleet Admiral's command console reading the morning messages and looking over the big board. This was the Fleet Admiral's War Room - the central hub of activity in fleet headquarters. The room in every way resembled the flag bridge of an Explorer or Cruiser. These were the two types of capital ships that normally carried a fleet or squadron commander. A flag bridge was outfitted with the latest tactical and communications equipment that enabled the Admiral or Commodore commanding the fleet to coordinate the activities of an entire cluster of ships operating together.

The war room was one step above the flagship command; it allowed monitoring and coordinating the efforts of an entire fleet. The room was composed of row after row of monitoring stations each with a specialist or officer seated in front of the console. The displays monitored various sectors and fleet activities. Each of the sectors channeled into the overall fleet status. The big board, which was an overlay of the solar system, updated every fifteen seconds to indicate the latest known position of all Union ships and known or suspected positions of enemy vessels. Lines of yellow indicated areas of space controlled by the enemy - at the present time there was a lot of yellow, since the Crimbians controlled most of the inner solar system. Ship positions were colored either blue or orange. Blue positions were based on solid information and reports, whereas orange indicated reports based on assumptions and analysis. All known or suspected enemy positions were shown in red. As encounters and incidents reports came in the board was being continuously updated.

There were display monitors all around the board, which showed views of various Union operations being conducted. On the left side was the Fleet Marine Force status and on the right was a list of all Fleet ships and the current status known. A Fleet Headquarters senior officer was always on duty in the room. The watch officer was assigned to monitor and make decisions of a routine nature just as if the Fleet Admiral was seated in the chair. Most decisions were of a routine nature that were covered in the standing regulations. When the decision required a significant command decision, the watch officer immediately called the Fleet Admiral and she would make the final decision.

War room watch was an eight-hour watch, which came up in rotation only about once a week, since there were so many senior officers on headquarters staff. To stand watch as the war room duty officer, the officer had to be a full Captain or above that had previously commanded a ship. Even the Fleet Admiral herself and her Chief of Staff took a turn at the position. In fact this morning the Chief of Staff was seated next to Mike in the Duty Officer's Chair. Admiral Thomas Watson had been composing an outgoing message when a young specialist arrived and handed him a vellum.

The specialists gave Mike a little wave. He smiled and waved back at his youngest daughter. She was looking more and more like her mother every day. One of the few pleasures he had serving at fleet headquarters was the daily contact he had with his daughter. All of the other children were grown and scattered all over the solar system.

Tom scanned the message quickly and passed it to Mike.

"I think the Fleet will want to see this right away."

Mike scanned it quickly - another setback for Union forces.

BEGIN TRANSMISSION

FROM COMMANDER LUNAR RESISTANCE FORCES

TO FLEET ADMIRAL

SUBJECT: ATTACK REPORT

TOP SECRET BLUE

ATTACK BY PAN CRIMBIAN FORCES AGAINST APOLLO BASE X 6JAN2228

2200 SUCCESSFUL. RESULTED IN SIGNIFICANT DEFEAT OF RESISTANCE FORCES. HUNDREDS KILLED, CAPTURED OR MISSING. HAVE RETREATED WITH ONE SMALL REMAINING GROUP INTO THE CAVES ON FARSIDE.

ESTABLISHING NEW BASE DESIGNATED PARKS. CURRENT EFFECTIVE FIGHTING FORCE NOW 28 (TWENTY-EIGHT).

IF YOU DECIDE TO ABORT DROP OF AUGMENT FORCE PLEASE ADVISE. IF YOU DROP AUGMENT FORCE NEW DROP ZONE WILL BE GRID RRX0004 BIX0123. ADVISE AS TO EXACT DROP TIME WE WILL PROVIDE SUPPORT AND COVER.

WE ARE RESOLVED TO CONTINUE THIS RESISTANCE

KEEP THE UNION SAFE

EARNEST MACLEAN

MAJOR FMF

END TRANSMISSION

Corporal Lucy O'Brian came around to the Fleet Admiral's chair where Mike was seated. "Daddy, can I talk with you?"

"Sure, what have you got in mind."

"Well, there's an opening for a Sergeant Communications specialist on the *Galileo.* I've applied for the job. But, the first officer will not allow me to take the position unless mother approves."

Mike chuckled to himself; he could easily understand the dilemma of both the girl and the first officer of *Galileo*. If he accepted Lucy and the Fleet Admiral was displeased things could be made unpleasant for him. Lucy on the other hand wanted to advance and go out on a ship. As much as Mike hated the thought of her going out, especially on the *Galileo*, he would have to talk with Maggie.

"Okay, I'll talk to her on your behalf. I can't promise anything. But, whatever decision is made you will live with and accept – agreed?"

It was obvious from her expression that she didn't like the terms, however the alternative was even less appealing to her. "All right, Daddy."

Mike leaned over and gave her a little peck on the cheek. "Run along. I have to take this message to you mother."

Lucy hugged the old man and was gone in an instant.

Mike said out loud, "And I thought they were trouble when they were toddlers."

Tom chuckled. "I've never married, so I can only envy your problems."

****

Chapter 2-3
0700 Monday 14 January 2228
Marine Barracks
Sidney Base, Mars

As Don walked into the squad bay, he

immediately got everyone's attention. The squad all knew he was coming. Some had been there for a full month just doing odd jobs like maintenance and setting up equipment. Today was the first day of training. From now on they were in isolation, a full company had been assembled, and most were unaware that within another week a full Marine Division would be together for the first time in more than ten years. Usually Marines were scattered in small groups all over a given sector. The only ones that were stationed in this desolate training base were the instructors and support battalion. There were eleven in the squad and Don would make twelve - a full squad.

"Fall in for inspections," he called out.

The eleven bodies scrambled from whatever position they had been in to attention standing in front of their individual Armored Pressure Suit - affectionately known in the Corp as an APS. A Marine without an APS was just not a Marine. A Marine's APS kept him or her alive. Don walked down the aisle looking over the group. His first impression was good, they all looked to be healthy and in good physical shape. They were a variety of complexions and sizes. Three were women and two were corporals. The rest were privates - all had proven themselves capable and were Marines, or they would not have been here at all.

"I'm Nighthawk. Other than the two

Corporals I know that all of you are fresh out of boot camp. We need to get to know each other, but we also have to become an effective fighting team in a short period of time. I just spent the last couple of days being briefed on the upcoming operation. We are going to drop in on a target and take it from space. As I walk down for inspection tell me your name and your Corp name."

Each member of the Marine Corps was given an official name by the Corps. This name was used primarily for communications, so that there could never be two Jones' or Don's talking at a given time on a circuit. But, over the years it became more than that. Some names were passed down within families from father to son or daughter. Names could not be reissued until the former member had died or given up the name from retirement. Other names such as East, Viper, or Orange were chiseled into the granite face of the Marine Memorial and would never be issued again.

He stood in front of the first Corporal.

"Corporal Lewis Brach - I'm Diver."

He looked the man over carefully checking his coverall uniform for proper insignias, all flaps were properly secured and boots were shined. Everything was as it should be. Next he stepped to the APS, he looked it over carefully ensuring it was clean and lubricated. Next he punched open the chest plate and depressed the computer menu display. The computer reported that all preventive maintenance service had been performed and the suit was in A-1 condition.

He stepped to the next man and repeated the process. Then each of them in turn introduced themselves as he went around the room inspecting each individual marine and APS.

“Corporal Mason Stevens - Falcon.”

“Private Jessie Trent - Bullfrog.”

“Private Lena Sampson - Flash.”

“Private Bond Noble - Wolf.”

“Private Alvin Duncan - Grit.”

“Private Festus O’Toole - Acid.”

“Private Susan Ann Weathers - Wasp.”

“Private Brent McKnight - Croaker.”

“Private Jerome Arken - Snowflake.”

“Private Solemn Carpenter - Pepper.”

Nighthawk spent about a thirty minutes going around the room. Most of the suits were brand new or freshly reconditioned. He found some preservative still clinging to the outside of one suit and another was reporting a non-vital circuit malfunction. But all in all, the squad and the APS’ seemed very ship shape. He checked the clock on the wall - it was almost time for the squad to meet the Gunny.

“All right in your suits and outside in formation in five minutes, ready for drill. Dismissed.” Everyone moved in a flurry of activity; Don had carefully gone over his suit and done all of the pre-operational checks before arriving this morning. In fact he had worn his suit when he came over from headquarters, it was certainly faster that way. His suit was hanging on the rail just outside of the squad bay; by the door of this temporary building. Don didn't waste one second. He bounded down the hall and onto the porch, with two steps up over the rail then down into the suit.

Each suit was tailored to fit a specific person, it took a specialist about three hours to make all of the adjustments on an armor suit so it contoured exactly to the body of the individual. The torso of an armored suit opened up with seams down the side, once your feet are planted in the boots and hands are in the gloves, the motion of leaning forward and bringing the arms together across the chest closes the torso. The helmet visor was an integral part of the neck of the suit. To close the helmet and pressurize the suit all one had to do was depress the chin button. This ensures the head was clear for the helmet to slide into place and seal the Marine in his suit.

He left the helmet open and was standing there, with his hands on his hips as each of the squad came stumbling out one at a time. Marines dressed in APS' stand about seven feet tall because the large power packs are located in the feet of the suit and they look somewhat like knights of old in armor. However, that is where the resemblance ended. A Marine Private in an APS would have been able to take on an entire company of old knights on their horses without even getting out of breath. He remembered reading about tanks that were used back on earth during World War II – a single marine or soldier could easily take on 10 of those old-fashioned tanks as well as the air ships that supported them.

"Helmets open," Nighthawk snapped. Two came out closed up. He looked down at his timer it was over five minutes when the last one was in line. "Let's get one thing straight - right now. When I say five minutes - I mean five minutes. Don't leave me standing around waiting for you all to get pretty again." Then he shouted at the top of his lungs, "Do you understand?"

"Yes, Sergeant," they shouted back in unison.

"We are going to platoon training. Attention!" There was a loud clanging sound as the metal boots of the suits snapped. Had they been in space of course no sound would be heard, but they were in the atmosphere of Mars. Don liked hearing the sound in unison. That gave him some reassurance that his marines were already trained in the basics.

"Right face," Another audible metallic crunch. "Forward March!" The squad stepped out together just as they should. He let them get together for about thirty feet then came the command, "Forward, double time - run!"

Immediately the pace increased as the group moved out. Marines in power suits do not run a normal pace. The immense weight of the suits in the lighter gravity of Mars kept then down on the surface. The suit had hydraulic controls, which amplify the normal motion of a person. Anyone wearing an APS was faster and stronger than a normal person. A Marine wearing an APS could easily grab and hug someone in a regular P-suit and crush them to death. Nighthawk looked down at his controls. They were doing forty miles per hour, a good pace for Marines in APS.

The APS was the invention that made men and women truly equal in combat. In the past women lacked the strength to be the equal to a man in combat, but with a suit all were equal in strength. Agility became more important than strength. Now it fell on the intelligence and daring of the individual. Marines were not stupid, if they were; they would not be able to qualify as Marines. For every ten applicants to the Corps only four would go to boot camp; out of the four only three would graduate. The Marines still considered themselves the elite fighting force of the Solar Union. The fact was that many of the Marine dropouts eventually became Army Troopers or military support technicians, but not Marines.

The organization of basic marines builds on sets of three. A basic fire team is 3 riflemen, usually privates. So Don's squad is three fire teams each led by a corporal and he himself would lead the third. Three squads would compose a platoon, three platoons would make a basic rifle company, however to make a full company there would be 3 additional platoons a heavy weapons platoon, a scout sniper platoon, and the headquarters service platoon. A full company is commanded by a Major, with an aide and an executive officer (2nd in command usually a captain or 1st lieutenant). Rifle squads are used for basic assault – they are the infantry. Heavy weapons are missiles, cannons, and other weapons used to breach. Scouts and snipers do what they have for centuries: scouts collect intelligence on the enemy and the snipers eliminate specific enemy targets. The support company are the cooks, medical, and logistics personnel needed to support operations.

Suddenly a group of buildings appeared on the horizon - Company Headquarters. Nighthawk stopped his squad just outside the perimeter and continued to march them into the area. Some squads were there already. Gunnery Sergeant James A. Travis was standing waiting, Don halted his marines at a pre-designated position for his squad. He halted his squad then placed them at parade rest. More and more squads continued to arrive. Soon all six platoons of 'A' company were in formation.

Gunny Travis walked up and down the ranks. When he spoke his voice boomed,

"Ladies and Gentlemen you are now 'A' Company of the Tenth Battalion of the Solar Union Fleet Marine Corps. As such you will conduct yourselves in the proud tradition that preceded you. I'm Cobra your platoon gunny and I'm also Major Markel's aide. We will all get to know each other very well in the upcoming weeks."

Major Markel came out of the Quonset hut, he was the only marine not in an APS. Gunnery Sergeant Travis shouted in a loud and commanding voice, "Attention!" Two hundred and twenty four men and women that composed 'A' Company snapped to.

Major Markel looked over the group. The Major picked up a hand mic that would transmit his words into the earphones of every marine standing before him. "At ease." He commanded. No one actually moved, but several could be seen slumping down in their suits. He continued, "I'm laying it out as much as I can. We are tasked in an upcoming operation. A combat operation. You will be told about the actual target once we are underway. Don't bother asking your squad or company sergeants, because as of now I am the only one who knows our actual objective. You duty now for the next few weeks is to train. I expect you to train hard. You must learn to fight as a cohesive unit. Welcome aboard. Gunny take over."

With that he walked back inside. Major Markel reflected to himself, *after over a month of planning briefings, training and movement of personnel he finally had a full company. Now he could begin the intensive training for the upcoming operation.* He glanced out the window at his marines. He wondered to himself, *how many would survive?*

****

Chapter 2-4
1610 Tuesday 15 January 2228
CE-46 Galileo, Wardroom
Mars

Combat Explorer *Galileo* was in orbit around Phobos base. The external cradle and rigging had been removed. Now the massive ship could be seen for the first time in months. *Galileo*, one of the largest and fastest ships in the Union fleet, is a massive ship is over five miles long and almost three quarter of a mile in diameter. Only seventy-one of these giant ships had ever been built. The cost was in the billions to build an explorer ship. *Galileo* was the only explorer in the inner solar system that was not old and decrepit. All the other explorers were in the outer regions. They were rushing back, but for now *Galileo* was the most modern of the big ships.

Galileo was now in the final phase of being fitted out for a space voyage. The ship was lying in orbit off the larger of the Martian Moons Phobos. The ship was lit up on the outside with portable lights to enable the civilian workers and technicians working outside on the hull to move about and work. The illumination could be seen from miles in space and even from the planet below with the naked eye. Yard tugs were attached to each end working together holding the ship in a stationary position in space.

Galileo had a crew of over two thousand enlisted fleet personal, more than two hundred officers including the flag staff, and a short battalion of Marines, almost three hundred, normally commanded by a Colonel.

Admiral Lorraine Wilson entered the wardroom followed by her aide Jonesy. Everyone in the room came to attention. This was the first meeting of her flag staff. Lorraine took a seat at the head of the table. All of the Warrants had made sure that the seating order was by seniority of officers going down the table. Commodore Doyle was seated on her left and a Marine Brigadier on her right. She did not know everyone at the table since this was an operation being thrown together at a fast pace.

"Welcome Ladies and Gentlemen, I am pleased that all of you could make it for this meeting. Some of you have only gotten your assignment with in the last few days. Let's go around the table, each of you in turn please introduce yourself." She looked at Doyle. "Please start, Commodore."

"Rob Doyle, I am the flag captain in command of *Galileo* and the combat ship task force."

Doyle was a middle-aged man who appeared to be still in robust health. His hair was gray but his temples were white.

He stood only 5'6" and had a stocky build. A fair complexion, green eyes and heavy lines were starting to build around his eyes. He had a large full mustache that was also showing streaks of gray.

The Marine Brigadier was next. Another middle-aged man in his fifties. His gray hair was cropped close in a regulation Marine haircut. He had brown eyes and a smile. He was taller than Doyle with a medium build. He had obviously been physically active his entire life. "Steve Ridgeway, I'll be commanding the Marine landing force."

Back across to the Captain seated next to Doyle was a handsome man in his forties he was tall well over six four and probably massed over two twenty earth weight. "Captain Snicker, Commanding the transport *Guardiant*, I'll be commanding the transports with General Ridgeway's Marines embarked."

Back across the table to the other Captain, "Bud Kadel, First Officer of *Galileo*."

Bud had served with Doyle previously. On their last mission he had been with Doyle when they had successfully conducted the first bombing mission on the Pan Crimbian homeland. Bud had been injured but he had healed and had been advanced to Captain. As a Major Bud had commanded a small picket while carrying the breveted rank of Jr. Captain. Doyle had also served with Bud earlier in their careers, so Doyle selected Bud to be his second in command.

Another Marine was seated next to Captain Snicker. A woman with fiery red hair and dark penetrating eyes, "Colonel Isabelle Davis. I'm in command of the Marine Detachment aboard *Galileo.*"

The little Major seated next to Captain Kadel spoke next. "Joe Banks, flag operations and communications officer. You all will be sending your reports to me during this operation."

Three Warrants were seated at the end of the table, Jonesy and Mike O'Brian were seated together the other one was a woman.

"O'Brian, Aide to Fleet Admiral."

"Jones, Aide to Admiral Wilson," holding up his hand.

"Patty Sue Smith. I am Commodore Doyle's new Aide and *Galileo's* Senior Warrant"

Everyone at the table knew who she was. Her father Admiral Bull Smith had been one of the most respected officers in the annals of fleet service, and until his death only a few months ago had been Fleet Admiral O'Brian's Chief of Staff. Patty Sue's mother had died when Patty was a young girl and she had enlisted long before her father had remarried Doctor Arlene Smith. She had never tried to use any of her perceived influence. She was too proud and over the years she had several disagreements with her father – so she would have never asked him for help.

Patty Sue was a strikingly good looking woman with high cheekbones and a well-defined shape. She was a weapons specialist who had enlisted right out of school and had immediately gone off on several long exploration voyages. On these voyages she had proved herself to be competent, intelligent and able. She had advanced steadily to the rank of Master Chief, which she had held for several years despite twice having been recommended for promotion to warrant. In the peacetime fleet there were simply no openings, and in the fleet if there was no billet there could be no promotion. The fact was there were very few billets for Warrants in the fleet. Most ships had only one, just as there is only one commanding officer. On an explorer there are only seven warrant billets.

When she found out that Doyle had been selected for command of the Galileo and that his Warrant Earney MacLean, who had served with him for so many years, had been advanced and re-assigned somewhere, she took a bold chance to get the job. She waited for Doyle, camped out by his door at the BOQ[1], and waited for him to return from the opera one night. Doyle did not know Patty from Adam nor even made the connection of her name to her famous father whom he had worked for briefly. So he

---

[1] BOQ – Basic Officers Quarters – evolved from old earth military term that originally stood for Bachelor Officers Quarters. Fleet Officers can rent quarters for temporary visits, the rooms are similar to hotel rooms.

found her waiting there with her record and asking for the job. At the time he was considering several others but her strong reasoning and record convinced him that she was the best person for the job. It was only after arriving on the ship that Jonesy told Doyle that she was Admiral Bull Smith's oldest daughter.

Lorraine looked around the table and smiled. She was sure that she had a core group that could handle any situation. "This operation against Eros is going to be called Pecan Pie. Not because it is going to be easy as pie; in fact from all the data we have it will be a tough nut to crack. Jonesy, will you please begin."

Jonesy stood and presented a series of slides and visual clips for the next hour. First he showed how the area had looked before the Pan Crimbian invasion - just a sleepy little outpost of less than a hundred military stationed there and a little more than three thousand civilians. Primarily Eros had been a fueling depot and a way station for ships to stop off. The only mineral of value that had been found on the rock was thorium, a low level radioactive ore – most of which had been mined out years ago. During the mining heyday a very nice space station and dock had been built. After the mining boom played out, the little community lived on at about one tenth of the size. They existed by location alone. Since it was one of the few rocks between the orbit of Earth and Mars in the solar system. As such it now took on strategic significance. If the Union could retake the little planetoid then they would have a base within striking distance of Earth. The Union would be in a position to send raids to Earth and Luna.

The Pan Crimbian forces had hit Eros less than two weeks after they took Luna and Freedom. A squadron of warships and two battalions of crack troops took less than one day to capture the outpost. Once the military forces had been defeated, the civilians surrendered. They had only a few recon photos and limited information about the area since the Crimbians had taken over. It appeared that the enemy had made a large effort to build the outpost into a full-scale military facility. The space station was being expanded and equipped with defensive weapons and the rock was being heavily fortified. There were at least fifteen ships in the area at all times.

The plan was fairly straight forward comprising of three phases. First, the fleet units would engage the ships and either kill, capture, or run them off from the area. Obviously capture would be preferable since there was more profit in that. Second, the Marines would invade the space stations and take them while the fleet forces concentrated on pounding the rock. The fleet ships had to keep enough bombardment with missiles and canons so the forces on the rock could not attack the Marines assaulting the space stations. The final phase would be a combined Marine and Fleet force to take the rock. Hopefully, the enemy would surrender before this phase started. But the Union forces were finding that since the Pan Crimbians were religiously motivated, they didn't surrender willingly – in fact they would rather die in battle than surrender. They had some Crimbian religious belief that if they died in battle they would go directly to heaven. But, if they surrendered, it was a sin that would require several lifetimes of isolation in purgatory or whatever they called purgatory.

When Jonesy finished speaking and the lights came up Lorraine looked around the room. "I don't really need to remind everyone here that the discussion of Pecan Pie is limited to this group. Mr. O' Brian do you have anything to add?"

Mike was brief and to the point. "Your people will receive a final briefing after departure. Even the fact that *Galileo* is operational again is being kept under wraps. If anyone in the press notices the ship is missing we intend to tell them that the ship is undergoing some tests. We intend to stick a lighted barge in place of the ship. The Marines involved have already been isolated and each ship will leave Mars sector separately and join up enroute. Admiral Wilson and the Fleet Admiral intend to keep this a low-key operation; if the enemy gets wind of this they may reinforce the objective and your chances of success will be greatly reduced."

****

Chapter 2-5
0900 Thursday 17 January 2228
Headquarters Pan Crimbian Moon Command

Sky Marshal General Custus was in a very good mood. The report in his hand indicated that the barbarian resistance on Luna had been broken. They had captured hundreds of Union military and civilian personnel who obviously had been responsible for most of the terrorist attacks that had been occurring in the past few months. A lot of good and faithful people had died from these barbaric acts. He sat in his chair waiting for his breakfast. A little bell rang and one of the women barbarian slaves appeared bringing his breakfast on a silver tray.

After the woman left he said his prayers and then asked for God's blessings for the Oracle and Ruffus, the two divine messengers of God who blessed the holy mission of the Pan Crimbian Holy Forces.

What brought Pan Crimbian to a position of world domination was the Oracle. Religion had always been mankind's greatest detriment and its greatest natural enhancement. Just as the world was emerging from the dark day of bitter strife, two things occurred which placed the Union and Pan Crimbian civilizations on their course of destiny. Everything evolved from something else. The Crimbian religion was a combination of Islam, Christianity and Old African native beliefs. They took much of their organization from Christianity, but the aggression and rightness of dying for God came from Islam and the old African native religions. Anyone of the faithful Crimbians who killed while on a holy mission (particularly an unbeliever or barbarian) was made stronger with God. Since Sky Marshal Custus had used the holy weapons many times he knew that he was in good graces with his God.

At the beginning of the twenty-first century there had been over six billion humans on the planet. But that was before the plagues brought on by immune system diseases. What started as one disease was finally discovered to be more than 20 different diseases. By the time the first barbarians landed on Mars more than a quarter of Earth's population had died. The barbarians were only interested in ravaging the gold and minerals from the new planet. While plagues raged on Mother Earth these people made themselves rich on material things. The disease had hit the hardest first in Africa then in Asia. Before World War III started more than half of the population of Africa had died.

Africa contained 20% of Earth's landmass, and at the turn of the 21st century had 20% of the world's population. Had not the plagues reduced the population, it would have been done by other means. Earth simply could not feed its population. The number of people increased beyond the carrying capacity of the planet, so they suffered wave after wave of terrible famines.

Finally, the Crimbian Priesthood took hold and regulated the population, so each of the continents controlled by the Pan Crimbian Empire was environmentally balanced. All of the non-believers and barbarians were systematically eliminated from the gene pool, leaving only the faithful and genetically faithful. The official population of Africa allowed today was only about 100,000 or roughly what it had been in 1840. Once the people died off, the animal population again expanded, reclaiming the wild natural space, which had been lost to the human population.

After the great loss of population, a new civilization evolved. The priests carefully selected the proper couples to have children. These children were stronger, smarter, healthier, and resistant to the diseases that had so ravaged the planet. With so many other parts of the world devastated, Africa became one of the few safe areas, a natural selection for the capital of a new civilization. People from Europe and Asia emigrated and intermarried with the native Africans. This also occurred in South America thus making the stigma of race less of a condition. The new condition of persecution and oppression became religion. The barbarians in space and in Australia shunned and belittled the pure of faith.

The Oracle was born sometime just after 2100. No one had heard of him until 2135. At that time he was just a little unknown evangelist preacher who traveled from town to village spreading the Word. His childhood was spent in India serving in some type of monastery of unknown religious persuasion. He was somewhere in the northern part of Africa in an area called Sudan when he was abducted by Moslems and imprisoned for three years in a dark dungeon. Whether he was released or escaped is uncertain, however six months after his release he started converting the unbelievers to the new faith. He was now the Oracle of God. The believers of the Oracle were so strong that it took less than seven years to convert the entire continent to Crimbian. It would have spread even faster had not the Moslems taken offense and started a religious war. A war which the Moslems lost, as they were pushed completely off the African continent. Still, even today they did not have any strong followings even in the Middle East where once Islam had reigned supreme. By 2143 the Pan Crimbians had sacked Jerusalem, Mecca, Baghdad, Tehran, and India. They had burned the cities to the ground and then systematically destroyed everything left. All that was left of a once great civilization that formed the civilizations of Islam who ruled the Middle East for centuries was now empty vast deserts. The Hindu's were converted to Crimbian or killed.

These barbarian spacers should have looked at the lessons of history more closely. Or they would never have treated the followers of Crimbian with such contempt. Now they were paying the price of their ignorance.

Custus finished his breakfast and called for the barbarian woman to remove his dishes. He was now ready to receive the Lunar Commander. He rang and General Weams entered. He saluted and knelt in prayer briefly, then stood. Weams was a very tall man standing over seven feet and weighing almost 300 on earth. He had a dark complexion with very curly light hair.

"I bid you welcome Sky Marshall," Weams bowed paying homage to his commander. "My prayers thanked God for your safe trip to this humble outpost."

Custus replied, "You have done well despite the problems of occupation. Come forward."

General Weams came to attention and stepped up directly in front of Custus. Custus took a box from his desk and took out a medal, which he hung around Weems' neck. It was the Royal Order of Holy Conquest. The highest military award that could be given to a military man in the Crimbian Empire. Weams was overwhelmed as Custus gave the blessing of the Oracle.

Custus continued, "Since you have been so successful you are being given a new holy mission. We are forming a new fleet from the captured enemy vessels. Most have been refitted. You will be going into deep space to stop any new advance attempts by the barbarians. You have already secured your place in heaven. Ruffus knows they will send their fleet from the outer reaches of the solar system to try to reconquer the Moon and Earth. So if you can stop the barbarians by crushing their outer system fleet, you will have a place beside the Oracle. The outpost of Eros will be the sector command center for your new efforts. Go with God"

"What will happen to my command here?"

"Now that this sector is fully under control it now becomes the mission of the High Priesthood. They have the holy mission to convert these barbarians to the Faith. The military presence does not require a General of your stature anymore."

****

Chapter 2-6
0430 Saturday 19 January 2228
Marine Barracks
Camp Sidney, Mars

Nighthawk was up and moving as soon as his bedside alarm sounded. His coffee maker was on automatic. He made a quick stop in the head[2] then he drew himself a cup. He stepped out on the squad bay porch. He liked the early morning just before sunrise. Don tried to give himself about ten minutes of quiet concentration. He was standing outside in only his shorts and tee shirt, it was a comfortable seventy eight degrees.

---

[2] Head: Old seafaring term for the water closet or toilet. Marines and Fleet personnel tend to use many of the old nautical terms as tradition.

Today's main training objective was target practice. Don always enjoyed going to the range. He was a fairly good shot. In-fact, all Marines had to qualify as a sharpshooter. But there were actually four levels of recognized proficiency: Sharpshooter, Marksman, Expert-Shooter, and Master-Shooter. Don had over seven years in the Corps and had spent much of his free time studying and practicing; last year he had finally achieved the rank of Master-shooter. Most Marines who worked at it might make Master after fifteen or twenty years; some would never make it in an entire career. That was the main factor in him making Sergeant as young as he was. As a Master he was automatically an instructor whenever they went to the range.

He had applied to become an Armory Sergeant, but the war had brought that to an end at least for now. Armory Sergeant was a prized position within the Marines. In an earlier century an Armory Sergeant would have been called a gunsmith. Don liked to work with guns of all types. His walls at home was covered with all kinds of guns, both real and pictures. He had attended the Basic Armory School for a year and had done well enough in the course to be recommended for advanced training. He thought he was on his way towards the goal, but then the war came.

Well, time to get the Marines moving. At five to five he started pounding on doors. Physical and team training was the responsibility of the squad sergeant, a responsibility that Don took very seriously. He was a strong believer in the old axiom *'the more you sweat in training the less you bleed in battle'*.

He had served with the platoon of Marines assigned to *Pegasus* on a secret raid to bomb the Pan Crimbian homeland. *Pegasus* was an old cruise ship that had been pressed into service. They had made a fast crossing to Earth and had managed to hide from the Pan Crimbian sensors by hiding in the tail of the Lorenzo comet. After the bombers had left, the Pan Crimbian war ships had showed up, they sent wave after wave of crack troops to board and take the space liner. What followed was a pitched battle that lasted more than seven hours. The Marines blocked all attempts to board. Finally, the enemy got a toehold; Don went with the colonel and sergeant major to lead a counter attack that failed. Both the colonel and sergeant major were killed and the enemy landed a troop shuttle in the bay.

The bombers returned lead by some crazy Commodore (who was now Admiral Wilson) who had escaped from the Pan Crimbians. She was flying a Crimbian War Bird and the enemy did not realize immediately that she was a threat. The bombers and the war bird cut the enemy troops on the outer hull to pieces. One of the bombers crashed right into the shuttle bay. Don had been able finally to get the upper hand with a lot of help from some kid gunner, Fleet Corporal

Ed Carter who went berserk killing everything in sight. The Pan Crimbian troops tried to retreat but Don and the kid had them in a crossfire. The First Citizen gave the Carter the Medal of Honor and Don got the Gold Cross of Valor. As far as Don was concerned the kid deserved two Medals of Honor and a million bucks too.

Don knew from that experience that combat was not to be taken lightly. Nothing would go as planned and his squad had to be ready for anything. No one was ever going to say that Don didn't give his Marines every precious minute of training time. He didn't know everything about the upcoming operation, but he knew about officers. They were training the Marines hard and were still being nice to them – this must be a real crappy operation where a lot of good Marines were going to die. *The nicer the officers were - the worse the job!* That was a military truth and had been for all time, even before the days of Alexander the Great.

The Marine squad bay in a barracks was laid out exactly like a marine squad bay on any large ship. One big room in the center with fourteen doors. Twelve sleeping quarters with a front and back door. A massive table with seating benches ran the length of the bay which could be lowered flush with the floor by a simple flip of a switch. Each Marines APS and primary weapon was mounted in a rack on either side of the door to his room. Each enlisted Marines room was small, just enough room for a bunk, a small desk, and a head. In fact, everything is arranged very compact and folded away when not in use. Everything had a stored position the bunk, desk, shower, toilet, and sink. The bunk had an entertainment center at the foot and the desk had a computer, although this computer is not necessarily for entertainment. The actual purpose was so the Marine could study – there was always something to study. Wall lockers for the Marine to store clothing or equipment took up every other bit of free space. Everything had a place. All in all, the little room provided a private, very condensed little living space.

Don didn't even get halfway down the row of doors before all of the squad was out and standing at attention; they were learning the ways of their new sergeant already. Everyone was dressed exactly as Don in shorts and T-shirt. Walking down the line, he stopped in front of Grit. His T-shirt was full of stab holes.

"Private, what happened to your shirt?"

"Bayonet qualification drill, sergeant."

Don shook his head. It was obvious the man was a greenhorn. Bayonet drill was a form of amusement. First you found someone very green then the troops would explain that a good marine should be able to use a bayonet even blindfolded. First, they would let him or her stab at the dummy when they could see. Then somehow they talked him into taking off his shirt. Then the victim was bind folded. His shirt was placed on the dummy. Now the person starts thrusting the bayonet while his shipmates cheered him on. The result was a shirt full of stab holes. Oh what humor – only in the Marines.

“Get a new shirt,” Don told him sharply.

“Yes, Sergeant,” came the reply.

Don would have to talk to the corporals about this, but later and privately. Don switched on some music. The soft sounds of another great Marine, John Philips Souza filled the room.

“Stretching exercise,” Nighthawk ordered.

This was just the beginning. A good five minutes of stretching then a period of warm up exercises and finally some lifting exercise. One limitation to working out on a planet rather than a ship was that on a ship the Marines can go outward toward the higher gravity decks and get a better workout. Don never let them stop for twenty minutes; they rested by changing the pace. This was only considered a warm-up period for the day.

“Okay, showers and formation in fifteen minutes.” Actually it took about seven minutes to shower, dry, get dressed and get the room squared away a room.[3] Don had

---

[3] Squared away: Marine slang for putting thing in order or stored properly and neatly. It can refer to a person also as opposed to being a foul up; he or she is a squared away Marine.

straightened and cleaned his room the night before and had his clean uniform coveralls hanging ready. He wasted no motions by showering, shaving, and brushing his teeth at the same time. A minute later he was dry and dressed. He checked the time seven minutes thirty seconds had passed. Five seconds later he was in his APS and walking out the door to the porch. Already about half of the squad was there. They were learning.

Don made it a point to assign those that arrived after him to extra details such as dumping trash, sweeping, etc., but the really crappy jobs such as cleaning out the garbage dumpster was reserved for anyone who got caught on inspection with something wrong. Rooms, APS's, and primary weapons were inspected daily. If any one of the three was not up to Marine regulation standards then there was grief for that Marine. Whenever everyone else had free time at the end of the day Don found something extra for that person to do. It didn't take long for the others in the squad to realize that the last person out or especially anyone late beyond the fifteen minutes would also catch some misery.

When Croaker complained the other day that there was not enough time allowed to square away the room, get cleaned up and ready for formation, Don's reply was the same that sergeants had used over the centuries of military training. 'I am sure the enemy will give you enough time. Adapt, prepare, accommodate - you have to be ready at all times.'

All this regimentation had a point. Every piece of equipment the Marine used had to be ready for use at all times. Whenever a weapon ran out of energy – it's reloaded immediately; there may not be time later. If something on an APS malfunctioned fix it immediately - because you wouldn't have time when the enemy attacked. All these routine things have to become second nature, a kind of built-in trained instinct, so the Marine was free to think about fighting and surviving in the most hostile conditions ever encountered by mankind – space.

****

Chapter 2-7
0200 Friday 25 January 2228
Ready Room – Raider
In orbit over Luna

The twelve were already dressed in their APS suits with helmet visors shut and sealed. Each man was strapped in a launch insertion rack. They were ready for the drop. Jake was worried. They were late and now they had been redirected to drop in a new zone. He was enclosed in the tight space and fastened to the rack. If anything happened now everyone would die fast. Jake and Gus had checked everyone then carefully checked each other. Finally the fleet Master Chief had strapped in Jake and Gus.

There was nothing new about troops

dropping. These type of drops went back to the twentieth century only then it was paratroopers dropping from airplanes – now troops dropped from space ships on the planets or any rock in the solar system. Instead of using parachutes (which they could if they were dropping onto a planet with an atmosphere) now each man used an individual power pack that was fastened around each APS. The IPP (Individual Power Pack) was now an integral part of the APS. Each person would be an individual pilot coming down on the lunar surface. This concept was as old as space flight itself. The first men who landed on the Moon and on Mars used this concept. The IPP would be jettisoned once they were down.

The pilot of the ship was the most important part of this operation. If he or she was off even a half of a degree one way or another the troops would end up in the wrong location. Drop type insertions were primarily Marine and Fleet exploration methods of landing on the surface of a new rock, but the military applications were obvious. Marines were trained to make drops using the IPP to land on rocks or the outer hull of ships. Once the Marines dropped on the surface of a rock or surface anywhere, their job was to establish a landing zone for shuttles to land with more troops. Establishing a LZ can mean a lot of tough fighting surrounded by an enemy until the landing shuttles arrive. This was one of the toughest military jobs in the Union. However, in this case it would hopefully be a little different. This should be a clandestine drop without the knowledge of the enemy.

Jake was strapped tight but he still felt the slamming of acceleration as the pilot maneuvered to get into position. This was such a terrifying feeling of entrapment many could not adapt – anyone who couldn't adapt would never become a Marine or fleet explorer specialist. The small raider was coming straight in trying to slip in between the enemy patrol ships and satellites on constant alert.

Jake's earphone crackled alive, the pilot was talking. "Marines stand by for insertion launch in one minute."

Slam they were hit with at least seven G's as the ship pulled up into launch position. Jake was thinking about the woman he had been with on the last night before they left Mars; he had a feeling that it would be long time before he would have another date again. "Fifteen seconds," the voice announced.

Jake knew that he and Gus would be the first ones out, one hand gripped the control throttle and the other gripped the weapon handle. He was ready to come out shooting.

They could hear the count down, "Ten, nine, eight, seven, six, five, four, three, two, one." At eight the hydraulic pressure went to 30,000 psi and then at three the pumps wound up to full RPM. Jake never heard zero because in the next instant he was punched out. He was in free space with the little ship above him and the moon landscape below.

There was no time for sightseeing. A quick scan of his display console indicated that the only contact was Gus and the raider. Two seconds later the next pair was launched. This was precision egg laying. Through the next ten seconds the pilot held his ship steady hovering over the same exact coordinates while compensating for the movement of the moon and his ship. He was literally shooting out men like bullets at a target. Jake could see the man had done his job exactly because they were all falling in the same trajectory toward the lunar surface below.

Now it was time to pay attention to where they were going. There was supposed to be a beacon it wasn't there. Jake called Gus – "Lightfoot, do you have any signal?"

"That's a negative, Laredo." Came the reply

"Crap, Crap." Jake thought to himself. When he looked up the *Raider* had already boosted and was fading from sight fast. Well, at least he was doing what he was supposed to; the longer a big object hung around the more likely someone might realize there were smaller objects. Even though the APS and IPPs were shielded from sensors one felt real exposed just hanging above the surface. They had been dropped at fifty miles and were already down to thirty miles. The idea was to get down fast but if

they had to maneuver it was easier to do while they were still fairly high up. Simple physics. If you have to change course one or two degrees at fifty miles it is better than ten or fifteen degrees at ten miles up. Jake made a decision. There was a bunch of hills off to one side. If there were any problems - better to have some cover. He took a bearing and it was fairly close to the grid coordinates. Suddenly there was the beacon.

"I got it," Gus called out in a calm voice.

"I'm on it too," Jake replied. Then he gave the order, "All Raiders steer towards the beacon. If you don't have the beacon stay with me or Lightfoot."

"Aye. Aye," came a group of voices.

Jake shifted frequencies "Red Dog this is Laredo. I hold your beacon. Do you copy."

Earney replied, "Come on in, Laredo, and bring your children. The coast is clear."

The drop was going well, Jake thought to himself.

Jake applied his thrusters easy to start slowing down. He took a moment to do another sensor sweep while they were still up in altitude. Actually it was Gus' job to keep watch while Jake was busy directing everyone down to the landing zone. But, another set of eyes never hurt. Jake was sure that Gus would be double checking his navigation.

At one mile up he started applying the

thruster steadily and slowed down until he was hanging about twenty feet off the surface. He looked up and Gus was hanging just above his left shoulder. A lone suited figure in an APS came out of the shadows. Jake concentrated of landing near the man in the APS suit below. Jake set down by Earney. Within thirty seconds the rest of the team was grounded and gathered around. Jake took a head count – *all present and accounted for.*

The last two down were carrying two boxes of delicate equipment. Other containers in unmanned drones had already settled into the lunar surface.

Earney looked around at the small group. They sure looked good after what his people had been through. "Hope you guys brought some beans. We are down to licking the cans and ration wrappers."

Jake replied, "I think we can do a little better than that. Should we get under cover?"

"You bet!" Earney replied.

Gus called out, "Alright let's get this stuff undercover. Leave nothing on the surface. Last man dust off all of our prints."

This order was necessary because anyone walking on Luna left foot prints in the dust. All foot prints must be removed to ensure they left no evidence that they had been here. In fact, someplace on the other side of the moon was a memorial park where Neil

Armstrong and Buzz Aldrin had walked on the moon for the first time. There footprints were still enshrined for all time.

****

Chapter 2-8
2235 Sunday 27 January
Pan Crimbian Warship Ark

Commander Zepherine Chin looked at the view screen carefully. There was a Union Frigate approaching. *Excellent,* He thought the barbarian was coming into the trap just like a fly into a spider web. Actually, the *Ark* had originally been a Union Frigate. It had been captured in the great holy battle of conquest last May. The barbarians had surrendered and then were taken to a Pan Crimbian reconditioning camp.

It took months to refit the ship, because the barbarians had set incendiary charges that destroyed most of the computers, communications, navigation and weapons systems. After months of reconditioning only one of the crew had converted to Crimbian religion and was of some assistance in teaching the barbaric systems to the Pan Crimbians. Of course that man had been left behind to teach other crews the barbarian ways.

The hatch opened and a Daughter of Crimbian entered - she was wearing the green uniform of a Union Officer. She certainly looked out of place here among the gleaming white, blue, and lavender uniforms of the faithful.

"You wished to see me Commander of the *Ark*?"

"Yes, Daughter." He indicated to the main viewscreen. "We have an enemy Frigate approaching."

She went forward to the screen and looked carefully at the controls. Then leaned over the display operator and verified his readings. She came back to the Commander.

"Do you have your missile ports open"?

"Yes of course. I intend to wait until the enemy ship is in point blank range and then shoot."

"Have they made any effort to communicate"?

"Of course, but we are maintaining silence." The commander was irritated at this woman questioning him.

"Are his missile ports open?" she asked.

"No."

She turned in contemplation. "If he follows procedure he will come in close and make a pass. He does not see us as a threat yet since he is looking at a Union frigate. Then he will lie off and send a shuttle to establish direct communications. By this time he will be suspicious so the element of surprise will be lost. The Union still uses light communication between ships. Why don't you let me use the blinking light to make some halting communications with him in plain English - with his guard down he will come in thinking we are badly damaged and in need of assistance. You can shoot and if he is not ready he cannot have time to shoot at this close distance. Just remove the interlocks that prevent missile detonation close to our ship."

The commander thought about this. He liked it. "Very well Daughter, go with the Radio Chief. He will assist you and keep me informed as to your progress."

They dropped down several decks to the 'A' deck, which was the no-weight deck on all Union Fleet ships. Then they went forward into the bow compartment. The bow compartment is a shuttle launch bay with an observation bubble going around the forward edge. Mounted on a revolving track is Navigation and Visual Communications. They pulled up onto the track and released it from the normal ship rotation. Both of them belted in she manned the big searchlight and the Radio Chief plugged into the communications network.

"Ready?" she asked. He nodded yes.

She studied the sector and pushed the controls until the track was maintaining position on the incoming ship. She waited several minutes until she could see the other Frigate in the visual sights clearly.

She started pulsing, 'A - A - A -A'. This was a series of dots and dashes much like the old Morse Code except with flashes of light using the standard Union Military

Code. She waited about thirty seconds then repeated. She knew it would take several minutes for the other ship to respond.

Finally a response. "Union CF- 81 *Saipan* identify yourself with Vessel ID & Pass code."

She tapped out the response "CF-73 *Hastings*. All communications out. Plague has killed most of the crew. Please do not fire on us - May Day - May Day."

The Radio Chief spoke for the first time, "The Commander is firing missiles."

Sara watched as the missiles streaked across the black space and impacted against the nearly motionless Frigate *Saipan*. It took less than two minutes for the missiles to reach and impact on *Saipan*. *She could only feel pity for the poor misguided souls on board. There was no doubt in her mind that the missiles would be fatal to the Union ship. It was unfortunate that they stumbled across their holy quest. She knew that the Faithful Commander of* Ark *would be proceeding immediately. He wouldn't look around for survivors. As a Holy Daughter Sara had a mission to fulfill, and Arks mission was to deliver Sara.*

****

Chapter 2-9
0300 Monday 28 January 2228
CF-81 Saipan
Location Unknown

The fires were finally out. Warrant Mickey K. Horton was dressed in a standard

P-suit; he was in the control room, or what was left of the control room. It was sickening the missiles that hit the ship must have contained some type of oxidizer, he was thinking. Nothing could have burned this hot without oxygen, maybe hydrogen peroxide. He started checking the suits still strapped in at their battle stations. They were all dead. With the Captain and First Officer dead he needed to find one of the officers still alive to take command.

Union Frigate *Saipan* had been underway alone for Mars from a Saturn moon. It had been a long voyage. They had departed on this voyage long before the May attacks against the Union. When the word had reached *Saipan* about the destruction of the Lunar Fleet Mickey's captain had been order to change course for Mars

Mickey was still trying to determine the ships condition. He had gone forward while his friend Abe was checking aft. Already he knew main and vital power were out – only about six hours of power left in the emergency batteries. There was oxygen in bank four; and the atmosphere, for now was contaminated and holding in the compartments that could still be pressurized.

Chief Abraham C. James came in and moved toward Mickey. “Mick, it's not good.” Abe said. “Is the Skipper dead?”

“Yep, along with the first officer there.” Mickey pointed to a still form. “No officers alive forward."

"All the officers in engineering are dead too," Abe replied. "All main and auxiliary engines are out. The young kid Drew thinks he can get number five Aux on the line. Of course there are a lot of life support equipment out. The hull is breached in at least three places. Be a while before we can spin the ship. They knew just where to hit us and do the most damage."

"Is anything working?" Mickey commented rhetorically.

"The forward shuttle and my wristwatch. Which says you're in command and time is running out!

"You're sure? No one senior to you Abe, besides me?"

"No one moving. That I've found."

"Okay, for now I'm in command and you're the First Officer and Engineer." Mickey said.

"Did you see anyone alive that can fly the shuttle, besides you and me?"

"Johnston's a sergeant pilot. He should be able to."

"All right, get everyone together in sick bay."

Mickey watched as the tall string bean of a man moved away. Abe was not dynamic but he was quiet and steady - a good man to have around in a tight spot. Mickey went to the chart rack and rummaged through it to find a vellum chart of this area. He went back to the chart table and pushed the body of the watch officer off the table. He spread it out to study. He knew approximately where they were from eight o'clock reports last night, somewhere between the orbits of Earth and Mars. Earth was at 220 degrees and Mars was at 98 degrees, his captain had plotted a course between the two running along the plane of the Mars orbit. They had been avoiding the Earth-Luna sector.

Right now *Saipan* had been on a heading for Mars generally and Mars was coming nearer every day. There was not much in this area. The asteroids were mostly out between Mars and Jupiter, but there were a few between Earth and Mars. But in years past a few asteroids had been moved in along or near the orbit of Mars.

Finally, he found what he was looking for. In the old days before the development of fusion reactors there had been a series of outposts. Some were constructed, some were asteroids that had been moved. These small stations had provided navigation beacons and military observatories. Astronomers had even used some as great observatories, while others were taken over by mining companies and used as supply stations. None had been manned in more than fifty years. Most were abandoned - relics of another age – and which were marked on charts so that ships could avoid them. Station P14F9 was nearby.

The survivors were all in sickbay when

Mickey arrived. Everyone was in a P-suit a red blinking light on the wall indicated the atmosphere in sickbay wasn't fit to breathe. He had already decided not to waste their time by going through the details of their grim situation. "As you all can see we are in one hell of a situation. I've assumed command. I'm determined to get all of you and this ship back to Mars. Sergeant Johnston will take two specialists and get underway with the shuttle. Once you've launched, stay connected to the tether umbilical. You'll be taking the ship in tow. We can't go very fast. There is an old station nearby. We will try and make it there. I'll be in auxiliary control. The rest of the able bodies will get as many compartments gas tight as possible."

One of the old cooks waived for attention. "We think the auxiliary section can be made gas tight. Except for the stern room A deck will hold."

Someone else chimed in, "The Bow compartment is still holding."

"Okay, let's get a couple of portable scrubbers up there and start removing the CO_2. Move all of the causalities alive up to the bow. Take everything the nurse wants. Take whatever we need to keep warm. You guys know what to do."

The room became a flurry of activity. It did not take long before the room was empty. With no spin on the ship the bodies were weightless. Every one formed a line along the 'A' deck. The injured in their suits were passed down the line in the same manner that the crew loaded groceries and ammunition.

Mickey went up to auxiliary control. This area had not sustained the severe damage that had occurred on the bridge. He decided to move the three bodies still strapped into their station out before going to work. It was not hard, but it was nasty leaving him nauseated. He sat down and started on the aux computer. He needed to get a navigation fix of some sort so he could figure out which way to go.

Mickey Horton had spent thirty-three years in fleet service; he was going to be fifty this year. A year ago he had been planning his retirement for this very month. Now this war had changed everyone's plans. He looked down at the screen of the plot table. With the power off he looked at his reflection. His hair was gray and the lines in his face were starting to show his age. His mustache covered the scar on his upper lip. Mickey was not tall just over five seven, but he was wide in the shoulders and massed almost two twenty, but he still carried himself like a younger man. He liked serving on small ships. In fact, he had never served on any cruiser or explorer – *Saipan* was the largest ship he had ever been on. He had never before been given any opportunity to command.

On advantage to serving on small ships you learned many other specialties that you might never be exposed to on a large ship. He knew weapons, engineering, auxiliary systems, but most of all he knew how to pilot and astro-navigation to a degree.

Mickey thought, *I always wanted to command. Just did not have the education or opportunity. The weight of responsibility makes one feel older. I must save the survivors."* Another grim thought occurred to him, *'Now I get the chance to command and I probably won't live long enough to even get paid for it.'*

****

****

"In order for a war to be just, three things are necessary. First the authority of the sovereign. Second a just cause. Thirdly, a rightful intention." *Thomas Aquinas*

Part 3 - Preparation

The Holy Priests had already started on the work but now a new wave of Priests arrived on the moon of Earth to begin the difficult work of converting the barbarians to the faith. They took over the old administration offices which was left of the old Union military complex at Tyco and also the deluxe suites in J City. The barbarians had evacuated Tyco bases using a scorched earth retreat – anything that could not be taken was destroyed, and if that was not enough they fired high definition missiles from the frigate Carthage *into the complex destroying large sections of the base. The Holy Forces destroyed the frigate* Carthage *months later when it again attempted to interfere with the holy quest. In the months following the occupation it had been a priority-building program to reconstruct domes and facilities over Tyco. The barbarians who could not be converted to the faith were being pressed into labor, as was only fitting since they had so utterly devastated the lunar landscape. The newly completed facility became the Holy Mission Headquarters where the grand inquisitor could perform his vital mission.*

Holy History of Crimbian, Vol VII

Chapter 3-1
0900 Wednesday 30 January 2228
CF-81 Saipan
Station P14P9 Asteroid 162.44/99

The little station looked bleak, less than a mile wide and almost three miles long. It had been tumbling along since the last men had visited almost nine years before. This particular station appeared to be more rock than metal. In fact, it was a converted, mined out asteroid that had been moved to this location. Whether the asteroids had been part of a planet that broke apart as some theorized or was just a collection of rubble that had failed to form a planet at the proper distance from the sun was still a matter if scientific inquiry. This particular rock however had contained a volcanic fuser. In that volcanic turbulence that had occurred eons in the distant past, the raw atoms of carbon had been compressed under tremendous pressure as only Mother Nature could; the result was a rich vein of the most pure diamonds ever found. After all of the diamonds had been mined out, the gutted rock had been moved and refitted to be a station. The last active use had been forty-two years ago.

Mickey led a boarding party dressed in APS's down to evaluate the situation. They found the little abandoned station loaded with potential.

The miners had drifted in following the vein, along the way it had been necessary to dig side caves which became the container for living quarters; ultimately even larger rooms had been dug for storage and processing of the diamonds. In its day, the operation had been a big one. Then they lost the vein. Some felt there were other pockets, so side shafts were dug to no avail. In sheer frustration, late one night one of the miners got drunk and planted explosives between the two larger side shafts. He caved in almost four hundred feet of shaft and made the main shaft unsafe. It became a losing operation without any money ore being produced. Thus it was decided to shut down the operation after more than twenty-five years.

An old man who couldn't give up talked the partners into letting him stay by himself and continue the search. They gave him six months and the use of a skip loader. He moved and sifted the rock left in the cavern. Because he was by himself, all he did was shove the rock out the mouth of the cave creating thousands of additional little asteroids that floated along with the main asteroid. Finally, even he gave up.

What was left was a hollowed out asteroid and a large pile of rubble drifting haphazardly all around the little rock. When the Union took over the rock, it had been located out near Jupiter in what is known as the Trojan area. A large ship just came in and hooked up to the little planetoid. The ship applied power along the line that the asteroid was traveling and soon they were on their way. It took more than a year for the relocation effort almost seventy-five years ago. Along the way everything was gutted and refitted to be an observation station. For over thirty years the little station was manned and a thriving community of over a hundred. But when the little station was finally shutdown anything useful at the time was stripped out and taken away. Now it was just a lifeless hulk spinning near the Mars orbit line yet in between Mars and Earth with its own orbit around the sun.

This is what greeted the weary crew of *Saipan* when they arrived. If *Saipan* could be placed into the cave and if the area could be pressurized then maybe the holes in the hull could be repaired. *A lot of ifs?*

The crew had actually accomplished a lot in a couple of days. They had been able to do a complete assessment of the damage to the ship. There were actually five major holes in the outer hull; the largest two were into the engineering compartment. One was big enough to drive a shuttle into. All long-range communications systems were totally destroyed. All but one of the main engines had extensive structural damage. They were being used as spare parts in an attempt to repair the remaining reactor and engine.

Most of the sensors were now junk. *Saipan* was cripple, blind, and deaf.

There were some positives in this bleak picture; they had managed to get one generator going so there was some power available. There were actually two banks of oxygen still intact, and the main hydraulic system had very little damage considering the extent of the damage. They had managed to use spare high pressure hoses to bypass around the damage. Surprisingly enough all but one of the remaining tactical missiles were fully functional. Still without power and navigation they were oversized hammers. With minimal amounts of power available they had managed to reboot the auxiliary computer, which allowed some of the heaters and scrubbers to run and really determine the extent of the damage.

Had there been any other option, such as another ship in the area it would have been best to abandon *Saipan*. Since there was no other option, it was best to stay with the ship; it seemed to be the only chance of survival. P-suits, escape pods, and shuttles only have a limited duration so when a spacer abandoned ship - they only have a finite time to be rescued. There had been no time to send a distress message.

Space is a harsh mistress - there is no air to breathe, no heat and a lot of radiation. Once exposed to the vacuum it takes only about a minute for the life to be sucked out of any living organism. Spacers stayed alive by technology, wrapped in pressure suits or encased in a ship. One small mistake is fatal. Spacers have an old saying, '*old black space forgives no errors and death never takes a holiday.*' Many a spacer have died in a suit after running out of oxygen, power for heat and CO_2 scrubbing, or just by having a seal leaking. Traveling from planet to planet is one thing but surviving the rigors of space is another.

Ships are layers and layers of technology that protect spacers from the outside. So now, with all of the layers removed it becomes a fight for survival. The ship that had fired on them and then left had violated one of the most sacred laws of space travel. Any ship that finds wreckage or distressed spacers must make all possible attempts to rescue. Even in war when the battle is finished, every attempt is made to pick up the survivors. Union ships that have engaged in battle send shuttles afterwards to pick up the survivors. That's what should have happened in this case.

If they got back, Mickey would report this high crime to the Space Admiralty Court. The Space Admiralty Court was a branch of the High Court; they even have authority over the military and civil courts. Even the Senate and Executive Council had to abide by their decisions. If the authorities could find the responsible Captain, he or she would be brought up on charges. Not for firing weapons into the ship and killing the crew - that's war. No, he would be charged for not attempting any rescue of the survivors. If found guilty in Admiralty court – it's a capital crime in the Union. The ultimate penalty is death, normally by being spaced.[4]

There were some very foggy theories on execution back in earlier civilizations on Earth. Some went from one extreme to the other. In Germany during World War II over six million were executed simply for being Jewish. Yet, the other extreme prevailed in the United States and most of Europe afterwards. For some strange reason they felt it was uncivilized to execute so no one was executed. The results were staggering crime rates and a society that lived in fear. For some reason they failed to realize the civilization that they created was a living thing also and in order for it to survive you had to eliminate the cancer. Because left untreated, it grows and destroys the entire civilization.

If a person by their individual actions against other citizens proves themselves unworthy of being part of this society then it is the duty of society to protect itself and eliminate the cancer. Of course, a civilization cannot go crazy killing everyone

---

[4] Spaced is one of the two acceptable forms of execution in the Union, the other being firing squad. A person who is spaced is simply locked out of a ship or shuttle without a Pressure Suit. Usually for formal executions a remote site is selected and the body is left. Execution is normally only used for crimes of murder, treason, forcible abduction, or abandonment. However, in some of the more remote frontier places vigilantes often use this practice to reduce crime or for crimes against women such as rape.

like the Germans did or fail to eliminate the members of society that would destroy it for whatever reasons. Mickey was already resolved; if he got through this, he would hunt down that rogue captain and drag him up before the Admiralty Court. Mickey was personally ready and able to carry out any execution sentence. *Elimination of someone like that would never cause a second of remorse on his conscious. Mickey had given all remorse to his crew while they stacked the bodies in one compartment.*

Now Mickey and Abe were measuring the old mining cave to see if there was sufficient room for *Saipan.* Mickey had been holding one end of the tape measure while Abe had been stretching the tape back from the entrance of the mine (all electronic measuring devices were out of commission). The ship itself was over six hundred feet long, but they would probably need at least a hundred feet more to give themselves some working room.

His earphones cracked with of voice of Abe, "Don't worry, Mickey, my captain. I'm back over eight hundred feet, and there is still plenty of room."

"So what are we going to about this entrance?" They had already measured the opening to the mine and it was only seventy-five feet across. That was a problem since Saipan was a hundred and eighty three feet at the widest diameter.

"You forgot I came from a mining family.

I found some FLSC[5] and we will just cut the door out a little larger. You can let go of the tape."

Another voice came on the line, "Skipper, you need to come in here. I found something."

Mickey worked his way back to where Abe was. Young Blake Sims had opened one of the sealed side tunnels. The place was filled with supply canisters: oxygen, food, water, even containers marked as explosives stacked neatly against the rock walls. They walked back more than a quarter of a mile before the tunnel ended.

Blake asked, "Why would they leave all these supplies?"

"Cheaper to leave it rather than haul it back somewhere," Abe retorted.

Mickey was delighted - this might be their salvation.

****

Chapter 3-2
2230 Saturday 2 February 2228
Yacht Geosearch
Venus Sector

Freda and Ben were jarred awake by the shuddering of the ship; something had hit

---

[5] FLSC - Old term for Flexible Linear Shape Charge - It's a high velocity explosive that looks like an angle iron piece of metal; but it can be bent and is used to cut precision openings. Back in the twentieth century when it was first developed they used petin nowadays it is more commonly produced with DXT double velocity thermite.

the hull outside. They had been sleeping; both were absolutely nude as was their practice over many years of marriage. They were in a long voyage mode and there was nothing (at least that's what they thought) around them. In fact, they'd had no contacts on the sensors in over two weeks. Space was a big place.

Both went through the motions of throwing on pants and a shirt. Ben managed to get out of their big bunk just ahead of her. He dove headfirst in the low weight conditions of the little ship towards the flight deck. Freda was right behind him. They could see a large ship through the forward viewport. All she could think about was why didn't the sensor alarms go off warning them of the contact. She grabbed the computer display and read.

FROM: COMMANDER PAN CRIMBAIN PATROL SHIP

TO: COMMANDER INTRUDER VESSEL INTO PAN CRIMBIAN SPACE

SUBJ: IDENTIFY

YOU ARE HEREBY DIRECTED TO IDENTIFY YOUR CRAFT AND STAND BY FOR BOARDING BY HOLY FORCES.

****

FROM: COMMANDER PAN CRIMBIAN PATROL SHIP

TO: COMMANDER INTRUDER INTO PAN CRIMBIAN SPACE

SUBJ: IDENTIFY

YOU ARE HEREBY DIRECTED TO IDENTIFY YOU CRAFT AND STAND BY FOR BOARDING BY HOLY FORCES. A WARNING SHOT WILL BE FIRED UNLESS YOU RESPOND IN ONE MINUTE.

****

FROM: COMMANDER PAN CRIMBIAN PATROL SHIP

TO: COMMANDER INTRUDER INTO PAN CRIMBIAN SPACE

SUBJ: IDENTIFY

YOU ARE HEREBY DIRECTED TO IDENTIFY YOUR CRAFT AND STAND BY FOR BOARDING BY HOLY FORCES. THE FORCE YOU FELT WAS A WARNING SHOT YOU NOW HAVE TWO MINUTES TO RESPOND. THIS IS YOUR LAST CHANCE!

Freda realized that the Pan Crimbians had fired some type of pulsar weapon just to get their attention.

Ben was mad. "The bastards are not coming on board our ship."

She was thinking hard. The fact was that they made a good pair because they tended to complement each other's weaknesses. Ben had a tendency to take everything head on – he was a bull. *Suddenly she realized there was too much at stake and this was a situation that called for a little finesse.*

"No, Ben, we've got to think of the boy. Remember he is more important than either of us right now."

He paused and settled down as her words sunk in. "What have you got in mind?"

"First let's invite them on board. Maybe we can bluff our way out of this."

She leaned over, pulled out a screen, and put in the reply message.

FM: YACHT GEOSEARCH

TO: COMMANDER PATROL SHIP

SORRY FOR NOT RESPONDING SOONER. THIS IS A FAMILY SHIP AND EVERYONE WAS ASLEEP. WE WERE UNAWARE THAT THIS WAS YOUR AREA. WE ALWAYS WELCOME COMPANY. WE ARE NETURAL IN THIS WAR – OUR REGISTRY IS ARGENTINA.

She depressed the button and the message went out.

Ben looked at her. "They ain't going to believe that crap."

"Maybe if we stick to the same story long enough. Lock up the computer and purge any indications of where we've been. I'll get the kid; he's going to be our son not a passenger."

She turned around to see the boy standing in the doorway to the bridge. "Listen kid, we're about to be boarded by the enemy. I hope you have your package well hidden. It's time to be stupid. You don't mind being our son for a while, do you? Can you pass for twelve?"

"Don't worry the package is already hidden. I won't mind pretending to be your son. If it will help I'll try and pass for twelve?"

"Probably! It's best if you seem as non-threating as possible."

"Okay." Alex replied.

While the quick exchange had been taking place, Ben's hands had been dancing over the control panel. They felt the change as he took the spin off the little ship. They were now in a weightless condition. Then he ran a test sequence. The results were irritating.

"The alarms are not working. This is a hell of a time for them to crap out."

Ben pulled out his bottle, took a drink, and handed it to Freda. "Have a drink it might be the last one for a while. Alex, you definitely look twelve." While she took a sip from the bottle Ben reached into a drawer and pulled out two pieces of mole skin and place two flat metal objects on the adhesive. He pulled up his shirt, "Darlin, if you would, please slap these on my back."

She went through the motions of fixing the skin to his back, and smoothing it down. "That's as good as it's going to get," she counter while pulling his shirt back down.

They felt the bump of the Crimbian shuttle coming in contact with the hull

With only moments to go, he went to work on the computer. Freda had spent about a week purging their most recent trip to Luna from the computer. She was actually very good at this purge process; she had devised a program for navigation that was a series of overlays. The actual navigation history was broken into four separate files that were meaningless without the others. As a further safe guard, each file was locked with a voiceprint. If anyone other than she or Ben tried to open the files, a computer virus would be opened and start scrambling the entire database. As an additional safeguard he opened the bottom drawer of the computer and pulled out a small crystal rod from the board. He took a Band-Aid and taped the crystal under one of his toes, then pulled his boot back on. Without the crystal, the navigation computer was useless. The last thing he did was to enter a special code into the computer and then lock in the code. He picked up a small scribe and twisted to the standby test position. The test was good so he slipped it into his pocket.

Meanwhile Freda had gone back aft with the boy. Alex went to his stateroom and got dressed while Freda did the same. There were four men, so Freda had to cycle the lock twice for all of them to get on board.

The man opened his helmet. “Woman, I am Lieutenant Flets of the Pan Crimbian holy forces. I want everyone onboard together in one place.” She was not sure at first what he had said because his basic English was so bad. Once she realized what he had uttered she motioned for him to follow. She stopped at the first door going up the passageway and motioned for Alex to follow. He had dressed in simple clothing that was common among spacers. It was loose fitting and colorful. However, he had put on a jacket. Ben met them in the lounge.

Freda started the introductions, "This is my husband and commander of *Geosearch* Ben Papers."

Ben forced himself to be nice. "Welcome, gentlemen. You've met my wife here Freda and this is our son Alex. We three compose the entire crew."

The lieutenant waved his hand at the men and they went off. "My men will search the ship for contraband. May I see your registry and papers?" The lieutenant was obviously not interested in meeting the people on *Geosearch.*

Contempt was thick in his voice. "What is your cargo?"

"This is a Yacht; there is no cargo other than what food and trinkets my wife has bought." Ben handed the man a notebook of various vellums. This was one of six different notebooks that the secret service document people had supplied him. Now he was going to find out how good they were. The lieutenant started leafing through the vellums.

"I see certificates here on you and your

wife but I don't see anything on the boy."

Ben pointed to another section. "There is a birth record there for two children Ben Jr. and Raymond, there twins. This is Ben Jr. He goes by Alex after my father so the two of us are not confused. Notice the middle initial is A. Raymond is in Argentina with his grandmother. Children not of age do not normally need certificates."

"What is the purpose of your trip?"

"Pleasure. My wife here has a heart condition. So the doctors recommend low gravity living. We live on the ship and just travel from place to place."

"Like a group of gypsies?" The man spoke in Spanish.

"Guess you could say that." Ben replied in Spanish.

It was obvious the lieutenant was more comfortable in Spanish. Actually, he spoke very clearly with a strong Argentina accent.

"You're not of the faith are you?" the lieutenant said in an accusing voice.

"No," Ben replied. "We are Catholic. I guess we are not very good ones either."

The men returned from their search of the ship and reported finding nothing. The lieutenant stood and went forward. He was calling the mother ship. These guys made no decisions on their own. Any Union Sergeant who could not handle this kind of situation would be demoted. The Pan

Crimbians micro-managed everything. Even their commanders had very strict guidelines. Anything not specifically covered by a rule or regulation had to be passed up the line. Since they had found no contraband and their certificates seemed to be in order, there was no precedence to follow.

Ben looked at Freda and shrugged, she looked back rolling her eyes. They knew each other so well his motion communicated clearly the meaning, *'I've tried and given every bit I could.'* Her reply was, *'let's hope it's good enough.'*

The lieutenant finished talking with his superiors. He turned and came back.

"What is your destination?"

"I really haven't decided. We have just been cruising trying to stay away from this war. We are neutral."

"It's not possible to be neutral. We are taking you into custody and impounding your ship."

Ben came up with a bolt and had the lieutenant around the throat. Ben was not a real big man but he was strong. He got one hand around the Lieutenant's throat and squeezed with all of his might.

"You dirty son of a bitch you have no right..."

That was all he got out before two of the other troopers clubbed Ben unconscious. The other one slapped Freda so hard with his gauntlet fist that her mouth was cut and she was knocked down. Alex lunged at the man when he stepped forward to hit Freda again. He kicked Alex in the stomach knocking out his wind. They pulled Ben's unconscious body off the lieutenant. The lieutenant was still gasping for air and making gargling sounds. *Freda thought to herself, well at least he would not be talking very much. Hell that wasn't much of a loss. He couldn't talk very well anyway.*

****

Chapter 3-3
2230 Sunday 3 February 2228
Fleet Headquarters
Mars

Mike answered the door. He smiled instantly, recognized Samantha Norris. He stood aside and motioned for her to enter. Samantha was one of the few headquarters staff officers who could come unannounced and was welcome in Mike and Maggie's home. Samantha was not only the fleet intelligence officer, she was Maggie's oldest girlfriend. The two had served together only twice in their careers, but they had been roommates during three years at the Fleet Academy. During those early years they had shared everything, this had become a lifelong friendship that had spanned more than forty years. Over the years, she had become Mike's friend also. Often they went out as a threesome.

"You're looking especially radiant today," Mike commented. "You're expecting Rob soon."

Samantha smiled and giggled most uncharacteristically. *Mike could only smile to himself.* "She's in her study."

He watched her walk away towards the study. She stopped at the bar and mixed herself a drink. Mike looked carefully at his friend for the first time in a while. He realized that she was still a good-looking woman. Of course, she referred to herself as a skinny broad. She still looked forty even though she was in her early fifties. She was tall for a woman standing six-one and massing about 140 at one G. Her black short hair was just showing the first hints of gray, but it went well with the dark eyes and fair features. She had always been self-conscious about her nose, it was large, but it suited her pleasant features. There were outward signs that she had been a warrior there were some old burn scars on the left side of her face and neck that she always carefully covered with makeup.

Samantha finished her drink, walked lightly to the door and knocked lightly before opening the door. Mike sat back down in his reading chair and picked up his book. Reading and cigars were the only vices he indulged himself often.

Maggie looked up from her terminal, "Evening, Sam. What brings you out this evening?"

"We've finally heard from Luna," she said handing Maggie a vellum from her tunic.

BEGIN TRANSMISSION

FROM: COMMANDER LUNAR RESISTANCE FORCES

TO: FLEET ADMIRAL, FLEET HEADQUARTERS

SUBJECT: STATUS REPORT

TOP SECRET BLUE

DELAY IN RE-ESTABLISHING COMMUNICATIONS DUE TO LOSS OF POWER SUPPLY TO EQUIPMENT. APOLLO BASE ATTACKED WHILE OUT INTERCEPTING DROP. LIST OF DEAD AND MISSING ATTACHED. REGRET TO REPORT THE DEATH OF DR. PARKS HEAD OF APOLLO PROJECT.

DROP SUCCESSFUL WITHOUT INCIDENT. ENEMY HAS MADE CONCENTRATED EFFORT TO LOCATE AND ELIMINATE OUR SMALL FORCE.

HAVE LOST TWO MORE PEOPLE IN SKIRMISHES. HAVE CONCENTRATED ALL EFFORTS IN SCOUTING AND LOCATING SUPPLIES. WE ARE DESPERATELY SHORT ON FOOD, WATER, OXYGEN, AND AMMUNITION. STILL HAVE PLENTY OF ROCKS TO THROW.

BELIEVE THERE HAS BEEN A MAJOR CHANGE OF COMMAND ON LUNA. PAN CRIMBIAN HOLY MEN HAVE BEGUN GATHERING UP CIVILIAN POPULATION. APPEAR TO BE INTERNING THEM INTO CAMPS POSSIBLY USING THEM TO SUPPLEMENT THEIR WORK FORCE. WE

ARE STARTING TO GET REFUGEES FROM THE BREAKUP OF FAMILIES. NOW BEGINNING TO TRAIN THESE NEW RECRUITS; THEY ARE WELL MOTIVATED.

SERGEANT MAJOR AGUSTUS B. COLLINS NOW BREVETED 1ST LIEUTENANT, SERVING AS MY FIRST OFFICER. CHIEF JACOB A. SUTTER BREVETED AS 2ND LIEUTENANT, SERVING AS MY AIDE. MONTY P. SIMS, CIVILIAN SCOUT, SERVING AS CHIEF SCOUT AND INTELLIGENCE OFFICER.

HAVE SENT YOU A MOST IMPORTANT GIFT. BEING CARRIED BY SERGEANT ALEXANDER D. SAVAGE. HE IS INSTRUCTED TO GIVE IT TO NO ONE BUT THE FLEET ADMIRAL. HAVE COMMANDEERED GEOSEARCH TO DELIVER ON PRIORITY AAAA. PLEASE HONOR PAYMENT TO CREW. PLEASE MAKE NO RESPONSE TO THIS PARAGRAPH.

INTEND TO INITIATE ACTION AGAINST PAN CRIMBIAN SUPPLY DEPOT. PLEASE ADVISE WHEN DROPS CAN BE ARRANGED FOR AMMUNITION AND ARMS. ANY INFORMATION ON CURRENT PAN CRIMBIAN LUNA EFFORTS OR OBJECTIVES WILL BE APPRECIATED.

KEEP THE UNION SAFE

EARNEST MACLEAN

MAJOR FMF

END TRANSMISSION

Maggie looked up, "Sorry to lose old Doctor Parks. He was a man I really liked and respected. He was one of the truly great minds. It's another hard loss. So what kind of gift do you suppose that Mr. MacLean is sending me?"

"We haven't a clue. I was hoping you might be able to provide some insight." Samantha took a deep breath. "Maybe he stole a piece of important information that might help us. I guess we will just have to wait and see. Rob Doyle has great faith in MacLean. By the way Doc Parks granddaughter Jill is among the missing and presumed dead."

Maggie didn't speak right away. "This is a hell of a war. Of course there are no good wars. It's a shame about Parks' granddaughter." Then she changed the subject. "Speaking about Doyle, what have you hear from him?"

Samantha had been reluctant to even discuss it with her best friend, probably because Maggie was now her commanding officer; but she had to talk to someone. Maggie had to be aware that Rob was calling her on a regular basis.

"Maggie, I spent my entire life only concerned with my career. By any standard if I never advance again, my career can be called a success. For the first time I have met someone who is not threatened by me and for some strange reason I can't help but be attracted to him. It could not happen at a worse time."

"There never is a good time and if he is the one, you have no other choice but to go for it."

"I just don't understand. Why is it happening to me so late in life?"

Maggie looked at her friend and shook her head, "Who says there is a certain time for anything in life, especially in our occupation?"

"You know I have frozen eggs that I put away when I was twenty. I certainly thought that they would be used before I was thirty-five. He is talking about a contract. God I loved being the aunt to your kids and even to my brother's kids. But now I'm over fifty and I don't think I could raise kids."

"Jesus, you were a commanding officer. In a lot of ways it's like babysitting. It's just an earlier phase. I think you would make a great mom."

"Thanks. Nevertheless, with him going out to face the enemy, I can't help but think it's doomed before we start. This is shaping up to being a bloody awful war." Samantha took a drink.

"Listen, Doyle is a survivor – he's like Mike."

"I know. Maybe I will make a contract. Then if anything happens I can always have a part of him." Samantha decided to change the topic. "What's this I hear about you leaving headquarters for some meeting?"

"Well it's hush-hush, and it's not set yet. The First Citizen has agreed to a meeting with all the governors. They don't want to have it on Mars. There are some that think we are too vulnerable here."

"I don't think it's a good idea for you to be running around the solar system."

"Well, it isn't my decision to make. Don't worry. I'll have Mike with me."

Samantha choked back her thought. Mike was getting too old to be her protector forever.

****

Chapter 3-4
1945 Tuesday 5 February 2228
CE-46 Galileo
Warrant Quarters

Jonesy felt overwhelmed for the first time in years. There were just not enough hours in the day. He had worked at outfitting an expedition before but this was ridiculous. Lorraine was pushing everyone including him beyond the limit. The *Galileo* was not ready yet; the main engines had failed every major test trying to get them on the line too fast. Ion engines powered by proton boron fusion reactors were not tinker toys. These reactors had been torn down for a complete overhaul. That was just the start. There were problems with the weapons systems, life support environmental systems, less than half of the main computer functioned, and main hydraulics which controlled the ship's spin was out again. Finally, after four hours of no-weight he felt spin starting up again.

They were supposed to have more than thirty war ships in the force, there were less than twelve that were listed at 100 percent. Four ships that had been assigned to the force were missing; a cruiser, a frigate and two corvettes. The auxiliary force was in even worse shape. Out of twenty-two ships only five were listed as fully operational. While ships continued to order supplies, the logistic depot was out of almost everything they needed. Oxygen, fuel catalyst, and missiles could not be obtained for love nor money; in fact, toilet paper was even in short supply.

He had just left the Admiral and she had raked Jonesy over the coals. He had gone in and explained the situation. She had told him in no uncertain terms that she expected results not excuses from her Warrant. He was sitting at the table no longer studying the clipboard with a list of his problems, when Patty Sue Smith came in.

"Jonesy, I got a beef with you. You deferred a supply barge, bound for *Galileo* to *Guardiant.*"

"Listen, Patty, I have others to think about other than this ship. There is just not enough to go around."

"I just got raked by Doyle. He wants this tub ready for space trials by the end of the week. I couldn't tell him that it just was not going to happen."

Jonesy thought about it for a few minutes. "You know, we've tried to do things by the book and all legal like; I guess it's time to bend some rules."

"What have you got in mind?"

"I think it's time for some afterhours Christmas shopping. Have you got four people you can trust?"

"Yes."

"Get that old Logistics Chief and a shopping list. I'll meet you in shuttle bay four in twenty minutes. Bring your APS!"

It took Jonesy almost fifteen minutes to clear the work shuttle for the Admiral's use and log in an approved flight plan for the shuttle. He had just started the preflight checks when Patty arrived with her co-conspirators. Jonesy took a few minutes to explain in detail what he intended and then offered any of the group an opportunity to back out. He knew everyone in the group. He had a new respect for Patty Smith, because this was just the type of people he would have picked.

Jerome Oakland was a big man who had served with Jonesy on the old *Saratoga*. Jerome had been known to drink a tad too much and was considered a womanizer. However he was one of the best fleet specialist he had ever known, as long as they were away from any port. He was a first class who would never make chief unless some miracle happened. Carry Ann Gilpin was a scrounger from way back. Every ship needed a Carry Ann. Someone who could cut corners and get things that could not be ordered through regular channels. She was a Chief Environmental Controls specialists. In addition to working on the environmental systems she was a good farmer. Environmental specialists grew plants to help with the carbon dioxide on the ships; Carry Ann like so many others planted crops to supplement the canned vegetables. She was good at it and even Captains who had to bust her in rank would keep her around for long voyages. First Class Barbara Ryan was a very thin and unassuming person who had been accused of being trigger-happy guess once she started shooting she couldn't stop. The last man was the joker in the deck - Roy Burke, an excellent sergeant science specialist who many believed had spent almost as much time in the brig as he had on exploration missions. Of course, he had never been accused of being disloyal – just drunk and a thief. Yes, this was a good crew for this operation.

Jonesy drove the shuttle forward until he reached the limit of the umbilical then released flying into space. He headed immediately for the graveyard of ships floating near Phobos, which was getting bigger by the day. There were rows after rows of shuttles that were perfectly serviceable; but were obsolete or specialized for exploration and had no real value in war. After the war was over there would be a lineup of shuttles used for combat that would have no real value for exploration.

Jonesy landed on the top of a shuttle which bore the exploration symbol of *New Canada* a cruiser that Jonesy had served on before the war had started. After he locked on, the group dropped down the ladders and went inside. While Jonesy had been flying to the graveyard he had his crew reviewing the startup and operations of this particular make and model of shuttle. Jonesy maneuvered then counted inward from the last one in on a row then landed on the sixth one from the end. As soon as a seal was made all they had to do was drop down and move outward towards the edge of the row leaving one pilot with each shuttle. Each of his intrepid little group would now be flying their own shuttle.

Jonesy didn't even look at the checklist that was posted on the instrument panel. Suddenly, he had a strange feeling that sent cold chills up his back. The last time he had taken out a shuttle like this one, he had lost his whole crew, and one of his best friends Harvey Drum. It was at the beginning of the war. Jonesy had been sent with a small boarding party to try to keep the explorer *Magellan* from re-entering the atmosphere of Earth. Everything had gone wrong that day; he lost his crew, the *Magellan* went flaming into Earth as a massive meteoroid, he lost the shuttle, then ended up as a prisoner of war down in the middle of Africa. The only good thing that came of the incident was that he was tossed in with Lorraine Wilson. She had been a Commodore then, not an Admiral. They had managed to escape and even help some with a military operation. He looked around just before he disconnected, no one was there, but he sure felt like Harvey was watching.

Jonesy flipped on the comms and spoke, “Form up on me when you have a green board.”

When all shuttle systems were functioning normally, the green indicator lights formed a row across the top of the pilot’s console. He watched as each one unmoored and came alongside. Down they went towards Phobos into the main supply center auxiliary hangar bay. It was night so no one was there. There was a sleepy civilian guard just sitting there. Jonesy handed the guard his forged pass.

“Sergeant Nathan Graham,” he declared. “We’re here to pick up supplies for the Fourth Marine Division.”

The man scratched his chest. “Didn’t know there was a Fourth Marine Division.”

“There is now,” Jonesy replied as he walked down the corridor.

“This way.” Patty Sue pointed down another passage.

Down they went more than a quarter of a mile. The massive metal doors were of a solid construction. There were two locks on each door one electronic and one manual.

Roy attached a probe to the electronic lock and selected from a computer menu and within ten seconds the lock popped. While the electronic lock was being opened, he had taken out two slender plastic probes, which he inserted around the locking device. There were a series of clicking noises then finally the lock cracked open.

Jonesy shook his head, "I thought these electronic locks were supposed to be too complex to be opened."

"They are by a man. But another computer as you can see makes short work of it. Actually the more complex the unit the more ways around the safeguards." The man was obviously proud of his skills. "I used to work for a lock and safe company."

The room was several miles long and at least a mile wide. It was full of every supply that you could think of. Two factors caused this. One was getting the money from the correct fund to cover the cost. The other was that the Fleet Logistics Officer wanted an emergency stockpile so these items were kept until actual supplies came in, then the older things in stock were sent to the fleet.

Patty Sue went over to a terminal and started entering codes of items needed. He knew she would start with the parts needed for *Galileo's* reactors. There was a row of hover lifts so he went over and unplugged one and backed down to where she was working. She printed out a vellum with a list of quantities and locations and handed it to

Jonesy.

"Get to work we've got a lot to steal and only a short time to do it." Everyone lined up ready to look for loot. Jonesy took off down the first row. *He was thinking if they got caught they would be spending the rest of the war in the brig. What the hell - he already knew that the Union jails were preferable to the Pan Crimbian ones.*

****

Chapter 3-5
1415 Wednesday 6 February 2228
Quivero Test Range
Camp Sidney, Mars

Sergeant Don Thompson was at this time Nighthawk and as Nighthawk he was upset two members of his team were dead and another was down with his APS out of commission. Things were not going well. He was supposed to be facing an enemy dug in of equal strength – obviously that was not the case.

"Falcon, report!" Nighthawk called out snapping his voice in his sharpest sergeant manner.

Corporal Stevens – Falcon was in a higher position in the rocks above him; he was hoping that he would have a better view of the situation. "Falcon here. Looks like they got an M-200 up there. That's how they got our guys."

Now he knew the enemy was not playing fair. That brought his blood to a slow boil.

He had sent the other fire team around to the flank "Wolf, let me know when you're in position. I want you to pour on the fire from the flank."

"Almost there," came the reply between grunts.

Don took out his grapple. A grapple was not usually used in this type of position. They were designed for use in space to grab onto the hull of a ship. But now they were in a cave, this should work. The grapple looked like an old fashioned harpoon that used to be used for hunting whales. He inserted the explosive squib then fired the grapple upward into the ceiling hundreds of feet above – now he had a skyhook.

"We're ready," came the call.

"Fire at will, keep their heads down!"

He watched as Acid, Wasp and Croaker fired and advanced under the cover of the rocks. Nighthawk threw himself upward while reeling himself in on the spooling device at maximum inhaul speed. Up he went into the blackness above. He had the opposing squad in full view on the ledge below. They were shifting the M-200 to a new position to kill the fire team advancing on them. He had his Chattergun ready. Firing at the ledge on the fly, he got all but one on the first sweep. While the remaining one was looking up trying to find the target firing from above, Don released the grapple cable and dropped straight down on the hapless figure below. Firing as he came in, the enemy suits locked-up.

The objective of the training exercise was to capture the high ground for the opposing force. Nighthawk's squad was part of the blue team that was trying to overcome the red team holding the objective. War games like these were as old as any military force. He quickly checked the entire area to ensure everyone was dead –dead in accordance with the rules of the game. The Marines were not really dead – once the sensors of the APS sensed a hit by the training weapon, all power to the servomotors were shut off immobilizing the Marine. Now Nighthawk's squad held the high ground.

"Cobra, this is Nighthawk. We control the overhang. You're clear to advance."

He looked up to see the Sergeant Major Cargile descending on his position on a wire from above. He was wearing the Orange suit and had his beacon light on. He was one of the Umpires.

Sergeant Major Cargile said, "Sergeant Thompson you are in violation of the rules of the game. You are out."

Don was still mad at the situation, so he let his mouth run away. "Like it was fair for them to have an M-200."

"You're out of line, not another word." the Sergeant Major shot back.

Don suddenly found himself immobilized too. The umpire had the controls to lockup anyone in violation of the rules. There he remained for almost two hours. He could hear the progress of the mock battle as the red team continued to advance on the blue team. Falcon took command of the squad and continued the battle in his place. Don remained frozen in place with the twelve of the blue squad he had killed and two others of his squad.

The cave they were training in was part of the Grand Cave system in the southern hemisphere of Mars. This particular cave was not as big as the great cave of Valla, but it was at least three-quarters of the size. The cave was over fifty miles long and almost thirty miles wide. The ceiling was almost two miles high in the center and tapered down to about seven feet on the sides. Like all caves, the internal temperature was maintained at a constant seventy-six degrees. Where Valla had been built into a grand city this cave had always been used by the military and still looked pretty much as it did when it was discovered. The grand caves were formed in some strange pooling of lava during the millennia of the formation of the planet.

Don didn't have time to sit back and enjoy the natural beauty of the cave since the Sergeant Major had left him bent over looking at the dirt at his feet. Don was quite unaware of the conversations taking place about him.

"Major Markel, Sir," the Sergeant Major expounded. "The man broke the rules. He needs to be taught a lesson. I recommend him for extra duty."

"No," countered the Major. "List Sergeant Thompson as having completed the training satisfactorily."

"You're setting a bad precedent," the Sergeant Major argued. He was in a position to argue with the Major since he was not only the umpire but worked for the general.

"I don't care," Major Markel replied in a tone that left no room for further argument. "The man showed initiative and flexibility when confronted with a situation where there was no solution. That is the kind of Marine we'll need in battle. Anyway, we didn't tell them they were forbidden to use a grapple. We just assumed that he wouldn't have one since it was not part of the equipment load out for the exercise."

"Yes Sir," the Sergeant Major relented. "I just want to be sure all of the squad commanders are properly motivated."

"Don't worry about Sergeant Thompson's motivation - he has plenty. I knew his uncle who was my training commander. His uncle was killed at Flora."[6]

****

---

[6] Flora Industrial Complex had fallen to Pan Crimbian conquest on 14 July 2227. Retired Warrant Mason Thompson was one of the defenders who refused to surrender and was killed in action along with his 314 fellow citizens.

Chapter 3-6
2030 Saturday 9 February 2228
CE-46 Galileo
Commanding Admiral Quarters

Jonesy came in with the vellums of the daily messages and the eight o'clock reports. He handed them to the Admiral and then took a seat waiting for her to review the reports. *Galileo* was underway conducting space trials. The tradition called 'eight o'clock reports' is older than space travel, going back to the old sailing days of ships on the seas of Earth. Once a ship was underway there was no day and night routine because the watches were manned around the clock. Eight O'clock reports were a daily summary of all conditions taken at twenty hundred. It doesn't make much sense but that's just the way it has been done for centuries.

Around-the-clock routine set a different lifestyle clock on all involved. Spacers evolved a six, twelve hour watch routine. So, if the ship is on a six hour routine, the mid-watch goes from midnight to six in the morning. The morning watch runs six to noon, with the afternoon watch from noon to six at night and finally the evening watch from six to midnight. To support this pattern the ship's galley served meals every six hours. The oncoming watch eats first a half an hour before time to relieve the watch, while the off going can eat when relieved because the galley is open until a half an hour after watch. On most ships there are four watch sections, which allows six to eight-hours routine for sleeping. Of course, six hours of watch is not the normal workday for a fleet specialist. There is always something to be fixed, maintained, or serviced.

If that is not enough, there was always studying to be done. The one thing that was constant in fleet service was change. Systems and equipment were constantly being upgraded and improved. This placed the burden of constant technical study on the specialists. Jonesy realized that in his lifetime alone the science of navigation within the solar system had improved steadily. When he had first joined fleet service, they were still using light scopes to determine light intensity that gave a constant bearing and range from the sun. In fact, since the sun is the center of the solar system it is still the primary object for all navigation fixes. However, now it is more accurate to use low band electromagnetic waves and ultraviolet light than visible light. Bearings are taken with a bipolar electron telescope, which improved navigation accuracy dramatically.

While Lorraine was reading, Jonesy had turned on the vid just to catch the news. It was drearier than ever. The newscasts also had caught the Pan Crimbian official newscast. It was played with English overlay translating the comments of the Pan Crimbian talking head. Then they flipped to news footage showing the Pan Crimbians celebrating the conquest of Venus Station.

Venus had been a very remote Union outpost. Venus is almost the same size as Earth, but the resemblance ended there. The planet was proven to be totally inhospitable, not only was the gravity oppressively heavy but the atmosphere was mostly carbon dioxide; down on the surface one was exposed to pressures in excess of five atmospheres, with winds whipping between two hundred and five hundred miles per hour. The worst thing is the average temperature - over nine hundred degrees F. Every expedition down to the surface has been suicidal. No person ever survived longer than four hours on the surface - in fact, no one who had ever gone down to the surface of Venus had ever returned – no bodies to bury either. Even the most sophisticated robot units built for exploration on the planet ceased functioning within weeks on the surface. Even though Jupiter, Saturn, Uranus, and Neptune also had harsh condition - none compared with Venus.

Circling around Venus was a science station that had been built more than fifty years ago. Scientists from the University of Luna and Old Dome University on Mars mostly staffed it. Jonesy remembered that there were less than five hundred on the station at any given time. They should've been evacuated rather than leaving them to be captured.

“Admiral, look at these morons.” Jonesy

pointed the footage now being displayed from Pan Crimbian with the men somewhere on earth shooting projectile bullets up into the air in celebration. "Don't those fools realize that the bullets have to fall back down somewhere? Even the silly newscasters overlook that fact. Even an expended round can fall back and kill someone."

Lorraine chucked, "You'd be better off trying to explain green to a blind man than tell either the newscasters or those poor souls down there such an obvious fact." She changed the subject instantly. "Have you looked these reports over?"

Jonesy shook his head yes.

Lorraine continued without hesitation. "Doyle is doing well on the trials. It was fortunate that the vital spare parts were found." *She gave him an opening - which he ignored!*

"Admiral you've studied a lot of history. Why do the Crimbians feel the need to attack us? We believe in live and let live. I sure don't understand their motivation."

"Religion throughout the history of mankind has been the most powerful force to affect the course of history. Most modern civilizations make a distinction between religion and the government. Only by doing this can a government survive without being completely controlled by the emotions and passions of religion."

"Sure everyone learns in school that we

have freedom of religion and a separation of religion and state. That's guaranteed in the Constitution of the Union."

"But that separation and freedom of religion is not the same as freedom from religion. Almost everyone I know is religious in some fashion. In fact in our society it's impolite to ask someone their religion – and even more impolite to try and talk about religion anywhere other than your own home or in church."

He looked at her carefully trying to understand the meaning. It was hard sometime because this woman was so intelligent. "But that doesn't explain why they have the need to impose their religion on us. There are people in the Union that believe in Crimbian, admittedly not a lot, but they don't seem to want to impress the religion on everyone in the Union."

"I had a lot of time to think about this very subject during our time of captivity. In fact this was one of the subjects that I wrote a report on after we escaped." She paused to let the words sink in. "The key is in how they refer to us. Remember we are the barbarians or not of the faith. Think back into old western civilization to the fall of the old Roman Empire. They were sacked by the barbarians or the unbelievers. In the early days of Rome, they were tolerant of all faiths and cultures. This tolerance allowed them to hold a large area with a minimum of internal strife. Nevertheless, multiple religions caused them tremendous problems until

Rome became Christian. Remember that by the fifth century Rome had embraced the Christian religion completely. Therefore, the outsiders were the unbelievers or the barbarians. Rome had become intolerant to all other faiths. This created multiple wars which chipped away at the civilization."

Jonesy interrupted, "The barbarians finally caused the end of Rome?"

Lorraine was on a roll now. "Well in a way that's true, but there were many other factors too. You need to read Gibbons to get the full picture. However, the point I'm making is that there is every possibility that the civilization could have evolved again to a new level if the church had not come to dominate the government and rulers. This repression and complete control by the church probably more than anything else blocked any real technological advances during the Middle Ages."

"So you are saying that religion is bad?" Now Jonesy was on the defense.

"In a way too much of anything is bad. Everything must be kept in balance. Religion is one way humans get in touch with their spirituality. I certainly don't know what it is, but each of us has some spirituality and for most people, religion allows each of us humans to reach out to this inner spirit. But, like everything else this must be kept in balance. You will not find this written anywhere but I think that there are six areas that must be developed in every individual for them to achieve what the old philosophers called happiness."

"That's an interesting slant that I don't believe I've ever heard."

"Thomas Jefferson or maybe Ben Franklin called this lifelong quest as the pursuit of happiness. Using the original definition the Pursuit of Happiness is a lifelong quest for fulfillment or satisfaction that one can only look back on after a full life and determine if happiness was achieved."

"So what are the six areas that must be kept in balance?"

"I like to think of them as a circle: Spirituality, Family, Social, Career, Intellect, and Art."

"I understand what you are calling spirituality, but intellect and art?"

"The words I'm using are not necessarily the best words; it just a word to group a cluster of Ideas. Intellect means learning over the course of a full lifetime, until wisdom is achieved. Art doesn't necessarily mean creating art, but it could. I'm referring more to the appreciation of goodness and beauty no matter what form it takes. Family is not only love but also the proper rearing of children to carry on your memory and to continue with the works of your civilization. Social is not just getting together with friends – it also contributing, bettering or protecting your community, city, country or civilization. Career is a personal development which allows you the freedom to achieve all the other by providing shelter, food and an environment for you and your family."

Jonesy was quiet for a moment. "It sounds so simple when you put it like that. So why are these ideas and concepts so difficult?"

"Each of these areas is equal and just as important as the other. If there is not a balance and the person ignores an area or carries one thing to excess then it becomes a detriment. Most churches call these excesses sins. If someone murders or deprives someone else of property or freedom then they have failed in their social obligations. A miser usually achieves at career but fails in other areas. The same applies to any addiction such as alcohol, drugs, sex, or workaholics – this becomes the controlling factor in their life."

"That explains the poverty and harsh living conditions of the Pan Crimbian people we witnessed. They have forfeited in other areas for the excesses of their religion."

"Sure, that's what I was telling you. Even if they win the war – their people lose! If we lose, the excesses of religion will hurt all of mankind. Each person needs a personal relationship with their God, which must be kept in balance with the other things God has given them. Religion used properly gives us a path to our sprit or soul or being.

Remember God may have made mankind – but mankind made religion."

Jonesy stood up. "Thanks for the insight."

"One more thing," she stopped him. "I received a series of messages today marked 'Eyes Only'. It seems that there have been some thefts at the main supply depot. I am going to assure them that none of our people could be involved. I'm going to let you investigate. If you hear about anything that I should know about, just let me know."

"Yes Ma'am."

Jonesy went out the door thinking. It was tough working for someone so sharp. Fortunately she was more interested in her mission than how the support actually occurred. He hadn't fooled her at all. That was good in this situation. They didn't really need any secrets.

****

Chapter 3-7
0230 Sunday 11 February 2228
Unknown Approach
Mars

Sara was flying a small one-seat craft. She had been in the little craft for days since being launched from the frigate. Its inside was littered with trash, charts, and clutter of all types. She finally realized the end of this trip was over. Being confined in a small cockpit wearing a pressure suit for four days was not unbearable, but she would have avoided it if she could have.

She swung the little craft and entered the flight path followed by so many others coming in from Deimos. Deimos is the smaller of two moons, which orbit Mars. Phobos is the other moon, but it is the main fleet military base for Mars. Deimos on the other hand handles all commercial traffic on and off the planet. There are very narrow travel lanes going to and leaving Deimos. Sara was flying an old mining craft from the Alliance Corporation, one of the largest conglomerations in the Union. She had followed the beacon in and now was carefully following the beacon down to the surface of Mars.

She really wasn't very good at handling the little craft in the atmosphere, but after a few minutes, the autopilot took control so she released the stick and let the flight controllers take over. Twenty minutes later, the ship settled down into Alliance's main yard.

A young woman met the ship with a smile. "I don't have this flight scheduled. Who are you?"

Sara just looked at her; "I am the person who Alliance contracted with to return your ship. I certainly don't care what your schedule indicates. I need a shower and a place to get cleaned up before answering any more dumb questions. Just give me a signed acknowledgement for receipt of the ship and it's yours."

"I can't do that," she replied. "You're not on the schedule."

"Fine, then I'll just get cleaned up and fly out of here with Alliance's little ship. Maybe I can sell it for my time. I am sure your boss will be very happy with you for not accepting an Alliance craft because it was not on your schedule."

"Sorry," the woman capitulated in a very flustered manner. It only took a few strokes of the pad and she reproduced a small vellum and handed it to Sara. "Here's your receipt. You can clean up over there in the women's pilot's lounge. Come on back over to the dispatch office and we'll get you checked in. If you're interested you can probably get another run."

"Thanks," Sara replied. "Is there a bunk? I've got to get some shuteye before anything else."

"Oh sure." The woman looked up to see another shuttle coming down. "Got to go." She jumped into a little cart and accelerated down the little rutted road to the next landing.

Sara took less than a minute to pick up everything she could grab in the little ship. She walked across the hundred yards to the women's lounge. Once inside she checked first to see if anyone else was there. The place was empty. It was also unbelievably filthy and stank. The showers were community affairs of gleaming stainless steel; from the looks of it, in another life, the shower had been a storage tank of some type. After depressing the hot water lever and testing it, some heat came through giving hope that it would be hot when she was ready. Quickly she stripped down and shoved all of her clothes into the trash slot marked 'incinerator'.

She stepped into the shower with the special tube of soap; the steel deck was cold against her bare feet. The water was too hot so she gradually adjusted the valve it to get an acceptable temperature. She had to dance around and find the warm steel for her feet. She applied the soap liberally to all parts of her body, especially her hair. When she rinsed the color of her hair and skin changed. The brassy blond and fair complexion went down the drain. She looked at the distorted reflection of what she saw in the gleaming metal. Now she had brown hair and her normal complexion. A spot had been missed on her side, another soaping and rinsed again. She put some drops in her eyes and they turned from blue to her natural light brown.

She dried herself on the disposable towel provided and shoved it down the incinerator slot too. She dressed with her military style boots and pants, then put on a checkered shirt. She unwrapped a full evening dress robe with a hood and put it on over her clothes. Everything she had used as the pilot, including the receipt went down the incinerator too. Five minutes later Sara walked out of the yard past a sleeping guard and disappeared into the city.

****

****

"There are not enough Indians in the world to defeat the Seventh Cavalry."
General George Armstrong Custer

Part 4 - Armada

Following the sudden attacks on Luna, Freedom space station and the fleet units around Earth, the Union called all major forces back from the outer regions of the Solar System. It took more than seven months for the first of these units to arrive in the area around Mars. By this time, several major battles had already been fought. Nevertheless, the replacements and fresh ships were needed badly by the Union forces.

Journal of Solar History

Chapter 4-1
0418 Monday 11 February 2228
CC-141 Arial Control Room
Underway Ganymede Sector

Sam Waters was the Officer Of the Deck (OOD). He enjoyed having the mid-watch. With the Captain and First Officer asleep, he was in command of this impressive new cruiser. The control room of a ship is the brains; from here, every key activity of the ship is monitored and controlled.

They had just spent the last ten days conducting space trials. For a new ship, there were only a few systems with problems. The one thing that concerned the

Captain was the weapons systems. There were problems with the new software for missile control and tracking. In addition, the test missile they had fired with the new multi-sensor warhead had failed to respond as it should have. However, other than that everything else was functioning as a well-lubricated machine should. Sam had overheard the new Captain speaking to the First Officer. She was pleased with the crew even though she had not actually selected most of them.

They had left the test area and were transiting back to Ganymede. The rings of Jupiter are crowded; the sector contains many small-uncharted rocks much like the asteroids and the rings around Saturn. Other than Callisto, Ganymede and a couple other remote settlements the areas around Jupiter were relatively sparsely populated. Unlike the rings of Saturn, which had proven to be a treasure of raw minerals, Jupiter's rings had been essentially bypassed. So the fleet used the area for testing of equipment and training for exploration missions.

Sam stepped down to the chart table and picked up the dice container. He handed it to the Chartsman of the watch.

"Roll us a new course, Haney," Sam said.

She picked up the dice cup and depressed the plunger. Pop the dice came up with six – three – one.

Sam looked at the pilot. "New course zero – six - three azimuth one hundred." The selection was arbitrary based on the dice. Since they were at war, the Captain had ordered a zigzag course. This was a variation of the base course.

Sam took a seat back on his couch that overlooked the pilot's controls. He watched as the man carried out his last order. He input the new coordinates to the control computer - there was only a slight feeling of movement as the maneuvering thrusters along the hull fired in sequence. The new ship responded smoothly to the touch on the controls.

"Steady on zero-six-three by one hundred," the pilot reported back.

The routine of the watch continued as the other stations took new sensor readings, navigation took new fixes and computers were calibrated for the new course. It was unusual for the Sensor's Chief to have the mid-watch but with a new crew, there were many unqualified watch standers. Therefore, the Sensors Chief and his First class were standing twelve-hour watches, with junior sensor specialist under instruction.

The young sensor specialist was running detailed sector scans for practice. It was routine to check the baffles just after changing course, but it was not normal to conduct a detailed sector scan. She was shocked when the anomaly appeared. There should not be anything there, but there was so she checked again – it was still there.

"Chief, what's this?"

He looked at what she had done. "You forgot to pre-calibrate before the scan. Watch this!"

The Chief carefully showed the young specialist how to conduct the calibration procedure then he rescanned the sector. The anomaly was still there!

"Mr. Waters, we've got company."

Sam sat up with a jolt, "Are you sure?"

"We ran it twice. It's a ship and not one of ours. There is no ID beacon - I've already tried to interrogate the IFF[7].

Sam had his standing orders. He depressed the handset on the cradle next to his console. "Captain, this is the Officer of the Deck, I have an unidentified contact aft 120 relative at 40 azimuth - range ninety miles."

Her voice was sleepy. "Repeat range."

"About ninety miles," Sam repeated back.

"Battle stations," she snapped back as the near proximity sunk in.

Sam had been ready since that's what he wanted to do, however it is still the job of the Captain to send an entire crew to battle

---

[7] IFF Identity Friend or Foe - All union ships have a transponder which can be interrogated and return an Identification signal. This system is to prevent unintentional collisions and conflict between friendly ships. This very old system dates back to the development of aircraft in the twentieth century.

stations in the middle of the night. He turned the emergency switch to battle stations with a touch of the keypad. The battle alarm sounded throughout the ship. Men and women of the crew came out of a sound sleep and into P-suits. The bridge crew who were not already in P-suits pulled them on. They had no way of knowing whether this was a drill or an actual event, but they were trained spacers who responded immediately.

A series of events took place when a ship went to battle stations. Not only was the entire crew turned out and sent to their stations but the weapons were readied and manned and the ship was sealed in a gas tight envelope. Everyone on the ship had to get into P-suits and would be strapped down once they were at their station. Some watches changed on the bridge as the specialists who were assigned battle stations on the bridge relieved watch standers so they could hustle off to their own battle stations.

Gas tight integrity is required – this means the ship must be sealed gas tight, all doors and hatches are shut. This places the ship into a cohesive fighting condition. A cruiser is divided into twelve large compartments that become self-contained areas once battle stations are set. The only access between these areas is on 'A' deck at the center of the ship. It took almost six minutes before the last station reported in all stations were manned and ready; the large hatches between compartments were activated and shut. The big tactical board had a series of green circles than were illuminated from a red open to a green shut line.

The Captain was now in the control room looking over the Sensor Chief's shoulder at his console. Now Sam reported directly to her. "Battle stations manned and ready. The board is green and straight. Six minutes and five seconds."

"Very Well, Lieutenant. Workup a firing solution and open the outer doors missile tubes port one through eight. Take the spin off the ship."

He knew that she had concluded that the ship out there posed a threat. With the spin off the ship and the outer missile doors open, Arial was ready to maneuver and fire missiles at a moment's notice. Sam liked Captain Thomas. She was confident and sure, she certainly seemed to know how to handle a potential battle situation. He responded immediately to comply with her orders.

His suit crackled, it was the voice of the first officer in auxiliary control, "Lieutenant what's going on up there?"

In the event the control room was lost or damaged auxiliary control would take tactical command of the ship. The First Officer as the second in command always manned this vital position in battle. In addition, from Aux control, all damage control efforts would be coordinated.

Sam answered, "Unidentified contact, I am feeding you the tactical now."

"Very well," came the reply.

Another voice came on the line. He recognized the Chief Engineer's voice. "Maneuvering ready for one hundred percent power on all mains. All reactors are up and ready."

"Acknowledged," Sam responded.

Arial had four proton boron fusion reactors which were capable of putting out ten thousand terawatt-hours (TW(e).H) of electrical energy. A Fusion reactor essentially is a reactor that controls the combining of hydrogen to make helium with a byproduct of energy, just as the sun does, except that the process is controlled in the reactor.

Captain Jackie Thomas was ready now. She looked up to see the tactical displays that now indicated the update reports. "All right, Mr. Waters, let's get this shiny new toy turned around. I'd like to check out our shadow." She paused for a new breath. "Pilot, new course 162 degrees azimuth 355." Then as an afterthought she finished, "Captain has the con."

Standing orders indicated that when the commanding officer issued orders to the pilot, she automatically becomes the conning officer; Jackie wanted to ensure there was no doubt. During long voyages often the Pilot is the conning officer, which would relieve the Officer of the Deck for other duties.

However, in battle it is usually the practice for a captain to take the conn, since the ultimate responsibility and safety of everyone on board now depended on her.

The new course would take *Arial* back down a reciprocal course to the unidentified contact. Sam watched the displays as their bigger ship turned and settled on the new course. As soon as they were steady on course, speed was increased to enable the ship to close faster.

"Captain, what makes you think this contact is the enemy?"

She leaned over and whispered to him. "Call it a hunch, woman's intuition, or whatever. Somehow I always know. Maybe I'm a reincarnated witch."

Ninety miles out in space in the solar system is close, a ship as fast as *Arial* could close that type of a distance in a matter of minutes. Jackie had no intention of running down the raider. This was Union Space and she had every intention of allowing the other ship to identify themselves. However, if it was an enemy vessel, she did not intend to let them get the first shot at her. This radical maneuver was calculated to catch the enemy by surprise. Jackie waited until Arial closed the range to twenty miles before initiating contact.

"Communications Chief, hail the unidentified vessel on the emergency frequency. Request ID and intentions."

As soon as the comm chief started talking, the sensors chief started, "she's turning and opening all outer main missile doors. Vessel appears to be a Union frigate."

That was not good, thought Jackie. *A union frigate carried enough firepower in their main missiles to kill* Arial. *What the hell was a rogue union frigate doing posturing against another union ship?*

Jackie responded without thinking. "All cannons standby to intercept incoming missiles. Missile room standby to launch one and two as soon as the enemy fires or when I give the word." Jackie depressed the launch key in her console the lights indicated that the Weapons Officer and the Deadman had also closed their keys. It took three officers to agree to launch offensive weapons. *Arial* was ready for battle.

"Two missiles launched from enemy vessel." The sensors chief announced in a calm voice.

Jackie depressed her missile launch button. There was a shudder as *Arial* released missiles also.

"Only one launched," the weapons officer reported. "Frozen in the tube. Standby we are launching another." *A hell of a time for a missile to malfunction* thought Jackie. The lights on indicating tube four was ready – Jackie depressed the button and *Arial* shuddered again. "Number four launched!"

Jackie opened another frequency, "Bos'n Mahoney and Major Greer, get ready, I want a boarding party ready to go as soon as possible." Then she spoke to the Pilot, "Evasive action. Ahead 30 seconds boost from mains. Left ten degrees."

Major Greer was the Marine detachment commander and Bos'n Mahoney was the ships Warrant who should already be at his battle station in number one shuttle. Now she was determined to take this ship. *A rogue Union frigate was bad news for other Union ships in this sector. Must be the one captured last May.* She needed answers and she would get none by standing off and pounding the frigate into dust. The Pilot Chief now had the controls in hand. Everyone could feel the motion as the pilot obeyed the captain's orders; rolling the ship and snapped the huge mile long ship onto a new course to evade the incoming missiles.

The sensor chief was reporting again, "Our number one hit and did not detonate. Enemy missile still incoming."

"Chief Pilot, turn towards the incoming missile," Jackie ordered. He was responding even before she had finished talking. The incoming missile had the advantage of maneuverability now. A mile long ship just didn't have the maneuverability of a missile. It was the difference of a fly and a cow – right now *Arial* was a cow. Jackie keyed the weapons circuit. "Port battery, standby. Your turrets will get the first shot at this bastard. Make every shot count."

The outer hull of the cruiser was covered

with turrets of pulsar cannons. Now that their missiles had failed to get the enemy frigate, it was up to the turrets of cannons to protect the cruiser. Computers fed in the coordinates of the attacking missiles to the fire control centers and targeting information was supplied to the gunners. Mount 44 was manned by Corporal Arnold Kelly, Corporal Sally Martin, and Apprentice specialist Jolly Carns.

As the ship turned towards the threat, time seemed to move in slow motion, as the two objects came together at better than a thousand miles per hour. Mount 42 saw the missile first and 41 started firing at the same time. Ten seconds later mount 43 started shooting - none were able to hit the target. The missile had closed to less than one thousand yards when mount 44 started shooting. Mount 44 hit the missile on the second shot causing the five-kiloton nuclear warhead to detonate. The crews in turrets 41 to 45 were killed by the blast effect.

Alarms sounded as *Arial's* pilot fought the controls on the big ship. Sensors on one side of the ship were stripped back, and the hull was breached by the blast. Fortunately, though, a cruiser is built tough.

"Captain, this is Major Greer. My force and the shuttle are ready."

"Very well," Jackie answered. "Standby for untethered launch." She was working all of the options now. "Pilot, get us in close to this frigate. Let the starboard turrets get some shooting practice."

She could see from the tactical display that the port cannons had some damage, how much had not been determined. Damage reports were being made. There was structural damage, radiation, and a fire in section number three. She knew that teams of specialists were already fighting the fires. Now, the primary concern was to get this frigate! The distance was closing fast.

The sensor chief reported again in a calm voice. "Missile number four impacted on second enemy missile. It failed to detonate. The enemy missile came on and just passed by *Arial*.

Sam looked at the Captain. "What happened?"

"The missile is too close to their ship now. It will ignore all targets within a mile of the ship that fired the missile. We are inside the envelope now. Sam get down to section three and see how bad the damage is."

Arial came in close and now the frigate was within range of the cannons. The turrets started firing right away. Immediately they scored hits on the frigate. No frigate can stand and fight with a cruiser at close range, but they tried. In less than a minute, the turrets on the frigate were out of commission and *Arial* gunners started on the vulnerable antennas and sensors of the frigate. First, the sensors and antennas were swept away, then fire control had the turrets concentrate fire on the hull at vulnerable points. Soon there were three breaches in the hull.

Jackie opened comms to the attack shuttle. "Bos'n, launch will be in thirty seconds. Tell the Marines to get those bastards – they've killed *Arial* crew. I want that ship." "Cease fire. Chief put us alongside."

Ever so slowly, the two ships came together. At the end of the thirty seconds the shuttle launched into the void. Bos'n looked down to see the ship floating below; he drove in by line of sight. When he got close, he fired the grapnel into the hull of the frigate. Once the grapnel hook went deep through the outer hull, he winched in on the cable.

"Major, standby I'm not going to come all the way down on the hull. There are too many obstacles." Jackie told everyone on the circuit.

"That's okay," the Major replied. "Hold her and we'll slide down the cable."

The Marines went out the belly hatch on the shuttle and slid down the grapnel cable. They jumped one at a time through the breach in the hull. This was what Marines were trained for fighting inside a ship. Down they went, deck by deck, then they split going forward and aft, securing the ship. Most of the crew surrendered when the Marines came in. A Union frigate only has a crew of about a hundred and ten. This one had about a hundred and thirty. More than forty had already been killed in the battle with *Arial.* Four of the senior officers attempted a counter-attack against the Marines that held the control room. They were killed in the attempt, but they did manage to wound one Marine. Major Greer was ordered to capture the Captain. He failed in this task, because the Captain locked himself in his stateroom and took his own life.

Sam returned to the bridge. "Captain the fires are out, and our guys have the breaches plugged."

"Good. Major Greer has control of the enemy vessel. Lieutenant, would you like to become the Prize Master?"

"Yes Ma'am."

"Get together with the First Officer and Warrant Mahoney and pick a crew after you get relieved from watch. Call the Chief Cook and find out how long it will take him to fix breakfast."

Sam stepped down and went to contact the cook. The Master Chief Nurse arrived and handed the captain a list. At the same time two other reports were arrived on her command station monitors; along with another update from the Damage control and Major Greer's initial report that the Frigate was secure. Jackie took a moment to grieve for her dead and wounded crew.

Jackie opened her helmet and picked up a hand mike and keyed the 1MC the first general announcing circuit.

"This is the Captain," her voice boomed to every part of the ship and out to the shuttle and even to all of the Marines. "I want to congratulate each of you for a job well done. This morning we went to battle stations to investigate a ship that appeared to be following us. When we turned to go back - the ship fired on us. Our missiles misfired and failed to stop this attack. One of the enemy missiles detonated close to our hull causing some damage. All fires are out and our ship is in no danger. Fourteen of our fellow crewmates have been killed this morning. Four others are seriously wounded. Please join me in a moment of silence to thank these gallant people who helped to save this ship by their actions."

After the pause where she gave a little prayer for the lost souls she continued. "Between the work of the gunners and the Marines we have captured the enemy vessel. There will be prize bonus money for the entire crew and maybe we can find out find out what these people were up too. We are going to alert status two and as soon as the cook is ready, we'll start breakfast. Stay alert and be ready. This guy may have friends. Again, well done *Arial* crew."

Jackie clicked off thinking the capture of this ship certainly wasn't worth the lives of any one of her crew. She was angry at the failure of the missiles – those misfires had cost valuable lives. By God she was going to find out why.

****

Chapter 4-2
0945 Tuesday 12 February 2228
Crimbian Detention Center
Venus Station

Freda was seated in a cell. It was not much of a cell, but it was all she had known for the past ten days. There wasn't room enough to even stand up in the cell since it was only about five feet high by four feet wide and maybe seven feet long. The walls and floor were made of metal - it was unpainted and rusty metal at that. A honeypot hole was located in one corner. The place was illuminated from indirect lights, which were never turned off. There was a pad about four inches thick that had been tossed in on the floor for her to sleep on. The only way she could stretch out was to lie down. She now knew what it was like to be a rat in a cage.

She was still wearing the clothes she had been wearing when they dragged her off her beloved ship. When they had arrived on the enemy patrol ship she had been shoved in a closet by herself and ignored. The first thing she noted about the Pan Crimbian ship was that it stank. These people were dirty.

Freda had spent two days in the closet. The only time they opened the door was to let her use the head or hand her a bowl of some type of smelly gruel. When they arrived at Venus station, she was again dressed in her P-suit, then stripped again to her clothes and place into this cell. She had no idea what had happened to Ben or the young man Alex.

A key turned in the locking mechanism and the side of the cell opened. The boy was standing there wearing the same clothing that he had on when they were boarded. The Pan Crimbian guard motioned for the boy to climb up in the cell. Freda grabbed the boy and hugged him close. The guard was not through. He dropped their P-suits on the deck and motioned for both of them to suit up. Once suited the guard again poked at her arm until she understood that he wanted it extended. She stuck out her arm and he snapped a locking shackle cuff on the wrist of the P-suit. It had about three feet of chain attacked with a matching shackle on the other end. He snapped the other cuff on the boy's P-suit wrist. He then made them crawl back up into the cell, then shut the door without uttering a word.

"You okay?" she asked.

"I'm all right," he whispered. "I'm not sure I can eat anymore of the slop they are feeding us."

"Have you seen Ben?"

"Not since they clobbered him back on the ship."

"Where have you been?"

"In a box like this one with two other kids. I think they're getting ready to move us."

"Well I guess this mission is a bust since

we lost your package."

"Not exactly. I disassembled it while we were in transit and sewed the parts into my clothing. It doesn't look like they are concerned with providing us any other clothing. So it's safe for now."

Freda thought, *Well even though we have the package, it doesn't look like it's going to ever get to where it should!*

An hour later they were transferred to a ship.

****

Chapter 4-3
1810 Wednesday 13 February 2228
Ganymede Base Admirals Office
Military Headquarters Ganymede

A buzzer sounded twice. His aide was signaling that the expected visitor had arrived. This was one visitor that Admiral Juan Gonzales was glad to welcome. He needed an ally badly and the woman arriving potentially could provide that. He buzzed back to indicate approval for entry and the door opened. There she was Admiral Veronica P. Unger. She was still the tallest woman that he had ever known.

She stood well over seven feet tall, she was slim but had to mass almost two hundred at 1 G - and it was all muscle. She had jet-black hair, a dark complexion, and high cheekbones that some found appealing framing hard gray eyes. She was wearing a plain tunic that didn't display any of the numerous exploration awards she had received. Veronica was classified as the greatest living explorer in the Union.

"How are you, Juan? It's good to see you."

He had stood when she entered and had come around his massive ornate desk to greet her. They had first served together when they both had been young lieutenants and again when each had commanded their own ships. They hadn't seen each other in more than eight years while she had been out on several outer system exploration missions and he had done a tour as a squadron commander then had been the chief of staff to the former Fleet Admiral. They couldn't help it. She hugged him as these two had been lifelong friends. She had been by his side when his wife had died and he had been by her side at her husband's funeral.

"So why are you not at Fleet Headquarters?" she asked.

"I got fired. It's plain and simple. You know Navarro[8] was blamed for the fiasco on Luna and Freedom. What the hell could he have done sitting on Mars about a surprise attack is beyond me."

"Damn the politicians they always have to

---

[8] K. Barker Navarro, had been the Fleet Admiral in command of Union fleet when the Pan Crimbian invasion began. The new First Citizen requested Navarro's resignation after the loss of fleet forces around Earth. Margaret O'Brian had been advanced to Fleet Admiral.

blame someone besides themselves when something goes wrong. If anyone is to blame it should be Clark Edwards. He was commanding the Lunar Squadron. Of course he is missing or dead so they couldn't blame him."

"Would you like a drink?"

She just nodded yes and followed him over to the bar. His office was really nice, as an Admiral's office should be. A fully stocked bar took up one side of the room. The other side of the room contained a full size conference table. She took a seat on the barstool while he fixed her a drink. After all these years he didn't even have to ask her what she drank - he knew. He sat the Scotch whisky and water drink in front of her and made one for himself.

"It's too bad you were in the outer system when this war broke out. As the next senior Admiral you should have gotten the Fleet position."

"You didn't get along with Maggie I take it?"

"Mostly I didn't get along with that wild Irish man she's married to. That was probably my down fall."

"Mike O'Brian. I remember him. I had him once. It's difficult to control a Medal of Honor winner, especially one that's married to a Commodore. Yes, he thought he had the right to command the squadron. But, he had guts I say that for him. I ended up recommending him for a Gold Cross. Did you know he has five? I'd have to believe that he is the most decorated person alive in fleet service. I thought he retired."

"He did, but she re-activated him to be her aide. The other problem with him is that they have money and not just a little. What they're doing in fleet service is beyond me." Juan paused to take a sip from his drink. "Remember she was a Smith of the Lyle Smith family that invented and built the mass energy generators that link most fusion reactors today. In addition to that, Mike O'Brian was on the second Saturn mission where the large moons of pure Uranium and Thorium were discovered. He got wealthy from that mission alone."

"So now you're outcast here. Looks like a very lavish brig."

"I'm here to build ships. I've got practically an unlimited budget. By God if this is my lot – I'll build more than anyone else has ever built. We will show these Pan Crimbians what real space ships are. Within two years we will build an armada the likes that has never existed in the history of mankind."

"So how many is a lot?"

"Would you believe that I have orders to build almost five thousand ships? Of that twenty two hundred are to be combat ships. Also more than twenty five thousand shuttles."

"Within two years – you're kidding."

"Actually, we're ahead of the schedule. We've gotten a lot of workers here who escaped from Luna after the attacks. They're a lot of really pissed off people. Their anger has rubbed off on the others. These people work like you've never seen anyone work before. The ships that were already under construction have been completed, and we converted fifty merchant ships to be troop transports. The crews are already conducting space trials."

"I've got forty–four ships in my squadron many of which are in need of repairs after a long hard voyage." She drained her drink and handed him the glass to be refilled. "What kind of priority can I get"?

"You already know the answer to that. When I got your message I cleared several cradles for your ships."

He handed her another drink. She spun around in the chair, then turned back to Juan. "Listen I've been studying every message and every Fleet after action report. So far, this war hasn't been fought very well. Admiral Watson's battle at Castillo appears to have been a complete debacle. First it must have been only sheer luck for him to have found the enemy; and with the losses he took I don't see how Maggie can call it a victory of any kind. Yes, I have decided to challenge Maggie for the Fleet Admiral position. But this is going to require some finesse, not a head on attack."

He grinned – *this was even better than he*

had hoped. “How can I help”?

“First, I need to understand in detail how she is operating Fleet Headquarters. I hope you can give me a lot of insight. I think I need to take down this new Admiral, Lorraine Wilson. That shouldn’t be too hard since she lost the Magellan in the initial attacks on Luna.”

“She has become a very popular Officer since her escape and subsequent hand in the Pegasus attack.”

“Only a minor detail. Remember, I am related to the Prefect of the Senate. This First Citizen is only serving with a slight majority. He can be manipulated politically.”

She handed him two vellums then continued. “You need to study these. One is a plan for readying my squadron for action. I need to add another fifteen or twenty ships if possible so I command a superior force. After I have a victory, then the second vellum will come into play. I have been working on this plan for four months – I want you to study the plan and let me know where there are holes.”

“Gladly. You don’t know how refreshing this sounds.”

“Then if you want to be chief of staff again it can be arranged, or, if you want to stay here it will be your choice.”

Juan picked up the two vellums and placed them in his top desk drawer. “Don’t worry this will never leave my possession.”

"I know – or I would never have given it to you. We'll not only win this war – but we'll get rich in the process. You are going to have a very comfortable retirement, Admiral."

****

Chapter 4-4
0810 Thursday 14 February 2228
CF-81 Saipan
Asteroid 162.44/99

It was a somber group gathered - there were now twenty-nine survivors. The crew assembled in a semi-circle around the opening of what used to be a small mineshaft. The bodies of eighty-five of their fallen shipmates were hanging below on the walls of the old mineshaft. Next to the opening a large slab of stone had been made to close off the tomb.

Mickey Horton opened the old-fashioned book he was carrying. He had no idea about what to say until he had found this book in the Captain's cabin; it was full of all types of ceremonies -weddings, celebrations, and funerals. He had placed a marker at the proper point where he needed to start reading. Abe came out of the tomb and indicated that everything was ready. *God how he hated doing this but it was becoming difficult with all of the bodies on the ship.*

Abe barked, "Crew *Saipan* - Attention for final respects." Everyone was dressed in a P-suit and came to attention.

Mickey started reading, "Each of us holds

some Supreme Being in reverence, whether they call it God, Allah, or Buddha. No matter what name is used, the knowledge that there is something greater than ourselves allows each of us to find our souls and have a faith in the hereafter. Those who serve this Union are from many cultures and faiths that have formed a common bond of humanity on the foundation of the exploration of space and the discovery of the mysteries that our individual God has left for us to discover. Our fallen shipmates died in the service to this Union protecting their fellow citizens. Nothing more can be said in tribute to those who give their life in the service of their Union and civilization. They have given the last full measure that can ever be required of a human soul. We, the survivors, now pass on to you these gallant souls – please accept them and cherish their greatness as we will cherish their sacrifice. We the living solemnly swear that we will continue to protect the weak and discover the mysteries of the universe. Amen!"

There was a low rumble of twenty-nine different voices repeating many different words of final reverence.

Abe hollered, "Standby – Fire in the hole!"

He flipped a switch on the detonator box and the roof caved in sealing the tomb. Four of the crew carried a huge flat stone that was more than ten feet in diameter and two foot thick; they leaned it up against the pile of rubble. They used mining drills to melt the rock around the edges, sealing the slab to the edges of the tomb. Everyone could read the inscription that had been neatly carved into the stone with pulsar lasers.

'HERE LIE EIGHTY FIVE GALLANT UNION FLEET MEN AND WOMEN OF COMBATE FRIGATE 81 – SAIPAN. KILLED IN ACTION 28 JANUARY 2228.'

The name and rank of each of the eighty-five was carved below the inscription. They were listed in alphabetical order along with a date of birth and rank.

"Dismissed," Abe called out. "There will be a meeting of all key personnel in the crew's lounge in fifteen minutes."

It had taken two day of backbreaking work to get the ship into the main bay of the outpost. Since they only had one shuttle and no thrusters on the big ship, any kind of normal docking was out of the question or was it? The abandoned supplies had been put to good use. Somewhere in all that junk was a mining donkey engine with a winch. The cable had been on the winch so long that it would not uncoil; the strands of steel had taken a permanent set. With practically no gravity it was possible to move the winch into position and weld it down to the floor of the cave. Then taking the wire off became a nightmare. Eight people worked the problem for almost a day. Every time a wrap was removed it kinked up becoming another large piece trying to wrap back around the winch.

Finally, after Abe had blown a larger

entrance door to the main cave, Mickey used the shuttle. He nosed in, took the end of the cable and backed out unreeling the whole mess. It was now floating as a big ball a thousand yards from the asteroid. They then unreeled the stern bay's shuttle launch cable and attached it to the winch. Another four hours of pushing and pulling with the shuttle got *Saipan* into position. Finally, they attached the shuttle to the bow to keep a slight outward pull while they winched in with the donkey winch on the stern. There were a couple of minutes of concern when the donkey winch stopped working. Abe tinkered, kicked, and cussed, and it started again. Finally, the entire ship was in the outpost. Four hours later, they had a seal. It took three days between the outpost life support and the ship's damaged life support to set up a proper containment that was safe to move around in freely.

They started on the outer holes in the hull first. Between the metal in the mining supplies and what was in ship's supplies, there was more than enough. The real problem was that the hull of the ship was mostly titanium. The metal found in the mining supplies was high-grade nickel enriched steel - you can't weld steel to titanium without special equipment which they didn't have. So they used Elasto-Bond. Yes, the silly stuff that is used to temporally plug small holes. The only problem with this stuff, that when you used a lot, it took time to mix. When you spread it on over a large surface and then take time to set the piece of metal from the inside, the stuff was already set up. Abe solved that problem by cooling the metal which slowed the chemical reactivity time. It was a tedious process which took time.

Yesterday, Mickey finally decided to have the funeral after the propulsion specialist got a main engine started. Now it was possible to get underway so he decided to get that unpleasant task over with and put the funeral behind the remaining crew.

It only took Mickey five minutes to get out of his P-suit. He sat down at the table in the crew's lounge. Normally meetings like this took place in the wardroom but until today all of the bodies had been there. Even though they had buried them, it still seemed to be a sacred place. He had his handwritten journal which he had been keeping since the first night and a cup of coffee. He leafed idly through the book that by now he knew almost by heart. He grimly logged the events of the day including the burial of the crew.

Finally, everyone was gathered in the crew's lounge.

Mickey looked at the group. They looked haggard and tired, but no one had complained about the backbreaking work. He kept no secrets from anyone. Everyone had a stake in this venture.

"I want to thank everyone who helped with the ceremony this morning. It was a lot of extra work, but it didn't seem right to get underway with our honored dead shipmates." He could see in the faces of the group - everyone agreed.

He pulled his systems list out of the notebook. "It looks like the main computer and most of the communications systems are down for good. We have one main engine jury-rigged and Abe thinks he might get another up. We won't get there very fast and it will be dead reckoning navigation but there's a good chance we'll get home."

Someone called from the back, "Are we going to be able to shoot back?"

"Yes. The missile systems haven't been damaged. About half the turrets are functional. Actually, we really don't have enough people to man all of the stations. Once we get underway, it will be on a modified port and starboard watch bill, some of you will be covering stations that you have not previously had any experience. I'll post the proposed watch bill today so you can study any systems or equipment necessary. Of course, if you feel incapable of covering the assigned areas come, and talk with me."

"How do we tell the Union ships who we are?" someone else asked.

"I don't know yet. Let's take it one step at a time. Okay everyone has work to do. If there are no more questions you are dismissed."

As the group filed out Mickey was thinking. 'Without communications there was no way to let friendly ships know that Saipan *was friendly. In their present condition, even a passing meteorite or drunken miner could kick a breach through the sides. Any encounter with a warship would probably prove fatal'.*

****

Chapter 4-5
1650 Saturday 16 February 2228
Bunker Hill Sector
Luna

Jake was lying down looking out towards the supply depot. He had already studied the ground around this area. There was a large enclosure around more than six square miles of supplies. He didn't have to look to see row after row of pressurized warehouses down below. The Pan Crimbians were using the same area for storage as the Union. They had not changed anything as far as he could see concerning the security arrangements. This was a fairly remote location. Guess they thought it should be safe.

Right now, Jake was not thinking about the tasks before him. He was remembering. As a boy he and his friends had sneaked into this depot and had lifted a few items for use. It was crazy but kids will do anything. He wondered what had happened to his friends in the ten years since he had been here.

He felt the tug on his leg as the other suited figure shook his leg. She crawled up next to him and smiled, indicating that she wanted to look through his binoculars. He handed them to her. Two hours ago they had been in her camping tent together. God how he wished they were back there now. This was rapidly becoming a crappy assignment. Everything was rationed and little time for women. Well, maybe that's why they say war is hell.

There was no talking on the P-suit circuits; too much danger that the enemy might be listening. Jake reached over and took back the binoculars and placed them in the clip on his chest. They crawled back down to the tunnel. It had taken weeks to dig this tunnel and if it was done right they should be right under one of the main storage areas.

The biggest problem had been shoring of the tunnel because most of the rock in this area was soft volcanic almost pumice; it had a tendency to cave in. The problem was solved by stealing scrap metal from the spaceport where great mountains of metal were left unguarded - so the raiders simply drove up, loaded up their trucks and then drove off – bargain basement pricing. There were plenty of ex-miners who knew how to cross brace the beams to hold up the ceiling of the tunnel. It certainly wasn't pretty but it worked.

By the time Jake arrived, the tunnel work crew was ready for the final break through. The lock[9] was closed and the short tunnel

---

[9] Lock – refers to pressure lock doors common to all spacers. Usually involving two gas-tight doors; step in.

segment was pressurized. It certainly would be complete disaster if they broke in and caused a pressure drop. That would surely set off all kinds of alarms.

Monty had the drill and he pushed it forward until it popped through. It was only a half-inch hole. There was a slight surge of pressure then it balanced. Monty withdrew the drill and poked an optical fiber up the hole. He flipped on a monitor and they were looking into the dark room. Slowly he pushed another wire up the hole with an infrared light attached. The room was a mess. There weren't the straight even rows of a Union warehouse -it looked like a dump. He pushed more and more cable up until it was ten or twelve feet above the piles. He twisted and turned as everyone looked at the view - no guards or internal sensors. Monty stopped and panned down. There was a drain grate.

"Let's dig over a few feet and use the drain to get in."

So they went to work - soon there would be supplies for the entire resistance.

****

Close the outer door then the small area is pressurized allowing the inner door to be opened. To leave, the process is reversed.

Chapter 4-6
1305 Wednesday 20 February 2228
Old Dome Refugee Center
Mars

Susan Walker was seated at the camp table working on the weekly Red Cross charity report. She was finding that it was a very difficult task to be an executive of charity funds. There were so many deserving and not enough funds to cover all of the expenses. Her husband had been a wizard at coordinating these types of efforts; she knew that she lacked his genius, but with determination she was learning. Her husband had been Allen Walker, business executive, philanthropist, and much to her surprise, a reserve Union Admiral. Al was persuaded (or volunteered) to return to active duty soon after they were married. He went out and never came back – all she got was a medal in a box and the thanks of the First Citizen.

When she first met her husband, Sue had been working as a reporter. She had been sent to get the story about the refugees. She found Al working behind the scenes at this same table. It had pieqed her interest. What was a millionaire doing living in a tent and helping all of these poor people? Her first tactic was to come in head on and bully him. For the first time in her life she found a man that couldn't be bullied or charmed by her good looks. Only after weeks of digging did she find that the Old Guard Admirals had forced him out of Fleet service. Al had been in command of a bad situation that got out of hand and resulted in the deaths of over thirty fleet specialists and marines. He took responsibility and left the service. Five years later he was rich and bored with making money.

Sue fell in love with a man who wanted to help others and asked for no recognition or reward. This man only wanted to help. His only reward was the self-gratitude he received from helping. This caused Sue to look at her own life. As a reporter she had spent her life exploiting the misery of others. She resigned, married Al Walker and went to work continuing his work. After he was killed she didn't want to continue but the charity work and a group of nuns carried her through all of the dark days.

Mother Superior came in. "Sue, I have a strange situation."

"Okay, what?"

"There's a woman wandering around taking care of children who appears to be middle aged. But she doesn't know who she is."

"How long has she been here?"

"No one knows. Sister Mary Ann noticed her last week and tried to talk to her but she ran away. It's taken her a week to get close enough to her so she wouldn't run. After talking with her she discovered that she is mentally confused and seems to have some type of amnesia. Finally she took a lock of hair."

Mother Superior handed Sue the small plastic bag with a lock of hair. "Can you get someone to run an identification check on her?"

"Sure. In the meantime let's get the doctor to look her over. You know a lot of the treatments used for Alzheimer types of diseases seem to work well for the types of traumatic mental confusion problems we have here."

She took the hair, marked it and placed it with a dozen others that were being sent in for routine identification.

****

Chapter 4-7
0830 Wednesday 20 February 2228
Royal Flagship Oracle
In Lunar Orbit

General Ulisses C. Weemes was admiring the grand warship. Even though he had read and been briefed endlessly on the specifications of the converted ship, it was still impressive in person. Its size, if nothing else, simply took one's breath away. The ship was over eight thousand meters long by eleven hundred meters in diameter – which calculated out to more than eighty three trillion cubic meters of space inside the ship. It was bigger than most cities.

The ship had been captured during the battle for the Union Freedom Space Settlement now renamed Ruffus Station. The barbarians had called the ship

Armstrong II after the first man to walk on the moon. Now it was named after an even greater man, the Oracle who founded the Crimbian religion. The Pan Crimbians had paid a great price to have this ship. One battleship and six cruisers sustained major damage, and thousands of Holy troops were killed or wounded to capture this ship. Because of this ship thousands of barbarians were able to escape on smaller ships outward towards Mars and the Asteroids. The battle for this great ship lasted for more than a week. During this time he developed a respect for the fighting ability of the Union Marines. They only surrendered after they ran out of ammunition and power cells. Some of them even fought hand to hand to the death. This was the one thing that still bothered the General – the fact that the Marines fought so hard not for their religion, but just for money.

But what caused the most damage was that while the bulk of the Pan Crimbian force fought this ship, two frigates destroyed most of the military facilities on the moon. It took a lot of work and expense to rebuild the Lunar shipyards. General Weemes was proud of the fact that he had been able to rebuild the shipbuilding yard in less than four months. He had pressed the barbarians into service to rebuild what they had destroyed.

Trumpets blared and hundreds of Holy Crimbian soldiers came to attention. The shuttle carrying the General landed in the main shuttle bay of the vast combat Explorer ship. The barbarians only carried a crew of about two thousand on this grand vessel, but the Holy designers had refitted the ship to carry a full army of Holy troops plus ten fighter shuttle squadrons. The Pan Crimbians would have more than three thousand crew and more than ten thousand troops on board. The ship would now carry a mighty force. Pan Crimbians didn't clutter up a war ship with laboratories and exploration equipment and systems. There was no need for wasteful exploration since the Holy words of Crimbian revealed all knowledge worth knowing.

As General Weemes stepped from the shuttle, the trumpets blared the Holy Roll of Military Prayers. He walked up the rows of troops inspecting. He saw nothing out of place. He really didn't expect to find anything since the first three rows were the holy league of the Oracle in their yellow Armored Pressure Suits. These were the elite of all Pan Crimbian Troops – Genetically Pure of Faith. These men never married – they took the Holy Oath of Priesthood - they were married to the Crimbian faith. They were guardians to keep the faith pure. Behind the rows of yellow were the rows of brown pressure suits of the common foot soldiers and space crews, the pride of Pan Crimbian. He didn't bother inspecting any of the brown suits.

He walked carefully up on the platform

that had been assembled. Behind him was the pure while flag with the symbol of the Oracle in the middle taking up most of the wall. On either side of the giant flag were the pictures of the great ones: Ruffus on the left and the Oracle on the right. The symbolism was there for the benefit of all the troops. All of the arrangements had been made – his image and voice were to be projected to all of the ships in this force. Once he got behind the podium he started speaking.

"I assume supreme command of this Holy force as directed by the Space Marshal and Ruffus our Holy Leader. Those of you that have served with me before know that I only expect the best from each of you. We have brought together with in this fleet the mightiest armada ever assembled in the history of mankind. Someday you will be able to tell your children that you were part of this glory. We will be underway in a matter of hours - we will be over nine hundred ships - a mighty sword for the faith. We will defend our outposts and crush the enemy in his lair. When we went to the moon, there were those that doubted our ability to defeat the barbarian. We have proved ourselves – you are the finest military in history, not just because you have defeated a mighty enemy on his own ground, but because our cause is right and blessed by God. Let us pray"

All of the troops at attention bowed their heads.

"Oh, God of Crimbian, we ask your blessing as we depart on this Holy Crusade. Give us the strength to vanquish the enemies of the faith. Protect Ruffus as we depart from mother Earth. Give us the strength to defeat and convert the barbarians to the ways of the Faith. You have given us a mighty force. May we use it wisely in your service. Amen"

Another voice called out, "Attention!" The image of Ruffus came up on the viewscreens. He was seated in his formal room surrounded by the familiar ring of daughters.

"I have spent the last few days in prayer and meditation to ensure the success of your Holy Mission. Let us go forth with my blessing into the void. Return with glory and your place in heaven will be assured. Those of you that fear – fear not because, if you die, you will be in paradise with all of the others who have sacrificed before you. Amen!"

His picture gradually grew in the screen until his face filled the entire view screen. Then gradually it faded to the symbol of the Oracle.

"Prepare to get underway," Weemes then turned left the podium.

The Grand Holy Sergeant Major waited for the general to clear the bay then he shouted the command, "Dismissed!"

****

Chapter 4-8
1935 Thursday 21 February 2228
Fleet Headquarters
Mars

Mike was seated in his office when a young man came in with several vellums.

"Hot messages for the Fleet Admiral."

"Thanks," Mike answered back taking the vellums. He hurriedly looked at the messages one he read the other he couldn't. So he would take them to Maggie. She wasn't sleeping well recently and it worried Mike. He was trying to take as much of the load as he could. Mike now had a staff of his own to keep track of all of the different operations going on. Mike walked into her office and handed her the messages. He waited while she read.

BEGIN TRANSMISSION

FROM: FIRST CITIZEN OF SOLAR UNION

TO: FLEET ADMIRAL

SUBJECT: WAR COUNCIL MEETING

TOP SECRET BLUE [PROJECT OMEGA]

INTEND TO HOLD HIGH LEVEL MEETING OF WAR COUNCIL ON GLENDA ASTEROID. THIS IS PRIMARILY A POLITICAL MEETING BETWEEN THE SENATE AND HIGH EXECUTIVE COUNCIL. HOWEVER, I WOULD LIKE FOR YOU AND THE COMMANDANT OF MARINES TO ATTEND. THIS MEETING IS

TO BE KEPT QUIET. TRAVEL BY PRIVATE YACHT OR SMALL UNARMED SHIP IS PREFERABLE. MY MOVEMENTS WILL BE COVERED BY A HOSPITAL STAY, WHICH WILL NOT HAPPEN.

PROVIDE COVER EXPLANATION FOR YOUR ABSENCE. ENSURE ONLY THE MINIMUM NECESSARY PERSONNEL KNOW OF YOUR ABSENCE AS WELL AS MINE. THE MEETING WILL OCCUR EARLY IN MARCH EXACT DATE YET TO BE DETERMINED. I WOULD LIKE A CRUISER TO BE ASSIGNED IN THE AREA FOR SUPPORT IF NEEDED.

WM. PRICE

ADMIRAL FOR COMMANDER IN CHIEF

END TRANSMISSION

The second message required Maggie to place her thumb on the pad to open the message for reading.

BEGIN TRANSMISSION

FROM: FIRST CITIZEN OF SOLAR UNION

TO: FLEET ADMIRAL - EYES ONLY

SUBJECT: ARIAL ENCOUNTER

TOP SECRET RED

AFTER REVIEW OF CC-141 ARIAL INCIDENT ON 11FEB28, AGREE WITH YOUR RECOMMENDATION THAT ALL SHIPS WHICH DO NOT RESPOND WITH NORMAL FRIEND OR FOE

IDENTIFICATION OR NORMAL COMMUNICATION TO BE CONSIDERED HOSTILE. IT IS UNFORTUNATE THAT THE ENEMY IS USING UNION SHIPS AGAINST US.

DIRECT YOUR COMMANDERS TO SEEK OUT AND DESTROY ALL SHIPS WHICH MAY BE ENEMY OR SUPPORTING ENEMY OPERATIONS. YOU ARE AUTHORIZED TO SEND OUT SHIPS ON SEARCH AND DESTROY MISSIONS. TASK FORCE SENTINEL MISSION UNDER THE COMMAND OF ADMIRAL UNGER IS APPROVED.

KEEP THE UNION SAFE

VERNON QUILTMAN

COMMANDER IN CHIEF / FIRST CITIZEN

END TRANSMISSION

Maggie handed the message to Mike. “Looks like we’re going to get off the ground again. I’ll leave the arrangements up to you. Remember we can’t take a battalion of Marines.”

“Don’t worry, my dear. I’ll figure something out.”

“Send the Sentinel message to Admiral Unger.”

“Okay. I take it you’ve decided to do nothing about Veronica.”

“If she decides to make an issue about seniority, I’ll deal with her then. On the other hand if she follows orders I’ll let her keep her command."

"You know that she is in league with Juan. Those two will be up to no good."

"Sure, but I think they both love the Union more than they hate me. Let's wait and see if she is as good a warrior as she is an explorer. If she is only half as good she should be a real hellcat!"

Maggie ruffled through her desk and pulled out a message which she had been working on. She looked it over made one change by hand and handed the vellum to Mike.

"Send this out, Dear."

Mike quickly scanned the message.

BEGIN TRANSMISSION

FROM: FLEET ADMIRAL

TO: ADMIRAL VERONICA UNGER

SUBJECT: OPERATIONAL ORDERS

TOP SECRET BLUE

ADMIRAL VERONICA UNGER IS APPROVED BY ORDER OF THE COMMANDER IN CHIEF AS COMMANDER OF THE WAR EXPLORATION TASK FORCE DESIGNATED DELTA. THE FORCE WILL BE COMPOSED OF THE GROUP YOU BROUGHT IN FROM THE OUTER SYSTEM, USING THE EXPLORER WERNER VON BRAUN AS YOUR FLAG

BASE SHIP. YOU MAY ADD TO YOUR FORCE FROM SPACE READY SHIPS AT GANYMEDE.

AFTER YOUR FORCE HAS BEEN REFITTED AND IS COMBAT READY YOU WILL PROCEED TO EARTH SECTOR. YOUR MISSION IS TO ATTACK AND DESTROY ENEMY SHIPPING AND PERFORM MILITARY HARASSMENT. I BELIEVE THE BULK OF PAN CRIMBIAN FORCES HAVE LEFT THE SECTOR. YOU ARE PERMITTED TO KILL SATELLITES, ENEMY SHIPS, AND IN GENERAL CAUSE AS MUCH DAMAGE TO INFRASTRUCTURE AS POSSIBLE.

NO DIRECT ATTACKS WILL BE MADE ON THE LUNAR SURFACE OR THE FREEDOM STATION. YOU ARE PERMITTED TO DISPERSE YOUR FORCE AS YOU SEE FIT TO ACHIEVE THESE GOALS. RE-SUPPLY IS BEING SETUP, SO YOU CAN SUSTAIN THESE OPERATIONS. YOU MAY BE ASKED TO PROTECT AUSTRALIAN FORCES ON THE PLANET.

YOUR OPERATION IS IN DIRECT SUPPORT WITH THE COMMANDER IN CHIEFS' TIMETABLE FOR RECAPTURING LUNAR AND EARTH SETTLEMENTS.

ENGAGE THE ENEMY AT WILL AND KEEP THE UNION SAFE

MARGARET G. O'BRIAN

FLEET ADMIRAL

END TRANSMISSION

**

*****

*

Chapter 4-9
1330 Friday 22 February 2228
CE-26 Wernher von Braun
Admiral's Flag Quarters

"Captain Jacqueline Thomas reporting as ordered."

Jackie was standing tall in front of Admiral Unger on her flagship. She had spent the last two hours in transit to the explorer *von Braun.* She had not been offered refreshments or any of the usual amenities accorded a commander of a ship. In fact, she had been left standing in the Admiral's outer waiting room for almost an hour.

When she had finally been called in she was surprised to see that not only Admiral Unger was present but Admiral Gonzales too. Jackie had never met Veronica Unger before and had only seen Juan Gonzales once before. She was surprised at the sheer size of the woman. Both were seated at a conference table and Jackie had been left standing.

"Captain, I have reviewed your after action report on the recent battle you fought. I'm not impressed. A small ship should have never been able to inflict such damage on you. If it were up to me I would relieve you of your command. You are obviously to young and junior for such a command."

Veronica paused to let the words sink in. Jackie was angry but she held her temper in check. This was a powerful woman who knew how to use power. She not only had the power of her rank but she came from an influential family with money.

Veronica continued, "*Arial* has been reassigned to my command. Most of the ships of my force have been refitted and re-supplied. We will be departing the area soon. When will your ship be ready for the voyage?"

"The ship can be ready in another couple of days. Most of the damaged turrets have been replaced. My crew is running final testing now."

"Very good, that's what I like to hear."

Jackie could no longer control herself. "What about the problems of the missiles not detonating on impact?" Jackie turned and spoke directly to Admiral Gonzales. "I noticed you omitted the fact that the missiles were defective from the report you forwarded to Fleet Headquarters."

Juan had been just listening to the conversation, but when accused he reacted. "Listen, young lady, you do not have the experience. I spoke with my Superintendent of Weapons; he assured me that the missiles were not defective and that you or your people made a mistake. However, be assured if there is a problem, my people will take care of it."

"Maybe he should speak with my Chief Missile specialist. She has some ideas after the incident about what the problem may be."

Veronica interrupted, "That's enough, Captain! This is what I am talking about. The fleet has a mechanism set up to take care of problems; you will follow procedure. Admiral Gonzales here has plenty of competent people and if there's a problem it's theirs to deal with. You have a ship to run or as my grandmother use to say, 'tend to your own knitting'."

"It was my people killed by the defective missiles."

"Get it through your head. Your people were killed by an inexperienced captain. I've looked over your record. You like to operate independently and take your own initiative. That type of behavior has gotten you into trouble in the past. Under my command you will refrain from such independent actions and you'll follow my orders or you will no longer command. Do you understand?"

The silence that hung over the room was so thick it could be cut with a knife. Jackie realized instinctively this was neither the time nor the place - *Time to survive.*

"Yes, Ma'am."

"Dismissed," Veronica declared.

Jackie turned and left the room. It was a long ride back to her ship. *After she came to grips with her emotions, she started to think clearly. Along the way she came to the conclusion that this Admiral was dangerous. Then it hit her. The Admiral had never been in combat or she wouldn't have acted that way. Jackie needed to be very careful, not because this woman had tried to intimidate her; but because Jackie was not going to allow this Admiral to get any more of her crew killed.*

****

"He who fears being conquered is sure of defeat." *General Napoleon Bonaparte*

Part 5 - Luna

It is written in the holiest of all laws of Crimbian that only the pure of spirit and heart can enter into the graces of Crimbian. Even the barbarian can enter heaven but first the soul and spirit must be cleaned; made ready to receive the blessings and word of the faith. It is the work of the most dedicated to mold a barbarian into a useful subject for receiving the faith. Not only must the barbarians be altered genetically they also require mental healing to cleanse impure thoughts. These dedicated servants of Crimbian need daily prayers to sustain them in this distasteful duty.

Code of Prayers for Pan Crimbian Evangelist Soldiers

Chapter 5-1
0418 Saturday 23 February 2228
Barbarian Reform Center
Luna

The light startled Jill Parks, as hands reached in and pulled her from the dark box she had been imprisoned in. She could not stand, so someone grabbed her on both sides and half carried and half dragged her down the passageway. She had no idea what day it was, nor any idea of time whatsoever. She was sure that it had been days or weeks since she had been brought here and shoved in the closet, but it could have just as well been months or years as far as Jill was concerned.

They took her into a room and placed her on a table of cold metal. One of the men in yellow robes came in and looked down at her; his face clouded with disgust. "This barbarian is filthy and stinks. Clean her before I minister to her." With that the yellow robed figure turned and left.

Down the hall the guards dragged her all the way to a shower room. She was shoved in clothes and all. Sprays of warm water alternating with cold water beat her exposed areas. The men left when two matrons came in. They pulled off her clothing that was literally rags. Her clothing was tossed into a wash bin and cycled through. They pulled her erect under the shower and finally with the warm water she was able to straighten her legs. Her back and abdomen were painful and her legs felt like pins and needles as sensation started to return. Long minutes passed before she was able to stand unassisted – classic symptoms from being folded up in one position for a long time.

The box that she had occupied as a prison was not big enough for her to standup or lay down. She had been kept in the dark for weeks. There was a hole on one side for biological needs but the stench was overpowering. She had been fed but in no set pattern or schedule. Some days she received one or two light meals while on other days she was fed six or eight times. Some meals were light soup or gruel while others contained more than she could eat. The little room was sound proof so there was nothing to listen to. The walls, floor and ceiling were all the same type of welded metal plating. She was also subjected to temperature oscillations on no set pattern. It was cold or hot there was no in-between comfort range. But the worst thing was just the isolation - in the dark with nothing to feel but cold metal walls, no sound and only one foul odor.

The shower stopped and the dryers started, soon she was completely dry. Moments later the bell rang on the clothes washer her clothing came out clean, dry and folded. Once dressed she was brought back to the inquisition room. The matrons strapped her to the hard table and left. Left alone looking up into the bright lights in the ceiling she soon had a headache. The priest in the yellow robe returned. He consulted a computer built in to the wall. Then he knelt in silence for a few minutes.

"Daughter, I have prayed for your sins and have asked God to look kindly on your soul."

Jill said nothing. She was disgusted and repulsed by the man. He looked at her for a long minute waiting for a reply. Suddenly he reached out and slapped her across the face.

"Listen, you barbarian wench, when a priest of the faith speaks to you - you answer! Or you will receive the punishment reserved for barbarian sinners - pain and humiliation."

Jill just glared at the man – it was hopeless so she just closed her eyes. He slapped her again. "You will tell me about the barbarian resistance that you were part of." Her expression must have changed. "Yes, the others told me of your betrayal to the faith. You will tell me about MacLean, who he is and where is he."

That was just the start. After that he took out a small whip-like plastic rod and systematically beat on different parts of her body until the desired effect was achieved - pain. The man was an expert at pain but this was just the softening-up. The real effort would be coming later. When she passed out, he sprayed her down with ice-cold water.

Somehow she knew in her mind that if she ever talked to him she was finished.

Jill was an academic. Her mind was in fine shape from years of constant use and study. When the pain became unbearable, she moved her mind from reality to attempting to solve a quantum physics problem that she had been working on for the past few years. Somehow deep in the back of her mind the pain lessened and she could see the mathematical symbols.

After hours of this treatment she passed

out in a shock induced trance.

The priest placed the electroencephalogram hood on Jill and looked at the readings. He adjusted the dials and checked the standards against the findings. Now he was angry. She had escaped.

He buzzed and the two matrons entered. "Prepare this one for transport to the Oracle Station. I am going to assign her to the Grand Inquisitor. He has the proper equipment to break open her mind."

As the two matrons prepared Jill he thought with a chuckle. *If Grand Inquisitor couldn't break into her mind then at least he could destroy it. Then she would never be able to escape mentally - because nothing would be left.*

****

Chapter 5-2
1015 Monday 25 February 2228
Office of Commandant of Marines
Fleet Headquarters, Mars

Brigadier Steve Ridgeway was seated at the table with Commandant Nathan Graham and Colonel Isabell Davis, when General George G. Evans came in and took a seat. George Evans had massive shoulders and iron gray hair; he was every inch what a Marine should be. George was somewhat of an outcast among the others since he had never attended the Academy. George had started his career as a private and had worked his way up holding every rank in the

Corps. Until a week ago George had been commanding the First Marine Division. He was not happy about being relieved.

Nathan started. "General Ridgeway would you please review the condition of your division."

Steve cleared his throat, "Early this morning my division began embarking from Mars to Admiral Wilson's ships. Hopefully, she'll have enough room for the entire division. Most of our planned, land-based training is complete. By tomorrow at this time Sidney Base will be almost empty."

"You understand what is expected of your force?"

"Yes, I believe so. We face an enemy that has had eight months to dig in and establish defenses. You expect us to take the objective no matter what the cost."

"Exactly! Your capture of Eros is a crucial first step in our overall plan to retake the Settlements on Luna and Freedom."

"Yes, Sir," replied Steve.

"Colonel Davis you are the second highest Marine officer on this Expedition, I wanted you here so you also understand the importance of this operation. I'm perfectly aware that Steve here is not bullet proof, so if something happens to him I expect you to pick up where he left off."

"I understand, Sir," she replied softly.

"God, I only wish you two really

understood. Only one other time were the Marines involved in an operation of this magnitude. I was there as a young major and George here was a first Louie. You're going to have to think in a broader context than the Marines normally function in. I am well aware that you haven't had the training time necessary for an operation of this size; I had three choices concerning this operation - and they were all bad."

Nathan took a drink of water before continuing. He had their full attention now.

"One I can send in an unpolished, ill prepared division - and hope for the best. Two, wait for the Army to be ready to support this operation in six months. Three, I attempt to bypass this enemy strong hold and hope they don't attack Mars while we are spread too thin. So I chose to send you in with the unpolished division. If you fail, it will be my duty to break you both, but it will be my fault."

Steve looked at Nathan. "Then why aren't you sending George, since you have doubts about me?"

"Steve, I have no doubts about you or Isabelle. The fact is you are going to be up against a bigger force and you have not been in combat as a General commanding a large force and neither has your Commanding Admiral. George is going to be my chief of staff for a while and he'll command three divisions of Marines when it comes time to invade Luna. George will have his hands full training the Third, Fourth and Fifth Marine Divisions for a Lunar assault."

George snapped alert. He had been wondering why he was here.

Nathan cleared his throat; "You both have all of the plans and goals - keep them in mind as you work. I give all Generals the same advice; it's easy to become isolated in a big operation. Lead from the front. You have to put yourself in harm's way to have moral authority and respect. Don't take command away from your battalion commanders. Of course you are probably a better battalion commander than they are, but you have to be the Commanding General, so let them command their battalions. Get out in the field and off the ships - you must feel the horror, the cold, the loneliness, and despair your Marines will feel."

He paused to let the words sink in.

"Depending on how you look at it, it's either a blessing or curse; but each of us are on the cusp of history. I know each of you will do your duty, but this is one of the times that require men and women to do more than their duty. I'd give almost anything to go in your place, but my duty is here."

"Don't worry, sir. We won't let you down," Steve retorted.

"Of that I have no doubt." Nathan waved his hand towards the view screen in the corner of the room. "One other thing – the media. You will have reporters on board. This is not my idea – the First Citizen insisted. He has a strong belief in an open press. I think I know how you feel about the press. Most of us have the same opinions. They are sensationalists, exploitive, insensitive, and they prey on misery. They also will write much of the history you are involved in. You must tell your side of the story as straight and factual as possible. They'll get in your way and they'll be a pain in the butt. Remember you can't kill the press."

"So what is your recommendation on dealing with the press?"

"When I was a boy I kept pet rattlesnakes. A very useful animal for getting rid of rats in the ventilation. You don't have to love them or even like them; but you have to handle them properly. But most of all you must feed them. Feed them what they like and you have fewer problems. Ignore them and they'll hunt for something to eat. Remember they are poisonous and unpredictable. They also are known to bite the hand that feeds them, whenever they take a notion."

Nathan looked over to George. "Have I forgotten anything?"

George looked at Steve and Isabelle. "The only other thing I can add is; be careful, don't burn out your staff or yourselves. Remember General George Marshall of the United States ran World War Two from Washington D.C. He took a nap every afternoon after lunch and went home every night by sixteen thirty."

"I want to thank you for listening to my little pep talk. Good luck." Nathan stood and walked with them to the door and shook hands again as they left.

Nathan walked back to his desk. It was a simple plastic desk much like most Marines had on any ship. George started to get up, but Nathan motioned for him to stay.

"George would you like a cup of my delicious coffee?"

"Absolutely, I never refused a cup of coffee in my life."

Nathan drew the coffee and handed it to George. He took a seat at the table across from him.

"I didn't invite you here to listen to the talk I gave them. I wanted you to be fully aware of their situation. Those two are among the best we have and I know they will do a good job. But the reality is, that at best, they only have a fifty-fifty chance of success."

"Then why commit to such a risky operation?"

"They're actually fighting a delaying action. The real truth of things is that the Union needs time. We are hoping that this battle will keep the attention of the enemy, giving us time. Now that you're here with me you'll need to read the upper level reports to come up to speed. The Army took a real beating on Luna and over half of the Army is in the outer areas. It will take time for those forces to get here. You've heard that we are authorized to form a fourth and fifth division – but the reality of the situation is somewhat different. The fabled fourth and fifth divisions only exist in a planner's computer – we don't have the Marines. We need bodies. I need you to work on recruiting to fill the slots."

"When do we start training for the Luna Invasion?"

"It will be at least six months. We are going to work out a special invasion command structure. As you have just learned you are my choice to command three divisions of Marines that will be the point. The Army will be right behind you with forty divisions. This will be the largest military operation ever planned. The logistics will be massive. Fleet Admiral O'Brian has a special team looking at the planning. I want you to join the planning team to look at the needs of the Marines. Several retired officers have volunteered to help in this effort. This is going to be so complex I can't even begin to explain the problems. But, your team has to try and identify all of the pitfalls and figure out a way around them."

"One other thing," Nathan added after a pause. "I have to attend a meeting off planet with the Fleet Admiral and our Commander In Chief. I'll need you to work with the Fleet Admirals Chief of Staff while I'm gone and while I'm gone the fewer people who know we're gone - the better. In fact if you're the only one that knows I've been gone when I return the better off we'll be.

"So, you want me to fill in here for you too and get a massive recruiting and training program going while you are away at this meeting."

"Yep, that's what is needed."

George looked hard at Nathan. The two had been friends for more than thirty years. "You going to tell me why I am going to command the largest force of Marines ever while you set back here on Mars?"

"There are going to be more operations than just your invasion. After Luna we are going to take Freedom Settlement back then we will invade Earth. The decision has already been made. Pan Crimbian Empire is not going to survive – they will surrender unconditionally or die."

****

Chapter 5-3
0500 Tuesday 26 February 2228
Barbarian Detention Center
Luna

Sub Priest Cessan was sorting the file cards on the various barbarians who met the special category for interrogation and special treatment. These were the barbarians who had resisted the benevolence of the Crimbian saviors. He still couldn't understand resistance to such a glorious privilege.

Suddenly he felt a pressure change; he

moved quickly to don his P-Suit. Cessan dropped his yellow robe and vaulted into his suit. In his haste he bumped the table of cards and knocked one box over spilling the cards on the floor. He didn't know what was going on but the duty officer would hear about this. As he went out on the balcony that overlooked the courtyard, suited figures were advancing in the yard.

Cessan stepped back into the shadows out of the light. Thinking fast he knew he had to take action. He moved down the walkway to the corner. There he found the fire alarm. He used his elbow to smash the glass and depress the alarm. Red lights started flashing right away and he could hear the alarm through the closed suit. Most of the troops would still be in bed, but this would bring them out fast.

Then he remembered the overflow armory was just two doors down. He slid along the wall staying out of sight from the barbarian troops below. He reached the door and felt for the latch. It opened to his touch as it sensed his priestly authority. Inside was row after row of captured enemy weapons. He wasn't really familiar with these strange guns but they would have to do. He grabbed the first one that look familiar; an older model Chattergun. The energy cells were in the next row back. Within moments he had the gun loaded. The display panel indicated the gun was ready for use.

As he came out the door he met one of the barbarians – Cessan fired by instinct and the man went down. The yard below was full of barbarians he opened fire raking across the area in his line of sight. Many went down.

Then the area around him came apart as the barbarians below shot back. They hit the ceiling above him and it collapsed on him. Cessan kicked and pushed the rubble off. As he stood he saw his gun sticking out from the rubble. He grabbed it and it came free. In less than 30 seconds he started shooting as one of the barbarians vaulted over the rail about twenty meters down the passage. He tried to pull the trigger, but the other man was faster – *Cessans last thoughts before he was enveloped in darkness was that he had been hit- he prayed that the faithful would destroy these barbarians.*

***

Jake looked down at the yellow suited figure. He was dead.

"First platoon, advance!" Jake called out over the comms. *He paused briefly thinking that was a gutsy little guy! Where did he come from?*

Two more figures came over the rail in a smooth motion. Jake signaled one to cover him from the right and motioned the other to check the door. The man in the yellow P-suit had left it open. Jake ducked in diving to one side – this was the room full of weapons - their intel had been correct. It was a good size room. Jake moved the length of the room then across. Finally, he was convinced there were no other enemy troops in the room.

"Red Dog, this is Laredo. I'm at the first objective. Ready to load when you get here."

"On my way," came the reply.

Jake started breaking all of the locks. He had an electronic ultra-low freezing device. It worked quickly and decisively. First freeze the metal then he hit the lock or the cable with a hammer and the metal shattered - crude but effective. By the time he had the first row broken others had arrived and started unloading the room. It took almost twenty minutes to clear the room. Eight of the resistance fighters worked like mad men, moving the weapons and energy cells onto the carts and sleds. As soon as one was filled it took off out of the Pan Crimbian center.

Earney started getting concerned. He could hear the increased chatter on the circuits as Gus' forces advanced on the Crimbian troopers. Apparently, they got some reinforcements or somehow had pinned down Gus and his squad. The room was about half empty. Earney motioned to Jake.

"Go help, Gus."

"We're gone." Jake shifted circuits and motioned to his guys, "Hey, Gus, where are you?"

"Down the first passageway. A Crimbian shuttle just landed with a load of those yellow suited priests. We're pinned down." Gus was thinking on the fly. "Why don't you come around from the outside and we'll attack from both sides."

Jake jumped on the mining cart with his squad of eight following. "Hang on!" Jake called out, as he gunned the loaded cart out the front door which was still swinging open from their initial assault. He snap turned the cart and ran a half-mile down the first wall. Another snap turn at the corner and then another turn - the Crimbian shuttle was parked by the back door service lock. As Jake gunned the cart at full speed, one of the men with a big rocket launcher jumped into the right hand seat next to him and started firing at the bigger Pan Crimbian shuttle. They were preoccupied and must not have seen the cart coming because on the third direct hit the shuttle burst into flames and exploded. Jake turned and drove the cart right through the back door.

The yellow suits were caught from behind. Jake's fighters had target practice. As Jake drove forward down the long hall; his guys were shooting at everything that moved. When he got to the end, Gus' fighters in assorted ragtag suits were advancing. The yellow suits were caught in crossfire – in less than a minute all were down. Most of the Crimbian yellow suits had major breaches – the priests were dead.

"Where's Gus," Jake Asked?

"He's down, but it took six of the bastards

to get him," one of the corporals pronounced. "I patched his suit but he needs help."

Jake lifted the man onto the cart with one hand. "Show me where!"

The man pointed the way and Jake drove the cart forward down another hall. Two men were bent over the form on the floor. When they saw Jake they motioned to him. The carnage was grotesque.

"He's gone," someone stammered. Gus was lying in the middle of yellow Crimbian suits.

Jake jumped out of the cart and tossed Gus' inert broken form into the back. "Hang on. We're heading back. We'll save him – he can't die." Jake was not ready to accept facts.

Earney came on the circuit. "Red Dog here. Mission is accomplished. Pick up all casualties and withdraw."

***

Hours later a Crimbian Cadet Priest returned to the room where Sub Priest Cessan had been working. His hands shook as he went about picking up the cards spilled on the floor and placing them back into the boxes. The longer he worked, the worse he shook. His mind wasn't on the task at hand. He couldn't help thinking about the barbarians who had so brutally attacked and killed. Inadvertently, he misplaced some of the cards into the wrong box.

****

Chapter 5-4
1505 Wednesday 27 February 2228
Hospital Complex, Fleet Headquarters
Mars

Doctor Arlene K. Smith walked down the passageway of the gleaming complex. She was wearing a typical hospital green smock and uniform pants. The smock was imprinted with her name and rank. SMITH – MAJOR (MD). Arlene was a middle-aged woman of slight stature and close-cropped blond hair. She had light brown eyes and an aura of confidence. Dr. Smith was considered among the best physicians in the hospital although she was not the most senior doctor in the hospital.

The nurse behind the desk looked up when she approached. Arlene leaned over the desk.

"You called me?"

"Actually, Dr. Naylor called. He has a patient he wants you to see."

"Where is Dr. Naylor?"

"Station seven."

Dr. Naylor was the duty resident and Arlene was the duty physician. Obviously he had something that required a second opinion. Minutes later she arrived at station seven. She didn't see any signs of Naylor but as she turned to leave he walked up.

"Good evening, Dr. Smith. I've got a real dilly for you." He handed her the chart vellum. "I've got an Army Colonel in here who does not know who she is. She was found at one of the refugee centers. They sent a sample for DNA matching. No telling how long she's been there or why she has been wandering around untreated."

"What have you done"?

"I administered a standard hyperbaric cloister treatment for amnesia. Strangely enough there is no sign of cerebral dysfunction on scans that I could see."

Arlene took out her medical reader and inserted the patient's chart vellum. She flipped carefully through the information and tests. Everything looked in order. Amnesia was no longer the mysterious condition it had once been. Cerebral scans usually showed the area where the disconnect was. Then it would be a simple matter to administer a straightforward adjustment to the nerves while the patient breathed hyperbaric oxygen and the problem was corrected. The treatment was almost a sure thing whether the episode was psychotic or traumatic in nature.

"Okay, I'll take a look at her."

Arlene Smith had been a widow for only a few months. Her husband had not died gallantly in battle he simply died of a heart attack. As a doctor she knew that there were only a couple of final diagnoses; and heart attack was usually the final cause of death in nine out of ten times. Her husband had been Admiral Bull Smith. His death had left her alone at the young age of forty-three. Her daughter Ruby was a cadet in the fleet academy and engaged to a nice young man, Ed Carter who was also a cadet.

Actually, Arlene couldn't complain, she'd had a good marriage to a highly respected man she had loved very much. They had a good kid in Ruby, even a couple of stepchildren from Bull's first marriage. She had also been lucky to have a good career in the fleet service. She had a shore assignment for the first time in years. Ever since Bull had died, she had put every waking moment into her work – the truth was that although she was surrounded by people who liked and respected her Arlene was lonely.

Arlene entered the room and looked at the woman wearing typical hospital pajamas. She had brown hair and smooth skin. The woman was not a beauty. Her nose was too large. Arlene already knew she was thirty-nine years old and a Colonel in the Army. That was young to be a Colonel in a peacetime Army.

Sara's records indicated that she had been on active duty since she had been seventeen. She had never been married and her parents lived in the settlement on Titan, the largest moon of Saturn. Her last assignment of record had been on Luna with the 1st Exploration Force. She had been listed as missing in action and presumed killed last May in the battle for Luna.

"I'm Doctor Smith, how are you feeling today Sara?"

"Actually, after the Recompression Chamber I feel better than I have in a while. I'm still a little confused about why I'm here."

"This is the Fleet Headquarters hospital."

"I understand that but why am I here in the hospital?"

"What did Doctor Naylor tell you?"

"He told me my name was Sara Samuels. Then he treated me in the recompression chamber. When that was done, he asked me if I remembered my name. I told him that he had told me my name was Sara."

Arlene pulled up a chair. "So what do you remember about your past?"

"Not much. I remember being in the refugee camp. There wasn't much to eat and it was cold there."

"Do you remember about your childhood or how you got to the camp?"

Sara winced deep in thought. "Nothing."

"I'm going to tell you some of the raw facts we have about you. Let me know if anything brings back any memories."

"Okay."

"You are in the Army and you were on Luna when the Pan Crimbian forces attacked. Everyone in your unit was listed as missing. Do you remember anything about the battle?"

"In my dreams there are always battles and death; but I don't know the faces I see or where it's located."

"I was there on Luna when it fell to the Crimbian forces. There was a lot of confusion. Obviously you got off the moon somehow."

"I wish I could remember. I want to."

"Amnesia is a funny ailment. One moment it's here, the next it's gone and your memories come flooding back. Most respond to the recompression treatments of hyperbaric oxygen and drugs. You don't really need to be in the hospital. What you need is a comfortable place to stay. I'll make you an offer. I live in a big place all alone why don't you come home with me? We'll work on your memory together.

"I don't want to be a bother."

"You won't be."

"Okay, I accept." Sara smiled. *This was going well just like it was planned.*

****

Chapter 5-5
1100 Thursday 28 February 2228
CE-46 Galileo, Shuttlebay 27
Location (classified)

Sergeant Don Thompson was supervising a gang of fifty-five Marines. They were moving a vast array of supplies onboard the big ship. As fast as the Marines could unload the shuttle, another would arrive to be unloaded. At the present time they were unloading weapons and explosives. As fast as the Marines took the boxes off the shuttle, other gangs of Fleet specialists were assembling the boxes into pallets. A pallet of an exact size was necessary for handling by the ships automatic storage conveyers. The boxes were specially designed to clip together to form a pallet.

Once the pallets were assembled, forklifts moved the pallets onto the conveyor and away it went. The logistic computer tracked and logged each pallet and it went down into the holds of the giant ship. Explosives had to be stored in a magazine. With all of the extra people on the ship they would need every space of the ship for storage. Four things would take up a lot of extra space: food, water, oxygen, and weapons. By the time the ship left on this voyage every space would be filled. Every deck would be lined with food. Nets would be screwed into the overheads or any available corner, which would then be filled with low mass objects, such as toilet paper, crackers, dried fruit, etc. Ten thousand men and women would literally have to crawl through the ship.

The big man, Warrant Jones, was overseeing the efforts of all the people working in the bay. Don didn't know why but he developed an instant liking to the big man. Don respected competency and the man exuded confidence.

The shuttlebay was over a quarter of a

mile long and filled with over two hundred people working at various loading docks. The shuttlebay was designed as a three level bay. Each shuttle tube was about thirty feet in diameter. That made enough room for forty –four shuttles to dock on each level or eighty-eight shuttles could be in the bay at one time if they did not double stack. A frigate for instance carried one shuttle forward and one aft. A cruiser had six bays that could hold twenty-four each. However, bigger explorers like *Galileo* had six of the big eighty-eight bays and ten of the twenty-four.

On exploration missions the exploration section would be filled with mostly recon shuttles and only a few landing craft shuttles. Now that they were outfitting for combat most of the shuttles were attack fighters and landing craft shuttles and only a few were recon shuttles. The marine landing craft shuttles also made great cargo shuttles.

The operation of the shuttle bay was amazing. Don had watched before but he never got tired of seeing the intricate operation. When a shuttle approached the outer door, the bay would be opened to space. The bay superintendent on the bridge would direct the shuttle pilot to the bay opening where he was to enter. Since the big ship is rotating on its axis the shuttle pilot had to chase his assigned bay and match speed with the rotation of the ship.

Each shuttle bay tube had a fleet specialist who is the launch bay operator, who controls the tube and the shuttle once it is captured. Once the shuttle is in position for recovery, the shuttle bay operator sends out a cable with a camera and probe attached to it. The launch bay operator's job was to capture the shuttle. The probe had small thrusters that powered the probe out. Every shuttle has a bow and stern attachment point for the probe to attach to – once the probe rams into the attachment clip it secures the shuttle to the mother ship. Then launch bay operator is in control of the shuttle – the cable allows the launch bay operator to steer the shuttle in addition to providing communications, power and breathing air.

With the cable attached process is simple and usually very routine. The launch bay operator specialist simply inhauls on the cable reel which bringing the shuttle into the ship and then settling it onto the capture skid. The outer twenty foot door is shut once the shuttle is in the tube and on the skid. Then launch bay operator equalizes the tube with the main launch bay. Then the inner door is opened by hydraulics, first the outer ring is rotated then the inner door opens by actuating a large hydraulic ram. The inner door opens and slides out of the way under the deck plates. Once the sensors indicate the inner door is locked open the shuttle can be slid into the shuttle bay. When the shuttle cradle comes to a stop and is locked in place by hydraulic latches, a basket of nylon strap netting is lowered to hold the craft in position. This entire operation usually takes less than five minutes.

The launch on the other hand is usually the reverse. The netting is raised, the cradle is unlatched and the shuttle and cradle are slid into the tube. The inner door is shut and the tube atmosphere is pumped to a large dump tank. The outer door is opened once the tube is equalized to space. The capture cradle slides out, now the launch bay operator gives the shuttle pilot control to fire retros taking a strain on the cable and the shuttle is slowly allowed to reel out into space. Sort of like a yo-yo on a string. The centrifugal force spin of the ship pushes the shuttle away. When the shuttle pilot is ready the launch bay operator released the shuttle cable and it is thrown clear of the larger ship. Navigation computers usually time the release so the shuttle can enter the traffic pattern on the correct course for its destination.

With such a large operation in progress there was a shuttle arriving or leaving every five or ten minutes. Everything was supposed to work each time and all systems had been thoroughly tested. But the real truth was that when the war had started *Galileo* had been gutted – the ship was in the middle of a long overhaul. In less than five months the ship had been reassembled and made ready for combat.

Don was standing where he could see the Marines in a line passing the explosives in a chain from one man to the next. Jonesy had everything in order so that the Marines walked from shuttle to shuttle down a line unloading. Once the shuttle was unloaded the crew went back aboard and it was slid back into the tube. They were on the sixth shuttle, so Don had learned the normal sounds of the shuttle sliding back into the tube. He was not sure what was wrong but he knew something was wrong.

The one inch cable creaked and groaned as took the strain. Something bound up – Don acted without thinking.

"Marines on the deck," he shouted. "Incoming!"

Most of the Marines acted without thinking, as they should. They were trained to obey instant orders like this. Most dropped instantly to the deck or behind one of the boxes. Jonesy had on a pair of earphones and was talking on the comms, so he could not hear Don's alarm. Don dove headfirst across the bay and tackled Jonesy.

When a one-inch cable under maximum strain broke, it cracked like a gunshot with a loud popping noise and snapped back. Anything in the path of the cable moving at velocity of over two hundred miles per hour is cut in half. It doesn't matter whether it was is a man, a steel pole, or deckplate - it's severed by the cable. One of the younger Marines, a private, had frozen and not reacted. A corporal had tried to pull him down, but he was not fast enough the private was decapitated. The cable tore out the launch tube console and slammed back into the bulkhead placing a thirty-foot long dent in the thick walls.

Jonesy stood up looking over the scene. *What a mess.* "Thanks, Sarge. I owe you one."

****

Chapter 5-6
1030 Friday 29 February 2228
Pan Crimbian Transport, Xennin

Arms grabbed hold of Ben and dragged him from the darkness of his cell. They stood him up and spoke to him in a language he didn't understand. Whatever they were saying became apparent when they started prodding him down the passageway. He stumbled and moved in the direction he was being forced. He recalled this had been a weight deck and now there was barely any weight at all. He pulled himself along.

Down several levels they went to the center deck; then forward to the control section. As he pulled along he realized that the normal lights were not on. The lighting was emergency lights. It came to him in a flash. This Crimbian ship was in trouble. The atmosphere was too humid and heavy – someone had been bleeding oxygen into the ship without stabilizing the ship environment – the pressure inside the ship was elevated. Crimbian ships had a natural stink of unwashed bodies and general uncleanness. That's why Ben hadn't made the connection just lying in his cell. This ship had troubles.

Up another series of ladders to the control room. Finally, Ben was standing before the captain. *Xennin's* captain was a big man, with a bald-head and bushy white beard. The captain spoke English and Ben could barely understand him with the thick accent and drawl.

"You are the Captain Papers?"

"Yes," Ben replied.

"My ship is without power and life support is on emergency. My engineers have worked for more than a day to solve the problems. They tell me it cannot be fixed without a repair facility maintenance crew. Would you take a look to see if you can solve the problem?"

Ben almost laughed out loud but he resisted the temptation. "What's in it for me?"

The big man was obviously angry but he visibly fought to control his emotions. "I could tell you that I won't kill you if you help, or argue that whatever happens to us will also affect you and the other prisoners. However, obviously I am in a difficult position so I will bargain with you barbarian. What do you want?"

"Not much, as you point out whatever happens to you also happens to me. I would like a decent meal and a bath. Also I would like to see my wife and son if they are onboard and be held with my family?"

"Your terms are not unreasonable. So be it – if we are still alive and the engines are running your request will be granted." The Captain turned and gave an order in the Crimbian language. He then turned back to Ben. "This is my Grand Engineer. Go with him. He speaks your language. A word of caution, if you perform any acts of deceit or violate my crew I will kill you myself along with your woman and son. Do we have an understanding?"

Ben shook his head yes. "I understand."

The Captain turned, picked up a phone handset and started talking again in the Crimbian language – he was finished with Ben. The Grand Engineer motioned for Ben to follow. Back they went to the engine room. Just entering brought a new wave of stench. Every component in the engine room was covered with rust. All of the piping was leaking – water, hydraulic fluid and hydrogen sulfide. The engines were old ion types. Ben had never seen anything like it. He had read about engines like this. This was something his grandfather might have used. The single main engine took up most of the engine room. There was no power because the generators were belt driven off the main engine. When the main stopped working they were forced on emergency generators and batteries. There were no fuel cells or power cells for emergency power. There were two water stills and boilers which drew power from the generators.

But the real nightmare was the life support scrubbers. They used some type of old-fashioned catalytic absorption fluid (probably amine) to pick up the CO_2 and pump it out into space. They didn't even convert the CO_2 back to oxygen - what a waste. This whole system was tied directly to the main engine like everything else. Ben shook his head and cringed to think his life depended on this junk.

Ben went back up the main engine and dropped down inside where the rest of the ship's engineering crew was working. Ben rolled up his sleeves and went to work. Two hours later he knew what the problem was. The ion exchange controller was not functioning. On an ion engine it was essential. Ben looked at the broken component for about ten minutes trying to figure out what to do about it. Probably no spare parts had been built for the exchanger in the past thirty years. The unit was monstrous about thirty feet long with unbelievably large contacts inside. It even had old-fashioned wires to carry three-phase alternating current.

The Engineer tapped him on the shoulder. He asked, "Is the exchanger the problem?"

"Yes."

"Can we build the parts that are burned out?"

"Do you have a 3D printer that can fabricate the exchanger body out of stainless steel?" 3D printers to fabricate parts were standard in any Union ship.

"Then no."

"What can we do?" The Chief Engineer said, almost in a whine. It was hard to believe this man was the Chief Engineer. He would not be qualified to be even an apprentice specialist in a Union ship merchant ship engine room, much less a warship. Ben realized sadly that these people were qualified only to run the ship. They had no idea how the engines worked or functioned.

"I'll build a new controller. You got something to write on?"

He was handed a pen and a piece of paper. Ben looked at the paper strangely. *What a waste of good trees, he thought.* He made a list of things he would need. Then he turned over the paper and sketched the box and the circuits that needed to be built.

The engineer took the paper and started talking rapidly. Runners left in three different directions. Someone handed Ben a water bottle, so he took a long drink. Within minutes the materials started appearing. Twenty minutes later he had the contraption breadboarded together. Ben ran a little test using one of the batteries it worked. Then the real trick was fastening it in place inside the engine.

The engine room crew was amazed when the motors started up. Ben was sitting just watching the controls when the two guards appeared and grabbed him. They took him back and tossed him into his cell.

****

Chapter 5-7
0700 Monday 3 March 2228
Fleet Headquarters
Mars

Mike O'Brian was seated at the conference table in the large room all by himself, which was preferable just now. Mike was feeling blue – the news from Luna wasn't good. He looked at his watch. Maggie should be here soon since there was going to be a staff meeting at 0800. He started to read the messages again when there was a tapping at the open door frame.

A man cleared his throat. "Excuse me."

Mike looked up at the rumpled man in the doorway. He seemed lost. "May I help you?" Mike asked.

The man looked down at his notebook. "I am looking for Senior Chief Warrant O'Brian."

"I'm O'Brian."

"Yes. I was sent to talk with you about some thefts."

"Thefts reported by…"

He looked back down at his electronic notebook. "Your Logistics Commodore's Aide."

"Ah, yes," Mike remembered. "You're

from the Federal Police?"

"Yes," the man replied after searching each pocket at least twice. He produced a gleaming gold badge. Centered in the badge was a visual image of the man looking at Mike. "Chief Inspector Herbert Kohler, at your service, Sir." Mike looked carefully at the badge and the man. Kohler was a big man with a big belly. Middle-aged, thinning sandy red hair and blue-gray eyes and an oriental heritage of some type. *Well Union spacers were a mixed breed.*

Mike flipped up his notebook and scanned through several files; finally, he found the one he needed. Two strokes later he had down loaded the files and reports and had a chip to hand to Kohler. "Personally, I think this is a waste of your time, but since the Commodore insists, here are the data files on the case. You will see the Fleet inspectors have already investigated it; they could find no evidence or suspects. When you speak to the Commodore, he'll give you a story that he believes that it is an inside job."

Kohler slipped his badge back into his shirt pocket and took the data chips from Mike. "I'll need a pass to permit me access throughout headquarters."

Mike handed him another disc. "Take this to the central pass office by the main lobby desk."

"Thanks." Kohler turned to leave.

"One more thing." Mike stopped the man. "This is a Fleet investigation ordered by the Fleet Admiral. Please report your findings to me."

Kohler looked hard at Mike and then smiled. "Of course. I owe you that courtesy. I like to do things in a logical and fair manner. However, you do realize that if I find evidence of serious corruption, I must file charges and arrest any Fleet personnel involved."

Mike liked this man. "The Fleet Admiral just wants to be informed; particularly if a member of the senior staff is going to be arrested. We wouldn't think of trying to interfere with your investigation or authority. You see investigations, no matter how necessary while we are trying to run a war, are a hindrance."

"I think we have an understanding," Kohler replied as he went out the door.

Mike rubbed his eyes. This was an aggravation he did not need. Now they had a Federal Inspector poking around. This just added to the glum news from Luna. Mike picked up the messages from the moon and re-read them.

BEGIN TRANSMISSION

FROM: COMMANDER LUNAR RESISTANCE FORCES

TO: FLEET ADMIRAL

SUBJECT: LUNA SITUATION REPORT

TOP SECRET BLUE

RESISTANCE FORCE HAS CAPTURED SUFFICIENT FOOD AND WEAPONS TO BEGIN NEW CAMPAIGN AGAINST THE PAN CRIMBIAN FORCE. BELIEVE THE FORCE ON LUNA HAS BEEN REDUCED IN MILITARY STRENGTH. A NEW COMMANDER HAS ASSUMED COMMAND HE IS A HIGH PRIEST IN THE CRIMBIAN RELIGION AND SEEMS TO BE A FORCE IN THE POLITICAL BUREAUCRACY.

THEY HAVE BEGUN SYSTEMATICALLY ROUNDING UP ALL CIVILIANS AND IMPRISONING THEM IN HOLDING COMPOUNDS. FAMILIES ARE DEFINITELY BEING SPLIT APART. THIS APPEARS TO BE RELIGION TRAINING AND CONVERSION OF THE GENERAL POPULATION. ANYONE WHO RESISTS THE CONVERSION TO CRIMBIAN IS IMPRISONED IN GENERAL LABOR FORCE OR EXECUTED IF ANY HOSTILITY TOWARDS THE PRIESTS IS FOUND. WE DISCOVERED A COMMON GRAVE WHERE MORE THAN THREE HUNDRED UNION CIVILIANS WERE KILLED AND BURIED.

HAVE CHANGED TACTICS WE NO LONGER OPENLY ACCEPT ESCAPEES ON FACE VALUE. TWO RECENT ESCAPEES WERE FOUND WITH TRANSPONDERS AND HAD BEEN CONVERTED TO BE INFILTRATORS.

INTEND TO ATTACK A LABOR CAMP TO OBTAIN ADDITIONAL TROOPS.

SERGEANT MAJOR AGUSTUS B COLLINS 4771882 FMF HAS DIED FROM WOUNDS SUSTAINED IN ACTION OF 26 FEB 2228 – CITATION ATTACHED. SERGEANT MAJOR COLLINS INTERRED IN MAMMOTH CAVE SIRIUS MARINE. INADEQUATE MEDICAL SUPPLIES AND MEDICAL SUPPORT. REQUEST A PHYSICIAN SURGEON AND FULL MEDICAL UNIT WITH NEXT RESUPPLY EFFORT.

KEEP THE UNION SAFE

EARNEST MACLEAN

MAJOR FMC

END TRANSMISSION

***

BEGIN TRANSMISSION

FM: COMMANDER LUNAR RESISTANCE FORCES

TO: FLEET ADMIRAL

SUBJ: COMMENDATION FOR SERGEANT MAJOR AGUSTUS B COLLINS 4771882 FMC

UNCLASSIFIED

RECOMMENDATION COMMENDATION FOR SERGEANT MAJOR AGUSTUS B COLLINS 4771882 FMC.

ON 26 FEBRUARY 2228 AT 0500 SERGEANT MAJOR COLLINS ACTING AS

1ST LIEUTENANT LED THE POINT UNIT ON AN ASSAULT AGAINST PAN CRIMBIAN DETENTION CAMP ON LUNA WHERE MUNITIONS WERE STOCKPILED THAT WERE VITALLY NEEDED BY THIS UNION MARINE FORCE.

1ST LIEUTENANT COLLINS COMPANY WAS SUCCESSFUL IN PERFORMING A SURPRISE ATTACK AND IMMEDIATE BREACH OF OUTER PERIMETER. HIS UNIT IMMEDIATELY ATTACKED AND PINNED DOWN THE PAN CRIMBIAN TROOPS WHILE VITAL WEAPONS AND ENERGY CELLS WERE CAPTURED. 1ST LIEUTENANT COLLINS' UNIT ABSORBED A COUNTER ATTACK FROM AN ELITE ENEMY FORCE (YELLOW SUITS) AND STOPPED THEIR ADVANCE ON THE EXPOSED UNIT.

AGUSTUS COLLINS DISPLAYED COURAGE IN BATTLE AND DEVOTION TO DUTY ABOVE AND BEYOND THE CALL TO DUTY. HE EXPOSED HIMSELF TO ATTACK BY A SUPERIOR FORCE TO SAVE HIS FELLOW MARINES. HIS WOUNDS RESULTED IN HIS DEATH. LIGHTFOOT WILL BE REMEMBERED BY THE MARINES WHO HAVE SERVED WITH HIM.

ADDITIONAL RECOMMENDED PURPLE HEART WITH CLUSTERS

RECOMMENDED FOR PERMANENT RANK OF 1ST LIEUTENANT

RECOMMENDED FOR MEDAL OF

HONOR (POSTHUMOUSLY)

PASS TO GUS' WIFE JUDY AND CHILDREN MY PERSONAL GRATITUDE FOR HIS SACRIFICE AND MY CONDOLENCES.

EARNEST MACLEAN

MAJOR FMF (BVR.)

END TRANSMISSION

Mike and Maggie had been over to the Collins house just before the winter holidays. Seven children; Gus and Judy's oldest boy was just seventeen. Mike already missed Gus. Judy was a nurse over at the fleet hospital. Guess he had to tell her. He would go over right after the meeting this morning. *It would be best if it came from him. God how he hated this war; come to think of it he hated all wars – such a waste of good people.*

****

Chapter 5-8
0815 Tuesday 4 March 2228
CC-141 Arial

Routine on a ship underway was essential. The crew expected to stand watches and work at specific times. This was life on any ship on a long voyage even during wartime. *Arial* moved silently on its prescribed course and speed directed by the task force commander. Little was left to the captain's control when a group of ships are on a prescribed course. The Admiral had laid out the flight plan with complete course and speeds for the next month of cruising. No variation would be permitted.

Arial was cruising, as all of the other ships in the force, with no running lights or sensor emissions permitted. This didn't allow the individual ships to even communicate with each other. Each ship became its own world as it settled into the routine. This was planned to be a long voyage so each ship had sufficient supplies to stay out for up to three years.

The trick of traveling anywhere in the solar system was that you had to know where you were going and what time you would get there. Speed, distance and time are the three factors that have been the same constant ever since mankind started traveling. If you know any two, then finding the other was simple. The main problem with travel space was that even if you know where you wanted to go, you needed to know where it's going to be when you get there.

When the first men traveled between planets, they followed elliptical orbits using Kepler's laws of physics to get the most use of their fuel. The first problem was to break free of the effects of a planet's gravity. Since men started from Earth, they used rockets to boost them up out of the atmosphere. Then a slight push and they traveled to the moon in about three days. Over ninety-five percent of the fuel they had was expended just getting off the ground. Spaceships such as *Arial* were built in space and couldn't land on a planet. Cruisers have fusion reactors to power them, so they boost going out to their destination and then turn and boost to slow down. The key is knowing the average speed over the course of a voyage.

War and exploration ships can average up to 8,000,000 miles per day, which is about 333,333 miles per hour. So it's no longer necessary to follow the efficient elliptical curves to catch up when traveling between planets. Most of the planets in our solar system are located in the same plane. If you looked down, all the planets are moving in a counterclockwise direction. The sun and all of the planets rotate in a counterclockwise direction (except Venus). Even the moons around planets rotate in a counter clockwise direction. Spacers boost up and over or down and under when traveling between planets. If you were moving inward towards the sun a captain goes down and under; conversely if you were moving outward away from the sun the rules require you to stay above.

So if a ship averaged 8,000,000 miles per day then all you had to know was where the planet you're traveling to was going to be when you get there. Earth is an average of 92.9 million miles from the sun but it can be as far as 94.6 or as close as 91.4. Jupiter on the other hand is nominally 483,600,000 miles from the Sun, but it too varies between 507 and 460.6 million miles. So in theory the maximum distance to travel from Jupiter could be 576,500,000 miles or it could be as close as 390,700,000. That makes the travel time anywhere between 73 to 49 days. Of course this is by relatively straight line on a plane. In practical application a ship has to drive an arc above or below the plane of planets to stay clear of particles. However, if the Sun is in the path of travel then almost every Captain will keep his ship clear of the Sun. Any ship passing close to the Sun will soak up too much radiation and heat. So even when the Sun is inactive the rule of thumb is to stay outside of the orbit of Mercury.

Arial would take fifty-eight days to complete this voyage. Since she had departed on 24 February then it would be 23 April before they would arrive in the Earth/Luna sector. Captain Thomas was determined to make the best use of all the time in transit. Jackie was waiting at the head of the wardroom conference table for everyone to finish breakfast. She had spent her time reviewing the projections of voyage time and energy available for boost.

When the last person arrived, First Officer Jane Polanski started. “Captain, everyone is here that can attend. Anyone not present I’ll brief off line.”

“Very well, let’s get started.” Jackie looked around the table. All of her senior officers were here. The person in particular she wanted was Science Chief Clarence Bell. Jackie was quite aware that Chief Bell had worked in weapons research projects. “I’ll make the situation clear. Last time out we went up against a ship that should have never been able to touch us. I am putting together a Tiger Team with the weapons officer as the lead. I want to know what's wrong with the missiles we have, and by gum I want them fixed before we get within range of the enemy."

Sam Waters looked at the Captain. "Ma'am weren't we ordered to leave well enough alone and let the civilian technicians at Ganymede solve the problems?"

Jackie looked at Sam. She really liked Sam but sometime he was a little naïve. "I wouldn't trust Admiral Gonzales to solve any problem, other than to figure out where his next meal is coming from." She turned looking at Chief Bell. "You once told me that you might have some ideas about the failure of the missiles."

"Ma'am, I was postulating on a couple of hypothesis concerning the failure to detonate."

"Well now you have your chance to prove your hypotheses. I want answers."

Jane Polanski handed a vellum to Chief Bell. "Here's a list of personnel with particular talents. Look it over and get with the Weapons Officer to set up a schedule. I'm sure one of the first things will be to open up and disassemble a missile.

Chief Bell took the vellum and nodded in agreement.

Jackie looked over this group. She knew this would be a real challenge, but she was convinced that they would be up to the task. Jackie only had one more comment. "We were faster and had more fire power. But they got to us and killed people in this crew. Next time we get someone in our sights I want weapons that work. By God I do not want to play games with the lives of this crew."

Everyone seated at the table now saw the fire in their new Captain. This lady had a pair of steel pants and now she wanted to be sure she had steel boots for kicking.

****

Chapter 5-9
1600 Wednesday 5 March 2228
Barbarian Reform Center
Luna

"I don't care what your list says. Prisoners here are held for political or security reasons." The guard on the Inquisitor's block was obviously upset.

The Sub-Priest in the yellow robe was exasperated. The audacity of this enlisted guard to question orders from the transport minister. "You want to take a chance that this list is incorrect and disturb the minister priests in prayer and meditation?"

The man thought about the results of such a decision. He remembered what had happened to others who had brought the wrath of the minister priests down on them. He had a good job, safe and warm for the most part and very little of the chicken regulations and work details. "Okay, take her! Your list is in order and has the proper authorization, however I am going to log that I questioned the order."

"Get her out here. I don't have all day to mess around with one barbarian woman who probably is not worth the time we have already wasted."

Minutes later Jill was brought out and shoved down. The priest looked down at the dirty woman. "You are called Jill Parks?" the man in the yellow robe asked.

"Yes," she answered softly.

"You're being moved to the Congo Labor Camp to work for the glory of Pan Crimbian Empire."

"I won't do anything for the glory of Crimbian," she replied evenly. "In fact I pray every day that Crimbian and all you scum that are infected with Crimbian drop dead."

Both men hit her from each side. The priest slapped her in the face but the guard drove his fist into her back about the level of a kidney. She dropped to her knees in pain from the blow.

The priest bent down and took her face in his hands. "Daughter, you are insolent and disrespectful. If you don't learn to curb your tongue, you'll spend a lot of time on your knees in pain. When I release you, stand and follow me exactly two paces behind me. Keep your eyes down. That is what is proper from a barbarian woman. Do you understand?"

She tried to shake her head but he held her head tight. "Yes," she finally managed dutifully from between clenched teeth.

When she stood the guard tossed her a P-suit. It was not hers but the standard prisoner suit issued to all prisoners. The suit looked like it had seen better days. Now she was going to Earth – what a nightmare. Just when she thought things could not get any worse - *they did*!

As she followed she swore a silent vow. *She would never convert to this religion of murder. They had killed her grandfather, all of her friends; and the man she loved might be dead as well. At the first opportunity she was going to exact every drop of vengeance possible. She hummed to herself – kill – kill – kill. Ten for everyone.*

****

****

"It seem to be a law of nature, inflexible and inexorable, that those who will not risk cannot win." *Captain John Paul Jones*

Part 6 - Elude

Even the Union had a seamier side. Contracts were made with private individuals to conduct exploration missions for profit. These private explorations and research made many discoveries of wealth and minerals. The Union Office of Production issued private ship operation permits for voyages of loosely worded goals. There were few rules and potentially large profits to be made. The types of people who seemed to gravitate towards this life were those who wanted few ties to official oversight. When they brought in gold or scrap radioactive materials for sale, few questions were asked. Most were considered rogues at best or pirates at the very worst. Not really criminals - but as close as one could get without really being one.

Journal of Solar History

Chapter 6-1
2220 Tuesday 11 March 2228
Aboard Privateer
S/S Amelia O'Leary[10]

Buck Cardif was a giant of a man. He had

to bend over to stand in the bridge. Over eight foot tall and would weight more than three hundred and fifty pounds at 1 G. The crew liked working for this man. As Captain of the *Amelia O'Leary*, Buck had made everyone onboard independently wealthy. They called themselves privateers. Buck had a charter issued by the Union Office of Production. Officially they were private explorers for profit; however the Pan Crimbians considered them pirates.

Buck was studying the sensor screens. There was a ship out there somewhere; when it was an enemy ship on the sensors he could feel it. There was no logic in the feeling and Buck certainly couldn't explain it – but he knew the bad guys were out there.

Buck looked down at his wife Amelia who was also his first officer and the duty pilot. "Lay in a course and bring her alongside."

"Everyone will have to strap down," she responded. "It's going to get ugly."

"Okay, make it so," the big man rumbled.

Amelia rang the general alarm. The horn sounded throughout the ship. When the alarm ended she toggled the general announcing switch and spoke in a clear and distinct voice. "All Hands, standby for no-

---

[10] Private merchant ships are designated by mission: i.e. S/S Space Ship, L/L Luxury Liner, C/S Cargo Ship, etc. Whereas fleet military ships are designated by either Combat or Support use: i.e. CE Combat Explorer, CF Combat Frigate or ST Support Transport, etc. See Appendix C.

weight and acceleration changes in one minute. Strap in! Be ready for battle when all maneuvers are complete."

Her hands danced across the controls. She input the coordinates of the unknown ship ahead. In less than fifteen seconds the computer had solved the basic ballistic problem of velocity and direction between the two ships and a recommended course and speed flashed on the tactical display. Across the top of the pilot's console was a series of lights. Each one of the eleven lights changed from blue to green indicating that all were at maneuvering and battle stations. She had to wait for the time to be correct. The computer timer was in a countdown mode. When it reached zero she thumbed the control to thrust the main engines.

The *Amelia O'Leary* was actually an old frigate hull that had originally seen over thirty years of fleet service. She had been decommissioned and tossed away on a junk pile left to float along with the rest of the trash in the Asteroid belt. Buck had found the old ship and started a project to restore it. The hull itself was actually in fairly good shape but the engineering, electronic and computer systems were junk. It took him almost three years to restore the ship. Of course most the refurbishment was done with parts of questionable ownership. The result was a ship that other than length and diameter - had very little resemblance to the warship it had once been, especially inside.

In Fleet service the ship would've had a

crew of about a hundred and thirty five. Buck commanded the ship with forty-five and he would be confident in taking on a Pan Crimbian cruiser. The ship ahead was nothing compared to a cruiser or even a frigate – it appeared to be some type of transport.

Everyone was pressed back in their couches. It was not so bad at first, but as the minutes ticked off, the pressure became unbearable, even in armored pressure suits. Suddenly relief. They were weightless.

Buck sent the message:

BEGIN TRANSMISSION

FM: COMMANDER AMELIA O'LEARY

TO: COMMANDER UNKNOWN VESSEL

SURRENDER AND PREPARE TO BE BOARDED!

END TRANSMISSION

They waited several minutes. Buck looked at the sensors. "Well, well - they are game." He toggled the comm switch. "Enemy vessel is preparing to fire missiles."

The weapons mate answered, "Yeah, we see. We see."

Buck watched as the outer hatch opened on the other ship. Suddenly the cannons on the Amelia started firing into the open missile hatch. They were rewarded with a burst of flame as the fuel and oxidizer exploded, moving the other ship sideways in space. For every action there was an opposite and equal reaction. Obviously the other ship was not prepared to counter the explosion of a missile. The Crimbian ship only had two missile hatches – it wasn't really a true warship. As the other open missile hatch came into view, Buck's gunners concentrated cannon fire until it also exploded. Once this was done, they shifted to firing on the stern section buckling the exposed parts of the ion engine. The big weakness of an ion engine was the negative grid – it's big and exposed on the stern of a ship. An ion drive ship without the negative grid is dead in space.

Buck came unbuckled and started moving while speaking to his beloved pilot. "Notify the boarding party to meet me at the forward shuttle. The bridge is yours my dear."

It was fairly unusual for the captain of a ship to lead a boarding party. But Buck had always made it his trademark to lead the attacks; anyway his wife was actually a better pilot, as well as being the only person that Buck trusted implicitly with his ship. *What the hell, it was just as much her ship too.*

By the time Buck arrived at the shuttle bay there were ten men and two women suited up and ready to go - this crew had a lot of practice. The shuttle pre-flight checks were already done, the pilot was just finishing. The outer door opened and the shuttle eased forward on the umbilical cable until clear then the shuttle popped out into the void. The pilot of the shuttle handled the ship with the ease of experience. It took him only minutes to turn and match speed with the enemy ship. Soon they were chasing around the spin of the ship keeping what appeared to be the launch bay in sight. Buck fired the grapnel. It went through the hull into a tank and held fast. Now they gradually winched in until the shuttle settled onto the outer hull of the Crimbian ship.

Two men were ready – while the shuttle pilot had been maneuvering into position they had been preparing a breaching charge. When the light came on indicating the shuttle was firmly moored the suited men jumped out. Shape charges were old technology, but very reliable. Practice makes perfect. The high velocity explosives were placed in a large rectangle while the first man placed the low velocity charge in the center. The second inserted the detonators. Both men clipped off to the hull and then swung out of the way. Only hand signals were used now and the radio transmitter of the shuttle was off. No one wanted the charges to go prematurely.

The signal was given both men clear and ready. Buck gave the signal, then announced, “Fire-in-the-hole.”

A stab of flame shot out - but since the only oxygen present was contained chemically within the explosives it was quickly consumed along with the detonation. What actually happened in a split second was that the high velocity shape charge split through eight inches of honeycombed titanium pressure hull like a hot knife through butter. The low velocity pounding charge detonated 0.13 seconds later and punched the nine-foot by three-foot rectangle of metal into the interior of the ship. There were a few reasons for putting the breach of the hull back into the ship. First, it was one less piece of debris floating in space and second, it might be needed to plug up the hole later. Most of all, if anyone was waiting on the other side, they would be crushed by the concussion of the rectangle metal piece of the hull. It was crude but effective.

The two explosive experts swung on the static lines into the breach – as expected, the tank was empty. The first layer of skin on space ships is usually tanks. One man moved one direction while the other went the other way shining light upwards towards the inside of the ship.

"Over here," called the detonator man. He had found the access hatch into the interior of the ship. He looked around just in time to see the big suited figure of Buck entering the tank. He stood there for a half minute or so tracing out the lines that went to the valves. Soon he was surrounded by everyone in the boarding party. He cycled the lock using the valves. There was only room for two in the access. Buck and the first man got in. Moments later the inner door opened and they dropped down into the empty passageway. They shoved the lock shut and the cycle completed dropping two more into the ship. By the time the lock cycled the third time Buck was ready to move out.

Down they went three decks before encountering anyone. The chattergun fired in Buck's hand knocking down the enemy crewman. He didn't think, he just acted. When he got the center deck he started forward. By now he had eight with him. They went through three of the hatches going forward until they reached the control section. That's when the crew of the Crimbian ship hit. They dropped down into the invaders from around the core and others started firing from the hatches all around. It would have been a good plan if Buck and his men had not been expecting it. They threw themselves against the bulkheads and Buck tossed a concussion grenade into the mass of suits. Buck's men were holding on expecting the force, while the attacking Pan Crimbians were hanging suspended in the center of the compartment. The explosion slammed the attackers into the bulkheads at a high rate. Most were knocked unconscious, the rest were dazed. Buck's men cut them down with their side arms and knives – it was over in less than thirty seconds. Within another minute all of the attackers who had been shooting down through the hatches were finished off. It was grisly work which was quickly done. Buck went up the ladder climbing three decks to the control room - there was no further resistance.

Buck opened his helmet since there was still atmosphere in the ship. He was facing a very angry and arrogant captain along with another Crimbian officer. "I am the Captain of the holy ship *Xennin.* I demand to know why you have attacked my ship."

Buck grinned then said. "I'm Captain Cardif and I'm in charge of this part of the solar system. You have crossed into our space. You have to pay the toll."

The Crimbian captain and the other officer looked at one another. The younger officer asked, "Captain, what is a toll"?

****

Chapter 6-2
1830 Thursday 13 March 2228
CE-46 Galileo
Underway

Patty Sue Smith was angry. She was sitting just outside of the common decontamination shower room for bachelor women located aft. She could hear and smell the retching of the young woman. The situation was disgusting. When the woman finished vomiting, Patty stood and walked in turning on the shower again. Patty directed the water to run the mess down the drain then soaked the sick, fully-clothed woman lying on the deck again.

"Hello in there," a familiar male voice called.

"Come on in," Patty replied. She had

been waiting for Jonesy.

Jonesy stepped in and looked over the situation in one glance. He knew instantly what the general problem was. The young woman on the deck had a weakness.

"Booze or patch?" he asked.

"Booze," Patty replied.

Alcohol was still a social drink among the Union spacers. Drugs, however were not sociable and spurned by Union spacers. The miners on the other hand had developed a habit of chewing a certain plant, which produced some of the effects of alcohol. Later it was found that a piece of the plant could be taped to the skin under a Band-Aid to produce the same effect over a long period of time, even while the person was wearing a P-suit. They called it patch. Unfortunately, much like alcohol, too much could cause dependence with certain weak individuals. The results were the same.

Fleet or Marine personnel who developed dependencies or displayed these weakness were usually sent off ships and left dirtside. Once that became a problem underway, were confined and dried out. *As these thoughts went through his head, he suddenly realized there was something unusual here or Patty would have dragged the woman down to sickbay all ready.*

Jonesy asked, "What do you need me for?"

Patty used her foot to roll over the

woman. She looked familiar. "This particular drunk is Lucy O'Brian the daughter of the Fleet Admiral. I need your help to ensure she is not going to be an embarrassment."

Jonesy sighed. This was the part of the job he hated. "Where is she getting the stuff?"

"She won't tell me. But you know as well as I do on a ship of this size there's always some enterprising specialist who is willing to risk it to make a few bucks. Usually it's just as well to let it alone. But she has it bad, so she must have been drinking a lot. Someone has a real big operation going on. With the Marines on board you can bet there are lot of willing customers."

"Let me talk to her for a few minutes," Jonesy retorted.

"Okay, I'll go and get us some coffee." Patty turned and left.

Jonesy picked up the folding stool that Patty had been sitting on. He carried it in the shower and sat down looking at the pitiful looking waif.

"Okay, Lucy, you're going to tell me about it."

"About what?"

"I've met your father and mother; both fine people and professionals. You come from good stock. What's making you drink?"

"You're just a big asshole – just like that

bitch that left."

"Remember, you're just a corporal and I'll not listen to any disrespectful talk against a fellow officer. Even if your mother is the boss of the whole fleet. So get your shit together and start acting like a corporal."

Lucy started crying. Jonesy just sat waiting. When she started settling down he stood and walked over to a locker and took out a towel. She sat up cross-legged and Jonesy tossed her the towel. She dried her head then looked up sniffling. He handed her a handkerchief; she blew her nose and wiped.

"You think you're the first ever to try and crawl into a bottle? I tried it once, got to feeling real sorry for myself after I lost someone I loved. No matter what the problem is – it's still there when you sober up."

"I'm not good enough. My chief hates my work and me too."

"I'm sure – If you're drunk all the time your work probably sucks."

"My father is a great hero. I'm scared all the time – I'm not good enough to be here," she blurted out. Before he could reply to the admission she continued, "The word is that this is a one way voyage to death. I was up there in the hangar when the cable broke and you were almost killed. I can't get the image of that Marine out of my head. He and I had had a couple of drinks together.

He was so nice. Look, I get the shakes just thinking about it. I can't sleep unless I have a couple of drinks."

"Oh hell, kid, we're all scared and none of us are good enough. But until the rest of the Fleet gets here from the outer regions they'll just have to use us. As far as this being a one way trip I can assure you that I wouldn't have come if I thought it was one way. I don't have a death wish. I plan to die of old age somewhere greater than one-forty."

"Really?"

"Yes, really."

"I heard our Admiral stood for a court martial for losing her last ship."

"Listen, I'm going to set you straight just this once. Yes the Admiral stood up for losing her ship. I was there. There was nothing that could've been done to prevent it. Any commander that loses a ship must stand in front of a court of inquiry. She was exonerated and promoted. Furthermore, I've seen her in action; we're lucky to have her – she is good. You mama wouldn't have put her here if she wasn't."

Lucy started crying again. Patty Sue came back with three cups of coffee.

Jonesy took the coffee and handed one to Lucy. He stepped out into the outer hall. Patty followed. Jonesy looked at Patty. "You dry her out and I'll find the still."

"Thanks."

Jonesy left and went forward. What a hell of a mess. Both he and Patty were guilty of neglecting the crew. They were supposed to keep things like this from happening. Everyone was so intent on getting the fleet ready and heading out that they had overlooked some of the people things. The trouble was he had only been aboard a short time and really did not know the crew. Even though it was a big crew it wasn't that big. *Who were the operators?*

He took the tube forward and got off in the exploration section. Since the ship was not really exploring, the exploration section had been turned over to the Marines. He stopped at one of the information terminals and punched in the name he was seeking. It listed the section and quarters for the man. Ten minutes later he opened the door to the squad bay of the 1st Platoon of A Company. Two privates were sitting reading and two others had an APS suit laid on the table and were working on the internal controls. When one private looked up and saw a warrant he snapped to attention. "Attention on Deck – Officer in the Bay." All four came to attention.

"Carry on," Jonesy spoke crisply. "I'm looking for Sergeant Thompson."

The Marines relaxed but remained standing. The closest man spoke, "He went to work out in the gym, but that was a couple of hours ago. You will probably find him in the armory; he likes to work on guns."

"Thanks.' Jonesy turned and departed. It took only a few minutes to drop down two decks to the weapons lab where the marines had set up their armory. He found Don standing at a workbench with a chattergun disassembled. Don came to attention along with the rest of the Marines NCO's in the room. Jonesy waved for them to relax.

Jonesy spoke, "Sergeant, good to see you again. Can we talk for a few minutes?"

The other man standing nearby was a gunny. "Is there a problem, Sir?"

"Not with the Marines. I need some help. I was hoping the Sergeant here could be of some help."

Don spoke, "This is Gunny Travis my Platoon Commander. Warrant Jones."

"Glad to meet you." Jonesy replied sticking out his hand. The Gunny shook his hand.

"Don't I know you? Jones, you were a Marine once?"

Jonesy chuckled, "Guilty."

Don asked, "What can we do for you?"

"I've got a problem with a still. I want to find it and put it out of business."

Gunny asked, "Why don't you just have the master-at-arms find it and get rid of it?"

"Well there's two reasons; first I don't want an official report. Second, I want it gone and to never come back. I figure a couple of Marines can put the fear of God into these people."

Don realized he actually had information that could help. "Wait here. I'll check it out." With that brief statement he was gone.

Travis looked hard at Jonesy. "So when I'm Cobra what do you answer to?"

Jonesy paused before answering. "You'll keep it to yourself."

"Sure."

"Well, my name was Hermit."

It came to Travis in a flash. He had heard the stories of Hermit, and there was more than one story. He thought that Hermit was dead - not transferred to the Fleet. If even half of the stories about Hermit were true, this man had at one time proved himself as a Marine.

"So why did you come to Sergeant Thompson for help?" Now Travis was curious, since he knew better than to probe a sensitive area of Hermit.

"The kid helped me out last week and I realized he was a fast thinker."

"Yeah, he is a fast thinker. He certainly should have been an officer by now. Some just don't have the opportunity."

Don returned silencing the conversation between Travis and Jonesy. "That wasn't hard. The boys have a steady supply coming from environmental control section. Those farmers have found better uses for corn other than for eating."

"Let's go," Jonesy ordered in an offhand manner. Don reached up into the gun locker and took down a Carter 350 handgun and Travis tossed Jonesy a Ballistic Model 2201B pistol. Travis picked up a matching gun. The ballistic was an interesting weapon it fires solid explosive projectiles at an adjustable velocity using a miniature hydraulic compressor and could deliver energy pulses from a cell for over an hour of continuous use. The problem with a weapon that can shoot either projectiles or energy pulses was that it needs to be aimed - that takes skill. To help overcome these problems the Model B had an advanced computer sighting system. You just looked in the little screen and place the target in the cross hairs. That's what the gun will hit when fired.

Jonesy checked the loads and set the safety before sticking the gun in his belt under his tunic. They probably wouldn't need guns, but it's always better to be safe than sorry. The three dropped down two decks and went forward to the junction tube where they caught the people conveyer that ran forward and aft in that quadrant.

Galileo was so big that in addition to the center no-weight tube going forward and aft through the ship there were four other full-length of the ship also. With over three hundred levels it would be too much for everyone to have to go down all three hundred decks or any portion of them to go between each section of the ship. Elevators and conveyers were placed to run from the interior section all the way out to the outer hull. So to move between sections a person would have to get on the level with a transit tube or at the center 'A' deck.

They dropped off in the environmental section and started outward. They had to move through decks of lush plants. Some were obviously vegetables grown to supplement the normal packaged foods eaten by spacers, and some were flowers that brightened up things considerably. But most of the plants were strange and were grown only because they had an ability to give off a lot of oxygen and absorb carbon dioxide. Jonesy realized that it was one of the obvious places for an illegal still. The environmental specialists worked almost in autonomy. No one ever paid much attention to the specialists in this remote area. Not only that they grew a lot of the basic ingredients needed to produce liquors or patch.

When they reached the destination deck they moved forward through the cornfields. There was a path and Don took the point moving forward as Jonesy and Travis fell back on either side staying under cover in the fields. Don met the specialist in the middle of the path. His insignia indicated a sergeant; Don was surprised to see a man in such a dirty uniform.

"Hey, Jarhead. You lost?"

"I hope not." Don was hesitant acting reluctant. "One of my buddies told me that I might be able to get some alcohol down here. He said you guys have the good stuff."

"Anyone with you?" The man looked around in the direction, which Don had approached.

"I don't think so."

"You know officially it can't happen."

Don held up a money clip. "We're going to have a party. I want two gallons. One of my boys Alvin Duncan sent me here."

The specialist licked his lips. That was a lot of money. He was greedy. "Come on."

Don followed the man down the path to a shed. The combination was punched in and the door opened revealing row after row of plastic bottles.

"Quite a supply," Don noted.

The man was confident now. "We got ready for this voyage. Let your buddies know there is plenty more."

Travis stepped forward from the field. The man dropped the bottle he was holding. He turned to run. Don stuck out his foot and tripped the man.

He looked up to see an officer. Jonesy said a single word. "Busted!"

The man lay on the soft ground; his expression showed plainly all thoughts of running or fighting was gone. "What're you going to do?" The specialist was scared now.

"I'm not going to do anything," Jonesy declared. "You are!"

"What do you mean?"

"You're going to destroy this supply and any other stashes you have. You are going to destroy the still and the parts are going overboard. Furthermore, you're going to tell us who your associates are. You do that and it ends here. If not, you know who I work for. I'll take you up before the Commodore so fast your head will spin. I can just about guarantee that you will spend the remainder of this voyage in the brig."

The man stood there without answering. Jonesy kicked the plastic bottles and several broke as they fell down to the ground. "Answer me," he growled. "Make your decision – and make it fast."

"All right, you win."

Jonesy looked at his watch. "I've got to go. Gunny can you and the sergeant finish this job for me?"

They nodded yes.

As Jonesy turned to leave he heard Travis. "Get to work butt-head. Pour this crap out."

Jonesy retraced his steps heading aft to the Flag Section. Five minutes later, he fell into a chair for the eight o'clock report meeting. The Admiral looked at Jonesy.

"You're late."

"Sorry, Ma'am. Working with Patty Smith on a little project."

"Anything of importance?"

"No," he responded. "Let's face it so far it's been a dull voyage." Jonesy just leaned back, smiling while listing to the various reports.

****

Chapter 6-3
0415 Friday 14 March 2228
S/S Amelia O'Leary
Underway

Buck's little wardroom was full. He had the captain and first officer of the Pan Crimbian ship sitting there. One of the chiefs from the Amelia was standing in a corner with a chattergun keeping guard on the two Crimbian officers. Amelia and two of the mates were seated on the other side of the table. Ben and Freda Papers were seated at the other end of the table. Even though both had had a bath and a meal, it was obvious even from the most casual observer that they were suffering from mistreatment. Buck thought the two *'looked like death warmed over.'*

Buck looked at the two Crimbian officers. "I've called this meeting to decide what to do with you two and your crew."

The Captain looked at Buck. *Even though he was in a tough spot, he was sure he was the one that had been wronged. In his mind Buck was nothing but a pirate.* "If you know what is good for you, you will release us and beg for forgiveness for attacking a Holy ship on official business."

"Well I guess I don't know what's really good for me," Buck replied dryly.

The Crimbian captain glared at Buck defiantly. "I'll pray for you to become enlightened."

"Don't' waste your prayers on me - I'm on my way to Hell. You'd better pray for yourself."

"So now that you have robbed my ship like a common thief, you're going to murder me and my crew as well."

Buck looked at his wife. "Please read the charges against the prisoners."

Amelia started reading from a monitor screen. "The Commander of Pan Crimbian ship Xennin is charged with the following violations of Solar Admiralty Law:

Article 47 – False imprisonment of Union Citizens without a trial of charges being declared; to whit holding of 64 Union citizens.

Article 91 – Negligent death of two of the prisoners from maltreatment and basic human rights To whit allowing citizen Raymond C. Mason age 44 and citizen Bethema C. Randolf, age 4 to die from starvation.

Article 124 – Transport of stolen Union commercial property; to whit attached list of gold, platinum, textiles, and war materials.

Article 7 - Unlawful transport of Union Citizens in a manner of slavery.

All officers in the command structure are indicted as conspirators, see attached list of officers. Articles 7, 47 and 91 each hold the maximum punishment of death by execution." She looked up directly at the two defendants. "How do you plead to the charges?"

The Pan Crimbian captain sputtered, "This is ridiculous. You have no authority. I refuse to accept your right to conduct this inquisition."

"Unfortunately for you no one here cares whether you accept this authority. As for rights, I have the right by the simple fact that you lost the battle. This is not an inquisition. This is an admiralty court martial. I could've just as easily spaced you and your entire crew. But you're lucky. In the Union we have a rule of law and as such I must as the captain who has captured an enemy ship, conduct a hearing."

The Crimbian first officer must have realized the gravity of the situation. "We were just following orders."

Ben interrupted angrily. "That defense won't wash. The military officers of Nazi Germany tried to use that excuse. Your government signed the Treaty of Admiralty accepting the laws of space travel. As a Captain and First Officer commanding a ship in this solar system, you must abide by the law."

The Crimbian captain replied, "The only law we are accountable to is Holy laws of Crimbian faith and the Holy edicts of Ruffus our prophet and king."

Buck sighed and shook his head. He was already tired of these two. "Let the record show the two accused refused to enter a plea on the grounds of their religion. Furthermore let the record show that they stood defiantly refusing to explain their actions."

Amelia continued. "As First Mate on this ship I have conducted the following investigation." She held up a vellum. "I'm entering the following facts into the record as witnessed by two admiralty officers Captain Ben Papers of the *Geosearch*, his First Mate Freda Papers and son Alexander." She then looked at the two. "Do you have any objections?"

The two just stood at attention looking straight ahead.

Buck decided he had enough. "As Captain of the *O'Leary* I find you guilty as charged. How say the other officers of the board."

Amelia coughed, "Guilty"

Ben's anger flowed through, "Guilty!"

Freda snapped, "Guilty!"

There was a pause then Buck passed the

sentence. "Having been found guilty of capital offenses you are sentenced to death. Normally, it would be my duty to transport you to the nearest Port Captain for justice. However, in this case I have a higher obligation to your victims. I will abandon you here with your ship. However, if for some reason you survive, this report will be filed with the Admiralty. If you are again apprehended after the war the sentence will be carried out."

The Pan Crimbian Captain turned white with anger. "You are nothing but a pirate using this mock trial to kill me and my crew. I will pray for the Oracle to deal with you. Never fear. If I survive your abandonment, I will file charges of piracy and the theft of my cargo. You had better hope my crew and I do not survive because there will be a death warrant for you and your ship."

"Captain, you command a ship of death. Death is only fitting for the likes of you. Space will take care of the likes of you and your crew." Buck motioned to the Chief. "Get this vermin out of here and off my ship."

After they were gone Buck opened a drawer and took out a familiar looking container of liquor. He set four glasses on the table. "I don't know about you all but I need a drink after that. Anyone else?"

All four nodded yes. Buck poured the drinks then took a big gulp. This was a tough situation. Ordinarily Buck would have just taken the Crimbian ship in tow along with the crew and cargo. The ship itself was worth quite a bit. He hadn't been prepared for over a hundred Union captives. The four of them had discussed their options last night, after Amelia had finished her investigation. The Crimbian crew had been slowly starving their captives because they already had a shortage of food.

The Pan Crimbian ship had been in bad shape even before Buck had attacked it - now it was almost a hulk. The attack had damaged life support and environmental systems. Thus an evaluation of the resources aboard the Pan Crimbian ship concluded that there was insufficient oxygen or water on board for the remaining crew alone to reach Luna or Earth, much less being towed to Mars or the Asteroids.

With the additional bodies onboard *Amelia* there was going to be short rations it they voyaged outward to Mars. Buck decided to take additional oxygen and food from the Crimbians for the Union prisoners and leave the Crimbian crews to their fate. He logged in his voyage record that he had left sufficient stores for the Crimbian crew to make it to the nearest Crimbian facilities. Maybe it was true maybe it wasn't. It was a tough situation, however, it being war - none of the options were pleasant.

The speakerphone crackled. "Buck, all secure ready to get underway. What course?"

"Just give me a few minutes," Buck answered back switching off the phone. He turned to Ben. "I know you have a burning desire to go to Mars, but even with the bounty being paid for rescuing refugees, it's not necessarily a profitable trip. Any way I'm not anxious to go there since the bounty will be paid no matter where we go."

Ben needed leverage. Buck, like many who explored privately, liked to keep a distance from any government authority. "How about if I make it worth your while? Say an extra ten thousand when we get there."

"I would prefer it in advance."

"Well, I really don't have it on me but when we get to Mars I can get it."

"Okay, let's make it twenty thousand on arrival at Mars."

"Done."

****

Chapter 6-4
0900 Saturday 15 March 2228
Luna Far Side Underground
Marine Field Headquarters

Earney looked down at the man on the table. He was dead. Earney felt no remorse for the man. He was a traitor who had taken the easy way out. Rather than talk the man had taken his own life. The man had been one of the many Luna captives that had escaped from Crimbian custody. He had joined the resistance then had been caught passing information to the Crimbians. He gave up the location of the Crimbian detention center where he had been converted. But what Earney really wanted to know was where Jill might be, if she was alive? The man had managed to swallow a suicide pill that they never thought to look for.

It was just as well. Had he not died, Earney would have had to convene a court and go through the pains of a trial. The result would probably have been the same - death for this unfortunate wretch. This had been a most unpleasant task. Since Earney ordered the interrogation, he had sat and witnessed the entire procedure. As the Commanding Officer he felt it was his duty. Such a waste of time - the man had died without telling anything of any use, other than spouting the Crimbian crap in the end.

Earney excused himself and went to the toilet. Once there - he vomited. After several times, he sat next to the bowl and tried to clear his head. His mind was racked - where was Jill? *He thought God three weeks ago they had attacked the actual detention center. If he had known Jill might have been there - he could have rescued her then. Could he justify another attack? Probably not!*

Jake found him sitting there five minutes later. He came in to the small area designated as the head. Jake sat on the floor next to Earney. He reached into his pouch and took out a bottle of Johnny Walker Scotch Whiskey. "Nectar of the

Gods." Jake handed the bottle to Earney. "I've been saving this for a necessary occasion – looks like this is one of them."

Earney took a drink of the raw whiskey. It actually settled his stomach some. "What a gruesome job. It's unfortunate that we failed."

"We found out there is something to hide. Or he wouldn't have been willing to die to keep the secret." Earney handed the bottle back to Jake. Jake waved in a long motion while speaking, "What is so confusing is why would an apparently upstanding citizen become a traitor and attempt to kill one of us?"

"There is nothing new about brainwashing. Placing people in a situation of sensory deprivation or isolation has led to some very weird mental changes. If we had the lab tools I'd bet the man's DNA was tinkered with. The Crimbians have developed hybrid genetics to a grand scale."

Jake wiped the top of the bottle then took another pull on the bottle before asking, "So when do we attack the Detention Center again?"

"We don't! I cannot justify attacking the place just to rescue my girl. The risk would be too great - they will be ready for us this time.

Jake held up the bottle. "This stuff makes me think clearly. We don't need to attack the place to rescue your girl. We need to rescue all of those who have resisted and are being held within the compound. They'll become the core group of our force. Anyone we rescue from that place we will ensure they're free of the Crimbian infection, like that guy had in there. If we do it right we can separate the sheep from the wolf's wearing sheep skins."

Jake wiped the top again before passing it back. Earney took another drink. "I think you might have something there. To pull this off we'll need a good old-fashioned diversion. I doubt if we can really change their plans – but we can sure as hell cause a lot of delays."

Jake smiled then said. "If any place ever needs to be completely destroyed – that's the place!"

"No," Earney hesitated. "I've got a better idea – these guys need to learn what it's like to be mistreated. We need to give the Crimbian persecutors a taste of their own medicine." Earney took another drink and handed the bottle to Jake. "You know it's unseemly for two grown men to be sitting in the crapper drinking whiskey."

Jake grinned then said. "It sure is."

"We'd better move camp before we attack. I want some type of mental screening ready on all the Lunar recruits we have already. We don't want any more traitors. Also before we attempt to pull any more people out they also need to be screened."

"Wasn't Carson some type of a security guy at Apollo Lab?"

"He sure was," Earney replied. "Let's talk to him about screening everyone as soon as we move."

Earney suddenly felt better. Yes, he was ready to take the offensive again and the possibility of getting Jill back helped a lot. Suddenly he had a wild idea. Earney quickly talked through the plan.

Jake placed the cap back on the bottle. "You're crazy – but I like it!"

****

Chapter 6-5
1915 Sunday 16 March 2228
Fleet Headquarters Mars
Major Arlene Smith's Quarters

It had been a long day for Arlene so the smell of the steak surprised her when she opened the door. Then she remembered that she was having guests this evening. Sara was standing in the middle of the kitchen trying to do everything at the same time.

"I'm sorry." Arlene felt bad that Sara was making preparations alone. "I should've been earlier. I just lost track of time."

"Think nothing of it. I've enjoyed being able to do something useful. Your guests are due at twenty hundred so you've got time for a shower."

"Are you sure I can't do something?"

"After you shower you can do the salad."

"Okay." Arlene raced to the shower. Within a minute she was standing under the running water. As the tensions of the day washed out she suddenly realized that she had become use to having Sara around. It wasn't just that Sara was helpful on days like today. She had developed a real fondness for the woman. Even though Sara's memories of the Lunar battle had not returned, she was much better and now remembered her childhood and early service years. Arlene knew Sara would have to return her to regular duties soon. Meanwhile it was nice just having someone else around.

This was just going to be an informal evening with old friends so she dressed comfortably in a loose fitting shift. Fifteen minutes later when Arlene came back into the kitchen, Sara had all of the makings for a salad laying out. Apparently Sara had gone to change too. Arlene went right to work. Sara returned wearing slacks and a loose shirt of the latest style. Arlene had gone to the Army paymaster and had talked them into paying Sara on a regular basis. He couldn't pay any back pay or housing per diem, since Sara was bunking in with Arlene. But this did allow Sara to buy some uniforms and clothes that fit.

"What smells so good?" Arlene was curious.

"Cornbread."

"Oh, good. Mike will like that."

"Am I dressed all right? I've met Generals but I've never been close to the top echelons. Never met the Army Field Marshal before, much less the Fleet Admiral."

"Don't worry. She's just a regular person. Just relax and go with the flow and you'll do okay."

"So who is this other lady coming to dinner?"

"Samantha Norris is the Fleet Intelligence Office."

It was all Sara could do to keep from gasping. Now she was worried. She went back in the kitchen and checked on the various dishes. She could only hope that Arlene had overlooked her obvious nervous gestures. Sara placed the various dishes on the server, which would keep the each dish at the proper temperature, and serve them once everyone was ready to eat.

The door monitor sounded. Sara could hear Arlene greeting her friends in the other room. When Sara came in to the front room she was introduced to Maggie and Mike O'Brian along with Samantha. She relaxed somewhat since everyone was wearing civilian clothes. They had just completed the introductory small talk and everyone had sat down with a drink when the door sounded again. Before Arlene could answer the door opened revealing a young woman and man. Apparently, one of them had the access code.

"Ruby!" Arlene exclaimed. She jumped up and hugged the girl, then the young man.

Arlene brought the young couple in. Both were wearing cadet officer uniforms

Sara recognized the image of the girl, since a large twenty by twenty photo hung on the wall of the living room. Ruby was Arlene's daughter. The young man was introduced as Ed Carter, Ruby's fiancée and classmate. Mike stood and shook the young man's hand.

Sara greeted Ruby, "I almost feel that I know you already from your pictures around the place and your mother's continual praise about you. "

Ruby replied, "Mom has had nothing but nice things to say about you too."

"Do we have enough for Ruby and Ed to join us for dinner?"

"Of course," Sara replied. "In fact, if everyone is ready, we should eat now."

Arlene motioned everyone towards the dinner table as Sara rushed to set two more places.

As everyone was taking their seats Arlene said, "I have to confess. Sara prepared everything. I stayed late at the hospital and nothing would have been ready yet."

The conversation was lively and gay as the group went through the meal. All agreed that everything was perfect.

Mike looked across the table to Ed, "So

how is school going?"

"Just swell," he replied.

"Don't be so modest," Ruby interrupted. "He's already completed his missed high school work and is taking a full load of freshman college courses."

"That's nice," Maggie replied. "I'm glad to hear that someone listens to my orders."

Ed blushed. "Well, I have to admit it's not as hard to study as I once thought. It's easy to study things that are interesting. Also, the way they handle the classes is much better than my old high school."

Samantha chuckled, "It's usually a shock to students at the academy to find that there are actually so few actual classes. Mostly the class interactions are symposiums, rather than lectures."

"I'll say," Ed replied. "I hated sitting in nice neat rows. The high school I went to was considered enlightened, but at the academy all instruction is really individualized."

Samantha was on a roll now. "Actually, I seriously studied to become a teacher at one time. I studied the various philosophies of education. Since most of the Union's original settlers came from the old United States, many of our schools used the pattern of those schools. It's hard to believe now but the simple change of a basic premise changed all of our schools forever."

Ruby asked the obvious question, "What

was the change?"

"In the later periods of the United States they were obsessed with rights. Children had the right to a public education. Therefore, no matter what the child or student did, they couldn't be denied an education. Also the schools were free, publicly supported."

"Why that's the silliest kind of school I've ever heard of," Ruby retorted.

"The change was simple. As you well know, you don't have the right to an education you have a privilege. You can attend school so long as you obey the rules and don't interfere with anyone else's learning. Of course you or your parents are obligated to pay the teacher."

"I don't understand," Ed said. "Who paid the teacher in the old Earth schools?"

"The taxpayers, even those who didn't have children in school paid. Oh, our taxpayers supplement the schools because no family could afford the total costs of a school. But the tuition your parents pay covers most of a teacher's salary."

"That seems like a very strange way to run a school," Ruby murmured.

"I agree," Samantha said. "But it was even worse than that. They had special school police who went around picking up kids who didn't want to go to school and forcing them to attend. Then, just to make school fair, they made the courses so easy that even a moron could pass. You might not believe this. To make everything equal the teachers couldn't discipline or flunk a student."

"You're kidding!" Ed was incredulous, remembering back to all the garbage details or cleaning details that he had been assigned as punishment for failing to obey some rule.

"No, not at all. If you study World War III carefully you'll find that the reason the United States lost the battle for Europe was that most of the sailors and soldiers couldn't read technical manuals for the more complex systems. This became a problem as systems were damaged in battle and couldn't be repaired."

"Okay," Ed remarked. "You have my attention now. I'll make an effort to look up those historical facts."

"Actually, this is also critical to our present situation," Samantha continued. "We've had some people studying the Pan Crimbians. They have failed to read history. Their enlisted soldiers and spacers are just warriors and watch standers. Only the officers have any technical training. Admiral Lorraine Wilson was down there recently and wrote a report noting the possibility that this could easily be their Achilles heel. Only well-educated forces have been successful militaries since industrialization. The longer this war goes on, the more of a problem it will become for them."

Arlene looked at Ruby. "Have you decided what you are going to major in?" Ruby was actually older than Ed and was officially listed as a sophomore. As such she had to declare a major before becoming a junior. This had been a long-term tension between Ruby and Arlene.

"Medicine."

"That's nice dear, I'm glad you finally made a decision." Inwardly Arlene was pleased. She was sure that her daughter had finally made a decision that suited her talents.

Mike looked at Ed. "Son, have you thought about a major yet?"

"Sure I knew the day I started the Academy – Science and Exploration."

"You have to score high in math don't you?" Mike asked knowing the answer.

Ruby chimed in immediately, "Don't worry about him. I scored in the ninetieth percentile to qualify for medicine. His scores were even higher than mine. Since he scored so high, he got one of the academy's top math instructors for a coach – a Lieutenant Mako."

Mike coughed, "Yes, I know the Lieutenant. She is very pregnant right now. When is she going to have the baby?"

"She's due in July," Ruby replied. "She is such a nice lady."

"Speaking of Lieutenant Mako,"

Samantha interrupted looking at Maggie and Mike. "I received an interesting report on her."

"Interesting how?" Asked Maggie.

"Interesting in that she has only been over there a couple of months and the Commandant is going to convene an academic review board and award her a Ph.D."

Maggie was surprised. "You mean she has already written a thesis?"

"Not just a thesis, but a presentation of mathematics which several of the math professors are still trying to figure out. Our girl Dolores may be the one of our generation's most insightful math geniuses. Maybe on the level of Einstein or Newton."

"I don't understand," Mike said. "How can the professors want to give a Ph.D. to her if they can't figure out what she has done?"

Samantha smiled at Mike. He was always so direct and predictable. "Mike you have to understand things at that level. She was sent as a graduate student but in the process of writing this paper apparently she had proven herself to be equal to or superior to her professors. When Isaac Newton first wrote his work no one understood it because he had to invent calculus to explain the concepts he was explaining. Apparently Dolores has also invented new concepts in math to explain her theories. Our most learned professors have to learn the type of math she has invented."

Maggie leaned forward. "What is the practical outcome of such a finding?"

Samantha replied, "I really don't know, but she is talking about how to drive ships much faster than we do at present and possibly how to achieve an artificial gravity."

"My God," Mike burst out. "That would revolutionize the entire spaceship engineering concepts and the way we travel in space."

"Exactly," Samantha agreed. "But what caught my attention was the possibility of a new type of encryption and possible changes in communications methods."

Sara couldn't contain herself. "Now I'm confused. What does gravity and space ship power plants have to do with encryption and communications?" Everyone leaned forward and stopped eating. There was only silence.

Finally Samantha said, "Well it does on the face of things seem to be a far stretch. However I'll attempt a simple explanation given to me by the resident professor at the academy. First none of these concepts can be explained in vocalized language. They can only be explained in mathematical terms."

Maggie almost whispered so as not to break the mood. "I got all A's in math including calculus. No one can command a ship and navigate without understanding high level math."

"Actually, the professor referred to trig, geometry and even calculus as arithmetic. He said these concepts explain things that are tangible and made of matter or energy. What Dolores has done is to go a step further and explain how energy, matter, and whatever is not energy or matter are related and how they interact. But to answer your question about communications let me first ask a question. How long does it take for sun light energy to travel from the sun to the Earth or Mars?"

"That's an easy problem," Ed responded. "The Earth averages ninety three million miles from the sun. Light travels at one hundred and eighty six miles per second so it takes about five hundred seconds or about eight point three minutes. Mars on the other hand is a hundred and forty one point six million miles so the light travels in about seven hundred and sixty seconds or twelve point six minutes."

Everyone at the table just looked at each other. Ruby beamed. "See, I told you he is good at remembering things, especially numbers." Ed turned beet red with embarrassment.

"That's all right, son. You're exactly correct. You see I worked it out on a computer earlier today. I can't solve a problem like that in my head." Samantha took a drink before continuing. "Messages sent between planets and ships are limited by the speed of radio waves and light waves. As far as we know today nothing can move faster than the speed of light. But what would happen if there were ways to send something faster than the speed of light. Then we would be able to call any planet or ship just as you can now call anyone on a planet."

Maggie almost groaned. "This should set physics on its ear. It's one thing to slow down the speed of light; hell half of our technology rests on our ability to control the speed of light. However, if the maximum speed of light is no longer a constant in physics, then the whole world of physics will change."

Samantha replied "No doubt about that. Dolores also is working on the second paper. She tells me her work isn't finished yet." Samantha stood up since everyone seemed to have finished the meal. "I need to stand for a while and I want to hear more about your trip, Maggie."

Arlene pushed the button on the server and all of the utensils and leftovers were whisked off the table. Within a half a minute, the table was clear and fresh flowers were in place in the center. Arlene glanced into the kitchen briefly as the server went through the process of sorting washing, drying, and then storing everything for the next use. It took only a few minutes for everyone to gravitate to the balcony. Mike had already lit a cigar. Samantha, Ed and Ruby joined him with their own brand of cigars. Sara was standing just out of sight behind the curtain, listening intently.

Maggie looked around. She did not see Sara. “Please don’t talk about my trip. Not everyone on the staff even knows it’s going to happen.” Looking directly at Ed and Ruby Maggie said, “I’m going to a meeting of the high council off Mars and the trip is a secret, I am sure the both of you will keep this to yourselves.” Maggie continued just thinking aloud. “As a matter of fact I’ll be needing some help on the trip - it’s very much within the curriculum for two young cadets to accompany the Fleet Admiral. If you are with me you certainly won’t be talking to anyone else. Would you two like to come along?”

“Yes, Ma’am,” they both replied in unison.

“Mike, can you make the necessary arrangements?”

“Certainly, my dear. Best idea I’ve heard today.”

The sun was setting and the shadows grew longer. Everyone gathered out on the balcony just took in the view. As the sun became lower the red shadows cast bright shades on the landscape below. The quartz and pyrite in the Martian rocks were like little prisms, displaying a rainbow of colors. On Earth the oceans cast a blue sheen to everything. Here the iron rich rock was red during the day. Only near sunset did the little splashes of light show - it was beautiful almost like looking at a field of flowers.

"You know what bothers me about this war?" Mike asked. No one answered so he continued. "Just watching this sunset reminds me that we're on the verge of starting to ecoform other moons in the solar system. When I first came to Mars as a boy we lived in domes. It was a harsh environment to survive in. Now the use of more living space will be delayed. That would have provided an entirely new world for mankind's use."

Ed retorted, "Maybe we should take the Earth back."

Arlene looked at Ed. "I've heard loose talk like that, but this is not the point of this war." Ed turned red again, but everyone knew he was just repeating what many other citizens were starting to think and voice.

"It's okay, son. I know you mean well." Arlene wanted to change the topic, "Maggie, could you find a place on your staff for Sara? Physically she is fit for duty but I would like to keep her around and put all her memories back in place."

Maggie looked at Mike. "I have no objections as long as Mike can justify it."

"No problem," he replied. "We have three slots for Army liaison officers. And only two are filled now."

Sara was elated. This was even better than she had hoped for. Now, finally, she had picked up two very valuable pieces of information. First this Fleet Admiral was going on a trip and would be vulnerable. She remembered that the United States defeated Japan by shooting down a plane carrying Yamamoto Japan's best Admiral. Maybe history could be repeated. This math genius Dolores - she must be eliminated before she could complete her work. Such a mind would be a threat to the Pan Crimbian Empire.

****

Chapter 6-6
0200 Monday 17 March 2228
CF-81 Saipan
Control Room

Abe looked out into the void of space. He was seated all alone on the bridge of the frigate. He was trying to remember what his young son looked like. It had been over two years since he'd seen him. The boy had been four when he'd left. Then the war started and he had not returned. Isaac would be in school now. All of the kids would be in school now.

The young man who was on watch with him returned with coffee. Blake Sims was a tall, gangly lad in his early twenties, with a muscular build. He had blue eyes with a little smile that was often catching from his good since of humor.

"I made a round of the ship. Everything is secure."

"Thanks for the mud." Abe tasted it. Black was not his preferred mixture of coffee. There was no sugar and no cream. They were lucky to have coffee.

"Is it time to take a fix?" He wanted something to do. Normally every hour the watch fixed a position on the chart for the record and log. Abe was an engineer not a deck officer but he had already learned and had plotted the current position.

"Already done. You want to sit here in the pilot's seat?"

"Sure."

Abe got up and stretched as Blake slid into the pilot's seat. They were not even half way through this watch.

"What do you think our chances are of getting back"?

"At first I wouldn't have given us any more of chance than a dog left on a methane world would have. But since we got halfway repaired, I'd now give us a fifty-fifty chance."

"You know, I signed articles only for this one voyage?"

Abe realized that the young man must be a reserve fleet specialist. For the most part serving in the reserves was a good deal. A young person joined as a reserve and was sent to basic training then would make one exploration or military voyage to get qualified on a ship. Then he would go off to school or a regular job and draw a monthly pay of twenty percent of his basic pay. All they had to do was meet once a month for four hours of training and once a year for ten days of training. Some reserves would get bored with their job or get laid off so they would find a ship and sign on for a voyage just to keep a hand in. This arrangement was good for both the individual and the Fleet. It kept a reserve staff for just such an emergency that now had occurred and the individuals got to serve without really subjecting themselves to the rigors of the life of a Fleet specialist.

"A reserve? You in school or what?"

"Yeah, I was a senior at Old Dome State. I got behind and was doing more partying than studying so I decided to take a year off and get squared away."

"ODS. I went there. Graduated class of sixteen."

"Now with this war I'm afraid I'll never get back and finish my schooling."

Abe sighed then said. "I've got a wife and kids somewhere back on Mars that are pretty important to me. I have plans too, but after what we have been through and seeing so many people killed, our plans don't seem so important anymore. It looks as if the very existence or our way of life is under attack."

"Guess I should have though it through. If there's no Mars then there's no school."

"That's right. You need to look at things in another light. This war also provides opportunity. You are a sergeant now. If the war goes another year, you'll be a chief specialist. That's worth a lot in any job you want. As for myself, Mickey already told me that he plans to recommend me for OCS. I intend to take it. I've seen it before. When the war is over, there won't be enough billets for the higher ranks. Career people will be forced to accept a lower rank. However, when you retire, you retire at the highest rank you held honorably. That could be the difference between just getting by or living in comfort in retirement."

"I can see that even if we get this tub back, we'll all be reassigned to another ship as soon as they can."

"You can believe that is the truth. Where would you rather be? Out here helping out your fellow citizens or grounded waiting to be bombed out of existence?"

****

Chapter 6-7
0330 Tuesday 19 March 2228
CC-141 Arial
Captains Quarters

The alarm sounded and Jackie sat straight up in her bunk. The general alarm sounded again and announced, "All Hands to deep shelter. Cosmic radiation storm. Radiation on outer hull above 100 REM and rising. All Hands to deep shelter. - - This is not a drill!"

Jackie was up and bounded into the suit hanging on the back of her door. Out into the passageway and down she went to the 'A' deck in the center of the ship. Cosmic radiation storms from the sun were still one of the greatest hazards of travel in space. Even on the biggest ships, all anyone could do was go the shelter and ride out the storm. ‘A’ deck in the center of the ship was outfitted for an event such as this. They would be cramming everyone onboard into this deck. It would be tight and confining and promised high misery level. When she reached the deck, she went aft to the auxiliary control station.

Jackie found Sam Waters. He was the Officer of the Deck. “Is the muster complete?”

“Not yet,” Sam reported. “This one’s going to be a bad one. The outer skin is above one forty REM.”

“How high is the count here on ‘A’?” Jackie asked.

“Almost 80 millirem. 79.8, to be exact,” Sam said.

“Let’s get the hatches shut and get everyone into a suit” Jackie was direct, this was no time to take any chances.

“Shut the hatches,” Sam ordered. Jackie could hear word being passed. The sounds of hatches shutting aft were the first sounds.

Several young specialists started shutting hatches leading into the after control section. Eight hatches opened up into the center deck from above. They were heavy since each hatch was lead lined, just as the bulkheads of ‘A’ deck were lined. But in no-weight conditions became a mass that actually took some strength to get started. As the hatches came shut the against the mating surface, one specialist would stand with feet planted holding the hatch closed until another specialist could rotate the locking ring by hand making a gas tight seal.

Just as they were preparing to shut the last one someone yelled, “Wait. Wait!”

Chief Bell threw himself through the hatch just as it was closing. Jackie looked up to see the man hanging in the air in the middle of the room. He was wearing only his undershorts. She was taken aback by the sight of the man. Not only was he dripping wet, but he was the hairiest man she had ever seen. He was covered with long dark reddish hair on every part of his body. He was built heavy with great slabs of muscle. She didn’t know it but he had grown up on Neptune where the gravity was above one G, so he had naturally big bulging muscles that made him look almost deformed. In fact his legs were bigger than her waist.”

“Nice of you to join us,” Jackie teased. “A little out of uniform aren’t we?”

He flushed then kicked himself towards the bulkhead. He grabbed on and opened a locker. In one smooth motion out came a blanket, he proceeded to wrapped himself. “Sorry, skipper. I was taking a shower and didn’t hear the alarm at first.”

“It’s okay, Chief,” Jackie now had something else on her mind. “After you find something to wear and a P-suit come on back up here and let’s talk about your little missile project.”

"Yes, Ma'am." He shoved off from the bulkhead and started forward.

By the time Chief Bell returned minutes later, Jackie had a complete picture of the emergency. It was a bad storm and the radiation levels were extremely high in the outer levels of the ship, but the crew was safe for many days in the shelter. Nothing had really changed since man had first understood radiation. The type of radiation, time of exposure and level of intensity determined exposures. Radiation effects were accumulative, but at low levels, the effects were controllable. High doses over a short period caused permanent crippling disabilities or death. Shielding protected the crew from high-level exposures and extended the exposure periods to harsh cosmic, gamma and x-rays.

Jackie motioned for her group to gather. She, Jane Polanski, and Sam Waters took positions to permit easy listening. They were head first into the center with their bodies and legs going out like the spokes of a wheel.

Chief Bell began by outlining the situation. "First, the Master Chief Missile specialist and I studied everything we had on this new type of missile. The MK 22 has been under development for the last six years. Apparently, when the war started it was rushed into production. This appears to have been a political decision made at Fleet Headquarters. Someone spent a lot of Fleet money on the development of this weapon. The MK 22 was over budget and there were development problems."

Jane asked, "What's the normal development time for a weapon like this?"

"Usually it's only a couple of years, but a few have gone as long as four years. None have ever had the drawing board life of this one. As all of you are aware, the old MK 21 was also a proximity and contact detonation. One of the major shortcomings of the MK 21 was that it could be confused and it has been known to go after a friendly ship. The MK 22 was built with a very advanced brain – it is supposed to know the difference between a Union ship and an enemy vessel also there are about a hundred interlock safety devices which will prevent accidental detonation."

Jackie asked bluntly, "So how do we make it explode when we want it to?"

Sam Waters took over talking. "Well that's a good question. One that I've pondered over a lot during the past few weeks. Actually, there are only two conditions which permit detonation by the programs in the missile's brain." Sam paused, now was as good of time to tell the Captain about something he had done without permission. "I took the liberty of completely disassembling three of the missiles we have aboard. The Chief and I built a test stand and have been dropping missile warheads for over a week. The detonator is built out of substandard plastic parts which break on impact and fail to detonate the warhead."

"Is there any good news?" Jackie wanted to know.

The Chief answered. "Sure. The MK 22's main engine is far superior to the old MK 21 which will give you a greater range than any of the Pan Crimbian missiles that we know about. And the warhead is at least twice as effective as the older model."

"So what we have is an overpriced piece of junk with poor programming and tinker toy exploders." Jackie was incredulous. "What do you plan on doing now?"

Chief Bell said. "I plan to keep dropping warheads and modifying the detonator until I can get it to fire. And by fire I mean – fire every time. Meanwhile Lieutenant Waters plans on working on the computer programs."

"Have you got any idea how long this will take?" Jackie asked.

"Not a clue and it's so complex I can't guarantee that we can solve the problems."

"Give me the names of anyone else you need to help." Jackie said, then she turned to Jane, "Major can you revise the watch bill to relieve the Lieutenant here so he can concentrate all of his time to this effort."

Chief Bell pulled out a vellum. "Ma'am, other than Mr. Waters no other changes are needed right now. The Warrant has already given me anything I've needed. I have volunteers from the weapons department now and have help from the science labs. We have a couple of altered detonators that we are working with. If the solution is within the capability of this team, we'll solve the problems. I want to give you a venomous bite for this ship."

Jackie thought Chief Bell and Lieutenant Sam Waters were very capable. But, she was asking them to redesign the missiles before the ship went into battle. Could it be done with the limited resources of a single ship? A lot of lives would depend on it. But right now she wanted a ship with the ability to bite – and yes, by God, she wanted venom too.

****

"Some are born great, some achieve greatness, and some have greatness thrust upon them." *William Shakespeare*

Part 7 - Oceanea

The largest fleet ever assembled for the great work of Pan Crimbian Empire arrived at the outpost of Eros. More than two thousand ships made up the impressive armada. Actually, the fleet was so big that it took three days for the entire assemblage of ships to arrive. This massive array of manpower trained Enroute for the invasion into the heart of the Union. Under the leadership of the finest minds of Crimbian military and with the blessing of god, the massive fleet took position -ready to strike terror into the barbarians.

Holy History of Crimbian VII

Chapter 7-1
2220 Saturday 22 March 2228
CE-46 Galileo, 'A' Deck
Underway to Eros

There were over three thousand people crammed into 'A' Deck. The same solar storm that affected *Arial* also was affecting the rest of the fleet. There was no spot left vacant. Even on the giant explorer there was no comfort to be found; not even for the Admiral or the Commodore. As each hour passed the misery increased proportionally.

There were no showers or regular meals in shelter and everyone for the most part had to stay in a P-suit. After a day in a P-suit everyone started getting a little ripe. The only thing to eat was the prepackaged rations, commonly referred to as P-Rats along with some more colorful expletives.

Lorraine awoke from her sleep. She looked up and realized that she had been using Jonesy for a pillow. He was still snoring softly so she just lay there thinking. After months of captivity and being forced to sleep with Jonesy she was well aware of his habits. She was quite aware that most of their friends and shipmates assumed that there was a relationship between the two of them. But strangely enough, there was no relationship of an intimate nature - Jonesy would have never allowed it. She knew he was a natural gentleman. But somehow in the months of captivity they had developed a special bond and friendship.

This had to be a bad storm for it to keep them in the shelters so long. Of course she could remember one that had lasted almost five days back in fourteen - everyone alive today would always remember that one. Several ships were lost with all hands and many in deep shelters were affected by the severe radiation intensity. That was one reason why today all Union fleet ships now had even more lead lining on 'A' deck. Most storms are over in six to eight hours, but some last a day or two. For some reason the sun suddenly puts out a burst of energy. A lot of really brilliant scholars had studied the effects, trying to understand the inner working of the sun. Several had tried to come up with predictive models -all had failed. So the best that could be done was keep observatories aimed at the sun and when an eruption was detected, the solar flare warning alarm is sent out immediately in an attempt to provide an early warning. The problem with this method is that it's considered iffy at best. Because once the eruption of radiation begins all communication in the solar system was disrupted or blacked out. This meant that all ships no matter how big or small always had a sensor watch looking for solar flares.

Even right now there was no communication between her and the rest of the fleet. Fleet headquarters on Mars could not talk to anyone. Even communications between Mars and Phobos or Earth and Luna were out. Many of the smaller settlements would be forced into shelters. Only Mars and Earth had the protective atmosphere. However, if the storm was really severe it could even disrupt communications on a planet. Long range sensors would be disrupted as well. Fortunately, the newer short-range sensors allowed the fleet to track each other. At least that had the potential of keeping the ships from running into each other.

There was one bright spot in this whole situation. Fleet ships of the Union were prepared for and were equipped to handle the storms. The Pan Crimbians were not. However miserable the Union forces were, the Pan Crimbians were even more miserable.

Jonesy opened his eyes and looked at Lorraine. She sat up trying to push up her hair. The gestor was a waste of time in zero G. Her hair looked just as bad as before. Since they were weightless it was just a simple push off and she glided down the passageway in a smooth swimming motion. As she slowed it was a simple matter to use a finger on the bulkhead to keep the momentum going. As she reached the head she could see the line. The first person in line offered her a place at the front of the line. She took him up on the offer since she really had to go bad. She was in and out in minutes taking a few additional moments to wash her face and wet her hair. Lorraine used her hands to sweep it back and clip it into place.

She went back forward towards the control center to find Doyle. Bud Kadel was seated in the OOD's couch and Doyle was right by him.

"How is it going?" she asked.

"Good evening, Admiral," Bud responded. "The radiation has leveled off and is starting to drop."

"Any estimate on how much longer it might last?"

Doyle answered this time. "Sensors have

been running some predictions. It looks like four to twenty-four hours. This has really been a bad one." He turned the commander's console towards her so she could see the display for herself.

Lorraine pressed the menus that flashed status on the ship's systems. Her curiosity was satisfied. "Have you been thinking about the last message before blackout? Any ideas?"

Doyle reached into his thigh pocket and brought out the vellum. "That and this storm is all I've been thinking about." Bud looked at Doyle curiously. Doyle handed the vellum to Bud while looking at Lorraine. "Do you mind, Admiral?"

"No. Everyone will have to know eventually."

Bud read the message.

BEGIN TRANSMISSION

FROM: FLEET HEADQUARTERS MARS

TO: COMMANDER TASK GROUP CHARLIE

SUBJECT: ALERT

TOP SECRET OPERATIONAL RED 'EYES ONLY'

BELIEVE LARGE FORCE OF ENEMY SHIPS OUT BOUND FROM EARTH DESTINATION UNKNOWN. LOGISTIC REPORTS AND INTEL SOURCES AGREE THAT IT HAS ALREADY OCCURRED. NO TIME ESTIMATES ARE AVAILABLE.

HOWEVER, IT WOULD BE ONLY PRUDENT PLANNING TO ASSUME ALL OR PART HEADING FOR EROS OR VICINITY. YOU MUST PLAN FOR THIS NEW THREAT. ANY ADDITIONAL INFORMATION WILL BE PASSED ON AS SOON AS IT IS AVAILABLE. GOOD LUCK

KEEP THE UNION SAFE.

MARGARET O'BRIAN

FLEET ADMIRAL

END TRANSMISSION

"I don't suppose there is going to be another task force sent to help us?" Bud asked idly.

Doyle chucked softly in spite of the seriousness of the situation. "No, it's a sure bet that we're on our own."

Lorraine announced, "Well, unless anyone has a better idea, we'll just plant the Marines down, then pull back and meet the new threat."

The three all had the same thought. The Marines were going to feel awful naked without fleet support.

****

Chapter 7-2
0920 Sunday 23 March 2228
Fleet Headquarters
Flag Conference Room

Senior Warrant Chester Hale came into the conference room. He immediately recognized everyone in the room. His old friend Mike O'Brian, Admiral Tom Watson, Commandant Nathan Graham and Commodore Samantha Norris.

"Good morning, ladies and gentlemen. I certainly wasn't expecting such a distinguished group," Chester greeted everyone.

Mike motioned for him to take a seat at the table. The server had already set coffee in front of Chester's seat.

Tom Watson said. "Sorry to bring you out here so early on a Sunday morning, but war leaves little time for the little things in life. I want you to volunteer to go to Ganymede. Actually Senior Warrant O'Brian recommended you for this job. "

"That seems pretty far out of the mainstream of things," Chester replied.

"Show him your file." Mike pushed a stack of vellums forward.

Chester picked up the first one.

BEGIN TRANSMISSION

FROM: COMMANDER CC-87 LUNA

TO: FLEET HEADQUARTERS MARS

SUBJECT: AFTER ACTION REPORT SUMMARY

SECRET BLUE

INFO TO: COMMANDER GANYMEDE

RECENT ENGAGEMENT WITH PAN CRIMBIAN DESTROYER. FIRED THREE MISSILES NONE DETONATED. FORCED TO FINISH OFF THE ENEMY WITH CANNON FIRE AND ATTACK SHUTTLES. CAUSALITIES 14 - KIA 0.

BELIEVE DEFECTIVE LOT OF MISSILES ALL TECHNICAL TESTS SATISFACTORY.

CLINTON MAYNARD

CAPTAIN

END TRANSMISSION

Then he read the second one.

BEGIN TRANSMISSION

FROM: COMMANDER CF-211 ROSE

TO: FLEET HEADQUARTERS MARS

SUBJECT: AFTER ACTION REPORT SUMMARY

SECRET BLUE

INFO TO: COMMANDER GANYMEDE

ON 1 MAR 27 ENGAGED TWO PAN CRIMBIAN PATROL CRAFT IN ASTEROID SECTOR THUL. MISSILES FIRED, FAILED TO DETONATE. FORCED TO USE CANNON FIRE TO ACHIEVE BATTLE SUCCESS. CAUSALITIES 1 - KIA 0.

FIRED A TEST MISSILE AT AN ASTEROID - IT ALSO FAILED TO DETONATE. PLEASE ADVISE IF OTHERS HAVE HAD SIMILAR PROBLEMS.

EASTON P. VON RICTOR

CAPTAIN

END TRANSMISSION

After the second one Mike interrupted. “Don’t bother, they all say the same thing, Captains are having problems with the new missiles.” He handed Chester another vellum.

BEGIN TRANSMISSION

FROM: COMMANDING ADMIRAL GANYMEDE

TO: FLEET HEADQUARTERS MARS

SUBJECT: INCIDENT REVIEW REPORT

IMMEDIATE TOP SECRET BLUE

HAVE REVIEWED ALL FAILED MISSILES INCIDENTS. MY STAFF HAVE COME TO THE CONCLUSION ADDITIONAL TRAINING IS NEEDED FOR SOME CAPTAINS AND CREWS WHO ARE USING THE MISSILES FOR THE FIRST TIME. PLAN TO RUN ADDITIONAL SERIES OF TESTS TO DETERMINE IF ANY TRAINING IMPROVEMENTS CAN BE MADE.

JUAN V. GONZALES

ADMIRAL

END TRANSMISSION

“Okay, you have a problem. This is a job for a good weapons officer not an old obsolete Warrant.”

Tom Watson took the lead. “You’re

absolutely correct and you'll be going out with a first rate weapons officer. Major Gorball is just out of the hospital and can be posted to limited duty. He is going out officially as the Officer in Charge of this investigation. The problem is that he will be immediately subject to the orders of the Commanding Admiral in the Ganymede sector. You on the other hand won't officially be part of this investigation. You will be reporting back directly to the fleet intelligence officer using separate channels, so you will be able to pass any unfiltered information along to us."

"So what is my purpose if I am not part of the investigation?"

Mike reached below the table and brought out a large chart case. He pushed the case towards Chester. "Inside this case is a complete set of the final plans for the construction of the largest space craft ever to be built – for now we are calling it a Super Explorer 72. They have already started on the hull months ago, but soon they will need the inside systems technical specifications. It will be the platform for the Marines and Army units, which will invade Luna and maybe even Earth. Its very existence is Top Secret, no one except a hand full of top level engineers will even know what the complete ship will look like. You will report to Captain Porter and present him with his commission as Commodore; then work with him in the construction of this ship. This project has top priority and will utilize a separate work force from the ones involved in shipbuilding for Admiral Gonzales. You'll have plenty of time on route to review the plans and the entire structure of the new command along with the MK-22 issues. Officially you will be Commodore Porters Aide and Security Officer."

"How long do I have to decide?"

Marine Commandant Graham pulled his comm-link out and laid it on the table – the numbers of the time glowed. "About five minutes, since you only have three hours to pack and say goodbye to anyone. You and the Major will need to be on a ship that is preparing to get underway at fourteen hundred from Phobos base."

"Okay, I'm on my way," Hale said grumbling. "I'm getting too old for this crap."

"Don't give me that," Mike replied. "You love it - you'd die if we stopped asking you to help."

Chester stood and took the case. "See you when I get back."

When he turned to leave Samantha motioned to him. "One other thing - that case is rigged with a self-destruct mechanism. Use it if you must. Also inside are detailed instructions for your communications with my staff."

Chester could only groan inwardly as he walked onward towards the door. As his hand touched the door controls Admiral Tom

Watson called out. "Send in the Major will you? Also one more additional duty. Take care of Major Gorball."

A very thin man with black hair and a large nose was seated in the waiting area. He was wearing prosthetic power walker legs. Chester immediately made the connection. Gorball had been part of the group that had gone in with Doyle last year to bomb Earth. He remembered reading how Major Gorball had been horribly wounded in battle. In a coma for weeks the man had been almost given up for dead – but he had survived. Now, apparently somewhat rehabilitated he was being sent to the boondocks with Chester.

As the Major stood Chester said, "You're next, Sir. We can talk later."

Chester watched as the man used the handgrips to move his legs to the door. Moments later he stood alone in the big room. He had places to go and no time to get there. *Now he was carrying both secrets and bombs along with an incapacitated officer - a bad combination. Maybe the Union was in even more trouble than he ever realized. They were relying on an old man who should have been put out to pasture and a cripple.*

****

Chapter 7-3
0720 Monday 24 March 2228
Eros
Main Shuttle Bay

General Weems walked into the main entryway of the asteroid main bay. Two rows of troops were stationed in formation. They immediately snapped to attention as the General started down the landing ramp from his shuttle. Trailing behind were a dozen senior officers wearing the familiar yellow suits of the Holy League of the Oracle.

Brigadier General Solas greeted General Weems with the traditional prayer of welcome. The two men knew each other so there would be no preliminary discussion other than the formal ceremonies required by custom. Ten minutes later the two were alone in General Solas' office. Solas served breakfast while the others waited.

"Are you going to command the sector from this asteroid?" Weems asked.

"No. You will continue to command. However, I will give you reinforcements once the complete fleet arrives. You will be given two armies and a division of Holy Troopers. Your job is to hold this station. I believe that the barbarians are heading this way. It's logical that they'll want to take this rock back. I am going to let them come and attack. I will take most of the fleet away just out of range of long-range sensors. While they are busy attacking you, I'll come back and we'll crush them between us."

"Yes, my lord. I will pray for our success."

"One other thing. Tell your most trusted men of this plan. No one is to surrender – or they will face the wrath."

"Yes, my lord. I understand. It shall be as you will."

****

Chapter 7-4
2345 Tuesday 25 March 2228
Just outside old Tyco Base, Luna
(Renamed Pan Crimbian Holy Sanctuary)

Jake was lying prone in the small two-man pressure tent with Earney. Jake picked up the binoculars and looked down the hill towards the area below. Earney was napping while Jake watched. Everything was quiet for now.

Jake looked up at the temperature gauge. Sixty-seven inside the tent and minus two hundred and five outside. It was warm for a lunar night. The Union resistance had been moving into these positions gradually during the past twelve hours. There was only one watch tower manned and they had the lights on in the tower. The watchers inside couldn't see out across the dark plains of the lunar landscape. The video low light systems left by the Union were no longer operational. This gave the Resistance the opportunity to sneak up.

Of course, the Crimbians wouldn't be expecting anyone to approach during the night. It would be crazy. People who lived on the moon never went on the surface at night. In fact they rarely went on the surface. Most of the lunar cities were built underground and pressurized. This had been the way ever since the United States had started the first permanent settlement. The first landing had occurred in 1969 when Neil Armstrong and Buzz Aldrin arrived in Apollo 11, but it wasn't until 2037 that the first colony was established. That first settlement was only set up for scientific studies and astronomy. At least that was what everyone was told. Actually, since the group was composed of mostly military officers from the United States it soon became an open secret that it served military functions. They were in a perfect position to make detailed observations of Earth and monitor military movements on the planet. As the years passed and the influence of the United States waned - the settlements expanded the military significance increased. These new expansions came by digging deeper into the surface.

The first tunnels were dug for shelter, then minerals were found and the miners extended the tunnels quickly. Large boring machines were brought up from Earth and assembled. When the miners finished, the farmers moved in and started farming the tunnels. Water was initially a problem but ice was found in pockets. Water also was lifted from Earth in great barges built especially for that purpose. Environmental recovery of water became so efficient that water losses were minimal. Once farming started in the pressurized tunnels, oxygen became less of a problem since plants naturally produce oxygen. When World War III started there were over three hundred thousand living and working in the moon.

By that time the people existed completely independent of support from Earth. Luna was exporting more than it imported. Technically everyone was a citizen of the United States but most considered themselves citizens of Luna. The war started with the exploding of nuclear bombs in twenty of the twenty-six major metropolitan urban centers of the United States. The bombs had been smuggled in and set in place. All the money they had spent on military defense couldn't stop weapons set in place. Europe got only eighteen, but Russia and the old Soviet empires got almost thirty. Iran and China should have won, but even in their weakened states the United States and United Kingdom unleashed a holocaust of weapons against the Muslim nations of the Middle East. The survivors of the world were ravaged by starvation and disease. No elections were held in the 2032 cycle and Congress no longer had a quorum. The Supreme Court Justices all died off along with the Vice President, the Speaker of the House, and most of the cabinet. After the President died of a heart attack, the United States government ceased to exist.

Between 2053 and 2070 all support from Earth slowed. Finally in 2071 the citizens of

Luna realized they needed some form of government so they formed the Lunar Compact that was to become the basis for the Solar Union. The basic principles were adopted from the United States however they tried to drop all of the excess baggage that had been collected over the years. The primary limits built in were to control the powers of taxation and spending which had become oppressive. The Lunar settlers realized that limits were needed to curb wasteful government spending programs; particularly on things that the government had no business being involved in.

It was 2139 before the Solar Union was formed. By that time there were nineteen major settlements within the Solar System, each with its own style of local government. Some similar but some very different, all had been trading with each other and supporting each other for years. The concepts of terraforming were developed and would require more resources than Mars could afford. On Earth once again governments threatened the existence of the people who lived in space. There were actually some of these fledging governments on Earth who came out and claimed the moon as the property of their nation. The Constitution of the Solar Union was written at the end of one of the darkest periods of human history, after billions had died down on the mother planet from overpopulation, war, and religious excess.

Everyone in the Solar Union was

convinced the government had to pay for its needs. Any service provided by the government such as weights and measures was to be paid for by fees and fines. The government was permitted to engage in capitalism business and make a profit, but it couldn't be a monopoly. The government was not permitted to engage in any social services. There could be no government-controlled schools, religion, retirement programs, medical or health programs, or social welfare. All support of socialism or communism was forbidden. Elected or appointed representatives had to take an oath of ethics in which they swore never to benefit personally from any service to the Union. Also to be elected a person had to be a first class citizen. There was no set method of becoming a first class citizen but to advance to that level you had to demonstrate some type of service to the Union. Most satisfied the requirement by a term of service in the military, but it was just as acceptable to serve as a police officer, Red Cross volunteer, or even as a priest. It was not foolproof, but it seemed to work better than anything else had before. Of course, as with any human endeavor, when one set of problems were solved a new set was created.

The Solar Union was the first free social government ever created without a revolution. It was created by men searching for a loose bond to hold them together in a common protection. Most of the original writers of the Constitution of the Solar Union thought that the United States would arise again. Many of them had been born in space on one of the settlements, but they thought that they might once again become citizens of that old civilization again. But as the years passed by and with the United States gone, they gradually accepted that there was only the Solar Union.

Earney was awake. “Anything?”

“Nah, quiet as a lunar night should be. Thought I saw one of our other teams getting into position, but I could be wrong.”

Earney looked carefully at Jake. “I notice you’re always with a different woman. You ever find just one that you would be happy with?”

“I’d sure like to find just one. It would make things a whole lot less complicated. A lot of other men are sometimes envious I think. But the way things are set up, the women are in charge. They just use me for a good time then it’s so long.”

Earney chuckled. “You would have a hard time convincing most other guys that you are to be pitied for your plight in life. In fact, most women would scoff at such a suggestion.”

“Well I can’t help it; it’s just the way things are. I was reading an interesting article just before leaving Mars that posted much of the conflict we have with the Pan Crimbians is because they believe we have a matriarchal society and they have a patriarchal society.”

"Ugh! What does that have to do with the subject?"

"Everything. The way our society is set up no man can make the first move, it's always up the woman. We consider it good manners, but to the outsiders it would be a weakness. The Crimbian religion is based on a male-dominated society. Women are always submissive. But in our society we declare women are equal, but in most cases they dominate. For some reason women find me attractive. But they just use me for their own pleasures and then discard me." Jake paused then added, "Yes, I would like to find that special woman. The way you have with Jill."

"Sorry. It's just that I can't stop thinking about Jill," Earney replied.

"If I had someone special I'd be the same way. Actually, there was one lady that I really respected, but nothing could ever come of it."

"Why? Was she already involved?" Now Earney was curious.

"You could say that. She was a nun. When we evacuated after the initial invasion, she hid out and we managed to get a bunch of kids out of this hellhole. She was one of the few women that I could really respect and like."

"So if you got off this rock once, why come back?"

"Well that's tough to explain."

"It always is," Earney retorted.

"My grandmother was one of the original signers when they set up the Constitution of the Union. Most of all I was born here on Luna, and I saw firsthand what they were doing to the people here. Someone had to come back to help them and keep you out of trouble. I sure wouldn't want the old girl to come back. She was a tough old woman who could easily kick both of our butts without breaking a sweat."

"Guess that's as good a reason as any."

"So how does an old ship Warrant end up here as a Marine Major?

"Well they stuck me in school and I felt useless. Then there was a little job that had to be done, so I came. Then everything went south and I just happened to be one of the survivors."

Then Jake realized guys like Earney were always survivors. That's why he was sent here.

Earney looked at his watch. "Go ahead and get some shut eye. I'll watch for a while, It's going to be a long day."

Earney took the binoculars and started checking the lunar landscape below. Before he got half way through the sweep Jake was asleep, snoring softly.

****

Chapter 7-5
0230 Tuesday 25 March 2228
Pan Crimbian Empire, Earth
Gulf of Guinea Work Station - 50 Meter Level

Jill was awakened when the cell door opened. Two of the priests came in and gathered her up from the cold metal deck she had been sleeping on.

"Where are you taking me?" she asked.

No response from either as she was pulled down the passageway. When she got to the end another guard looked her over and then pushed her up against the bulkhead. He mumbled something in his language and the two on either side of her laughed. She flushed with anger and started to comment, but held back as other voices could be heard approaching from around the corner. The pushing guard stepped into what appeared to be a storage room and came out with a bundle. He tossed it to her and motioned to her. It was a very different looking P-suit. She looked at the wall and saw that it was marked with strange measurements - probably metric. He had been taking her size.

She pulled on the lime green P-suit. It had a very strange construction. It appeared to be constructed of vulcanized rubber compound and the insulation was markedly thin for use in space. She looked it over carefully there was some question as to whether it would be gas tight. But she was on Earth - you didn't need pressurized space suits here!

She was pushed from behind, bringing her thoughts back to the present.

“Move along, cow.” The man spoke in Basic English - very badly.

“Where are you taking me?”

“Shut up. You’ll find out soon enough.”

She was worried again. Jill had been here about three weeks. Locked in a cold metal cell.

Before that she had been outside someplace in tropical Earth - subjected to the glory of weather; something she had never experienced before. Even in March the weather was miserable. It rained every day and usually the humidity and temperature were both above 95. When outside she had stayed wet from sweat continuously. Jill decided that she could never again read about wind or rain and think of it as being as romantic as it was so often portrayed in literature.

Down on Earth nothing was controlled. The pressure of gravity was unbearable. Fortunately she had only been outdoors for a few days then they had brought her to this complex.

She realized they had drugged her. She went to sleep in one area and awoke in this strange place. In this strange metal place there were no doors or viewports, but there certainly was a lot of water condensation. They had issued her a white tunic, shorts, and a wraparound skirt. This was how all of the women prisoners were dressed. She was almost always cold in this strange place.

In space the environment is monitored and adjusted as needed to maintain a comfortable temperature and humidity. Jill had been born in space and had never lived even close to one gravity before. On all of her previous visits to Earth she had taken drugs and had worn power walkers. That was not an option on this trip.

Jill had been assigned to the sewing area. This was a big compartment maybe three hundred yards square. There were row after row of sewing machines. Inside hundreds of women sat all day long sewing military uniforms. The guards walked on platforms suspended above the work area. From this position they could look down on the women below. If you did not work hard enough, you were flogged.

It was the first real shock of her captivity. Seeing a whip taken to a human being was a defiling act. She would've thought the same if a dog or animal was whipped like that. The woman who committed the offence was taken to the nearest post and her hands tied above her head to a ring high up on the post. Then her back was bared and with precision the guard laid five strokes on the woman. Each one cut deep bringing blood to the surface. Then the woman was dragged away to the healing area. The woman was gone for two days but on the third day she was back at her machine next to Jill. Jill never heard her talk again. There were apparently worse punishments that were inflicted in private chambers. *Jill though grimly - and they call us barbarians*!

When they got to the end of the passageway it took two men to open the six-foot round hatch. All of a sudden Jill realized what was wrong - everything was backwards. The hatches swung the wrong direction. They were designed to keep the pressure out not in. She was underwater in some sort of seafloor habitat. She stumbled and the men caught her. They held on to her until they had guided her through the service lock into a miniature submarine. At the far end was a large bubble of Plexiglas. Through the glass she could see fish were swimming around the little submarine.

They sat her in a seat and strapped her in. Two men came in and took seats in the control station. She watched as they went through the undocking checklist. Even though they spoke another language she had seen similar procedures many times in space. It was only a short trip less than fifteen minutes to the next dome in the undersea city. As she looked around at the massive missile launch tubes there came a realization that this was primarily a military facility. This was a real cute idea. This facility located underwater couldn't be detected from the space ships in orbit above. She stretched her neck to look around to get an idea of just how big the entire complex was. Even with the lights and fairly clear water she was limited in vision. But she had seen several of the dome structures connected together by tubes. This was a real big place.

The small ship settled into a landing cradle and went through a typical docking routine. Once the pressure equalized, the two men unbuckled her harness and led her out into the complex. They passed through several sections. The bulkheads were green in the section where they landed, then changed to blue and finally light yellow. Stopping in front of a control sentinel, the two men placed their hands on an ID screen and answered into the machine in response to questions. She was taken into a little room with four chairs around a small table. They just left her. It was a long time before anyone came, probably more than two hours.

The door opened and a very tall man and a woman about her size entered the room.

"Good morning. I am Major Xene. This is Sergeant Arank. Would you care for something to drink?"

"Yes please," Jill answered politely since the man was being nice, unlike so many others. The woman sergeant went out apparently to get her a drink.

Major Xene motioned to the chair at the table. "Have a seat, miss. There appears to have been an error. You were not supposed to have been sent here."

"I certainly had no control over that," Jill replied.

The man chuckled. "No, you certainly had no control over that but I am still trying to figure out how you got here."

"Sorry, I really can't provide any insight. One minute I was in a cell on Luna the next they pulled me from the cell and shipped me out down here. Wherever this is?"

"You are in Oceanea one of the greatest achievements of Pan Crimbian Empire. As a scientist you should be able to appreciate the technological achievement."

Jill could only nod yes. The sergeant returned with cups of cold drinks. Jill accepted her cup and took a sip. It was sweet and cold - ice tea. It was good. This was the first refreshment she'd been given that didn't taste like something a dog left. She drank deeply and very quickly the cup was empty. Jill felt lightheaded - she tried to stand then collapsed.

The sergeant looked at the Major, and spoke in the primary Pan Crimbian language. "Is she going to die?"

"No," the Major replied. "Get her ready for transport back into space."

"Yes, Sir. I thought that no one was allowed to leave once they have been here in Oceanea?"

"Don't worry. She's going to the chief Inquisitor. She apparently was part of the resistance on the moon. When the Inquisitor is through with her, she won't even know her own name."

****

Chapter 7-6
0430 Tuesday 25 March 2228
Just outside old Tyco Base
Luna

Jake crawled forward along the trench just below the guard tower. He stopped and rolled over on his back so he could look up into the guard tower. The guards were oblivious to the outside. Rolling back over he moved up to the outside ladder. Slowly he eased up just in case they could feel any vibration or hear any scrapes from the outside.

It was strange he thought. Almost a year ago he was based here in Tyco and then was forced to fight and defend the base. After the battle was lost the base was devastated from space to render it useless. Now he was again attacking the same base. For over a hundred years Tyco had been the key to holding Earth's moon. Originally, it had been a large crater that had been covered over with a dome.

Over the years it was expanded many times; each time by adding a larger dome over the old one. Today Tyco was the most obvious landmark seen from Earth.

Jake cycled the air lock. There was no way he could tell who was in the lock but even a sleepy non-attentive guard would hear the valves being opened and the rush of air in the pipes. What Jake was counting on was that the guard would believe that the lock was being used by some Pan Crimbian officer checking up on him – not by an enemy so brazen. When the inner door swung open, the guard was shocked to see a stranger standing there. He just stood looking in amazement as Jake came toward him – finally the realization set in, but too late. As the man lunged for the alarm, Jake grabbed him around the chest. The upward thrust of a knife silenced the guard forever. Now the door was open and they'd have almost an hour before anyone would be checking on the guard.

Jake held a light up to the window and flashed the signal. They were on radio silence – the Crimbians couldn't understand the inter-suit chatter of the Union, but they could be alerted to their presence just by hearing the talking.

Jake went to work planting explosives. Earney wanted to make it very difficult for the enemy to figure out what had happened.

Down the ladder they went to the main detention center. This operation was different than any yet attempted. Most of their other operations involved slash and run. This was a completely different operation. There were thousands of Union citizens being held in this old base. Jake had done some scouting down deep in the old tunnels. The Pan Crimbians had not cleared out all of the old Union munitions and equipment stored in the deep bunkers.

Jake and Earney planned to make good use of the old battle supplies. But first things first.

Earney led his small squad from below to the communications center. On the outside of the door he scratched lightly. The peep hole opened and could see nothing but empty passageway. The door opened just a crack - it was enough. Earney launched himself across the passageway and was able to hit the door with full force. The door flew open sending the small man back against the wall. The Pan Crimbian Officer held his hands up indicating his surrender. The others in the room followed suit. These men were non-combatants. Earney gestured with the barrel of the chattergun for them to leave. This was just a simple communications shack there was no encryption equipment, so as far as Earney and his band of fighters were concerned the goal here was to eliminate this as a place where a warning could be given. As soon as the Crimbians left with Earney, a Union specialist got busy with explosives.

Earney had selected the old recreation center room as the holding room for the Crimbian prisoners. There were several dozen already being held under gunpoint when Earney arrived with his little group. Another group arrived while Earney was standing – this group was bedraggled from months of captivity. When they realized freedom might be coming there was a change of attitude among some and demanding –

typical Union Citizens Earney thought.

So Earney spoke to a group of the more belligerent. "You can be held with them," Earney pointed to the Pan Crimbians wearing uniforms. "Or, you can pick up a gun and guard them and leave with us."

A big man stepped forward. "Give me a gun. I'll take care of these bastards!"

Earney swung the bell of his chattergun into the man's belly. "You will guard these prisoners and follow orders – or you can join them. No one is to be killed unless they attempt to escape or unless I order them killed. Do you understand?"

The man didn't like it – Earney could see it in his eyes. "Yes, I understand," he replied reluctantly. The man's eyes changed accepting the situation. Earney looked at the others. They were either nodding yes or mentioning something positive.

Everyone felt it – the lunar surface buckled up – some stumbled. Then it happened again this time even more violently. Ceiling tiles came down, a ventilation duct came loose and a light swung free from one side. Dust settled around everyone in the room.

Someone called out loud, "What the hell was that?"

"That was the front and back door being shut!" Earney declared.

"The what?"

"Tyco is a big complex, but there are only two main tunnels coming in. We just collapsed more than a mile of each tunnel."

"You mean we are trapped in here?"

"In a manner of speaking. I would call it a fortified position. The enemy will have a hard time launching a counterattack."

Earney tossed the chattergun to the big man. "Keep these guys out of trouble. Don't worry. There's a plan and a way out."

Earney went out the door and ran into Jake herding another group of prisoners. Jake took them into the holding room and returned. Earney handed him a cigar. Jake took it and lit it.

"Well, Major, Phase one complete. Hope we live through Phases two and three."

Earney lit his cigar. "That would be good. Meanwhile, let's get to work and tear this place apart."

****

Chapter 7-7
1630 Wednesday 26 March 2228
Fleet Headquarters Mars
Fleet Admiral Office

Mike was seated at his desk going through a stack of routine correspondence. It seemed unreal but most everything of a routine matter had been separated already by his growing small staff. Most aides keep track of a multitude of things simply by using a computer and a fleet scheduling program. Mike had found at this level there was too much to keep track of for the Fleet Admiral, so now the most unprecedented had happened Mike now had aides. Of course, they were not called aide, they were just Warrant's or Master Chief's assigned to the Senior Fleet Chief Warrant.

There was a light tapping at his door Inspector Herbert Kohler was standing in the doorway. Mike had seen him nosing around during the past weeks. The man seemed obtuse so almost anyone would talk with him since he was wearing a badge indicating the highest security level.

"Would it be convenient for me to speak with you for a few minutes?" Herb's tone was almost apologetic.

"Sure, come on in." Mike motioned Herb in.

Herb came in and took the seat by Mike's desk. Out came the little electronic notebook almost as if by habit. He flipped open the cover one handed and took the little stylus and pushed a series of micro switches on the cover. "As you know I've been looking into the thefts from the main logistic warehouse." Herb paused and Mike nodded an acknowledgement. "Thought I'd come to you and talk about the results. Between the two of us I figured we could decide what to do."

"Okay, what have you got?"

"It seems that most of the missing supplies were removed in a series of raids conducted and lead by two of your Warrants – one Arnold Jones and Patty Smith now assigned to the *Galileo* underway for Eros with the invasion force."

"You're not supposed to know where either Jonesy or Patty Smith are – much less the fact that they are on *Galileo* on an invasion mission." Mike was irritated by the amount of information the man had about a top secret operation.

"That's the other subject I want to talk about – your security around headquarters is pretty loose. Of course, I'm unusually nosey after everyone stopped noticing me I just listened. I have been real busy. But, as you realize, I should've never been able to discover such information."

Mike rubbed his forehead – this was potentially going to be a mess. "Any ideas on why two very decorated veterans would take to stealing?"

"Well, it seems that your logistic department wouldn't sell them the supplies they needed to get the operation underway. Apparently, there is some rule about keeping an adequate reserve. They were enterprising officers trying to complete a mission – so they took the supplies that they had rightfully tried to purchase. I want to tell you I served in the Army and saw the same types of bureaucratic nonsense – that's why I am reluctant to send out warrants of arrest for them."

Mike was really angry now, not at Jonesy

or Patty, but at the fleet logistic officer. Not only had he been immensely stupid by not giving the highest priority ships the supplies they desperately needed. He then compounded the situation by ordering an investigation. As a federal police officer Herb could order the arrest of two very key people now getting ready to go into battle.

"What are you going to do?" Mike asked.

"I don't see how justice can be served by arresting the thieves. It would seem more appropriate to arrest your logistics officer. But, I can't do that without involving the thieves themselves." Herb punched out a chip from his pocket vellum and handed it to Mike. "I'll let you handle it at your level. They may not even return from their mission. In any case as a citizen, I can see no real crime has been committed other than by your fleet logistics officer."

Herb paused and held breastbone. "Heartburn," he explained before continuing. "Also on that chip are the security problems which I have noted. I understand that you are very good friends with the Fleet Intel Officer. I'll let you tell her and let's see if the holes are plugged. However be advised I'll be around – and if the same people have a problem with diarrhea of the mouth, then I'll take action."

****

Chapter 7-8
0830 Thursday 27 March 2228
Freedom Settlement (Renamed Blessed Faith)
In Geosynchronous Orbit around Earth

Ruffus was carried into the large compartment on the space station. Formally it had been the corporate headquarters for the Bethler Steel Corporation. In fact the Pan Crimbians were shocked to discover that the private offices of a corporation were more elegant than the government offices. On Freedom Station the government offices were among the smallest and plainest in the settlement. Since the Crimbians had no need for corporations the Holy command took over the luxury suites.

Four of the daughters easily carried Ruffus in the low gravity despite his large mass. Ruffus took his place on the center pallet constructed especially for him. Once he was comfortable with sufficient pillows he motioned for the women to leave. He pressed the call button to summon his war staff.

Space Marshal Custus was the first one through the door followed by Secretary of State Millerfrid, Grand High Priest Kaler, and Minister of Finance Drassic. Whereas Alex Custus was large and imposing, the rest were even more peculiar. Grand High Priest Kalen had blond hair and blue eyes which didn't go at all with his dark skin. Secretary Millerfrid was small with a rat like nose. He wore large spectacles and had very fair skin. The man was a genius. The finance minister on the other hand was an enigmatic man, with swarthy good looks that clashed with his personality - one of the most devious men Ruffus had ever known. Each of the men was fiercely loyal to Ruffus and to the Crimbian faith and empire.

Space Marshal Custus asked Ruffus, “Shall we start with a briefing of what is happening on the Moon?”

“We will get to that in due course,” Ruffus stated. “But I want to hear good news first so let’s hear from the minister of finance.

“Our prayers have been answered. From our conquests of the Moon and this station we have recovered sufficient gold and platinum to finance another three years of war. I’m going to approve and endorse Space Marshal Custus’ request for more ships. Our elite Priesthood will get the additional inquisitors needed to turn these barbarians into keepers of the faith.”

“Excellent. Excellent.” Ruffus rubbed his hands together. “Secretary of State Millerfrid you had a communiqué from General Weems, did you not?”

He handed the parchment to Ruffus. “General Weems reports that he has arrived at Eros and is preparing for battle with Union forces. Several of our intelligence operatives on Mars have reported that a large body of ships departed several weeks ago. We believe they are headed for Eros. With Eros moving ever closer to Earth’s orbit we cannot allow the enemy to hold it.”

"Lord Kalen, your report."

"Up to now we have been ahead of schedule on converting the barbarians to the faith. As I have explained before only about fifty percent of these space barbarians convert on the first attempt. But they seem to respond well after six months to a year of hard work in the labor camps. We get a lot of useful work from the unbelievers and it breaks them down and makes them more receptive to the ministers of the priests. We had a lot of the more difficult cases in the Tyco holding center. This latest problem will cause delays."

Ruffus looked at the group. "We must all pray that this unfortunate situation is resolved soon!" *No one in the group especially Marshal Custus missed the veiled threat.*

Space Marshal Custus was ready. "I don't believe things are as bad as they seem. Yesterday morning a small group of Union raiders broke into the Holy Sanctuary at Tyco. They detonated charges and shut off the two tunnels into the complex."

Ruffus asked, "So why have the faithful not tunneled back in and restored order to the Tyco Sanctuary?"

"More than three kilometers of rock was collapsed into the tunnels. There is no tunneling equipment immediately available. What is on the moon is barbarian equipment which none of our faithful know how to use. Not only that, the pressure in the adjacent areas was lost. So our people are digging by hand in pressure suits. I have ordered digging machines to be on the moon as soon as possible. The last report I was given was arrival within three days."

"Can we attack from the surface?" Kalen asked.

"Well, it's not so simple. The enemy chose an opportune time to attack. It's dark on the surface and it will take time to set up a real assault from the surface. If we drill a new tunnel it will take weeks. Of course, we could simply attack Tyco from space with heavy weapons. But the entire complex would be destroyed – but we want the complex intact."

So what steps are being taken?" Grand High Priest Kalen demanded. "I have sixteen High Priests that were in that complex along with scores of other faithful mid-level priests."

"I believe we should not be rash. Remember the patient are rewarded in heaven. We finally have the pesky resistance bottled up in one area. While they are there they can do no further damage. Meanwhile, we'll start digging a new tunnel and prepare for an attack when it is light on the surface. Either plan will succeed. The resistance commander has finally sealed his own fate.

****

****

"Victory has a thousand fathers, but defeat is an orphan." *John F. Kennedy*

Part 8 - Eros

The Battle of Eros actually started on 29 March 2228. This became one of the epic struggles of the Solar War as 28,000 Union Marines and Fleet specialists went against 137,000 of the Pan Crimbian Holy warriors. The Union forces were determined to take the rock and the Pan Crimbians were determined to hold it to the death. This struggle became etched alongside such other classic battles: Waterloo, Gettysburg, Tours, or Iwo Jima. Both sides were destined to suffer more than fifty- percent casualties fighting for the merest fly speck of a rock of in the solar system. Eros became a landmark of mass courage and individual valor on both sides. As the Union capital combat ships came into range, they started a steady bombardment of the rock and space around the small planetoid. Missiles and cannon fire maintained steady sweeps during the solar night. The Crimbian ships in the area were destroyed or fell back to avoid destruction. The first wave of Marines went against the space station early Sunday morning of the 30th of March. The Marines breached the outer hull of the twenty mile wide station but were unable to advance due to the heavy resistance. The first wave of Marines to hit the rock at noon suffered 80% casualties. Admiral Wilson was forced to close the landing zones by 1800. A second wave was launched at 2200 when the first wave ceased to be an effective fighting force.

Journal of Solar History

Chapter 8-1
2220 Sunday 30 March 2228
CE-46 Galileo
Launch Bay B42

Sergeant Don Thompson settled into the control rack on the side of the attack shuttle. He had already checked all of his Marines. He checked even though the Marines had already checked their individual equipment. Each corporal had checked their team and he checked the entire squad before strapping in. He knew that soon the Gunny would be checking over everyone. Each Marine just wanted to double check to be sure there were no mistakes.

If little details were forgotten, then the Gunny might be unsure of Don. Don was now Nighthawk, just as every Marine in the squad assumed their fighting name. Don felt his body quivering with anticipation, even though he couldn't move a muscle strapped in to the rack. He had told the psychological officer about how he shook before a fight. The Psych Officer had told Don it was just nerves and surges of adrenaline, like a horse or a runner before a race. Don didn't feel much like a horse – *just a target.*

The racks for Marine deployment had been installed in each shuttle for the drop. In this case since it was a large drop additional racks had been bolted to the outside hull as well. They were designed to hold the Marines in their APS, so there were twelve bodies lined up on the shuttle, like human bullets in a magazine. So if the shuttle carrying the marines to the launch point was attacked it was likely the exposed Marines hanging on the outside would be shot through to get at the marines on the inside. This made the Marines hanging on the outside feel very exposed. Of course, this was also the fastest way to get rid of the Marines in an emergency. *Get shot or drift in space – neither option was good.*

Each Marine was encased in his APS and encircled with IPP's. The plan was for the Marines to be set down on the rock in a specific LZ (for Landing Zone). However, if plans or the situation changed then the shuttle would release and drop the Marines in a position to get down onto the rock using their IPP units. Naturally, in this situation, the Fleet crew flying the shuttle was just as vulnerable as the Marines.

Each of the Marines and Fleet specialists

were wrapped in their own thoughts now. No chit chat was allowed on the battle circuit. The Marines and Fleet specialists had trained for weeks just for this landing event. Every waking hour for the past few weeks, except for the time spent in shelter from the storm had been used to plan and prepare for this invasion. General Ridgeway had proclaimed the division ready for battle just prior to arrival.

The circuits came alive. Don recognized Major Markel's voice. " 'A' Company standby for launch. The General tells me that things aren't going well down there. I expect that we can change that. Be ready for anything."

The voice of the shuttle craft pilot came on, "Shuttle launch T minus Five – Four – Three- Two – One!" The force of acceleration pressed the Marines into their racks. One minute they were bathed in the bright lights of the launch bay the next blackness of space. The pilot rolled the little craft and spun going down from the ship into the landing zone. The bottom shuttle doors opened for the Marines inside to be launched. There were arcs of light flashing as energy pulses hit targets nearby. They were being shot at by the Crimbian defenders – the Marines and Army called this 'going in hot'.

As the miles rolled by Don could see the near end of Eros getting bigger and bigger. Soon he could pick out suited figures down on the surface. Everything appeared in black and white through his visor. That was because the ships and landing zone were illuminated with only one band of light. There were thousands of bands of light in the visible and non-visible ranges. The ships emitted only one frequency at a time. The programming of the APS permitted it to adjust to the frequency of the current time light band period. This kept the Union Marines able to see visually even in the darkest areas, leaving the Pan Crimbians in the dark unless they turned on a spot light. Still, any spotlight turned on would instantly become a target!

Then it dawned on Don that the figures in the LZ were down and not fighting. This was the remnants of Charlie Company who had landed hours earlier. As the realization of what he was seeing reached him Don's stomach tightened into a knot. Broken APS suits with arms and legs missing indicated dead Marines.

***

The initial landing had gone smoothly. After all the hours of Fleet bombardment, barely a dent had been made in General Solas' well planned defenses. The wily Crimbians had just battened down the hatches and rode out the barrage. They let the first Marines land against light opposition. The Fleet bombardment had to stop once the first wave of Marines was down. It had taken an hour or so for the Crimbians to shake off the effects of the bombardment. By this time, the LZ's were piled up with men, women, and equipment.

Then the Pan Crimbians launched a counteroffensive.

The rock was honeycombed with bunkers and defensive launch sites. Every shadow and rock outcropping concealed a launcher. Boulders came alive with murderous energy pulse fire. Zero G mortars fell in wave after wave from concealed pits. Heavy artillery and anti-ship cannons were lowered to rake the LZ areas and incoming landing shuttles. Land mines had been strewn across almost every square foot of the surface. They detonated with killing effects allowing the Marines only to inch forward on the desolated surface.

***

Don knew none of this during the launch and descent. All he knew was that he and his little squad were being inserted into this LZ. Don's thoughts drifted back to the ship remembering the good nature kidding between the Marines and Fleet specialists. The Marines were telling them how easy the Fleet guys had it - always a warm bunk to sleep in and steady rations - never sleeping in an APS and lying alone out in the cold. Whereas the Fleet guys countered with the fact that most of the time the Marines just trained and rode along. They made a drop for a few hours or days and then were done for weeks or months. All the while the Fleet specialists stood six hour watches and were always exposed to attack from other ships. *It didn't look too healthy to be either one*, Don thought grimly.

A blast hit the landing craft to the right and the Fleet pilot fought to control the little craft as he tried to compensate for the loss of a thruster and a hole in the hull. He steadied up and held the craft still for a split second over the LZ. “Marines away,” the pilot called out. Eleven Marines dropped twenty feet to the surface with their equipment. Croaker was the first fatality of the squad - the blast that had blown a hole in the hull of the landing shuttle had gone right through him.

As the Marines looked up there was a moment of confusion and reality went through the squad. Eight stood there looking up. “Get down!” Don shouted.

They fell belly down instantly as the training kicked in. There was a pit or depression to the right. Don dove into in and motioned for the rest to follow. A blast arced off the rock near him his movement had been seen. The others tumbled into the pit as other arcs flashed. The sounds of someone vomiting could be heard over the comm net. So much for someone’s breakfast of steak and eggs.

Don’s moments of indecision were over - now Nighthawk took control. All landings seem to be boiling confusion. Everything seems to moves in a slow motion as adrenaline pulses through one’s body. But the Marines that are the best at control of the adrenaline flow and use it to be clear headed and calm. Encased in a suit, each Marine is alone. Most sweated profusely.

The life support blowers suck energy at an alarming rate trying to maintain the environment within the suit. They lay on rock at seventy-five below zero and the suit controls had to compensate for that loss of heat.

Don clicked on his squad circuit and he spoke in a calm voice. “Okay, everyone, we’re down. Let’s get the gear out and get to work. Time to give these Crimbians some of what they gave Charlie Company. Diver – Wasp, get that big gun out and ready on the lip. Falcon, get on the scope and look around!”

Marines are just as afraid to die or to be injured as anyone else. But they do have an ingrained compulsion about doing their job - and doing it right. Don tossed his IPP (Individual Power Pack) into the bottom of the hole. They would no longer need them now that they were down. The pressure proof boxes were opened and the big weapons were brought out. Soon each team had one. Falcon fired a couple of bolts into the surface and screwed in a plate. He then attached the periscope to the plate. The periscope went up and he turned in a three sixty viewing the area around them. Don could see the image clearly in his helmet along with the words of the computer analysis. It instantly identified other squads of Marines to the right and left and behind them, as it should have. Ahead towards the low hills was the enemy - Alpha Company’s first objective.

Major Markel's voice came on the line, "Time to move out."

Nighthawk pushed in his command acknowledgement button and switched circuits. "Saddle up, Marines. We're moving out."

Don went up and over the rim he went flat on his belly. His Marines followed. There is nothing about an advance on a low G rock like Eros that looks glorious. The Marines crawled belly down, staying in shadows, taking every bit of cover found on the craggy terrain of the surface. They fired only when necessary because firing in the dark revealed a Marine's position. Whenever a Marine does shoot he or she moves immediately to the right or left because to stay in that position could be fatal.

The surface beyond the LZ was strewn with not only the equipment from the first landing, but also bodies of their fellow Marines that had died on the first try for the high ground. *A silent reminder to everyone in the squad of the high cost of real-estate on Eros today.* So they crawled, slid, dodged, ducked, and slithered. But always forward towards their objective.

Screams could be heard occasionally over the comms as other Marines were wounded or killed. A hundred yards short of the low hills, the enemy counter attacked. They came boiling up out of the ground all around the squad. Three suited figures jumped on top of Nighthawk - one pressed a blaster to the side of his suit. Instinctively he rolled knocking the man's aim off. He shot one, crushed another with the advanced hydraulics of the APS, and kicked the other in the backpack of his Crimbian P-suit which ruptured his life support - killing him instantly. It was easy to distinguish the shapes of the Crimbians in their smaller P-suits. Nighthawk started firing along with Diver at the same time. In less than thirty seconds the enemy had been swept away adding to the carnage on the surface.

Nighthawk realized in a moment that the enemy snipers and cannon barrage had stopped to allow the Pan Crimbian attack. He lunged up and covered the ground in quick strides towards the base of the hill. He dove head first to cover the last ten yards and slid behind a rock. His quick movements caused the rest of his squad to follow instinctively. They now held the base of the hills. Their motions alerted the hidden enemy gunners. Sparks flew as the enemy tried to kill Nighthawk's squad. All they could do was hunker down and wait for a let up.

"Everyone here?" Nighthawk asked. Ten acknowledgement lights illuminated on his squad status indicators. He pressed the chin switch to speak on the battle command circuit. "Nighthawk reporting - Squad in position at the base of Hill 222. Commencing assault."

The Gunny answered, "Cobra here. Acknowledged proceed."

"Where is the Major?" Nighthawk asked since he was supposed to be the one answering on this circuit.

"He's busy. Get to work, Marine."

"Aye - Aye," Nighthawk responded. He shifted the circuit. "Falcon, take your team and move out. Cobra wants this hill."

Falcon and his team started up the hill on the right, while Diver took his team to the left. That left Nighthawk with the center. Bullfrog was with Diver's group and he spotted a concealed bunker. He tapped Flash and pointed ensuring everyone saw the opening. Bullfrog moved laterally along the hill then upward just above the opening. Flash moved upward just as twenty hand grenades came bouncing out of the opening.

Flash screamed, "Grenades!" She reached out and picked them up and started tossing them back into the opening. She managed to toss three back in before the other started exploding. Flash's APS protected her from the first two that detonated, but the third ruptured her hydraulics and the fourth cracked the seal on the suit. She never felt the others.

The rest of the squad had tried to crawl into the rock surface. They were far enough away from the explosions for any damage to occur. As soon as the explosions concluded Bullfrog rolled above the opening thrust his chattergun inside and emptied a full clip. He dove in head first and almost threw up at the sight of a half dozen mangled bodies.

There was an air lock in the back of the bunker but it was too badly damaged by the explosions to ever open again normally.

As he came back out Diver was placing a marker for the cleanup squad to find Flashe's body. Diver stripped the energy clips from Flash's belt pouch and her water jug. Diver was behind in the advance. He could see Nighthawk half way up the hill.

Nighthawk was nearing the crest of the hill when Grit next to him found a land mine. "Alert Squad," he called out, "Mines!"

"Mark them and move on," Nighthawk called out.

A solid wave of fire swept over the heads of the advancing squad as they worked their way up the final few feet to the summit. Anything that moved became a target for the squad. Sometime during this hour of fighting Snowflake came in contact with a mine and his APS was disabled. Pepper suffered a direct hit on the right arm that severed his hand. The suit's auto closure severed the arm at the elbow and applied a tourniquet along with an injection for the pain. Pepper never saw the final assault – she died quietly in her suit.

Falcon was the first over the summit. He advanced shooting at anything that looked human or threating. He ran out of energy clips after killing six Pan Crimbians. Three others jumped on him. Now it was hand-to-hand as the rest of the squad came over the top. They killed fifteen Crimbians to take the top. But there had to be more.

There was a cave opening on one side. Diver cut down the officer that charged out of the hole. A hand came out and dragged the still enemy officer's limp P-suit back in. Bullfrog, Wolf, and Wasp went in headfirst. Wasp had a torch. She lighted the flame then torched the cave killing twenty-five to thirty troops. Wolf dropped a backpack explosive charge as they backed out of the cave. The detonation collapsed the ceiling burying the enemy soldiers forever.

Nighhawk planted a transponder indicating that this position was secure. The Marines now had a very valuable hill. The price had been one third of his fighting force, 2 KOA, 2 WIA. Within half an hour Hill 222 was serving the Marines as it had the Pan Crimbians. Electronics were moved into place along with high-powered electronic telescopes and communications equipment – so by the time Major Markel arrived the Marines were already spotting enemy positions and directing other Marines to the next objectives.

****

Chapter 8-2
0700 Monday 31 March 2228
Fleet Headquarters
Mars

Admiral Thomas Watson was seated at the conference table when Mike came in and handed him the morning dispatches and messages. The red vellum contained all of last night's messages which had been decoded for the Fleet Admiral.

"You will probably be interested in the first one. It's started."

"Eros – Already?"

Tom opened the vellum using his thumb and code to actuate the Priority Blue message. It didn't use his actual thumb print. The computer took a sample of his DNA and compared it with the approval list. Tom read:

BEGIN TRANSMISSION

FROM: COMMANDER TASK FORCE C

TO: FLEET ADMIRAL

SUBJECT: FORCE ATTACK COMMENCED

TOP SECRET RED PRIORITY - OP IMMEDIATE UPDATE

COMMENCED ATTACK ON EROS USING APPROVED WAR PLAN C-006. CONCENTRATED ATTACKS BY 2ND MARINE DIVISION HAVE GAINED CONTROL OF FIRST OBJECTIVE SURFACE OF THE PLANETOID AND NOW CONTROL OUTER PERIMETER IN SPACE STATION. CASUALTIES HIGH - ENEMY GIVING MAXIMUM RESISTANCE.

FLEET UNITS HAVE SWEPT A TOKEN FORCE OF VESSELS FROM THE AREA AND HAVE DEFEATED ALL DEFENDERS. NO CAPITAL SHIPS ENCOUNTERED. THE LARGEST VESSEL NOTED 1 DESTROYER. DESTROYED 8 PICKETS, 4

TRANSPORTS, 1 CARGO, 2 SEARCH, AND 4 TUGS. CAPTURED 1 REPAIR TENDER, 2 TRANSPORTS, 4 PICKETS AND 1 SEARCH.

NO SIGN OF THE LARGE PAN CRIMBIAN FLEET.

CAUSALITIES - FLEET – 44 KIA - 142 WOUNDED 2 MISSING ----MARINE - 1,646 KIA - 14,722 WOUNDED - 647 MISSING. ALL SHIPS STILL FULLY OPERATIONAL. GENERAL RIDGEWAY REPORTS THAT HE STILL HAS AN EFFECTIVE FIGHTING FORCE DESPITE THE HEAVY LOSSES.

DISPATCH FIRST RESUPPLY VESSELS. HAVE USED 20 PERCENT OF ORDINANCE.

LORRAINE E. WILSON

ADMIRAL

END TRANSMISSION

Tom looked up. “Has Maggie seen this?”

“Oh yeah! I think she’s down vomiting up her breakfast after seeing the causality reports.”

“Look down at the next message.”

BEGIN TRANSMISSION

FROM: COMMANDER LUNA RESISTANCE FORCES

TO: FLEET ADMIRAL

SUBJECT: ACTION REPORT OP STATUS

UPDATE

TOP SECRET RED

HAVE TAKEN TYCO BASE AND LIBERATING AS MANY UNION CITIZENS AS POSSIBLE. TYCO APPARENTLY IS THE PAN CRIMBIAN BRAINWASHING CENTER. THE OBJECTIVE AT PRESENT IS TO PUT THEM OUT OF BUSINESS FOR A WHILE.

CAN ONLY HOLD THE BASE UNTIL IT IS LIGHT ON THE SURFACE OR THEY COMPLETE A RELIEF TUNNEL - WE CAN HEAR DIGGING. THE PAN CRIMBIAN COMMANDER HAS ATTEMPTED TO CONTACT US – HE ONLY WANTS ONE OF TWO THINGS. SURRENDER OR TO SET UP A DIALOGUE TO NEGOTIATE THE RELEASE OF HOSTAGES - WE HAVE NO INTENTION OF RESPONDING TO EITHER!

THE CURRENT POSITION PROVIDES EXCELLENT DEFENSE; WE HAVE SUFFICIENT FOOD, WATER, AMMUNITION, AND OXYGEN. WE INTEND TO BLEED THE ENEMY AND FREE AS MANY UNION CITIZENS AS POSSIBLE.

EARNEST K MACLEAN

MAJOR FMF (BR)

END TRANSMISSION

When Mike looked up, Tom chuckled. “Your friend Earney seems to be in a classic situation. He has fortified himself in the enemy castle. They have to burn down the castle to get him. I sure hope he knows what he is doing."

"So do I," Mike muttered.

"What time do you shove off?" Tom was changing the subject. It took Mike a moment to realize this so there was a hesitation.

"Around zero nine hundred."

"Anything I can do to help?"

"No. Everything is all set. But there is something you can do while I am gone."

"What's that?" Tom was now puzzled because there was usually nothing that could be done to help Mike.

"I met a young woman the other day. She is Army –Colonel Sara Samuels. Right now she is bunking in with Doc Smith. I know you used to have a lot of friends in both the Army and the intelligence community." Tom was nodding yes so Mike continued. "Would you use your contacts to check her out discreetly?"

"What do you expect to find?"

"Probably nothing. But I just have a hunch."

Tom probed, "So what do you think is the problem?"

"I don't know; it's just that there's something that doesn't quite fit."

"Why don't you ask that Federal cop

that's been hanging around? He seems to be a buddy of yours." Tom left the implications unstated.

"I would, if there was any real evidence of a problem. The trouble is, I already owe him a big favor. I just don't want to burden him down with this."

"Okay. So what kind of priority is this checkout?"

Mike replied very softly, "Let's say medium priority, but very quiet."

****

Chapter 8-3
1830 Tuesday 1 April 2228
CE-46 Galileo
Flag Control Center

A large monitor hung above the tactical displays indicated: "Eros D +2 H +9:23." This meant that the battle for Eros was two days, nine hours and twenty three minutes old. Below the large display was a list of units currently engaged in active operations. Lorraine was seated in her command chair listening to the discussion of the staff. The battle for control of the space station was finally making some headway. But the battle for the rock Eros was getting worse. The Marines, after two days of intense fighting, only held about half of the surface. They had been unable to break into the subsurface main fortress areas.

General Steve Ridgeway had one opinion and Captain Bud Kadel had another.

Lorraine looked over at Doyle. He was listening intently and not providing any input to the discussion.

Bud Kadel was talking. “We must hold a reserve force in the event this other fleet shows up. We could very easily be in a ship to ship battle.”

Steve Ridgeway countered. “I understand about the other fleet. That’s why we must end this battle. I’ll lead the final assault using everyone available, so we can end this quickly. I am tired of losing good Marines.”

Jonesy listened carefully. He had an opinion, but he certainly wouldn’t give it unless asked. Somehow he felt he was watching a significant event in history. Either man could be right depending on how the enemy reacted. He understood that General Ridgeway wanted to commit the reserve forces to the battle while Bud Kadel wanted to hold the reserve. Since causalities on the surface were more than four times the anticipated number, battle lines on the surface were getting thin. Ridgeway’s argument was that an overpowering force could now turn the tide and end the battle quickly. *Could it?*

Lorraine looked at Doyle. “Commodore, what is your opinion?”

Doyle cleared his throat and sat upright before speaking. “I don’t believe that one grand assault is going to end this battle. You notice how few prisoners we are taking? The enemy is fighting to the death. The enemy is either worked up into a fervor of religion or they expect to be reinforced somehow and soon. Maybe even a combination of both. I agree that we need to commit more troops to the landing effort. But I am reluctant to recommend that we charge in with everything."

Lorraine was thinking fast now. The thought was a glimmer then it formed. "I agree with Doyle. Also I'm still concerned about the possibility of an enemy fleet in the area. General Ridgeway you will land with half of the reserves and continue the battle on the surface of the rock. Colonel Davis will form a light battalion from various ship complements. We are going to split the fleet. A third of the force will remain to protect the LZs. I will transfer the flag to Captain Snicker's Ship. Commodore Doyle here will take the majority of the capital ships and scout for the enemy fleet."

****

Chapter 8-4
0930 Wednesday 2 April 2228
S/S Amelia O'Leary
Earth Sector

"What have we got?" Captain Buck Cardif paced the bridge. He was a pacer it helped him to think.

"Small freighter coming up from the surface," Sensors Chief called out from across the compartment. "The trajectory indicates its heading for Freedom settlement. Too small for heavy weapons. Looks like a resupply ship. Should be easy pickins."

"Battle stations," Buck called out.

The alarm sounded and all hands on the small ship started moving. Even on a private research vessel, the call to battle stations was answered immediately. This was wartime and every citizen aboard knew that the overall safety of the ship might very well depend on people being at their assigned battle station. Not only that this was an area near Earth with the possibility of profit.

Buck was looking at the screen – Ben Papers was the pilot on the controls. Buck and Ben had already become fast friends. They had a lot of common interests and Buck really liked the way Ben handled his ship. Ben had what was called the touch, Ben was someone who had a natural feel for handling ships. Most could be taught how to fly a ship given time and if they had a good understanding of mathematics as related astrophysics. However, there were few individuals who seemed to have a natural aptitude, who could feel the ship under his controls and react long before any problems developed. Yes, Ben was one of those few with the touch, Buck had already concluded.

Buck could see that Ben had already steered the *Amelia* on a course that would allow a slow overtaking of the target ship from behind. So far, the enemy ship seemed unaware that a Union ship was coming up from behind. Buck saw from his Captain's station that the missiles and turrets were manned and ready for action. Ben was busy running the computer checking his track of approach.

Buck asked, "How long to intercept?"

"About twenty minutes," Ben responded. "They should have seen us by now."

Buck realized that Ben's observation was correct. He looked over at the sensors console for confirmation. One of the Spec's was adjusting controls trying to make some sort of determination. She looked up shaking her head. "The ship is manned. I can see plenty of bodies on board. But their active sensors are off. Maybe they figure there is no danger this close to Earth. Their anti-satellite collision alarms should go off and warn them when we get closer."

"How many people do you figure are on board?"

"Looks like there could be twenty or thirty. Of course they could be hauling cattle."

Buck chuckle inwardly. He remembered when his ship had attacked another expecting to have a big battle. What they found on the other ship was a herd of cows. It seems that the signature of a cow looks almost the same as a man on shipboard sensors.

Ben sounded the warning, "No weight in one minute."

Everyone strapped down. Gradually everyone felt the sensation of weightlessness as Ben slowly took off the spin. He now held Amelia dead astern of the freighter. They closed the gap gradually to a quarter of a mile then to an eighth of a mile.

The young woman at the sensors called out, "They're not spinning. They are running at no weight."

Ben reacted immediately using some inner instinct. "They have made us. They're trying to run." The little ship started boosting and changed course to open the distance. It was too late for the enemy ship. Ben had already accelerated and was alongside.

Buck opened a channel to the weapons control. "Burn their tongue out."

Within moments cannon flashes sprouted from *Amelia* cutting off the antennas of the Crimbian ship. Now they couldn't call for help. Buck's crew was good and efficient in the gunnery department.

Ben fired *Amelia's* grapnels. The harpoon-like hooks buried themselves into the outer skin of the smaller ship. Bucks crew in the fore and aft compartments started reeling in the cable attached to the big winches. Now it was just a matter of time.

Buck came out of his couch making the announcement, "Boarding party, muster forward."

The smaller ship fired its main engines and the winches slipped paying out thousands of feet of cable. Ben adjusted and went with the smaller ship so the cables would not be parted. He had read about deep sea fishing on Earth where the boat and the fisherman had to work together to reel in the fish. The fisherman would let the fish run and get tired while the fisherman and the boat's helmsman worked together to prevent the fish from breaking the small line. Then after the fish was tired, they just reeled him in. In this case the small ship had no fusion reactor. It was just a matter of time until the ship expended all of its booster fuel. Then Amelia would reel in the ship just like the fish in the sea. It took about thirty minutes, either the fuel had run out or the pilot of the other ship realized the futility.

Buck actuated the probe and adjusted the camera on the end of the probe until he had the best view. He could see the cable probe reaching out wiggling and working its way towards finding the boarding hatch on the enemy ship's hull. Finally, he was able to attach at the bale by the forward hatch. Then he extended the snakelike tunnel. Now he waited as the computer program made a seal and pumped air into the tunnel.

Buck's voice came through on the comms. "Ben hold position. We have a soft seal."

Ben cut thrust from the engines. The grapnels now held the two ships together as one. The grapnels winches now gave Ben complete control of both ships.

Ben said, "Bella, let's do a complete detailed sensor scan of this entire sector."

Bella was the young woman at the sensors station. She was already working the scan. *Now would be a bad time to be surprised by a roving Pan Crimbian warship.*

"There's only a one-man crew," Buck called up from the boarding party. "The rest are Union prisoners. Real money. The Union is paying a thousand a head for the return of any citizen from Pan Crimbian custody. There are twenty-nine of them. I'll be sending them across five at a time. Log them in old buddy."

Ben looked over at the girl on the sensors. "Anything?"

Bella shook her head and announced, "Clear skies."

Ben knew the reality concerning this type of an operation. If the Pan Crimbians caught them, he would be spaced without hesitation as a pirate for piloting the ship, as would the Captain and First Officer. *Of course, at the present time he really didn't care about being killed by the Crimbians – it was better than captivity at their hands.*

"Who weeee." - There was a babble of voices jamming the network.

"What's going on?" Ben keyed open the command circuit override. He wanted to know what made everyone crazy.

A familiar voice of one Lester Scrugs came on the circuit. “Bridge, boarding party. We seem to have found a goody locker. There’s a whole hold full of all kinds of special foods. Probably for some big muckety muck! Surf and turf for dinner tonight. Big Buck says hold her tight until we can unload this cargo.”

Ben responded, “Roger.”

The first group came into the control room. Ben had never seen a more ragged bunch. He looked up at the first woman. She looked starved and was barely able to pull herself along in zero gravity. Her skin was drawn and pale. Her eyes were sunk back into her skull. She probably did not weigh more than eighty to ninety pounds. Ben knew these people would need some real care.

“Your Name and ID number, please.” She seemed confused so he continued, “For the log.”

“Jill Parks. Jillian D. Parks.” She hesitated almost ready to cry. “Sorry, I can’t seem to remember my ID number right now.”

“That’s okay,” Ben answered gently. “I’ve been there too. You’ll remember later. Go on down below and get some chow.”

****

Chapter 8-5
1515 Thursday 3 April 2228
Tyco,
Luna

Jake sat hunched over the big rifle. He was out of sight up on the top of the dome rampart which allowed him to overlook the entire sector by Tiger Pass on the approach to the outside of the base. He had used this type of rifle before when he had gone big game hunting in the Klana preserve. He had killed a Kodiak Bear that stood more than fourteen feet high and weighed over a ton. Of course, he didn't have this type of ammunition or load when hunting for bears.

The gun was a Glenda M-400 projectile rifle. Unlike most modern weapons this gun fired an old-fashioned projectile bullets. The M-400 is over eight-foot long and at one G it would weigh more than seventy pounds. The rifle has a built-in compensation system that allows a man in a suit to use the gun in low or even zero gravity. There is no gunpowder but a plastic explosive substance to launch the bullet. Without the compensation system when a rifle is fired in zero gravity conditions, the recoil force would fling the shooter back like a rocket engine. The compensators are small thrust rocket-like engines which fire at the same moment the bullet leaves the barrel to stabilize the big gun. The gun even has its own built in gyro to feed the computer with stability data. Even with all that, it was still best to tie down the barrel.

The bullets Jake was using are armor piercing and will penetrate the outer hull of a ship or shuttle at close range and could even be fired through the engine block of a tank. The bullets are 840 grains of titanium coated with Teflon VI which fires at a muzzle velocity of 16,410 feet per second - near the speed of sound in glass. The bullet would even penetrate through the armor of an APS P-suit. The gun also had the capability of firing energy pulses and could be sighted with laser or ultrasound. Without a doubt in Jake's mind, this was one of the most powerful hand weapons ever built.

Jake carefully made a sweep. The sight of the big gun was projected to a display inside his helmet. The display absorbed any visible light, ultraviolet or infrared light, as well as any heat given off by a body, and amplified it into the display. Even here out on the surface of the Moon, anyone in a suit would stand out like a tree on the outside of a ship.

Jake had been watching carefully. He had spotted two Crimbians who were attempting to crawl up to the outer dome. Over seven miles away, they probably thought they were being real sneaky. They were almost in range.

This was an ongoing saga. As the days passed, there was some new effort each day to probe the defenses they had built. First, the Crimbians had dug along the collapsed tunnels until they started encountering the land mines placed along the tunnel length before they were collapsed. There had been two explosions before giving up that method. Then the Crimbians had tried the ventilation ducts. Earney had anticipated this. With the ducts being so small, only one man could get through at a time. A box of hand grenades rolled down through the vent closed them and killed a group of attackers. Then of course, the Crimbians had shut off all utilities to the center. By that time there were seven rooms filled with water barrels and an internal generator already suppling the power to the complex. Venting the generator had been tricky but they had been successful at venting onto the Crimbian side so they couldn't work without a suit or breathing device.

Jake was starting to get cold. He had only been out less than an hour. The two out on the surface had been crawling up towards the dome for more than three hours, so they probably had been outside more than four hours. Jake could see no evidence of an external power pack, so the suits of the two must be pretty much used up by now. Pressure suits in general are designed to provide about three days of support. However, as any rock miner learned years ago, direct contact with rock will sap the heat right out of a suit. So the duration is just a matter of hours not days particularly, if you lay down on the surface of the moon. Even Jake would be out on watch in the exposed area only two hours. For longer exposures the practical thing was to have a tent which sheltered you from the cold and insulated you from direct contact with the lunar surface.

Jake opened the breach and extracted the projectile from the rifle. Jake looked it over carefully for any deformities or nicks. He found none, so he reinserted it and closed the breach. There was no sound in the void, but he could feel the breach lock shut with a distinctive click. He had already checked the round before, but it gave him something to do. Also by opening the breach he was sure that it was not frozen in place. He pulled two more projectiles out and looked each of them over too. They both looked good as well. He placed the two projectiles on the rest in front of him.

Now he looked carefully through the crosshairs moving the rifle until the enemy man was centered in the field. He flicked the switch to actuate the rifle warmup. The light came on indicating the gun was ready. He took a deep breath, let out a little and then held it as his finger applied a steady pressure on the trigger. The big gun fired. He automatically opened the breach and inserted a new projectile. He shoved in the next round and looked at his first target. There was a plume of gas venting from the back of the enemy's P-suit. He shifted to the next target and repeated the procedure, carefully sighting in before firing. The second figure flopped in convulsions from the big projectile before cooling off to the dark lunar temperatures of over two hundred below.

Jake worked the breach open and reloaded again. He started searching but there were no more targets. He was still searching for targets when his relief showed up an hour later.

“Anything?”

“Popped a couple of crawlers. Nothing since.”

“See yah later,” Jake called out as he unhooked and carried the big gun below. He still had to do post-operational maintenance service on the gun before he could turn in.

****

Chapter 8-6
0500 Friday 4 April 2228
CE-26 Wernher von Braun
Flag Control

Admiral Unger looked down and reread the orders. They made her angry. She still resented any orders from Fleet Admiral Margaret O’Brian. Yet, this was even worse. It was from Maggie’s Chief of Staff Tom Watson, an Admiral so junior that in Veronica’s opinion he shouldn’t command even a squadron much less fill the coveted chief of staff job.

BEGIN TRANSMISSION

FROM: FLEET HEADQUARTERS

TO: COMMANDER TASK FORCE DELTA

SUBJECT: ALLERT

TOP SECRET RED OP IMMEDIATE

HAVE INTEL INTERCEPT WHICH INDICATES A SQUADRON OF PAN CRIMBIAN SHIPS ARE OUTBOUND IN SECTOR 3.210 FOR MARS. BELIEVE IT TO BE THE RECENTLY REFITTED DREADNOUGHT & SIX ACCOMPANYING CAPITAL SHIPS WHICH MAY HAVE SURVIVED THE ENGAGEMENT WITH TASK FORCE ALPHA LAST FALL AND WAS INVOLVED IN DESTRUCTION OF FLORA INDUSTRIAL COMPLEX. YOU ARE DIRECTED TO REPOSITION YOUR FORCE TO SEARCH FOR THIS THREAT.

ENGAGE AND DESTROY. KEEP THE UNION SAFE.

THOMAS WATSON

ADMIRAL - FOR THE FLEET ADMIRAL

END TRANSMISSION

She had already spoken with the Commander of the *von Braun* and her staff. They all agreed with her that this would most likely prove to be a useless search. The chances of finding one of seven ships would be unlikely, even if the search was limited to a given sector. Still if a group of enemy ships with that much firepower showed up in the vicinity of Mars it could be real ugly. As much as she despised Maggie O'Brian, she was developing a deep seated hatred for the Pan Crimbian aggressors.

Last evening she had broken communications silence to summon all commanding officers to the von Braun for breakfast. It had been difficult, but the ships were spread out more or less in a straight line, so they had used visual laser signals to talk between ships. The others contacted the ships that could not be seen by the *von Braun* by passing the message on. Most had arrived during the night and she had been notified moments ago that the last shuttle was arriving. Although the message could have been transmitted through space on a high-powered linkup, but that would allow a higher risk of discovery by the enemy. Task force D was following a line that was more or less together at the same velocity and course, so the travel between vessels was relatively simple.

Her Warrant stuck her head in the doorway. "Admiral everyone is already in the main wardroom standing by for you."

"Very well." Veronica Unger stood and followed the warrant.

"Attention on Deck!" The warrant called out when they entered. All of the officers snapped to attention awaiting orders.

"Carry on, ladies and gentlemen. Let's have breakfast before we get into the discussion of the meeting."

Admiral Unger shook hands with several of the captains as she walked to the buffet table. Then she walked right past Captain Thomas and picked up a plate. The Admiral walked down the table filling her plate. It pleased her to know that there was still plenty of fruit. The other officers followed her down the table. Jackie was the most junior of the captains, so she waited until the others had gone, then brought up the rear filling her plate. She took her seat at the far end of the table away from the Admiral.

Actually, Jackie had been pretty much ignored by most of the captains. She thought it was to be expected since the others had been serving with the Admiral for years. She was the new captain, just taken on because the Admiral was forced to leave other cruisers behind for refit.

Everyone's appetite must have been peaked from the long night because there was very little conversation as the officers took their places around the large table. The flag wardroom of the giant ship was actually a very long room with a high overhead ceiling. The room not only was designed to serve as a galley and dining area for flag officer it was also intended to be used for meetings and conferences. High up were display screens all around which had the ability to project tactical simulations as well as plays and movies for the entertainment of the staff. The table could be extended out in a huge oval to seat up to a hundred. Right now it had been shortened to permit seating of the thirty-two officers present.

When Veronica had finished eating she looked around the room. Many were still eating, but she was impatient and wanted to get started. She stood, "Ladies and gentlemen, I apologize for not letting you finish before starting, but after all this is war. Please continue with your breakfast while I talk."

She now had everyone's attention. She started by quickly going through the contents of the message. Then she projected a holographic image of the sector in the center of the table. She pointed with a laser pen to the yellow lines across the sector. "Based on the information we have, this track is the most probable course the enemy will take. *Von Braun* is going to go right down that course. However, to ensure complete coverage of the sector I have worked out a search area for each ship. Each of you will stay within visual laser line of sight. Whichever ship spots the enemy they will pass the word and wait and observe until the full force of the fleet can be brought to bear."

Jackie Thomas could see that the sector drawn for *Arial* was on the outer most section of the sector. Admiral Unger was still angry with her and intended to keep her away from the center of the action. Well that was fine since the missile problem was not solved yet.

Veronica looked down the table at Jackie. "One more thing. As long as I am in command, there will be no cowboy captains. When you find the fleet, just report and monitor the movement of the enemy. Captain Thomas, you seem to take too much initiative. When I want initiative, I'll ask for it. Do you understand?"

"Yes, Ma'am," Jackie replied trying to maintain her composure at being singled out in public.

****

Chapter 8-7
0700 Friday 4 April 2228
Pan Crimbian Operations Center
Eros

Brigadier General Solas was seated at the communications console. He was angry, upset, and tired. The battle had waged for over seven days. He had expected General Weems to return long before now so that an effective counter attack could be made. While General Weems had been out playing cat and mouse with the enemy, Solas and his faithful had been bait in the trap. Well, the bait was almost consumed.

General Solas looked at the communications operator. The young man had served properly and had been wounded three days ago. Not bad, but in any other situation, he would have been relieved of duty and sent home for rest and recuperation. Now here on Eros after almost a week of constant conflict, no such luxury existed. "What is the procedure for contacting the fleet?"

General Solas had volume one and the operator had volume two of the command tactical communications manuals. Each was going through looking for information pertaining to the current situation. The young man looked spoke, "I found the frequency. It's very high and it refers to a recognition code in the first volume in section seven." General Solas looked carefully at section seven. A blast shook the rock some distance away and part of the ceiling broke loose. It drifted down slowly as a cloud of dust, never really hitting the floor it just followed the vent drafts.

"Here it is. This is the format for the message. Solas took out an old-fashioned writing pen and scribbled the note on a piece of dusty paper.

"Send this!"

As the operator started up the generator and started transmitting, General Solas said a silent prayer.

**
*****
*

Chapter 8-8
1145 Saturday 5 April 2228
CE-46 Galileo
Star Observation Deck

Doyle was seated in the astro-navigator's couch. It was comfortable and he liked it up here in the solitude where you could look out into space and see the stars. He never got tired of the view. Just now he was reading a book. This was another little joy that gave him a lot of pleasure. He knew that if he were down in the control room everyone would be conscious of his presence. They would be walking on egg shells just trying to be on their best behavior.

He had learned a long time ago that to get the best results from a crew he had to just let them do their jobs. If they couldn't do the job then it was his fault because in the end he hired them and had trained them. This was always the hard part, not knowing and waiting. He knew that Admiral Wilson was doing the same thing just now. She had not spoken, but she knew too. She could feel it and he was certain with no reason. The enemy was out here somewhere. If they had any chance at all of succeeding, he had to find that fleet. If he failed to find the fleet, all would be lost and the enemy could launch a counter attack that would mean the end of all of the good Marines down on Eros.

Doyle looked out again at the stars. It was ironic, he thought, that the son of a poor dirt farmer had now advanced in the Fleet to this position which gave him command of this grand vessel. He shut his eyes briefly. He could still see the gaunt form of his father standing there in overalls the day little Bobby had gone into space for the first time. Doyle had been twelve and was big for his age. His father wanted him to help work the farm. After all he was the older brother. He tried, or at least he told himself he tried, but he just couldn't do it. Finally, he told his father one day that he would never be a farmer and that all attempts to make him one were a waste of time.

It was ugly that night. His father stormed

and cussed. His mother cried and begged. Doyle stood firm, or as firm as any twelve-year-old can stand. When he got up the next morning, his father informed him that he had obtained a commission for him as a midshipman on a freighter leaving the following week. Apparently, the old man had stayed up all night on the computer going through the comm net and found this opening. He told Doyle that he was convinced that he was making a mistake, but he had given permission for Doyle to make a yearlong voyage. His father figured it would get all of the romantic notions out of his head and little Bobby would come running home to pick up his end of the load on the farm and be grateful.

That first voyage was over three years long and when they returned, Bobby had his high school diploma and an offer to sign on for another voyage. He only saw his family for a week that time, before he went for another three years. When he returned this time he was a qualified third mate. The captain who was a retired Fleet officer had arranged for Doyle to take the entrance exams for the Fleet academy. Doyle took the exams, passed and was accepted. Three years later he was a shiny new Ensign when war broke out.

Doyle went home after his cadet cruise while still in the academy. It was the last time he saw his father. The old man was sick and his younger brother had taken over the farm. It was better that way. His brother was always a better farmer than he was. His younger brother could put a stick in the ground a week later it would be a head of cabbage. If Bobby put a stick in the ground - a year later it would still be a stick. On the last evening he spent at home, he sat with his father on the little enclosed porch which overlooked the farm. It was in that moment that he finally understood his father.

'I wanted you to have all this, boy!'

'I never wanted to hurt you, but I could never do this.'

'I know, guess I knew from the time you were real small. You always looked to the stars.'

'Couldn't help it. Had to go!'

I know but you went too young. I loved you, so I wanted to keep you around more, to watch you grow up.'

'All we did was fight and argue.'

'Too much of me in you. Hear me well, boy. You have made me proud. You've brought nothing but honor to this family.'

Doyle remembered sobbing alone in his bunk for almost an hour, eight months later when he received the message that his father had died. He learned then that every man dies a little when his father dies.

Doyle was confident. He had been commanding ships for over twenty years. He had been selected to command a ship very young and now he was considered a senior commander. Actually, he didn't aspire to higher rank and he was now doing what he enjoyed doing the best – commanding a ship. Until last May, when this war started, he knew that Robert Doyle had no chance of ever advancing any further than captain. In the fleeting months of this war he had advanced, led a successful bombing mission of Earth and now commanded one of the most sophisticated war machines ever built by mankind. This was a good crew. Of course, there was a better crew. He remembered them fondly. His last crew of the *Carthage* had been lost in battle under the command of his handpicked successor. They had not gone down easily. They had taken many Crimbians with them. He certainly had no desire to lead this crew to the same fate.

A young crewmember came into the large bay. She was noisy and it was not difficult to hear her coming. He recognized her immediately, she came up to Doyle. "Captain Kadel sent me. He sends his respects and asked me to tell you that he has something interesting to show you down in the communications center."

"Thank you. Tell him I'll be right down."

The woman turned and left. Doyle was thinking that despite her initial problems fitting in, she seemed to be getting along all right now. He closed his book and followed her along the long passageways back down to the level of the communications center.

He stopped briefly and placed his book in a pouch by the seat of his chair in the control room. A quick glance at the status board showed no changes of interest.

When he went in someone called out, "Commodore in Comms." Doyle waved everyone down. "As you were."

He found Bud hunched over a console with two chiefs and a warrant communications specialist. Bud was seated in a most undignified manner. He had his rear on the back of the chair and his feet on the seat. Doyle realized it gave him the advantage of height being able to see both chiefs' display consoles at the same time.

"What have you got?"

"The chief here intercepted a transmission from the surface of Eros. It was a very high frequency which was scrambled and couldn't be understood. He probably wouldn't have seen it if he wasn't calibrating one of the receivers. There was an answer from another sector. The Chief got a bearing. I think it is the enemy fleet communicating with the force on Eros. We'd like to contact the Admiral's staff and give her this information. If they are monitoring and can get a bearing from their position, we might just find an enemy fleet."

"Do it!"

Doyle thought it's a risk but maybe, just maybe. Maybe I can make you proud again Dad.

****

Chapter 8-9
1745 Saturday 5 April 2228
Fleet Headquarters
Hospital

Sara settled into the closet to wait. She had become accustomed to waiting in the past few weeks. It was a medical storage room that had a vent, which allowed her to listen into Arlene's office. She had found that this was a way to pick up a lot of information. Arlene knew a lot of senior officers who seemed to feel free to talk to her about just about anything. Often they discussed acquaintances and about close friends who had been lost in combat or were missing. Occasionally, they talked about current operations. She especially found it beneficial when Commodore Samantha Norris visited.

"When do you think Maggie will return?" Arlene asked in the middle of a seemingly idle conversation.

"Why do you want to know?" Like any security officer Samantha was naturally curious whenever anyone asked something that was classified, even someone as close of a friend as Arlene.

"I've heard talk that the senior medical officer is looking for a doctor to go to the moon as part of the reinforcements for the resistance. I've decided that I want to go. I figure the best way is to get Maggie to allow it."

"What makes you think Maggie would allow it?"

"We're friends and, not only that, I am probably the best one for the job since I have experience. The reason I need to go to Maggie is that my Senior Medical Officer tells me that he can't spare me, and he won't approve my request."

"So why would you risk going over his head?"

"Actually, it's really not much of a risk. He is still scared of the reputation of Bull Smith. If I went over his head, he wouldn't do anything about it. Secretly, he is hoping that I will forget about the request and let it die. Remember Archie is getting up there in age and he likes being an administrator. With me here as Chief of Medicine he doesn't have to do anything but approve my requests and see a couple of political patients. If I leave, he has to get involved until someone else of my caliber comes along."

"The trip from Glenda will only take a couple of days but I don' think they are going to leave until tomorrow."

Sara almost fainted from the excitement. She had to repeat several prayers of penitence to settle down her racing heart. She wanted to jump up and run down the hall and shout success. She now knew where the Fleet Admiral was. Sara would pass along this information tonight. The Fleet Admiral would never return to Mars.

****

"In peace, sons bury their fathers. In war, fathers bury their sons." *Herodotus*

Part 9 – Dreadnought

Successful intelligence operations contributed to the battle victories of the faithful. The Union's weakness was a general independence of the individual citizens and soldiers. Religious freedom had become freedom from religion. This gave the faithful an advantage in this situation because, if they were loyal to nothing else, they were loyal to their God and the holy scriptures of the Crimbian faith.

Holy History of Crimbian VIII

Chapter 9-1
2340 Sunday 6 April 2228
Tyco Center
Luna

"The sun will be out soon," Jake said, reminding Earney that it was getting late.

"Well, you got to admit, we had fun with these guys for a change." Earney was looking over his handiwork. The six high priests were seated on barrels of nitroglycerin. They were wired to blow. Earney had carefully explained the set up to the priests while the specialist had hooked them up the Priests. Of course, he had assured them that there were several hidden switches that would detonate the drums. Actually, they would've to be incredibly stupid to set off the nitro, but Earney figured it would keep the Crimbian's busy removing the priests from the barrels.

Actually, Earney wanted the Crimbians to get the priests back. He had spent a week intentionally giving them false information. Earney and Jake walked back to the interrogation room. The Marines were giving everything one last wipe down and sanitizing the room. They wanted to be sure nothing had been left for the enemy to figure out their numbers or what they had been up to.

"How is our timetable?" Earney asked, once they were away from any enemy listening.

"The guys on the upper tunnel report that the Pannies are digging. They still have about eight feet to go. They have slowed down. Obviously they want to break through with a coordinated effort. Exterior perimeter watches report that there appears to be a large collection of vehicles over by Tiger Pass. We have observed troop transports in orbit around Luna. We think the two groups are preparing for an offensive. Could be as early as six hours or as late as twenty four hours."

"Your best guess?"

"Within twelve hours, probably sooner."

"Okay, go ahead and move all of our failed candidates to the rooms where the break-in is expected. After everything is checked and in place, I'll call to surrender."

"Do you really think that's a good idea?"

"Can't hurt - maybe we can reduce the causalities by talking to the Pannies." Jake looked at him. Could he be tired after all this time? But, he had been right too many times. Earney continued, "Pull the watches off the dome in two hours. Let's bring our defensive line down as small as possible."

Both Jake and Earney were busy for the next two hours working non-stop. Wires had to be checked, everyone had to be in place, communications had to be in just the right place and the enemy needed help with the surrender. When everything was ready, Jake called the guards off the dome and walked back to the command center where Earney was talking with the Pan Crimbian commander by voice link. "...But you don't seem to understand, sir. I offered to surrender."

As Earney put down the receiver Jake asked innocently, "Having trouble with the Pannie commander?"

"He won't accept our surrender," Earney said. "He says we can't surrender since we've already been tried and sentenced to death."

"My. My. What a surprise," Jake said. "That's very inconvenient of him. Did you offer to take the first bullet?"

"No, but I offered you to take it."

They both laughed together.

Earney picked up the receiver and spoke intensely. "Hey, dickless, come on down here and try and kill me. I've already sent a lot of you losers to your promised land. So come on down. I want to kill some more of your faithful losers." He listened to the yelling for about fifteen seconds before disconnecting the link. The two men looked at one another then both laughed together. Then Earney said, "I don't think he likes us."

Jake looked at his wrist chronometer. "I think we had better move up the timetable a little. If he could, he'll like to be here in about ten minutes with all the troops he can find - and boy is he pissed."

The radio crackled, "Major, this is Blister-One. They're really digging now. Break through will be any minute now." Another call came in on the heels of the first one. "Upper dome here. We got raiders breaking in - probably dropped from above."

Earney replied immediately, "Get out of there and follow your orders."

As Earney went into the passageway towards their hidden escape tunnel Jake pulled the pins on two proximity grenades. Anyone coming back into the room would set them off. Jake went bounding down the hallway singing a ballad he had learned as a child, but now with new words, "This is the way we fool the Pannies. Fool the Pannies . This is the way we fool the Pannies. This is the way we screw the fools, screw the fools, so early in the morning..."

***

Sub-Priest Zole was on the point when the boring tool broke through into the complex. He was the first man into the giant room. The machine had hurt some of the people in the room, but it didn't matter. They weren't dressed in Pan Crimbian uniforms or priests robes, so he followed his orders and started shooting. As other Crimbian troopers came in they too started shooting. The Union prisoners went down in a hail of shooting. Zole stopped shooting when he realized that they were unarmed and not shooting back. More and more troops poured in through the opening. Zole led thirty troopers down the passageway towards the communications complex.

The troopers moved tediously, finding all of the side rooms empty. Fighting the enemy was one thing but not finding any enemy was disconcerting. It was a big complex. As the Pan Crimbian crack troops spread out through the complex, they kept searching.

***

Two hours later Space Marshal Custus called the commander of the Holy Lunar Forces. "What do you mean you haven't been able to find anyone in the complex? They held the complex for almost two weeks. They didn't vanish into thin air. What about the hostages?"

"We found them and they're all right, but

physically tired from the ordeal. We found all of the high priests tied to explosives. The whole place was set with mines and explosive booby traps. I've already lost eighteen men in explosions."

"So what do the hostages say about the rebels?"

"They don't know. As far as they were able to overhear, the rebels were planning to fight to the last man."

"What about the Union citizens who were being converted?"

"All of the records in the complex were destroyed. As near as we can tell, there are about six thousand missing. The ones who were left are already loyal to Crimbian faith or incapacitated in some way. Most of the children are gone also."

"You moron. They've just recruited an army." Space Marshal Custus was so furious he could hardly talk. Finally, he forced himself to calm down. "Listen, somehow they got out. Find out how! Tear that place apart. I want those barbarians found and killed. Do you understand?"

"Yes, sir."

"If that's not plain enough if you fail to find and kill them and I am forced to travel to that God forsaken place, then I'll shoot you myself before I go after the barbarians!"

****

Chapter 9-2
0720 Monday 7 April 2228
Space Yacht Crystal
Location Classified

Mike sat at the controls of the little ship. As they cleared the perimeter of Glenda complex, he leaned over to the young man Ed Carter in the co-pilot seat and switched control to the right hand station.

"You've got it, Mr. Carter. Can you complete the checklist yourself?"

"Yes, sir." Ed replied crisply.

Actually, Mike had developed a lot of faith in Cadet Ed Carter. On the trip over, Ed had helped Mike all the way. The kid was not the greatest natural pilot, but he had good instincts and judgment. Most of all, he listened and followed instructions which made him a good learner. Mike had decided years ago that he would trade a dozen hot shots for just one good learner. As Mike watched Ed checked the controls carefully to ensure he had control then switched on the autopilot. This allowed him to bring up the checklist and take his time verifying the condition of all switches and systems.

Mike unbuckled his harness he moved easy in the low weight condition. After all a little ship like this could only get about 0.33 G spin, which was Mars normal. The pilot's control area was in the center or the zero G area. He kicked off from the edge of the center console with just enough momentum to send him in the direction of the door. His mind was on the collection of things that had to be done on this trip. Since the kid was handling the ship it was one less thing to be bothered with. The door opened as he touched it and he entered the main cabin, a combination galley, lounge, office, and dining area. The staterooms were off the passageway going aft from the main cabin to the engine room. There was one belly gun bay and a general storeroom - which accounted for most of the little ship.

Everything was luxurious. Certainly not a ship that would normally be used in Fleet service. However, years ago, a certain marine commandant had acquired it from a less fortunate individual who had to sell cheap. Nathan and Maggie were seated together going through a stack of briefing vellums. They would be busy during the entire return trip attempting to bring order to the complex plans and policy set forth from the meetings. Maggie had kicked off her shoes and was seated on the couch with her legs tucked under her. She gazed up with a questioning look on her face.

Mike could almost read her thoughts. Mike said, "Ship's in the groove. The kid's got everything under control." Maggie's eyes went back down to the documents in front of her. Mike looked aft towards the galley. He was hungry. "What's on the menu?"

Cadet Ruby Smith and Nathan's new aide Sergeant Major Sal York were in the galley preparing some breakfast. The little ship could easily carry fifteen people, so with just six onboard, there was plenty of room. Since this was the Fleet Admiral's yacht, a lot of goodies had been accidentally-on-purpose added to the roster of food provided for the trip. Mike had every intention of taking advantage of the situation.

"Have you found any of those fresh peaches or kiwis?"

Ruby was ready. She reached below the counter with one hand while she kept beating the eggs with the other. She handed him two small containers. One held the cut up peaches and the other kiwi. "Thank you, young lady. If I wasn't already married I'd propose."

"Remember I'm spoken for. Go away. We'll call when things are ready." Mike went over to the couch pulled out his IP (Information Processor). He had a lot of things to do. As he squeezed the pieces of fruit out one at a time he was thinking. *Obviously the man who said war was hell had a lot of documents to process.* Just before liftoff, a courier had handed Mike a large pouch of vellums. Mike needed to go through them all. He closed out all of the conversations around him and started going through the files of work. Many were routine most those of these he approved for Maggie, as she would never see the actual document. Mike tagged the ones that he though should be brought to her personal attention. One very curious document popped up.

BEGIN TRANSMISSION

FROM: SCWO CHESTER HALE

TO: SCWO MICHAEL O'BRIAN

6 APR 2228

MIKE - STILL ENROUTE. SPENT ENTIRE VOYAGE REVIEWING MK22 MISSILE DEVELOPMENT PROGRAM. YOU TOLD ME THAT THIS WAS A COMPLETE COPY OF EVERYTHING FROM THE ENTIRE PROGRAM. THE MAJOR HAS FOUND SERIOUS DISCREPANCIES IN THE RECORDS. THERE IS A LOT OF MONEY UNACCOUNTED FOR. EQUIPMENT TESTS WHICH WERE ORDERED PROBABLY HAVE NOT BEEN CONDUCTED - SOME OF THE RECORDS ARE GUNDECKED. I KNOW YOU ALWAYS ARE HONEST. WHOEVER GAVE YOU THE PACKAGE WAS NOT AWARE OF SOME SERIOUS OMISSIONS OR THEY WANTED TO DECEIVE YOU.

RECOMMEND THAT YOU VERIFY THAT THIS COPY WE HAVE IS COMPLETE. IF NOT IT MAY BE TIME TO CALL THE INSPECTOR GENERAL & FEDERAL POLICE.

THE GOOD NEWS - MAJOR GORBALL CONTINUES TO IMPROVE - NOW MOVING SOME WITHOUT THE POWER WALKERS.

YOU KNOW I WOULD HAVE NEVER ACCEPTED THIS ASSIGNMENT - EXCEPT THAT I OWE YOU. GUESS OLD WAR-HORSES LIKE US CAN ONLY

CONTRIBUTE FROM BEHIND THE LINES. NOW YOU OWE ME - I LIKE IT BETTER THAT WAY.

CHESTER

END TRANSMISSION

Not bad enough that we have an enemy to fight now have to endure an investigation into research and development fund misappropriations. What next?

****

Chapter 9-3
1920 Tuesday 8 April 2228
Asteroid Eros
Inside Tunnel Complex 774

Don was now only Nighthawk and Nighthawk was stationed with his little squad at a junction of three main tunnels. The cave that formed the junction was about a hundred yards in diameter. He had been assured his was a rear defensive position. The squad was being pulled out tomorrow for R&R. Officially, that stood for Rest and Relaxation; however there were various other versions - Rearming & Refit, Refreshment & Renewal along a couple of other off-color variations. What it really meant was that they were coming off the rock tomorrow.

The main battle was somewhere on the other side of the rock. He had been told that afternoon that the main body of resistance had been isolated and that General Ridgeway was leading the final assault. After a week on this rock, it was good to hear the rock was almost secure. This had originally been planned to be a forty-eight to seventy-two hour operation. This was now the ninth day. An APS suit was supposed to be good for thirty days, but not thirty days of combat. A suit is a lot of things, but no one can bathe in a suit nor can the men shave; and the ladies have their own needs. Every few days, you need to find a suit service station where the waste collection tank can be dumped, water tanks filled, oxygen replenished, CO_2 adsorbent changed, and batteries recharged. It also helps to connect the computers up to the mainframe and down load the latest programs and tactical information. But, it had been more than four days since the group had been able to service the APS suits. All the suits were low on power, water, and nourishment.

It didn't help that his squad had been reduced significantly nor had there been any replacements. Pepper was wounded in action (or WIA) with an amputation that would take months to graft on a new limb. Several of his team had been killed in action (or KIA) was: Croaker who had been killed on the way down, then Flash, but the rough one had been Grit lost two days ago. Grit had been on the point, leading the way down a tunnel when he had stepped on a mine. He had been killed instantly. There was nothing anyone could have done to help. So now his total force was seven. Seven very tired and overused Marines.

Nighthawk could feel the itchy growth of

his beard. He had thought several times about having a facial hair removal procedure done. Lots of guys did it nowadays. Some even had all hair removed from their head. The women especially loved the procedure. Most spacer women had body hair removed by the time they were fourteen or fifteen; especially, on the legs, arms, and other areas where hair was considered unsightly. The procedure had become cheap and available for all citizens. The trouble with an itchy beard in a suit was that it was hard to scratch. Nighthawk leaned up against the wall of the tunnel and rubbed his chin against the edge of his breast plate neck ring, it helped some but not enough. Finally, he gave up and crawled back to the right tunnel gun emplacement.

Snowflake was seated in the saddle of the marines biggest gun – a 44 cannon. He had been out of action for a while after a mine had damaged his APS. But the APS specialists had fitted him with a fresh one and he was back on the line. The number 44 cannon was a smaller version of a regular shipboard canon which could fire energy bursts. These energy bursts were enough to put a man in an APS suit down. It might not kill the person inside of a Union APS but the energy slugs could fry the electronics and cause major suit malfunctions. If a life support system could be affected, then it was possible to kill. The Crimbians suits were extremely inferior to the Union suits, so the 44 would definitely be exceptionally effective against them. Bottom line, it would kill any Crimbian troopers wearing their version of an armored pressure suit.

However, as they had found out several days ago the Crimbians had new weapon they were using effectively against the marines. A little mole type armored cannon operated remotely like a drone. It had a digger blade on the front, and a very effective pulse cannon. The mole could dig underground for a distance and pop out and start shooting. Their little 44 was not always effective against one of the moles.

Nighthawk had placed two Marines at each tunnel entrance leaving himself and Snowflake in the middle. The 44 could be swiveled to cover any of the tunnels. Since they were so lightly armed he had taken the precautions of planting detonation explosives down each of the tunnels for at least fifty yards. It was probably a waste of effort, but he felt better for having taken the precaution.

He decided to check his Marines. First, he went to where Diver and Wolf were situated. Actually, they had the best field of fire because the tunnel opening they faced sloped downward at about a twenty-degree slope for at least a quarter of a mile. All of this area was illuminated and was supposed to be the enemy front.

“Everything okay, Corporal?

When Diver looked up, Nighthawk saw his haggard expression. Don couldn’t help feeling that Diver still hadn’t recovered from a jolt of electricity that he had taken a couple of days ago.

"We're fine. Sure would like to have some more ammo. But can't have everything."

"You got that right." Nighthawk slapped him on the shoulder, which of course he could barely feel. "Just hang in there for tonight. We'll be back onboard the ship tomorrow."

Nighthawk moved to the left and checked the next position. This was the most vulnerable, covered by Falcon and Bullfrog. After a week of fighting, Nighthawk decided that these two were without doubt his best fighters. Bullfrog was a dead-on shot and Falcon was a close second. Nighthawk had given these two almost two thirds of the entire squad's ammo. He was sure they would make the most productive use of it. As Nighthawk looked through the energy clips, he could see that many had been used up. Too many were showing yellow on the band indicating they were almost depleted. He only found two clips that held full charges. This tunnel being held by Bullfrog and Falcon went up at a forty-degree angle giving them only a clear line of fire for about twenty feet. This was the direction from which he had determined the enemy would likely come.

"Tell me again why this junction is so important?" Falcon might be a good fighter but he had a tendency to question. It wasn't a bad thing but he was going to have to settle down a little more if he was ever going to make sergeant.

"Cobra says that we have caved in the tunnels in eight sectors. There are three intersections like this one. If they want to break out of their main cave they'll have to come through one of these intersections. That is why most of the guys are near the other two intersections. Cobra thinks there's not much of a chance of action here. However, if we get any action, all we have to do is call and Cobra and more marines will come running."

"Okay!"

"Hopefully, we'll just be a little short on sleep." Nighthawk was already moving to the third position which was held by Acid and Wasp. This was the largest opening, at least fifty feet high by two hundred feet long. They had the advantage of some natural cover from a pile of rocks near the middle of the opening. They had selected good firing positions. Nighthawk saw no need to move anyone.

"Did you place a listening device?"

"It's there," Wasp said pointing to a small junction box well into the tunnel opening.

"Good, Good."

Nighthawk moved on, back to the center where the big gun was mounted. Snowflake had the side panel off making some adjustments to the weapon. "Sarge, why don't you get some shut eye first? I've got another twenty minutes of diagnostics to do."

"Okay!" Nighthawk leaned back against the sacks of dirt that had been filled to provide fortification. He tried to think if there was anything that might have been overlooked. He couldn't think of a thing.

Of course, the squad needed rest and a decent meal. Suit rations were meager. There was only two choices neither good. Pull on the roll of tasty dried beef jerky and chew on it or suck on the tube of nourishment concentrate which came in orange, cherry, or peach. Either could be washed down with a good drink of warm recycled water which was sucked through a separated tube. Nighthawk pulled off a bit of the beef and started chewing. Nighthawk drifted off to sleep still reviewing all of the preparations that they had made. *He was sure that everything that could be done had been done.*

"Sarge!" Diver called through his headset. Nighthawk snapped awake instantly. "We got company." Nighthawk looked at his chronometer. He had been asleep almost three hours.

"They're trying to be stealthy, but they're making more noise than a herd of cows stampeding for dinner. They have at least three squads and they're bringing up some armor. Probably one or two of their little mole drones."

Nighthawk keyed his command circuit.

"Cobra - Nighthawk here."

"Go ahead."

"We have contact here. Expect some action within the next few minutes. It could just be a light probe. But, they have some small armor and it appears to be more than a single squad."

"Very well. I'll send help. Keep me informed."

"Aye. Aye. Gunny."

Nighthawk felt the first explosion. He smiled to himself. Apparently the enemy had found their tunnel defenses. He crawled over the fortification bags and swung Snowflake around with the big gun. "Don't fire until you can see something."

Wasp and Acid started firing at the same time. Nighthawk could see the energy bolts from the chatterguns. Nighthawk was up and moved two strides where he could look through the big opening. It didn't look good. All he could see were yellow-brown suits. Nighthawk started firing. Between the three of them they managed to knock down the first two rows and the rest fell back.

Snowflake was firing now giving support fire to Falcon and Bullfrog. Bolts of energy from the big gun bounced off the walls and went down the tunnel. But they were coming to a stop against the energy absorption layer on the mole advancing. The heavy gun of the mole fired knocking Falcon and Bullfrog out of their little shelter.

Snowflake was good. He used the 44 to strip off the antennas and sensors from the mole.

Before anyone realized what was happening Diver leaped onto the mole behind the guns. He opened the inspection port on the back and dropped in a grenade. He leaped over the side into a pile of rubble just as the explosion took effect. Before the smoke could clear Diver was back on top he pried open entrance hatch. He lifted the hatch and tossed a grenade into the interior of the mole, then slammed the hatch. This time the explosion was contained within the mole. Diver never made it off the mole. Crimbian troopers firing from behind the mole cut him down and peeled open the APS. Wolf and Bullfrog came around the mole hulk and started firing at the troops. There were enemy troops as far as the eye could see, but they fell back against the onslaught of just these two Marines.

The flashes of light caught Nighthawk's attention, so he helped Wasp and Acid as they fired at more troops advancing from the large opening. Snowflake poured it on using the big 44 as the Crimbian troops advanced. Something was different. The forward row carried power shields. The shields were six feet long, half round and clear allowing the enemy troopers to see through. Worst of all the energy bolts just seemed to bounce off.

Nighthawk depressed his command circuit, "Cobra, this is Nighthawk."

"Go ahead."

"Under attack from two sides. Seems to be a major push. I don't know how long we can hold this position."

"Hang on as long as possible. I've got reinforcements coming."

"We aren't going any place."

Nighthawk switched off. Suddenly he had an idea. He reached back and pulled out the bullet firing long gun. He jammed one of the cartridges in the chamber and snapped the receiver shut. He took aim and fired at the nearest shield. The yellow suit behind the shield was thrown back. The shield couldn't hold back a xenon coated bullet. Nighthawk knew the man that he had shot was dead. The xenon bullets were made to penetrate an APS, then detonate once inside. The man inside would be incinerated. The crimbian troops hesitated. Then, some began to fall back realizing thier shields weren't full protection.

"Report!" Nighthawk called out.

"Divers dead and Bullfrog is out of action," Falcon's voice boomed. "His suit is dead, so no vitals are possible. I can see that he is unconscious, most likely."

"Wasp here. I'm hit. Don't know how bad, but my legs don't work anymore. Also I think Acid is dead."

"Wolf here. Just reconned down behind the dead mole. Bad news. Looks like they're bringing up another mole. They seem to be massing a more troops for a charge up the tunnel."

"You stay over there and help Falcon." Nighthawk started crawling over to where Acid was positioned. It took some effort, but finally he was able to roll the man over. There was a large hole in his chest and all vitals were zero.

"Snowflake?" Nighthawk called out. There was no answer. Nighthawk looked over from the position and could see the suit slumped over in the saddle of the big 44. Nighthawk moved over to Snowflake. He pushed him upright. His vitals were reading zero. Looking through his helmet he could only see an unconscious marine. He didn't have time to make a full evaluation.

So he called out on the squad circuit. "Okay, people, heads up. When they come it will be from two directions. Let's hold on until Cobra arrives with the rest of the Marines."

Nighthawk wasn't sure what good these little pep talks did. Each of these Marines were now experienced warriors who would do their duty, no matter what. Each of them was fully aware of the gravity of this precarious position. Without immediate reinforcements there was no chance of holding the junction against such a force as they now faced. It always seemed as if the Union was outnumbered. Only superior technology of equipment permitted fighting longer and against greater numbers. But this?

"Wolf, you help the Corporal. I'll be with Wasp." Nighthawk crawled back to the jumble of rocks that sheltered Wasp. Nighthawk switched to one-to-one with her. "Are you in pain?"

"No, not really. Just can't move or feel my legs. The suit is okay."

Nighthawk looked over her suit. There were so many blast marks and dirt, he couldn't see anything. "Have you been listening?"

"Oh yeah. It sounds like the entire Pannie Army is down there. Just licking their chops. They figure it's time for dessert and it's going to be Union Marines."

"Could be." Nighthawk replied. "Let's make sure we break off some teeth when they try and take a bit of us."

As the minutes passed, the noise got louder as more and more equipment was brought into place. Nighthawk thought knowing where Cobra was, it would still be a while before they could get here. They needed to buy time. How to confuse the enemy about this position? Needed to make the Pannies think the Marine's position was stronger than it was. The idea came boiling up from the recess of his overly tired mind.

Nighthawk selected the one-on-one circuit again. "Wolf, you know what these guys would expect the least?"

"What?" He was tired too.

"They need an old fashioned Marine

attack. You lead your battalion down that tunnel and I'll take my battalion down this tunnel."

"Sarge, you've been on this rock too long. You're crazy. You know I only have a company backed up with armor." *Wolf knew they couldn't survive another attack.*

Nighthawk opened the circuit with the others of the squad. "Falcon, man the big gun. Wolf is leading the attack down the tunnel behind the dead mole. I'm going into this big cave. With Wasp providing covering fire."

Falcon was up and made the 44 with two bounds. "So what do you think my chances of making Sergeant are?"

Nighthawk chuckled in spite of the situation. "Probably a lot better than my chances of making Staff Sergeant." Nighthawk moved around and started collecting all the power clips he could find. He added Acid's chatter gun to his arsenal, since Acid no longer had any use for it. He picked up all of the remaining DRX grenades that he could find. He looked across the cave and could see that Wolf was doing the same thing.

"Wolf company report when in position for assault."

"Wolf company in position. Is Nighthawk Battalion ready?"

"Roger, Nighthawk ready."

Nighthawk dove through the opening. It

was dark as he bounded fifty feet down the tunnel towards the light. As he rounded the corner he saw a collection of yellow suits just milling around. Nighthawk opened fired cutting down the group. He tossed a grenade right and dove left into a cut. He felt the concussion of the grenade even through his suit. He pulled out the chattergun and started blasting the ceiling of the tunnel. Large chunks fell obscuring the visibility and adding to the confusion. As two yellow suits rushed from the haze Nighthawk cut them down without hesitating.

Wolf was up and running up his tunnel. He already knew the lay of the land. As soon as he turned the corner, Falcon started firing the big 44 down and into the wall of the tunnel. The large blasts broke of large chunks of debris creating a cloud of dust. Wolf dove in just under the second mole. It took less than five seconds to attach the limpet mine to the hull. Then he was up and moving forward. Every ten feet he stopped and slapped on another mine to the sides of the tunnel. Finally, he reached another intersection where two Crimbians appeared to be standing guard. They weren't that alert because Wolf was able to shoot the first in his comm unit and the second in the helmet. He then took his knife and finished off the first by cutting his life support supply and hydraulics just behind the helmet. The man couldn't move and he couldn't call for help. Without help, it would only be a matter of minutes before he died. He needed to put some distance between himself and the mines he had placed. He had only gone about ten feet when the first started exploding. At the end of the cave he found a big cave with maybe thirty to forty Crimbian troopers. Wolf dropped down and started shooting. Meanwhile a series of explosions continued every five to ten seconds. He could hear the heavy thumps of the energy bolts hitting him. He ran out of ammo and changed guns. When that was empty, he dove into a hole. It would be quite a while before they could go charging back down those tunnels.

Meanwhile Nighthawk was moving through the dust to an opening in the other side of the cave. He paused at the opening it was a ledge he was looking down into a large cave below. There were at least a hundred troops and two moles. Nighthawk unslung the heavy sack of explosives and clipped on a rope. Carefully he lowered the sack down until it was just above their heads. He planted a repeater loud-speaker into the wall of the opening. He tied it off and ran back to the other side of the tunnel. He found what he was looking for, a good size foxhole.

He switched on the comms to the loud speaker. "Alpha company charge. Bravo company charge." Then he detonated the explosives. Tons of rock and dirt poured down burying Nighthawk.

Initially Nighthawk was stunned and he waited for all movement to stop. He depressed his chin button for squad comms.

"Wolf, how do you hear me?" No reply. "Falcon, do you hear me." Still no response! "Wasp, report situation!" He clamped down on the command circuit. "Nighthawk can anyone hear me. Radio check." Silence! *Either his transmission antenna or transmitter was damaged or most likely he was too deep in the rock and dirt for a signal to get out or in.*

A person in an APS suit is tremendously strong. He could pick up large objects and carry them. Even in one gravity five to ten thousand pounds were within its capability. On the low gravity of a large asteroid, where gravity is less than a tenth of a G, actual strength is multiplied many times over. But, in order to use that hydraulic strength you must have something to push against. Nighthawk was trapped under hundreds of tons of rocks. So when he pushed up, if the rocks above were wedged tighter, then down he went. So he started moving in a swimming like motion sweeping the dirt and rocks around him.

Using the acoustics in the suit he was able to determine the direction of the least resistance. His display gave him proper orientation and direction. Even with the power of the suit it was a matter of moving inches at a time. He knew he had to get out to help his fellow marines. The exertion had him sweating within minutes. Finally, he was forced to stop and rest. His breathing was coming in gasps. All of the bio-indicators in suit were in the red or too high range. He moved out again. This time, he started using a jackknife like motion that appeared to work better. Even so he still had about ten feet to go when he felt the rumbling of another mole. It was probably moving across the rocks above him. He called out again to no avail.

Fifteen long minutes later he broke out into light. Down the tunnel he could hear or see the action. The enemy was in the process of attacking again. Nighthawk doubled his legs up and launched himself down the tunnel. He felt around his suit for weapons. None of the chatterguns nor his rifles were still with him. But he had a knife.

A knife designed to be used in space against an armored suit was unlike any other normal knife. The blade only stuck out about four inches from the handle and was protected in an open cage-like guard. To use the knife, the unlock button had to be pushed. If you are using the knife as a tool, you used setting one and the blade slides out in a couple of seconds. If you wanted to open a plastic you used setting two. However, if you want to drive the blade through an armored suit, setting five was used. This would shoot the blade out at a force of almost twenty thousand psi. Since, the blade was made of Inconel and coated with SuperTeflon,[11] it is strong enough to

[11] Inconel is a type of super alloy, a compound of austenite, nickel, and chromium. High strength metal. Extremely

pierce an armored P-suit.

Nighthawk hit the man from behind and tore out his antenna from his neck. Before the man had a chance to move, Nighthawk gripped his arms and triggered the knife into the vital area of the suit. The man dropped and shuddered. Now Nighthawk had a gun. He could see Wasp's suit broken open leaving no doubt as to her condition. Falcon was lying at the base of the big 44. Wolf was pinned in the corner fighting two Pannies hand-to-hand. Nighthawk shot the Crimbian trooper blocking his way to the big 44. It took only moments to climb into the seat, then he swung the gun around. There were at least twenty enemy troops in the room. The big 44 blew them apart. Nighthawk was in a state of total rage. He was no longer thinking logically. Some of the Crimbians started to move like they were going to get up. He fired the big gun until all of the ammunition was expended. Then he ran towards Wolf.

Wolf was down and the two Pan Crimbian soldiers were both shooting into his suit. Nighthawk used his knife on the first man and broke it. The other Crimbian lunged at Nighthawk. He fell back into the stand for the 44, but he couldn't get there. His hand closed around the hydraulic sledgehammer.

---

oxygen and corrosion resistant. SuperTeflon is generation fourteen PTFE Polytetrafluoroethylene (PTFE - a material produced artificially that is so slick it is still considered one of the most advanced lubricant known - it has to be molecularly bonded to another substance.

Swinging the sledge with all of his might, he broke open the front of the enemy trooper's suit. He then systematically walked through the downed Crimbian troopers swinging the big sledge. Some he just broke open the suit. Others he decapitated. Nighthawk killed any yellow suit that moved. Then he killed any yellow suit that didn't move as well. Nighthawk swung the big sledge until all his strength was gone. Then, he collapsed in the middle of the mess, gasping for breath.

When Cobra arrived with the reinforcements there was nothing to do but post guards and clean up the mess. The extent of carnage even shocked Cobra.

****

Chapter 9-4
0405 Wednesday 9 April 2228
CC-141 Arial
Captains Quarters

Jackie was asleep when the call came in. She had fallen asleep on the couch in her outer office. "We got something down here, skipper."

"What?"

"Contact. Maybe two out on long range." Jackie now recognized the voice of First Officer Jane Polanski.

"I'll be down in a few minutes."

Jackie knew that anything out at long range would take several hours to shape up into any real data. Even if *Arial* maneuvered to intercept, that could be another six hours to six days. She had time to freshen up. Since Jackie had slept in her uniform, she needed a fresh uniform and a shower. Anyway, she didn't want to show up acting too anxious.

One good thing about commanding a big ship like the *Arial* was that the Captain lived in deluxe quarters. There was even another small bunkroom at the back of the Main Control room just for the Captain, referred to as the steaming or day cabin. She stripped and jumped into the shower. The water was the exact temperature as soon as she hit the button. The shower computer knew how she liked it. She punched the quick shower button so she got thirty seconds of water. Thirty seconds of soap, then one minute without water to use the soap. Followed by two minutes of rinse water. Five minutes later she was dressed in a fresh pair of coveralls, with all insignias in the right place, boots on, and hair combed - she was ready. Well ready or not that's all they were going to get.

Almost fifteen minutes had elapsed by the time Jackie arrived in control. A collection of chiefs and officers had gathered around Jane. Jackie could recognize the flush of excitement in Jane's face, she said. "We think we're tracking at least two Crimbian destroyers. There are two further out and one is a lot bigger, maybe it's one of their dreadnaughts. Smaller than an explorer but much bigger than a Union cruiser."

Jackie could not believe it. *Arial* was never supposed to find the enemy ships. The Admiral with most of the ships should have been the one to find the enemy fleet. After all they had the superior firepower. Jackie studied the chart of the area along with the track lines of the enemy vessels. No doubt about it. These ships were underway for Mars.

Jackie thought back to her time on Mars last December. *The* Galileo *and her escorts were scheduled to leave soon even then. Once they were gone, that would leave just the ships in refit. Yes, it would be a bold move to go against Mars, but the Pan Crimbian's had already demonstrated they were capable of bold moves. Surely the Crimbians would have spies. They would know when the big fleet left. After all they had been preparing for war for years. The Union was still playing catch up. Even a small task force would be able to do a lot of damage. Yes, she decided the big ship had to be one of their battle dreadnoughts. It could do a lot of damage loose around Mars.*

Chief Bell was standing there. Jackie looked at him. "Well do we have anything to shoot with if we go to into battle?"

"I think so, ma'am. Basically, if we shut off all of the fancy stuff except for the old ship recognition programs and contact programs, it detonates in test conditions with the modified contact exploders I've installed. I was going to suggest a test shot before actually going into battle."

"Put everything back together. You're going to get a test shot against a Pan Crimbian destroyer!"

Chief Bell turned and hurried out. He knew he had a lot of work to do and very little time to do it. The old lady was on a tear now. He sure didn't want to be the one to hand her an unloaded gun.

Jane motioned to Jackie. "Captain, may I speak with you for a few minutes?"

"Sure," Jackie replied, holding one finger up indicating 'just a moment'. She turned to the display specialists on watch. "Have we figured out how long until the nearest destroyer can see us?"

"Yes, ma'am. About eighteen hours if both ships maintain course and speed."

"Very well. Officer of the Deck maintain course and speed. Let me know immediately if the targets change course or speed!"

"Yes Ma'am," came the retort.

Jackie motioned for Jane to follow. "First Officer, in my day cabin."

Two minutes later the two had gotten to the captain's day cabin and Jackie had drawn a fresh cup of coffee for herself and a cup of tea for Jane. Jackie had a feeling about what she wanted and she certainly didn't want anyone in the crew to hear this conversation.

"You're going to attack without waiting for the rest of the task force?" Jane understood the seriousness of what was about to happen.

"Yes. It'll take two or three days for the rest of the force to get here. If these guys spot us they'll run and be lost. It would be just pure luck to spot them again."

"But you are going against the Admiral Unger's orders. Are we looking for glory or revenge?"

"We are looking for neither. We have a job to do and right now it's to win this war."

"If we attack without waiting the Admiral, she will bust you for disobeying orders."

Jackie had been fighting to control herself, by keeping this conversation formal. *Jane also had a stake in this. As her first officer, she would be demoted too.* "Listen, remember the briefing we attended last fall? Mars is vulnerable right now. If we wait and are spotted then one destroyer will stay and fight while the rest change course and get lost. We'll notify the rest of the fleet, but we'll slide in and fight them all. The idea is to cripple the big ship. The rest will stay to protect it. We may be able to buy enough time for the rest of the force to arrive. This is no glory hunt. Given the circumstances, it seems the most logical tactic. It's no secret that there is no love lost between Admiral Unger and myself. The smart thing would be to just follow orders. But my conscience won't let me allow these ships to escape. If you have a better idea, I'm wide open."

Jane shook her head. "I just wanted to know that we were not going off half-cocked."

"I didn't make this decision lightly. Even if we succeed going up against superior firepower, if I survive in all likelihood, my career will be over. I want you to log a protest against my orders. That should protect you from the wrath of the Admiral."

"No, that's not necessary." Jane said.

"Yes, I insist. It's best."

Jane didn't answer. Instead she changed the subject. "Do you want a meeting of senior officers before we start?"

Jackie looked at the chronometer. "Yes, in two hours. I'll go out and pound out a tactical solution for maneuvering. You call the rest of the Fleet on the blinkers. Give them our position and the position of the enemy force. I want all personnel in the outer turrets in APS's and all reactors up and ready to go on line. Let's give Chief Bell and the Weaponeers as much time as possible. So plan on going into action in say, twelve hours."

***

The chronometer in the control room indicated 1754. It had been a busy day aboard *Arial.* They had started maneuvering almost two hours before, just after the staff briefing. They now had a clear picture of the enemy force. A single dreadnought supported by five destroyers. *Arial* was more than a match for a single destroyer and probably could easily take on two or three given the right circumstance. However, the dreadnought was a battleship, which was more than a match for even an explorer, such as the *von Braun*. It was going to be a long night.

When they reached the line where the enemy vessels should have been able to first detect *Arial*, Jackie had sent the crew to battle stations. Of course, she had ensured that everyone on board had had a good supper first. No matter what was going on, it was important that the crew had as much comfort as possible.

The ships ahead had made no indications or changes in course which might indicate that they had seen *Arial*. Jackie was intentionally coming up from behind. The ships were not blind behind them, but they trailed ions out into space from their reactors thrusting ahead. The ions were charged particles that created a lot of sensor interference and formed a baffle area that tended to obscure anything directly behind the ship. Union ships had special calibrated sensors, and a separate dedicated sensor operator who scanned the baffle sector continuously. The Pan Crimbian ships did not work a separate set of sensors aft. Jackie was hoping that she'd be able to get close enough to fire at least a first volley before the enemy ships were aware that Arial was there.

As the hours rolled off and the distance

closed, Jackie found it harder to sit still and just watch. She had the missile ports opened just before they entered the range of the dreadnought's short-range sensors. There was still no reaction from the ships ahead. Without a doubt she would get a reaction when she fired missiles. So Jackie maintained course and speed closing the gap. With the spin off the ship and massive thrust being applied, everyone onboard found themselves being pressed back into their couches like a big hand pressing down on them. Right now, *Arial* was boosting at almost two gravities. That in itself produced an exhausting strain on the crew.

Now, *Arial* crossed another imaginary boundary. They were within missile range. Still Jackie waited. She had to make the first shots count. The pilot turned and looked at Jackie. He wanted to know why the Captain didn't shoot. The bridge crew became more and more nervous as the distance closed. Finally, Jackie was ready to fire. Three times she had rechecked to ensure each missile was properly programmed. Each of the destroyers would get three missiles and the dreadnought would receive twelve. The closer they got the less chance that the enemy Captains would be able to avoid the onslaught of incoming missiles. At a hundred miles she had the missiles checked again. There was still no indication that the enemy had seen Arial. The Pan Crimbian ships should be changing course, going to battle stations, opening missile outer doors, launching shuttles, or at least talking to one another.

"Make ready to launch decoys."

"Say again?" The weapons console operator chief was startled. Decoys were fired by a ship running from another ship. Decoys were designed to confuse the enemy sensors when they were attacking. They were not designed to be used by ships attacking. So the Chief was unsure.

"Make ready to launch decoys." Jackie repeated to the Chief. "Let's confuse them about what they are up against." Jackie had finally made up her mind. There was no room for discussion now. "Launch missiles at twenty miles, unless any ship changes course or if they open their outer doors."

Now it was a different waiting game. Jackie switched the chronometer and the distance display to the ship wide display screens so every crewmember could see what was happening. Jackie fed coordinates into the ballistics computer for the decoys. Each one was given a course and speed and a given range to maintain from *Arial.* As the distance closed and reached twenty miles, Jackie ordered in a normal voice. "Launch missiles. Launch decoys."

Arial bucked and groaned as the missiles pulsed out of the tubes as her computers fired thrusters and engines to compensate for the changes that affected the base course and speed of the ship. It took almost three minutes to fire twenty-seven missiles and five decoys. As soon as the first missile left the tube and locked on to the nearest destroyer, they finally got a reaction. The ship increased velocity and *Arial's* sensor station noted a flurry of activity within the ship as the enemy crew went to battle stations.

Jackie snapped orders. "Start deceleration and match speed to the dreadnought designated as primary target."

"Start deceleration, match speed to the dreadnought, designated as primary target." The pilot answered almost exactly as Jackie had given the order. Now it was of utmost importance to ensure that all communications were clear. Ships had been lost in battle before because of failure to communicate properly.

Now, as the distances closed and the visual display came up, Jackie could clearly see the six ships ahead. Everything seemed to move in slow motion because of the vast distances and size of the ships. At eight hundred and fifty feet long the destroyers appeared as mere specks, as compared to the dreadnought which was almost three and a half miles long. Now the streaks of the outgoing missiles could be seen.

Jackie came up off her couch against the thrust. She leaned over the pilot. "Get close to the big guy, we're going to get very close to his stern. I know this is a bit unusual." Jackie patted his exposed hand for reassurance. Then spoke low in a tone only the Chief could hear. "I know you can do it, bring us up at a half a mile astern. Then hold our big girl steady at that range." Now was no time to question the captain. He was unsure about what she was doing, but the maneuver was possible so he changed course and speed to comply. Even though *Arial* was over a mile long she was an extremely maneuverable ship.

Jackie could just imagine what was happening on the ship ahead. Incoming missiles had set off alarms everywhere. Now the enemy sensor operators would be searching for the source of the missiles. Jackie was hoping that with all the ruckus they might just mistake the decoys as other ships. If she was lucky, they might even fire some missiles at the decoys.

The sensor operator called out, "Missiles fired from target A-1." *That would be the nearest destroyer.*

"Hit on target A-1!" The tracking station called out! "The dreadnought is launching missiles and shuttles."

As the minutes passed, Arial continued to close the distance towards the bigger ship. "We have multiple hits on the dreadnought. One- two - six - ten! Tracking six incoming!" Jackie watched carefully as the tactical screen displayed the situation. It took another twelve minutes for all of the missiles launched from *Arial* to complete their run.

Jackie pressed the open circuit mic button. All hands throughout the ship could hear her voice now. "Chief Bell and Mr.

Waters, along with the rest of the team, were successful at fixing our new missiles. We have successful multiple hits on all ships. Well done to everyone who contributed to the effort. We are still trying to figure out how much damage was done. The enemy has launched shuttles and missiles. Remember. No matter what happens, we drew blood first. We've hurt them."

As she switched off, the pilot reported, "Captain, I'm within a mile of the dreadnoughts stern."

"Good!" Jackie directed, "Continue to a half a mile then hold position."

Everyone in the control room watched the missiles coming in towards *Arial.* They were on a direct course. As the distance closed anyone who could see the tactical board waited for the explosion to occur. But, as the Captain had said, *Arial* had drawn first blood. Crewmembers out in the turrets now could see the missiles streaking towards the ship.

The first one hit *Arial* squarely and buried itself into the outer hull with only the rocket engine sticking out. The second one was a glancing hit and bounced off, tumbling out into space. The third hit bounced and hit again then was out of fuel or its engine was damaged by the concussion against the big ship. The fourth was hit by the gunners in the turrets. Others came to a similar fate.

"What happened?" The pilot asked. Others looked at Jackie with the same question.

"Arial is too close to the dreadnought for her missiles to be activated. Safety interlocks on the Pan Crimbian missiles prevented the detonation of the missiles within a mile from her outer hull."

A battle between ships in space is a slow motion dance to the death. Ships fire missiles, then move to a new position. Shuttles are launched from both of the large ships to fight in open space or attack the enemy ships. This potentially could go on for days. Jackie sat back planning her next move. This was what she had spent a lifetime training for. She had to keep her ship alive until the rest of the Union ships could arrive. *That might be easier said than done.*

****

Chapter 9-5
0915 Thursday 10 April 2228
CF-81 Saipan
Lost – Location Unknown

Mickey looked down at the blackened console. All of the navigation circuits were burned out. He dropped the circuit boards in disgust. Abe was standing next to him along with the young lad Blake.

"What now?" Abe knew full the gravity of the situation. The word had got out real fast - a simple electrical fire. Unfortunately, it was a fire in the navigational control panel. Everyone onboard knew that navigation was the key to space travel. Of course with the current shape of *Saipan* - that was a crippling loss.

One of the young specialists was curious. "Why don't we shift to the backup auxiliary navigation console?"

"This was the backup. We dragged it up here from aux control, remember." Mickey looked around. Everyone looked as if their dog had died. "Listen, we are basically on a good course. We know where the sun is. We will proceed - we'll find some sort of civilization eventually."

Blake muttered "The sleep of the innocent ---".

"Yes," Mickey completed the thought. "Yes we are a ship of fools. But we are still live fools."

Abe looked around. "I know this sounds crazy." He was thinking on his feet. "It occurs to me that the missiles have a guidance system of sorts. It's good enough to allow the missile to track the ship that launched it and it knows where the target is. Can we adapt one of the missile guidance systems to navigate the ship?"

Mickey shrugged, "It may be possible. However the missiles are basically stupid when compared with a shipboard navigation system. The missiles get last minute navigation updates from the ship's system before they depart. But, yes, they do have some minimal capability for navigation. Yeah we can try it but I'd be shocked if we have any ability to really navigate. We probably could detect whether we are steering into the sun, and maybe a general quadrant guess."

"That's better than nothing."

"Okay, I agree. However, if we are going to pull out missiles and mess around. I'd like to try and make one ready to launch. We are a big ship and traveling during war. It would be nice to have a missile ready.

"We'll get on it." Abe pointed to two of his skeleton engineering staff to follow him.

Abe was thinking to himself. Barely able to maintain headway with one engine and Mickey wants to fight. Some guys don't know when to quit.

****

Chapter 9-6
0045 Friday 11 April 2228
ST-19 Guardiant Flag Ship
Main Control Room

"I've got contacts on the screen - too numerous to count!" The display specialists was almost shouting.

The ship was a wreck. After two hours of battle the huge transport had been literally beaten to pieces. Several enemy missiles had hit the giant transport. Unlike a cruiser or explorer the transport couldn't take a lot of heavy hits. Lorraine was seated on the bridge. Captain Snicker was wounded, but he still sat in his couch commanding the ship. Jonesy came up and handed Lorraine a message - there was no need to make a comment.

BEGIN TRANSMISSION

FROM BRIGADIER RIDGEWAY

TO ADMIRAL WILSON

SUBJECT: BATTLE STATUS

GENERAL SOLAS BELIEVED KIA. ALL RESISTANCE GONE. ENEMY TROOPS HAVE COMMITTED MASS SUICIDE RATHER THAN SURRENDER. LESS THAN THREE HUNDRED PRISONERS. IN NEED OF FOOD, OXYGEN RESUPPLY, MEDICAL SUPPLIES, AND AMMUNITIONS.

COLONEL DAVIS REPORTED KIA. MAJOR LANDS NOW COMMANDING FORCES HOLDING STATION.

STEVE RIDGEWAY

BRIGADIER FMF

END TRANSMISSION

She folded the vellum and looked around the room. The thought jumped into her head, '*The price of victory.*'

General Ridgeway held the planetoid below. The last pocket of resistance had been broken. Colonel Davis had succeeded in taking the space station just before her death. Now the enemy fleet has arrived. Two other transports already had been broken apart. Thousands were lost in this latest space battle. The first ships had been easily repulsed, but now the capital ships had arrived. If the long-range sensors were to be believed then there were more ships coming in than she could handle – she needed her warships. A year ago she had gone through the same type of battle; overwhelming numbers of ships against her small support force. *Where was Doyle with the Union warships*?

Captain Snicker came over. Jonesy was suddenly standing beside her with Joe Banks.

"Admiral, we've been studying the long range sensors. Looks like hundreds of capital ships inbound. It's time to transfer the flag. Guardiant will not survive another attack like the last one."

"Damn, I hate to lose." She pounded her fist inside the suit. No one could see. "What are our options?"

Joe referred to his notes. "We can shift the flag to another of the troop support ships that are still in good shape. Transfer to the asteroid or to the station? All will be vulnerable from the incoming force. The largest ship coming in appears to be of explorer size. We were unaware that the enemy had any more ships of that size or capability."

Jonesy had been quiet up to this point. "Could they have refitted one of our captured explorers from the battle of Luna last year?"

"Sure." Lorraine was thinking fast now.

She liked none of the options that Joe listed. "Jonesy, ready us a large battle recon shuttle. Plan on moving within the hour. I want to be able to move. I don't want to be pinned down."

"Yes Ma'am."

Captain Snicker handed her a ballistic pistol from the rack. "Take this. It may come in handy."

"Thanks." She shoved it into her thigh pouch. "Joe, what's going to happen if we pull out the support ships?"

"The Crimbians will be pinned down, supporting a landing operation trying to take back the station and the rock. But from the size of the force it seems that they have more than enough ships to support a split operation."

"How long before the main body arrives?" Lorraine asked.

"About fifteen hours," Snicker replied.

"Okay, let's re-supply General Ridgeway and Major Land with every available body and all the supplies we have. Transfer the crew of any ship that must be abandoned to the asteroid. Strip the ships. Let's give the Marines on the rock everything we can! Get me General Ridgeway on the line. I'll give him the bad news myself."

That set in motion a series of events. The support fleet was going to leave. Now General Ridgeway and the Marines would be on their own. Lorraine could only wonder over and over. *Could the Marines hold until Doyle arrived? Where was Doyle?*

****

Chapter 9-7
0505 Friday 11 April 2228
Fleet Admiral's Yacht Crystal
Underway Location Classified

Mike was half-asleep when the first proximity alarms went off awakening him from his state of drowsiness. There was a big ship out there, but the simple sensors of the yacht *Crystal* couldn't tell him much about the contact at this long range. Mostly from instinct he gunned the engines and changed course towards the target rather than away from it. He raised the periscope and peered out into the void of space. He went fast at first trying to scan the entire area and then repeated the scan slower the second time. All at once he had it. A nearby object blotted out a section of stars. He snapped a silhouette image of the other ship and fed it to the computer. Maggie came in through the door and sat in the co-pilot's seat.

"What's going on"?

"Not sure. Another ship just snuck up on us. They don't have a Union transponder. I'm trying to get an ID now."

The image was processed and the computer displayed:

'PAN CRIMBIAN WARSHIP CLASS - DESTROYER LENGTH 850' BEAM 240'

CREW 600-700. ARMAMENT SHIP TO SHIP MISSILES CLASS II, ENERGY CANNONS FOUR GROUPS OF TEN ONE RECON SHUTTLE.'

"Do they see us?" Maggie asked.

"Oh, yeah. I get a feeling they've been tracking us for a while."

Just then the door opened to the cockpit. Ed stuck his head in. "Can I help"?

Mike snapped, "Get back there on the waist gun and let me know when you are ready to fire! I'll call out the target when you're ready."

"Yes, sir." He was gone in a flash.

Maggie asked, "You want me to fly?"

"Okay, darling." Mike didn't even hesitate. He knew his wife the Fleet Admiral was a better pilot than he was. She had the touch that only a few had. That was one of the many reasons that she had risen up so fast in rank. But when it came to fighting instinct, she always deferred to him.

"You've been thinking about this problem for a while. What have you got in mind?" Maggie asked as she took control of the ship.

Mike pointed to the display. "They are a big ship -they expect us to run so they can just pound us from a distance. Bring her in close up by the bow. We'll let Mr. Carter get in some gunnery practice. Let's see if he can burn off the destroyer's eyes while she is still spinning."

"I like that idea. Let's proceed."

Ed called up, "I'm ready to shoot and Sergeant Major York is ready to reload."

"See the dimple of antennas just about a third of the way back from the bow."

A pause then, "Yes, sir. I see the spot."

"Then get ready. When I give you the word burn off all the arrays as they come to bear." Mike said.

Ed responded, "Aye, aye."

"Maggie, range?" Mike asked.

"Eight hundred yards." She switched to the command circuit. Then she said "Gunner commence firing!"

Mike and Maggie watched as the Ed made a clean sweep – he might be still shaky as a pilot but he could definitely shoot. Maggie held the course steady. As the enemy ship rotated and the antennas came into view, Ed blasted them off. An energy cannon on the enemy fired and the bow of the little yacht erupted. When their vision cleared from the flash of light they could see the yacht's bow had been blown off.

Mike rubbed his chin. "Well, the Pannies thought they had easy pickings." He finished his though in his head. *So much for easy picking!*

Now there would be no give from either side. It would be a blind spider after a fly.

****

****

"If the highest aim of a Captain were to preserve his ship, he would keep it in port." *Thomas Aquinas*

Part 10 - Crystal

The Explorer CE-18 Thomas A. Edison *carrying the command of Admiral Homer C. Arrow had departed June 2227 from Uranus. Edison was leading a fleet of over forty-five ships, with seven cruisers and eight transports. General Carl G. Yang commanded the Tenth Union Army more than twenty thousand strong. Knowing that the Marines at Eros needed vital reinforcement and relief, Fleet Admiral O'Brian ordered the task force to replenish in space and proceed directly to Eros. Unfortunately, Admiral Arrow and the Army reinforcements would arrive after the battle.*

Journal of Solar History

Chapter 10-1
0305 Friday 12 April 2228
CC-141 Arial
Bridge Control Room

"The ship is lost!" First Officer Jane Polanski stated the obvious. The control room was a shambles and filled with smoke. After two days of continual fighting, *Arial* was no longer in a condition to continue the attack. The ship had lost power, life support, main propulsion, and auxiliary support. All missiles had been fired and most of the turrets were inoperable. Most of the shuttles had been severely damaged or lost in ship-to-ship fighting. In a last dying gasp, Captain Thomas had brought Arial alongside the larger ship and had fired grapnels into the hull.

Being grappled to the side of another ship was a mixed blessing. With *Arial* grapnel to the side of the dreadnought, she became a vulnerable target for the other destroyers to attack. But on the other hand, if they weren't careful they could cause even more damage to the dreadnought. Of course there were still two Pan Crimbian destroyers that were fully operational.

"Arial might be lost but we now have a chance to board the dreadnought." Jackie replied. Had she been able to see through the visors at the other officers faces, she would have seen looks of bewilderment on their faces. "Since Arial is no longer tenable I intend to take the dreadnought." Jackie cleared her throat. "Major Danforth take all weaponeers and blow a breach at shuttle bay four. Form your Marines there. Major your Marines will take the point. I will be right behind you with a bridge crew. First, take the control room and communications center. Major Polanski will lead the engineers. You will take the main engine rooms and maneuvering center. Lieutenant Waters, your objectives are the main missiles. Don't let the Pannies launch them just to keep them out of our hands. Bos'n Mahoney, you'll lead the explorers - take the shuttle bays and shuttles. We have shuttles out there I want them to have a bay to return to. Major Greer will take the main computer. Leave the damage control teams to fight the fires. If we can put the fires out there may be something of *Arial* to salvage. This is an all hands effort only the damage control fire fighters, the medical personnel, and the wounded will be left behind. Everyone still able-bodied that can fight will be coming with us. Any questions!"

Probably each person had a hundred questions. Most the Captain would not have an answer for. Each person here knew as much as she did. Captain Thomas had kept the crew informed during each phase of the battle. No one here could fault the Captain. Her actions had crippled the dreadnought and killed two of the destroyers before *Arial* had ever taken a serious hit. It was just the unfortunate truth that *Arial* was outgunned even with a determined crew and captain. *Arial* had been burning now more than twenty hours and most realized soon there would be nothing left. Almost an hour ago, the commander of the dreadnought had demanded the surrender of *Arial*, for the third and final time. Jackie had been given an hour to consider. When she had brought Arial alongside and grappled to the bigger ship, he already had part of her answer. She was sure the dreadnaught captain was busy getting ready to repel boarders. *She intended to give him the rest of her answer personally.*

Chatterguns were being passed out to everyone on the bridge and throughout the rest of the ship. She took her chattergun checked it then said, "Let's go."

Five minutes later the explosion rocked both *Arial* and the dreadnought. The Marines poured through the smoking hole. They were in an outer auxiliary machinery room. Down through the levels of the big ship they fought. Moving room-to-room, passageway-to-passageway, they fought for each inch of steel deck. Chatterguns fired until they almost melted from the heat. The Union Marines moved in their standard shipboard fighting teams, using one team to sweep an area then the next team leapfrogged ahead to the next area; always keeping one team in reserve in the event of a counterattack or when maximum resistance was encountered. Mostly it was hand weapons; Chatterguns, blaster rifles, and whatever weapons could be captured from the enemy. Some of the fighting became hand-to-hand especially in the missile rooms where a weapon discharged in the wrong place could detonate the entire ship. Both adversaries were equally motivated - the loser would get death! It would be the worst death imaginable - *slow death in cold space.*

When Jackie reached the control room she was informed that the captain of the dreadnought was dead. He had committed suicide rather than risk capture. The place was a mess however it was not nearly as messy as what she had left on *Arial.* Jackie took a seat on the command couch. She was exhausted. Everything that could be done was been done. A specialist came through stringing wires and soon a portable console was plugged in giving Jackie updates on the battle in progress. The first report was from Bos'n Maloney. His team had control of the shuttle bays. Then Chief Carter reported for Major Jane Polanski. They now had control of the power room. Jackie asked to be notified as soon as sufficient power to maneuver was achieved.

Jackie looked around at the enemy control room. Familiar faces were hunched over consoles trying to figure out the Pan Crimbian controls and indications. Several of the specialists had removed their helmets. Apparently, the atmosphere in the dreadnought was breathable. Jackie took off her helmet; *a little stuffy - but okay.* A Master Chief Pilot was working the controls carefully.

Jackie looked at the Master Chief, "Can you drive this tub once we get power?"

"Yes, Ma'am. It's fairly simple from a control standpoint. I'm marking the dials to change them from metrics to normal indications. I'll be ready when we get power!"

Ten minutes later the Chief called back. He had one engine on line and was ready for power orders. "Master Chief," Jackie said. Training period is over. Ahead slow.

Sensors, where is the nearest destroyer?"

"Moving away at high speed. It appears they have problems of their own. A couple of Union cruisers are chasing them."

Finally, the Calvary had arrived!

Reports started flooding in. Lieutenant Waters had captured and controlled the missile rooms. Then Major Danforth reported that the Marines now held all essential positions, as well as hundreds of prisoners. He was using one of the shuttle bays that the Bos'n controlled to hold prisoners. The damage control chief called in. All fires on Arial were out, but only after opening the ship to space.

The communications chief came up and handed Jackie a vellum.

BEGIN TRANSMISSION

FROM: COMMANDER UNION EXPLORER SHIP CE-26 W. VON BRAUN

TO: COMMANDER PAN CRIMBIAN DREADNOUGHT

DEMAND UNCONDITIONAL SURRENDER. YOUR ESCORTS HAVE ABANDONED YOU. YOU HAVE FIVE MINUTES TO RESPOND OR I WILL COMMENCE ATTACK.

EARL CATO

CAPTAIN

END TRANSMISSION

Jackie laughed aloud and handed the

message to the Master Chief. He also chuckled and passed the message around the bridge crew. Jackie grabbed a loose vellum and wrote:

BEGIN TRANSMISSION

FROM COMMANDER OF UNION PRIZE BATTLESHIP ARIAL II

TO COMMANDER WERNHER VON BRAUN

> UNION FORCES WILL NEVER SURRENDER. GLAD TO SEE YOU. NEED MEDICAL CARE FOR WOUNDED. UNION FORCES CONTROL ALL SHUTTLE BAYS. THE WELCOME MAT IS OUT.

JACQUELINE THOMAS

CAPTAIN

END TRANSMISSION

Jackie handed the reply to the communications specialist. She picked up the hand set phone to the engine room. After a delay, she recognized the voice of one of the engineering chiefs. "Engineering."

Jackie asked, "Chief can you spare the First Officer? I need the Major up here."

There was a long pause, finally the Chief answered after clearing his throat. "Ma'am the Major is dead. She was killed in action."

"Thank you, Chief." Jackie replaced the handset then turned to the Master Chief. "Chief you have the bridge. I'll be right back."

With that she was up and gone, down the passageway. She had no idea where she was going, but two doors down she found a head. Once inside she shut the door and was completely unprofessional as she threw up.

All she could think about was how many good people died because she decided to take on this dreadnought. Jane had been her friend.

****

Chapter 10-2
0500 Saturday 12 April 2228
Fleet Headquarters,
Mars

Chief Warrant Officer Lloyd Q. Reynolds knocked on the door of Admiral Tom Watson's door and entered. Lloyd was the Admiral's aide and had a longstanding working relationship with the Admiral. The Admiral was already up and seated smoking a cigar.

"What have you got?" Admiral Watson asked.

"We've finally heard from our allies on Earth in Australia, concerning information about Major MacLean. But the second message is troubling." Reynolds answered.

Lloyd handed the Admiral a communications vellum. The Admiral had to press the sensor with his thumb so the machine could read his DNA.

BEGIN TRANSMISSION

FROM: COMMANDER AUSTRALIAN

UNION FORCES

TO: FLEET ADMIRAL – HEADQUARTERS

SUBJECT: LUNA RESISTANCE UPDATE

TOP SECRET BLUE

OFFICIALLY WE HAVE LOST CONTACT WITH LUNA RESISTANCE FORCES COMMANDED BY MAJOR EARNEST K. MACLEAN. SINCE THE SIEGE OF TYCO, WE HAVE RECEIVED NO TRANSMISSIONS. ALL REPEATED ATTEMPTS TO REESTABLISH COMMUNICATIONS HAVE FAILED. OTHER LUNA LISTENING POSTS HAVE MADE ATTEMPTS TO GET MORE INFORMATION CONCERNING THE MAJOR TO NO AVAIL.

THE PAN CRIMBIAN MILITARY HAS BEEN CONDUCTING A HOUSE-TO-HOUSE SEARCH FOR ALL SUBVERSIVES. THERE HAVE BEEN REPORTS OF INSTANCES WHERE PEOPLE HAVE BEEN DRAGGED OUT, BOUND AND SUMMARILY EXECUTED ON THE SPOT. THE PAN CRIMBIAN PRIESTHOOD HAS TIGHTENED ITS GRIP ON LUNA IN THE WAKE OF MAJOR MACLEANS LATEST ASSAULT.

FRED N. YEN

COLONEL ROYAL MARINES

END TRANSMISSION

The next message was the real heart stopper!

BEGIN TRANSMISSION

FROM: COMMANDER OPERATIONS CENTER PHOBOS

TO: ADMIRAL WATSON - ACTING FLEET ADMIRAL

SUBJ: FLEET ADMIRAL O'BRIAN

EYES ONLY

TOP SECRET RED

FLEET ADMIRAL O'BRIAN'S YACHT CHRYSTAL HAS NOT ARRIVED AS PER SCHEDULE. FILED FLIGHT PLAN HAS NOT BEEN ALTERED. ALL ATTEMPTS TO COMMUNICATE HAVE FAILED. PLEASE ADVISE IMMEDIATELY.

TED H. GETS

CAPTAIN

END TRANSMISSION

****

Chapter 10-3
0400 Sunday 13 April 2228
Surface Sector 814
Eros

Lorraine was standing beside Brigadier Steve Ridgeway. They were watching the six shuttles being loaded with explosives. The bigger shuttle was the Admiral's official warship. It was also to be used for her escape if everything fell apart. But now she was loaning her personal backup transport to Jonesy for a wild scheme.

He had explained to her what they wanted to do yesterday afternoon and she had agreed because they were desperate and it was a scheme just insane enough to work. After days of sustained battle the Marines were losing. Now the shoe was on the other foot. Union Marines were trying to defend the rock much as the Pan Crimbians had done weeks earlier. The Pan Crimbians had now established LZs and were advancing on the Union positions. The Crimbians now outnumbered the Marines and Fleet specialists ten to one.

The shuttles were the older TR-10 model of recon shuttles. Most had seen long and hard service. The one Lorraine was looking at had a breach down one side. There was no doubt the craft could no longer contain an atmosphere. That didn't matter. The pilots who would fly these babies would be in suits. The shuttles had been stripped down, they only had an engine, a joy stick for piloting, and a basic portable computer. Just enough so that the shuttle could see well enough to get off the rock and not fly right back into it.

Lorraine turned and walked back inside through the air lock. This cave area had become her supreme headquarters for the operation. She and General Ridgeway were sharing the facility, such as it was. There was a large room filled with computers, portable consoles, navigation equipment, tables, maps, and statistical analysis display screens. Lights were bolted to the rock overhead or clamped to outcroppings. Since no real lighting plan had been used, it was haphazard, leaving harsh shadows all over. She took off her helmet and could hear the sounds of hundreds of specialists working, both marine and fleet.

The nearest specialist was at a communications console talking to a Marine detail. "Able One, we have no intel on that sector. Please report any contact."

At the far end of the cave were six doors - one led to a conference room. When Lorraine walked in, everyone stood up as a Marine sergeant barked, "Attention on deck for the Commanding Admiral."

"Carry on," Lorraine said. She needed to listen in on this final briefing. Seated around the room were the odd collection of Jonesy's cronies and one additional young Marine sergeant whom she did not recognize. So much was depending on this collection of oddballs being thrown together to form a team. She took a seat behind First Class Specialist Jerome Oakland, and for the first time she didn't smell alcohol on his breath. Chief Barbara Ryan had her blond hair pulled back into a pony tail and clipped. Although she was considered tall for a woman she was thin, she probably didn't weigh more than ninety-five pounds at one G. Chief Roy Burke was a ruggedly handsome man. Lorraine could see that it would be easy for any woman to be interested in him. The last woman on the team Lorraine had objected to. But she had allowed Jonesy in his ever persuasive way, to talk her into letting this obviously unqualified person go along. Corporal Lucy O'Brian was one person in this command that she did not want to lose, since she was the daughter of the Fleet Admiral. Sergeant Don Thompson looked tough and competent. He had a scab on his forehead that would probably heal as a scar. What she knew for sure was that they had all volunteered for this extra hazardous mission.

Jonesy had a plastic schematic rolled out. It was a cross section of the *Galileo.* He had drawn red circles around four areas and blue around four other areas. The red circles were primary targets and the blue ones were the alternative targets. Jonesy's voice was a little horse. "All right folks the idea is to kill an explorer. Even though the ship seems invincible, it's not. The differences between the *Galileo* and the *Armstrong II* are negligible. Now that we can see the ship visually it's been positively identified as the explorer *Armstrong II.*"

Jonesy paused to look around and ensure he had the team's complete attention. He pointed to each critical red areas as he spoke. "Roy, look carefully as I rotate the drawing. Your target is the overboard vent for number one and number three reactors. The two share a common vent. It shouldn't have been that way, but it is. Barbara, your target is forward shuttle bay seven. The detonation there will blow the main missile magazine. If you are successful the bow should be blown off and the ship will be blind."

He coughed and cleared his throat. "Jerome, your main target is the stern next to shuttle bay 266. God only knows why the hydrogen peroxide was centralized with the Amine[3]. Once the hydrogen peroxide is ignited, it should destroy the amine storage tanks. It doesn't take an advanced degree in bioengineering to figure out that the ship will not be able to scrub carbon dioxide from the atmosphere. Lucy, your target is the main water purification unit in the stern. A ship without water is dead. Your approach will be tight coming in between the main booster nozzles." She nodded her head, so Jonesy continued looking at Don. "Sarge, your primary target is amidships just above shuttle bay 44. There is an aux service work shaft that is closed off, but it leads to the flag quarters and near bridge control. You have two missiles. Put one in the shuttle bay and the other should open up the shaft. If you are lucky we should be able to kill everybody in the flag area and damage the main bridge computers and displays."

Lorraine looked around at the group.

---

[3] Amine - A compound derived from ammonia. First used by submarines to absorb carbon dioxide from a sealed atmosphere in late 20th century. Union ships use a synthesized form vastly improved from the original. When heated up amine absorbs 40 time its mass in CO_2. Then when cooled it gives off the CO_2 to reprocessing systems.

They actually believed it was possible to inflict mortal damage to the big ship. Well, why should she explain reality? Jonesy was gambling on trying to hit the Achilles's heel. She would have felt better about the attack if Doyle, along with *Galileo*, was available to launch five hundred missiles at the *Armstrong II*.

"Any questions?" Jonesy paused waiting before continuing. "I'll be flying the Admiral's barge. When you eject, I'll be along to pick you up. I want each of you to be wearing two transponders. Okay go out and check out you ships. Lift off in one hour."

A couple started to stand up, but Lorraine cleared her throat while motioning for them to wait. She waited until everyone settled back down. "I want to thank each of your for volunteering to participate in Jonesy's little plan. If it is successful, we may kill the enemy's flagship, which has been giving us a real beating for the last couple of days. Even if you don't kill it, your attack may be enough to cripple it until our capital ships arrive. Just remember, if they are fighting fires and repairing environmental systems they can't be launching missiles or shuttles for strafing." Lorraine rubbed her forehead. *It was always best for the boss to speak a few words. But, what was the right thing to say when you expect fifty percent causalities?* "I want all of you to come back. I already have enough letters to write." *It was a long standing military tradition for the commanding officer to write letters of condolence to the next of kin.*

The big man Jerome Oakley, who towered over even Jonesy, chuckled. "Don't worry Ma'am. I wouldn't want Jonesy to eat up my rations." Everyone laughed, knowing that Jerome was always hungry.

As the group stood and started pulling on their APS suits General Ridgeway came in. He watched as the group filed out one by one. Then he came over and sat next to Lorraine and asked. "You think this group can actually hurt the *Armstrong*?"

Lorraine nodded her head. "Oh yes. If they deliver the payload to the actual targets designated, they'll do considerable damage."

Steve motioned towards the group. "See that sergeant there." Lorraine looked at Don Thompson in the distance and nodded her head yes as Steve continued. "His company commander just wrote him up for the Medal of Honor. It appears he was the only survivor of his squad. They held a junction underground against a full company assault. He is one of four that have been recommended in the same action." He handed her a well-worn vellum. "I don't think I've ever seen anything as gutsy as this was. I'd like to give him a field promotion. If you approve it, I'll commission him in the morning."

Lorraine took the chip. "I'll read it first thing. Under the present circumstances I'll endorse your recommendation. Go ahead and commission him if he returns from Jonesy's trip."

"It sure would help if they can take some pressure off our people."

"What exactly is our situation, since you bring it up?"

"We are holding sixty percent of the surface and have blocked all attempts to come underground. Since you ask, intel gave me a new update about ten minutes ago. They expect a heavy assault within the next twenty-four hours. Apparently, they weren't prepared for the resistance we put up."

"I can't help thinking that I'm pretty useless here in this situation. I sure hope you don't think I am trying to take over your command."

"I haven't felt any pressure from you to take over or micro-manage my command. Not that there is much left at this point. If it makes you feel better, my Marine's morale would've been much lower if the commanding Admiral had flown away and left us here to rot. At least you're here and they know whatever happens to them will happen to you too."

"I've been trying to come up with a grand solution for days. It seems most of our options are gone." She looked down at her cold coffee and then drank the rest of the cup. "How much longer do you think we can hold out?"

"Maybe two days - maybe four days. Depends on how hard and fast they come at us. Have you given any thought to the surrender demands we keep getting?"

"I have already been a prisoner. I have no intention of surrendering. If you have any such intentions, you can forget them as long as I command."

"No, that's not why I asked. I just wanted to be sure that we were on the same wavelength. We burned them when they came at us. They didn't expect us to put up such a fight and we managed to sucker them into spreading out too thin. Next time, they'll be more organized and will come at us from eight or ten different directions. I want to place some massive cratering charges at the bottom of the holes where we will be making our last stand. They may defeat, us but I want them to pay a terrible price for victory."

"I agree."

***

Three hours later Jonesy was at the controls of the Admiral's shuttle, leading his little squadron to attack the *Armstrong II*. The little group was spread out and running with no sensors and on minimal power. Most spaceships or shuttles are easily seen because they fly with a beacon or a transponder to let every other ship in the area know where they are. But in times of war, the transponders are turned off. Most shipboard sensors were attuned to passive signs of a ship's presence such as visual sighting using photocells, heat signatures from the engines, radar, radio or ESE (electromagnetic signals emitted) from the targets. Large ships have inner-ship communications, navigation systems, and radiation signals which could be tracked. Also larger ships disturbed the patterns of cosmic radiation, which left a large signal to follow.

Jonesy had anticipated all methods of detection. Radios were off, no emissions were allowed and the shuttles were painted with a new reflective coating which masked engine heat and cosmic radiation disturbances. Jonesy had the only ship with a navigation computer. The rest were flying by keeping Jonesy's shuttle in visual sight. The other shuttles had been shielded by removing the outer covering and installing additional panels to cover the heat exhaust. The external fuel tanks had to be removed. That meant only the shuttle Jonesy was flying could make a round trip.

The reason it had taken so long to travel to the big ship was that Jonesy had plotted a long elliptical flight path out and around coming in through the enemy fleet. Jonesy sweated at the controls as he eased by several escorts and a couple of destroyers. Finally, he had the *Armstrong II* in sight - five miles of spaceship. He knew that at one mile the ship would pick up the little shuttles even with the precautions they had taken.

Jonesy turned on his mic, he made the only radio transmission on very low power. “Lucifer leader to group. Attack as planned.” With that Jonesy throttled back as the others increased speed to maximum.

***

Watch Chief, Lieutenant Ankrome was at his post on the bridge of the Royal Flag Ship *Oracle*, the former Union Explorer *Neil Armstrong II*. This was his first actual watch that wasn’t officially listed as under instruction. He was very pleased to be able to sign the logs listing his name and rank for the Holy record. With that in mind, he paced up and down between the consoles looking over the specialists shoulders. He was alert to every detail. So, when one of the sensor technicians reported that he thought he had noted a brief radio voice in English, he brought it immediately to Watch Chief Ankrome’s attention rather than ignore it since it was only a transient signal.

Ankrome came to the console and ran the brief signal through the spectrum analyzer to look at the signals himself. “Anyone else have any transmissions?” No one replied. It was tough when an eager beaver was running things. Ankrome rubbed his head. *His decisions within the next few minutes would prove him a fool or a worthy officer. However, he had a hunch. He remembered his instructor in divinity. ‘Trust your hunches*

- they are signs from God'.

"Scramble Alert One Squadron!" The Crimbian technician at the perimeter console was convinced this guy was overreacting; but orders were orders. He depressed the alarm in the duty shuttle bay. Every four hours the viper attack shuttles were checked out and the checklist was completed up to the final checks. The off duty pilots were in the lounge playing cards. Five seconds later they were in the hangar bay. Fifteen seconds they were in and strapped down and going through the final launch checklist. Thirty seconds after the alert had been called the shuttles launched.

***

The two shuttles squirted out of the big ship almost in front of Don. They were going so fast that the little vipers just blew by going in the opposite direction. That wouldn't last long. Don fired his missile into the shuttle bay and then his second towards the supposed location of the ventilation shaft. He watched as the first viper came around while the second went after another target, probably one of the other Union shuttles attacking the big ship.

Flames from the explosion of the first missile hit fanned out briefly into space until all oxygen was consumed. Then the second missile hit ripping a large hole in the outer hull. Don looked down at the display he had just turned on. The enemy viper was coming in fast. Don applied full power to the engines, dumped the shielding and hit the ejection controls just three hundred yards from the ship.

The little viper craft was game. He followed the Union shuttle right down the vent shaft. There was no spectacular flame when the shuttle detonated. Don could see the red glow down the shaft. A lot of Pannies would be busy fighting fires.

***

Jonesy watched as the two vipers came out. He was shocked that Pannies had responded so fast. It was unfortunate, to say the least. One turned and went for Sergeant Thompson. Jonesy figured that Thompson could take care of himself. The other went for Lucy O'Brian. Jonesy applied full thrust and tried to close the gap. She rolled and tried to maneuver, but her inexperience was plain to see. The enemy knew he had a kill. She could never out maneuver the viper. Her only chance was speed - fly fast and hard.

The viper fired his forward energy canons. Jonesy could see the effect. Lucy's shuttle detonated and exploded. All the Union shuttles were flying bombs.

Jonesy closed the distance and started firing. Two bursts and the viper was dead.

He made a quick flyby to check the wreckage -no transponder - no APS - no Lucy. Jonesy pulled around and vectored on the first transponder. He still had to pick up the other shuttle pilots. They were depending on him. The big ship was on fire. How bad he had no clue. Jonesy leaned forward and rubbed his nose on the visor of his helmet.

Now the rest was easy. All he had to do was pick up the other pilots, avoid all enemy shuttles and space junk and get back. Jonesy had to chuckle to himself. If he were at one of the big gambling casinos on the Thule asteroids, he certainly wouldn't bet on his chances of success. Also, with the loss of Lucy O'Brian, he had a sinking feeling deep-down. Admiral Lorraine Wilson was going to be very unhappy with Jonesy.

***

Watch Chief Ankrome received the reports of the detonation forward. Then, he felt the ship shudder from the explosion of the main missile magazine that blew off the bow. Another console operator reported the explosion aft that had ignited the hydrogen peroxide storage tanks. Before Ankrome could form a reply, the overhead caved in killing him and most of the bridge watch section.

****

Chapter 10-4
1715 Monday 14 April 2228
S/S Amelia O'Leary,
Underway for Mars

Freda was jarred from her bunk by the concussion of the first cannon blast hitting the outer hull of the ship. Alex met her in the passageway coming out of his room next door. They felt the ship go into no weight condition as the spin came off. Freda struggled, then Alex helped her move forward hand-over-hand towards the control room. More concussions from explosions rocked the ship. There was a light smoke haze in the ship. Then acceleration as all of the main drives pushed them down. Something bad had happed. Freda knew that Ben was the pilot during the afternoon watch - *she needed to know he was all right.*

As she entered the control room, she could see Ben strapped down at the pilot's couch. Relief flooded through her just seeing him there with his visor open. He was visibly sweating and looked drawn. He was watching the displays and looking at the flight control computer. The smoke was clearing. Obviously things were getting better from whatever had happened. So she hooked herself off a bulkhead and out of the way. She felt a bump and realized Alex was right with her.

She did not know why but during the past months, she had developed a real bond with Alex. The boy was extremely intelligent. They played cards and chess together. Maybe it was because he had no other family and she no longer had a child. Or, it could be just simple chemistry. Whatever she liked the boy. In the recent weeks, since the arrival of Jill Parks, the four of them had become inseparable. It had become almost a routine for them to play cards. Ben had introduced them to an old game called Canasta. A kind of a rummy played with two decks of cards. She and Ben used to play two-handed when they were younger, but they became too good, understanding how the other thought. It was only a matter of whoever made a mistake or the luck of the draw. Now, with four players, the game was once again a challenge. *Anyway, what else did one do on long space voyages when there were no Crimbian transports to attack*?

"Bridge. The fires are out," a voice from the speaker announced.

Ben and the others took off their helmets and gloves. "That was close," someone mouthed.

Ben announced, "Pass the word. I'm going to put spin back on the ship."

A suited figure came through the door like a shot. It was Amelia. Before anyone could say anything, she launched herself across the compartment twisted and landed top of Ben. She held a space knife to Ben's throat. Her finger was on the trigger - her hand was shaking and she was crying. "Why? Why? You killed Buck then left him like a sack of garbage! Why?"

Heavy beads of perspiration jumped out on Ben's forehead. "Easy you don't want to do this. Back off and I can explain."

While he was talking, she swung around in the low weight and wrapped her legs around his chest and hooked her feet together behind the pilot's couch. The knife never wavered. *Ben knew this was a dangerous woman. Any wrong move would be his last.* She could now let go of his neck ring that she had been using to hold herself in place. She used the free hand to slap Ben across the face. "I want an answer now!"

Ben looked up right into her eyes. "Buck ordered me to!"

"What?" Her eyes were wild with disbelief. She slapped Ben again even harder. "Why would he do that?"

"We were sandbagged. We spotted a freighter. Buck thought it would be easy pickings. It was a raider in disguise. When our boarding party blew the hatch, our team was gunned down by a team of crack Crimbian troopers. The ship had hidden turrets which opened up on us. With his dying breath Buck, ordered me to break off and save the ship. I just slammed on full thrust and broke free. We were lucky. Not one of the six missiles they fired hit us."

Long seconds ticked off as everyone on the bridge waited for her to decide. One of the watchstanders called out, "He's tellin you the truth, Amelia." She looked around at the other bridge watchstanders. She could see in their faces that Ben was being truthful.

She let go of the knife. It hung briefly in the air, then started ever so slowly drifting towards the deck. All she could do was cry she hugged Ben around the neck and sobbed into his chest. Ben was obviously embarrassed, but on the other hand, his heart went out for her great loss. He hugged her while she sobbed. Freda unhooked and came over to the two. Freda used her hands to disengage Amelia from Ben. After all he still had a ship to steer. Freda hugged the still crying Amelia.

Ben suddenly realized he had to snap her from this emotional state. "Captain, what are your orders?" He glanced at the console to verify the situation. "We're still widening the gap. The enemy raider doesn't seem have enough engine to outrun us."

By this time Freda had moved with Amelia to the bench at the other console. Amelia stopped and looked up. By tradition as First Officer she now became the Captain. "No! No! I cannot be the Captain. I'm more than competent as a first, but I am not a Captain. Ben you are now the Captain."

"Nonsense," Ben retorted. "You are the rightful next Captain. And you own the ship."

"No Ben. You must take this responsibility. I can't. What are your orders Captain Papers?"

"Okay, if you're sure that's the way you want it. But, if you change your mind, just let me know whenever you want to be Captain."

Amelia looked back at Ben. "Don't worry. I won't change my mind. Although, I still think we should continue heading back to

Mars."

"I concur, First Officer. Mars it is."

*
****
***

Chapter 10-5
0214 Tuesday 15 April 2228
CF-81 Saipan, Bridge
Location Unknown

Mickey was sitting in the Commanders couch of the ship looking at the displays. He had been studying the various displays for over an hour. He was trying to determine several things. First, what was actually going on between two ships out there in the void of space? Second, who the ships belonged to? Was one an enemy? If one was an enemy ship, what could he do about it?

He looked over at the motley little bridge crew. His pilot was an old chief who should have already retired. Two young men barely old enough to shave were operating the weapons console, one of whom was working with only one arm since the other was in a sling. Together they had twenty hours of training. The display operator was a reservist who tried hard but lacked the experience.

There was no more ignoring the fact that larger one had to be an enemy ship, just a little bigger than *Saipan.* He studied the various drawings of Crimbian ships on a vellum his captain had. He wasn't sure about the dimensions, but he concluded it must be a destroyer. The other small ship was some sort of Union civilian ship. Mickey leaned over the display console and adjusted the gain trying to get a clear picture. Everything was far out of calibration and had been overexposed to the elements and extremes of space.

Mickey wiped the moisture from his forehead. *If it was only himself. But he had the crew to think about. He had promised to get them home. But this was war and their primary job was to defend the Union at all costs.*

Abe came in and pulled himself alongside. Saipan was in a no-weight condition and had been for hours. "What are you going to do?"

"You say we have a missile that is operable?"

"Could be, all the tests indicate it's good." Abe tapped the chart table. "Only one way to find out."

"Let's find out," Mickey answered. "We have to get closer to shoot." "They should've spotted us by now. I don't know why they haven't reacted to our presence yet. I'm going to ease her in under a mile. That should draw a response from her proximity sensors. Go back there and make sure we have a hot missile to fire."

"Okay." Abe responded.

Mickey spoke rapidly to the chief pilot. "Steer new course zero-one-five; azimuth two-seven-five. Ahead full."

Mickey looked down at the display. Ahead full on *Saipan* in their present state was maybe half speed. He could only watch as the time passed. Both of the other ships were maintaining a steady course and speed. It looked as if the smaller ship was running from the larger one. On the other hand, the little ship could be leading the larger one. A very puzzling situation. It took more than an hour and half before *Saipan* was within a mile of the larger ship. He went over to the weapons console and reconfirmed for himself that the missile angle solver computer calculations were correct. They seemed correct. If the sensors data was correct, and if the ranges and if the distances were correct - and if the navigation brain of the missile they were going to use was correct. Fifteen minutes more passed and they were within three quarters of a mile. In space, this was the same as being in the other ship's lap.

Finally, Mickey decided he was as close as he dared. From this range it was unlikely that he could miss. There was an old term that came to mind - *point blank range.*

"Abe, open the outer missile hatch and standby to launch." Mickey looked over the two kid's solution again for missile firing.

"Outer door open! Ready to launch!" Abe came back.

"Launch." The ship shuddered as the missile flew out.

***

Maggie became instantly aware of the missile launch. Mike had been dozing at the controls in the right hand seat. Maggie smacked him in the arm. “Wake up missile launched.” She was already changing course and increasing speed. This was not the first missile that had been launched. Thus far, they had been able to evade them.

Mike keyed the intercom. “Standby in the turret - missiles launched.”

Ed and Ruby were ready. Ed replied, “Ready to fire.”

Mike looked at the display. “It hit the destroyer.”

“They shot themselves?” Maggie questioned.

“No, there’s another ship. They shot the destroyer. The destroyer has stopped making headway.”

Maggie kept turning the yacht and soon the Crimbian destroyer came into view. She applied thrust and flew back on a reverse course. Nathan came in to the cockpit. He stayed quiet as he watched. After about five minutes, *Saipan* came into view.

Nathan whistled softly commenting, “It’s a Union Frigate. Look at the battle damage. That ship looks like it has already visited hell!”

Maggie smiled, “Looks like an angel to me.”

Mike opened the comlink. “Union Frigate

respond." There was no answer.

Ruby called from the turret. "There's a flashing light coming from the frigate. Looks like Morse code."

Mike double clicked his mic to acknowledge receipt of the information. Maggie brought the little yacht around. Nathan started reading the light signals. C F S A I P A N - S T E R N L A U N C H B A Y O P E N.

Nathan asked, "Do you want to accept their hospitality?"

"Certainly," Maggie came back.

Nathan keyed from the engineering and weapons console behind the pilots couches. "Y A C H T C R Y S T A L F L E E T A D M I R A L O B R I A N C O M M A N D I N G."

Maggie brought *Crystal* around the stern of the Frigate. She could see the glow from the destroyer. They'd be busy for a while putting out fires. At the stern of *Saipan*, she found the aft launch bay. It was open in the center between the four larger boosters. The outer bay door was open and the launch recovery probe had been snaked out. With years of practice, she rotated the little ship and brought the stern around to the probe. Contact was made and the launch bay operator now had control as the yacht was pulled into the bay. They noticed immediately that there was no shuttle in the bay and that there was a substantial amount of damage to the entire bay. It took ten minutes for the bay to equalize and the ships specialists to gripe down the yacht.

Abe greeted her. He was shocked to see the gold pressure suit of an Admiral. He was even more shocked to realize that she was the one and only Fleet Admiral. "Excuse the mess Ma'am." He saluted smartly. "I didn't realize..."

As Nathan came up he said, "You were told to expect the Fleet Admiral!" Abe saluted, realizing that he also had another red and gold suit he recognized - Commandant of the Marines.

"Sorry, sir. I thought Mickey was kidding me." Abe was totally flustered now.

"That's okay Chief. I can see your ship has had a rough time. I'm not here to hold an inspection," Maggie remarked. Abe relaxed some with her words of reassurance. "Take me to see your Captain, please."

"Captain's dead. Warrant Mickey Horton is commanding. Guess you could say that I'm the First Officer."

"Very well, Mr. First Officer. Take me to Captain Horton."

Abe turned and lead. Out through the door to 'A' deck that ran through the center of every ship. Each of the visitors could see plainly the extensive battle damage as well as the makeshift repairs. As they went down the passage, the ship started to spin. As they climbed the ladder up towards the bridge control room, the first sensations of centrifugal weight were evident. It felt good.

When they got to the bridge, they found Mickey Horton. He was tired from his ordeal. Maggie started to appraise this middle-aged man. He had to be one of the bulkiest men she had ever seen. He looked fat at first glance, but he wasn't. It was all muscle. His clear blue eyes met Mikes, they both nodded - they knew each other. "Welcome aboard Fleet Admiral - Commandant." "I'm afraid you may have just jumped from the frying pan into the fire. That missile we fired didn't kill the destroyer. They just managed to start making headway again. Although, they're moving in a very peculiar manner."

Mike replied, "They're mostly blind."

"I believe that." Mickey looked at Maggie. "I wondered why we were able to slip up on them in this tub."

Nathan asked, "So why don't you just put another missile in their guts?"

"I don't have another missile that is operational. We don't have communications nor do we have navigation. *Saipan* only has one functional reactor and engine. But we do have a lot of hurt and tired people onboard."

Maggie looked at Mickey, "So Captain, what are you doing now?"

Mickey replied, "Same as you were doing Ma'am, before I interrupted. We are running from him. Maybe we can run faster. What we really need is navigation. Can your ship tell us where we are?"

"I think so." She turned to Mike. "Take Ed and let's get Captain Horton here connected to *Crystal's* nav computer."

As the group left Mickey, couldn't help himself. "Ma'am I don't mean to be disrespectful, but I'm only a Warrant. Would you like to take command of *Saipan*?"

"No, Mister. You've been commanding since the loss of your Captain and you know your ship. Also, you appear to have been doing an excellent job. As of now you are a breveted Captain and your Chief who is acting as First Officer is as of now a breveted Lieutenant. I have my hands full commanding a fleet. Thanks for your gallant offer but I cannot be bothered with one ship. Of course, Captain, I'll expect a full report on you voyage detailing the events concerning the loss of your Captain and the condition of the ship. As the senior officer present I am in tactical command of our two ships. Please feel free to ask for advice."

Mickey was overwhelmed. "Yes... Ma'am," he stammered.

****

Chapter 10-6
1648 Wednesday 16 April 2228
Union Military Control Center
Eros, Sector 241, Former Juan Mine

Jonesy crawled up the pile of rubble back

to the defensive position that he commanded. It was still awkward moving in an APS in the low gravity. Up until ten minutes ago, he had the job of holding and protecting the Union military control center, such as it was. In the cave below, the Marine command staff, Fleet flag staff, and tactical support centers had been combined. The entire command was now so small that only a single center was needed.

The cave had originally been a Union copper mine. The Pan Crimbians had blasted a series of tunnels to make a single large cave. The center controlled the vital communications links among the Marines to each APS and as well as the more critical computers that handled the encryption and decoding of messages. Also located in the cave, was row after row of display sensors and specialists attempting to monitor friendly and enemy ship movements. Much of the equipment had been damaged so the specialists were trying in vain to determine just what in the devil the enemy was doing.

The Marine engineers had left an hour ago. The cave was rigged with a nuclear bomb set in the middle of the room. An attack was expected today. If the Marines and Fleet specialists failed to hold the rock, then the comm center had to be blown. Vital equipment and data couldn't be allowed into enemy hands.

Jonesy had just come from meeting with the Admiral. Lorraine was very tired; Jonesy had tried to talk her into going with him in a shuttle. She would have no part of it. Things were going from bad to worse. There'd been no contact with the space station since yesterday. Now he had been told to go back and turn over his little command to a Marine 2nd Lieutenant. Jonesy had been upset, but had restrained himself. After all, this was a vital job, not one to be left to some inexperienced officer. When he reached the top of the pile, he could see an additional suit, with a shiny officer's crest. However, that was the only thing shiny on the suit. Blast marks indicated combat. No names or unit identification badges were readable, the suit was dented and gouged so badly Jonesy wondered if it actually held an atmosphere. Someone had spray painted over the sergeant stripes on the arms. The outer visor was open. Jonesy recognized Don Thompson immediately.

"Hell, I thought they were sending some REMF (Rear Echelon Mother F*****) from the General's staff. So you let them talk you into a commission? Congratulations, sir." Jonesy snapped a salute. Don was so startled that he was slow to respond. This was his first salute as an officer. Don returned the salute feeling very self-conscious. *No matter what the rank structure was, there was no way he felt senior to this more experienced warrant officer.*

"Thank you, Jonesy. I am surprised you didn't already know. I somehow figured that you'd put them up to this."

"Sorry, not guilty this time!"

"By the way, thanks again for picking me up the other day, I figured I was a goner without a transponder. I couldn't believe that both went out at the same time."

"Murphy's Law." Jonesy said. "I got lucky, but you're more than welcome. As you can see, I've been fairly busy setting up this area."

"I can believe that." Don replied looking around. "You've a good defensive position. Any chance of getting a battery of missiles or a Logan gun.12"

"No chance. If we had any not already in use they would be here. The brass decided on other arrangements."

"Other arrangements?"

"Oh yeah." Jonesy motioned for Don to follow him over to a white box. Jonesy took out a barrel key and opened the box. "Down below is a ten K nuclear device. You are not to let this area fall into the hands of the enemy."

Jonesy handed Don the key. Don took the key and locked the box. "I guess the insurance pay out for a second looey to my folks will be more than a sergeant."

---

12 Logan gun is a one man auto cannon which can be remotely controlled. Essentially it was a ship's single cannon removed from a turret and attached to a computer for use by Marines on a rock like Eros.

Jonesy fired right back. “Don’t count on your dad having all that money yet. Our lady Admiral is just taking out a little backup insurance of her own. Good luck Lieutenant.”

Jonesy held out his hand to Don the two gauntlet covered hands shook. *This was two warriors saying goodbye for what could be the last time.*

***

General Weems walked back and forth on the deck of the cruiser Isaac. He had already spent a long hour on a space transmission with the Sky Marshal Custus and his Holiness Ruffus. The transmission delay of several minutes made the transmission even more frustrating. Weems had to explain again for the fourth time how the Explorer had been lost.

The Sky Marshal found the explanation to be unbelievable. So Weems’ had to assured them that suicide attacks were the last desperate measures of a defeated army. He reminded the Sky Marshal of history. The Japanese Kamikaze attacks were the same. Then, he outlined to them his plans for the final assault to regain the planetoid. General Weems expressed his confidence that before the day was gone, he would be standing safely on Eros.

General Weems explained how he had outsmarted the enemy fleet. He reminded them that Brigadier Solas had volunteered to provide the defensive posture. He was aware of the risks and it was unfortunate that the General had been killed. The Union Marines were ruthless. Their cruelty was beyond belief. Finally, he assured the Sky Marshal and his Holiness that this would end today and that before the week ended he would be on the way to Mars to join the other group for the invasion.

***

Major Sidney Markel was the Marine duty officer and he was in the process of giving direction for the final displacement of the troops. This was a plan that had been hastily worked out late the previous night. Major Markel had been replaced as company commander after he had been wounded. Markel was seated because his knee had been totally disrupted in an injury three days ago. There were no power walkers here, so he was forced to get around with an crutch. General Ridgeway liked the Major, not just because of demonstrated battle competence, but because he had a fine tactical mind and good sense of humor.

Just then Brigadier Ridgeway came sliding down the hole into the observation room. Lorraine was seated on a box watching the tactical display. Steve took a seat on the box next to her. Everyone had their helmets off since the room was pressurized. Mud was banked along the edge of the cavern and water dripped from the ceiling. But the worst was the smell. In a room off the main cavern was the field hospital with the mixture of sweat, blood, and death permeating everywhere.

Steve smiled at Lorraine. “Everything is ready.” *So this was it. The Brigadier had finished preparations for the last stand.*

“So, General, how do you evaluate our chances?” It was an idle question. She did not really expect an answer. She already knew the answer.

“Somewhere between zero and none. By tomorrow we’ll start running out of rations and ammo. The only reason there is enough O_2 and water is that there are so few of us. So what happened to Doyle?”

“I can only assume that he has met with misfortune or he’d be here.”

Major Markel spoke, “General, the enemy has finished deploying their units across all sectors. Our observation posts report that the enemy is still landing and reinforcing the LZ’s. Just as you suspected, it appears they are massing for a maximum effort.”

“Thank you Major. Place the audio circuit on open speaker so we can listen.”

***

Commodore Doyle was standing looking at the tactical situation board. Captain Bud Kadel was standing next to him. “Well, Bud, it looks as if you were correct on your evaluations of the situation. There must be a thousand shuttles out there and I’ll bet they’re full of troops. It looks like an all-out effort.”

Doyle placed an unlit cigar in his mouth before continuing. "Launch all attack shuttles as planned! Captain Kadel you are cleared to attack. Pass the word to all ships fire at will when enemy targets come to bear. Sure looks like there'll be more than enough to go around."

Doyle then took a seat to monitor the tactical board during the next three hours of battle. He watched in pride as his smaller task force successfully attacked the Crimbian armada. The Crimbian troops were spread out in shuttles preparing to attack the Union Marines down on Eros. Union fighter shuttles came in and destroyed the unprotected troops in the shuttles. Doyle's ships had slipped in undetected, probably because the Crimbian's were so intent on the assault on the Union forces down on the planetoid.

The Crimbian's first indication of trouble was when the royal cruiser Isaac exploded in a ball of flame. One after another the Crimbian ships were attacked and destroyed. They were unprepared to engage engines and accelerate out of the area. Not only that, General Weems gave no order to disperse once the attack had started.

Doyle was prepared to use his ship against the Crimbian explorer - the captured *Neil Armstrong II.* What he found was a burned out lifeless hulk. This freed the *Galileo* to assist in fighting the other cruisers. The dreadnaught Ark broke off from the attack against Eros and flew towards the *Galileo.* The *Ark* broke up minutes later when it ran into more than a hundred Union missiles from the Explorer *Galileo.*

*

****

***

Chapter 10-7
1030 Thursday 17 April 2228
Fleet Headquarters,
Mars

Sara was set. It had taken her days to get ready. She knew that Dolores Mako would be here in headquarters today. Sara had a good view from one of the main ventilation ducts of the main gallery entrance to fleet headquarters. The main gallery under any circumstances was an impressive room, more than five stories high, and three hundred yards long by a hundred yards deep. The grand room had been carved right into a massive cliff.

Large pressure proof windows covered the open side. It was built in the era before there was an atmosphere on the planet. As such, the windows could handle pressure or vacuum from either side. Since the structure was of such a precise construction, any normal projectile-type bullet or energy pulse couldn't shoot through the windows. It would take a shape charge or repeated pinpoint energy blasts to put a hole in the windows.

Sara had already looked over the

windows. She was quite aware that she couldn't shoot towards the windows since the energy blast would bounce off and trigger hundreds of alarms. It had taken days to find and locate just the right spot. She had a view from her perch looking down a main passageway to the Fleet Admirals offices. Since Dolores seemed to be close to the Admiral and the Fleet Intelligence Officer she was sure that this would be the ideal spot to catch her.

She had meticulously cleaned the vent duct during the preceding days. She then covered the entire enclosure with plastic sheeting. This was necessary to contain any evidence that she was here. As soon as the shooting was over, she would remove the plastic sheeting and take it with her. Most average police efforts to trace anyone in a crime scene would start by looking for DNA. Any area touched left traces of DNA and a hair or fingernail clipping would be as good as leaving a photograph with your address written on the back.

Sara was dressed in the coveralls worn by the cleaning staff. Underneath she wore a sheer body covering quite like many actors and actress wore on stage to appear nude. She also wore sheer material much like the panty hose or stocking worn by women in centuries past. Her hands were covered with thin anti-static gloves. Her head was covered with a trooper's helmet and visor. Anyone who saw her would be hard pressed to even identify her as a woman.

Sara had an old rifle - an antique Magnum that fired seven-millimeter projectiles. Probably built in the United States in the early twenty-first century. There was no way to purchase any ammunition, but Sara had been hand-loading old weapons ammunition for years. It was a hobby of her father's that she had learned as a teenage girl. She had also learned to shoot proficiently as well. The gun was equipped with a scope that she used to look over the gallery and down the passageway.

Finally, she spotted Dolores. She was walking along the catwalk suspended about three stories up just in front of the windows. There was no shot yet. Sara waited. She knew that eventually she would get the shot she needed. Dolores was definitely pregnant. She paused to hold herself ever so often. She was walking with a Fleet Captain, someone Sara had seen before, but she could not place him right now. Then she had the name, Captain Kestler, one of the intel spooks. They reached the end of the ramp and Dolores paused again now holding her back. She was still in front of the blasted windows. Sara realized if Dolores turned down the passageway she would only have a narrow window of opportunity, since she was above the third level by almost a level and a half. The angle would block the shot after she went down the passageway more than fifty feet.

Dolores started walking again, but now

Captain Kestler blocked her shot the end of the catwalk. Then they turned into the passageway. Now Sara had her shot. She sucked in her breath and let it out halfway held it as she squeezed steadily on the trigger. Someone stepped into her view just as the big gun went off. It roared all around her. She looked again. Someone in uniform who had stepped in the way was down. It had been a solid hit. Her target Dolores was gone out of sight. Time to leave.

Sara jumped up and moved just as she had practiced. The gun was disassembled into four parts and placed into a box. She opened the inspection hatch and swung out. After she switched on the little pump it took less than thirty seconds to suck the plastic liner from the duct. While that was happening she removed the coveralls, gloves, and helmet. Everything folded into another box. She slipped on her working coveralls indicating her rank and security authorizations. Less than a minute after she had fired she was down the stairs towards the hospital compound. The first security officer arrived by the access vent within two minutes of the shot was fired. Two minutes and thirty seconds later, Sara was in an area where she belonged and no questions would be asked. Four minutes after the shooting, both boxes were hidden and she strolled casually down the hall towards the doctors' lounge.

Sara found Arlene in the lounge looking over some reports.

Arlene looked up. "Hi, what's happening?"

"Nothing much. I just got tired of sitting around your apartment and needed to get out. Went for a walk and just dropped by to see if you were going to get off early. Thought maybe we could catch a late dinner and a flick. I just hate to go alone."

"As a matter of fact things are slow and that sounds like a good idea." Just then a nurse stuck her head in the door. "Doctor Smith, can you come quickly? The duty doctor wants you in the ER stat."

Sara followed along far enough to be out of the way but close enough to see what was going on. The woman on the table was already attached to a heart-lung machine which was performing CPR and controlling the breathing. The doctor had just attached a bottle of synthetic whole blood. Sara watched through the windows. Someone came up beside her. It was another nurse. The nurse had seen Sara around a lot and knew she was Doctor Smith's roommate.

"Who are they working on?"

"Haven't you heard?" the nurse said. "That's Commodore Samantha Norris. Someone just shot her."

"Will she be okay?" Sara asked.

"Everyone is shocked that she's still alive. She caught it right in the back."

Excellent, Sara thought. If she couldn't get the primary target, the Fleet Intelligence

Officer was almost as good. But, she knew it would be even harder to get Dolores now.

****

****

"Nobody ever defended anything successfully. There is only attack and attack, then attack some more." *General George S. Patton*

Part 11 - Cosmic

Commodore Robert Doyle's attack against the Pan Crimbian forces at Eros became one of the greatest victories ever by Union Fleet ships. His tactics and preparations are now required study in the academy. Doyle's forces had no ships lost and only one man killed, shuttle pilot Hans Carrnka. Doyle sailed in with thirty-four ships and destroyed seventy-eight ships in a three-hour battle with estimates of more than four thousand Pan Crimbian crewmembers and troopers killed or missing. Additionally, Doyle's forces captured forty-one enemy ships. The great Pan Crimbian Armada was dead.

Journal of Solar History

Chapter 11-1
0730 Friday 18 April 2228
CE-26 Wernher von Braun
Flag Conference Room

Admiral Veronica Unger looked across the table at Captain Jacqueline Thomas. "So, Captain, do you think I should reward you for losing your ship and hundreds of your crew?"

"No, Ma'am." Jackie realized that she must look a sight. She had not slept well for the past several days. This morning, despite being summoned to the Admiral, she had not put on any makeup. She ran a quick brush through her hair and put on a pair of fresh work coveralls. All of her good uniforms were damaged on *Arial.* And now she was here standing before Admiral Unger.

During the past several days, there had been a group of more than twenty officers crawling over the dreadnought and the hulk of *Arial.* The Admiral had convened an investigation board. This was the accepted practice whenever lives were lost or a ship suffered extensive damage. However, Jackie knew the Admiral was looking for any excuse. O*bviously she had found it or Jackie would not be here now.* After the loss of her friend and First Officer she just didn't care. Jackie stood there looking bored – which further infuriated the Admiral.

The Admiral pointed to her computer console. "I have here the primary results of the investigation concerning the loss the Arial."

"Oh, my!" Jackie brought her hand up to her mouth and pretended to gasp. "I'll bet the result is that I am solely responsible for all deaths and the battle damage to my ship."

"I don't like a smart mouth. This is serious business, Captain, and you will treat this as such and display the proper respect to me as required by regulations."

Jackie flushed with anger. She knew the die was cast now no matter what happened. So she decided to let it all hang out.

"Admiral, put on your big girl pants. Respect is something that you earn. You have failed to earn my respect. Authority is granted by your rank. As such, I will obey your orders whether I agree or not."

Veronica Unger flushed red with rage she sputtered. "Why you... You failed to obey my orders. That's the simple reason you lost your ship."

"That of course is your interpretation of the facts. I of course respectfully disagree. I want you to know that I intend to enter in my report that you failed to come to the aid of a ship in battle. You dragged your feet while I fought your battle. On the official record it will go down as a great victory for your command. You and I know the truth. Because you don't like me, you took your time. I know the maximum speed of this ship. You could have arrived a full day ahead. Between our two ships, we could have sandwiched the dreadnought and crushed it like a piece of vellum." Jackie had to stop for breath, but she wasn't through. "Instead you chose to let me fight the battle alone to satisfy some sick petty jealousy you hold against me. I hope you sleep well tonight knowing that your action cost hundreds of Union lives needlessly."

Veronica slammed the cover of her computer thus stopping the recording of all conversation. “Captain Thomas, not only are you disrespectful but your implications accuse me, your commanding officer of being a coward or incompetent. You can’t make such accusations without evidence. Even so, I will overlook your last statements. They’re a feeble attempt to cover your incompetence. I won’t bring charges for the loss of Arial. However, a full transcript of the investigation will be forwarded to Fleet Headquarters. You will stand for a General Court Martial for disobeying my orders. I’ll let the Fleet Inquiry Board bring charges for the loss of your ship. If I had my way, I would space you right now. You certainly will never command a Union fleet ship again!”

“Don’t overlook any remarks on my behalf. I can live with them, if you can.” Veronica’s lips were pressed together in anger, so Jackie added. “I’m not making accusations nor excusing my actions. However, I want there to be no doubts between us as to what my opinion is. You have nothing to worry about from me. Slandering your reputation is not my style. So what happens now?”

“Fleet Headquarters has ordered the dreadnought back to Mars. You will command it home as prize captain. I have already informed headquarters that you will be coming. You can be assured that you will most likely be arrested upon arrival.”

Veronica waved towards the door. "Captain, you are dismissed."

****

Chapter 11-2
1140 Saturday19 April 2228
CF-81 Saipan
Bridge Control

"They will be sending a boarding party soon." Abe spoke aloud stating the obvious. Everyone in the control room could see and make the same determination for themselves. Even with the shaky displays that tended to flicker on and off the definite track of approaching combat shuttles could be seen. These were typical Pan Crimbian trooper shuttles holding thirty to forty troops and breaching engineers. The count was four shuttles; *one would probably be enough.*

Mickey looked over at Maggie. "You of course realize Fleet Admiral that all of this is to get you. Alive if possible. Dead for sure."

Maggie did not answer. During the past days on *Saipan,* she had come to realize that she had to be the sole objective of this attack. At first, the two ships seemed to be even in speed, but as the days passed the enemy had repaired something and was able to make more speed. Something even more insidious had occurred to her - *somewhere within headquarters was an intelligence leak.*

Slowly the gap between the two ships had closed. Now that they were within range the shuttles could reach *Saipan* from the destroyer.

"Maggie," Nathan spoke softly. "You must use the yacht to escape. No matter what else happens you must escape! You can fly out of here now and get back to Mars we will stay and fight."

Maggie shook her head. "When *Crystal* leaves the destroyer will follow, they would know I'm aboard. Anyway, if I leave, both you and Mike must go with me."

"You know that is not possible," he responded rubbing his forearm where the scars of an old wound showed. "Captain Horton does not have enough crew to fight - it will take everyone."

"Good then it's settled. All of us are staying." She knew she was being stubborn but it was necessary. "We must capture one of these enemy shuttles. Then if it looks as if the *Saipan* is lost, then the survivors will use *Crystal* and an enemy shuttle or two to escape."

Fifteen minutes later the first shuttle fired grapnels into the outer hull of *Saipan.* It took only an additional five minutes to breach the outer hull. That began the battle for *Saipan.*

***

Ed moved along the outer hull of the frigate very carefully. He was wearing an APS suit standard issue for a combat Marine. Space walking was an old method of working in space. It was first used first by a Russian cosmonaut and then by the Gemini

Project American astronauts. When you are weightless, you need a method of holding on and a way to move. An APS contained magnetic cores in the boots which when turned on, activated a switch when a boot was placed flat and released when the heel of the foot was raised inside the boot. That meant that you must to walk carefully always keeping one foot down. Ed had already completed training on External Vehicle Activity first on the frigate *Carthage* then again at the academy.

In one hand Ed held his umbilical. A umbilical was simply a bundle of hoses attached together. Down the umbilical came life support gas, communications (both voice and visual), sensor probe, and a strength member. Anyone walking on the outer hull of a ship underway wanted an umbilical with one end attached to the ship and the other to the walkers suit. No matter how the ship maneuvered, the walker would still be attached to the ship. Ed's other hand was full too, carrying a satchel of explosive charges.

He could see another shuttle approaching. He moved carefully to an antenna array to take cover. When he explained his plan to Sergeant Major York and Warrant Mike O'Brian, it sounded fairly simple. No one went outside of a ship underway, especially in battle. Once the shooting starts there's all kinds of crap and radiation flying around. A man in a suit, even an APS, is just too vulnerable. So he had convinced them that a lone man could move around and attach explosives to the shuttles once they grappled on. York had asked him if he had a death wish. Ed assured him that he didn't. Mike had been reluctant. But he had finally agreed to let him go, realizing it was one of the best chances they had of halting the boarding attacks. *Right now, Ed wished that they had forbidden him to go - too late.*

The shuttle passed over Ed and went around the ship. He could feel the vibrations of the grapnels entering the outer hull. He could see the first shuttle now he stayed aft and moved up by the engines. Neither the pilot nor copilot could possibly see him. He took the charge out of the bag and placed it on the hull of the shuttle. He opened the cover and pressed the switch that started a little clock counting backwards. He moved out in the direction he had seen the last shuttle go.

He looked down at the hull his location was etched clearly. "Sergeant Major, first charge set. I'm at frame 187 by 44. Where's the next one?"

"Keep going forward to 160 and around to about 180," came the reply.

Each frame on the outer hull of a ship is marked that are numbered starting at one from the bow. Even though the ship was perfectly cylindrical, at each frame there is a point marked 001 through 360 for each degree going around the circle on each frame. This is a basic and simple way to locate every piece of equipment on the outer hull and provides exact locations for anyone moving around on the hull. Five minutes later, he was at the next shuttle and moved to the next vector given to him by York. Two had set down right next to each other. This saved a lot of walking. Within two minutes he had affixed explosives to each of them. Then he moved out heading forward.

The last shuttle had landed up by near the bow. When he got to the forward navigation observation gallery, he could see the shuttle. It had set down facing aft, so he had to go around and come up from behind to keep from being seen by the men in the cockpit. When moving around with an umbilical, you plugged into a receptacle and moved out to the furthest limit of the umbilical. Of course each umbilical is equipped with a small jetting wand. This allowed a walker to move around in free space if he is not wearing walking backpack. When you plugged into the next receptacle, the last one disconnects and is retracted so the walker could move on to a new location, keeping constant communications and life support. The problem Ed had was that there were no receptacles in this area of the ship because of the temporary plates that had been welded in place to repair previous battle damage.

"Sergeant Major, there's no way to approach this last one. I'm going to have to free walk."

"Absolutely not. Return to the lock." The Sergeant Major knew the young man was not dressed for such an occasion.

Just then the ship shuddered as the first charge detonated. Ed was thrown free of the ship and floated into space. Pieces of the enemy shuttle went passed him like little meteorites. A couple of them bounced off his suit making an unmistakable clanging sound. He reached the end of the umbilical with a jarring stop. He tried to trigger the walking wand nothing. Looking down he could see nothing but twisted and mangled jets. With nothing else left to do, he started pulling himself back, hand-over-hand. Instinctively he felt like the target he was.

It didn't take long for the pilots in the shuttle to spot the walker. They started shooting at the apparently hapless suited figure. An energy bolt bounced off Ed's helmet leaving an angry ringing sound in his ears.

"Sergeant Major, can you hear me?" There was no answer.

Ed was carrying two chatterguns so he released the umbilical and started shooting back at the shuttle. The recoil of the guns propelled him back out into space to the end of the umbilical.

***

Nathan, along with three crewmembers, had been holding a passageway just outside of the dead number three-engine room.

When fighting from deck-to-deck within a ship it is not enough to have superior numbers, you also need the right tools. The Crimbians seemed to lack the proper tools. When attacking a ship from the outer hull, unless you carry a lot of very specialized shape charges to blast through reinforced bulkheads and decks, you had to use the doors to go to the center of the ship. That seemed to be the Crimbians problem.

There was only one door out of the engine room and Nathan had control of the door. He sat there around the corner with a chattergun and blasted anyone who tried to come through the door. There was only room enough for two to attempt any cover. Every time a Crimbian trooper tried to fire through the door, the old cunning old Marine cut him down. They tried what explosives they had to blast through the deck so they could out flank Nathan. They tossed grenades but it was a pitiful effort without any proper charges. They killed one of their own men in the attempt.

When the shuttle exploded, it came off *Saipan's* hull leaving a four-foot hole in the engine room. The explosive decompression of the compartment sucked out three troopers and caused the inner door to automatically close. There would be no opening it again until containment could be set and the pressure equalized. That effectively trapped the enemy troopers from that shuttle.

***

Crimbian troopers from the first two shuttles poured into the interior of the ship through the missile compartment. Mike, Abe, and Mickey were waiting with the bulk of the crew. 'A' deck was where the main battle started as the Crimbian troops dropped down from the upper decks, they were caught in a crossfire from either side.

The enemy troops moved slowly and weren't well coordinated or led. The Union spacers took no chances they cut them down as fast as they entered. Mike was puzzled, but this was no time to be taking prisoners. Then Mickey called out, "They're retreating. Advance!"

Mike was up and moving, the blood of battle was flowing again. The old man was engaged and useful he felt really good again for the first time in years. Moving forward towards the main missile hatch, he covered as Abe went on leading the point, with two more specialists. He could see the reflection of flashes as the chatterguns fired in the room above.

Blake moved forward through the hatch. Mike watched as Blake fired then took a burst into his chest from the side. Mike fired back at the side. All firing stopped and a suited figure floated up. Blood droplets drifted out from the holes.

Something moved out of the corner of his eye, he turned and fired - too late. Mike felt the impact of the energy blast rip through the pressure suit he was wearing. He knew he was hit. It had happened before. With his last waking effort he instinctively returned fire. The man in front of him exploded. No one in a non-armored suit can take a shot at short range. Old Mike lapsed into blackness his suited body floating in the zero gravity of 'A' deck.

***

Ed concentrated firing at the forward viewports on the enemy shuttle. There must have been a small imperfection in the viewport or the seal around it, because it should not have happened. Suddenly the viewport broke and shot into space. The shuttle must have been pressurized and the pilots were not wearing helmets because the grotesque body of one was sucked out. Ed tried not to look but he did. Forever was the sight of the man dying of explosive decompression in the vacuum of space etched on his mind.

Someone in the pair of shuttles that he had just left started shooting at him. He did not think he just reacted - Ed started firing both chatterguns out into space. The recoil started him descending back down to the skin of the ship. As he went lower, he fell out of the shooters line-of-sight. When one went empty, he managed to reload while continuing to fire the other.

Moments later he managed to click onto the hull. He stopped shooting and grabbed onto a support spindle as he gasped for breath. With all of the excitement he had over breathed the suit. The ship vibrated savagely as the other two shuttles detonated. It was fortunate that he wasn't hanging out in space. Ed was confused and getting angry. He thought the little prayer that all spacers had used from time to time. *"Please, God, give me a break and don't let me screw this up."*

Ed opened his mic one last time and called out to Sergeant Major York. There was still no response. Ed checked the loads. The shuttle sitting on the bow showed no sign of life. It took Ed just minutes to attach the last haversack of explosives to the empty hull. As he moved aft, he was looking for some way to get back inside. He came upon a hole and then realized the two shuttles had blasted this breach to gain access into the missile compartment.

Down he went through the hole into the missile room. Two Pan Crimbian suits were hunched down with their back to Ed. He opened fired as he advanced. He came to the end of his umbilical. With a sweep of his hand he disconnected it. Something hit him from behind. A man was on his shoulders. Ed jumped with all of his might into the overhead. The grip loosened just a little. This allowed him to swing his arm and point the chattergun back. A quick pull of the trigger and the grip relaxed, then was gone. Ed turned and looked at the man who had jumped him, he recognized the emblems of a Crimbian officer. He had to swallow to keep his stomach. *He had a job to do. Ruby needed him. Now Ed was really angry.*

Kicking off the overhead he moved around the big missile tubes and saw six suited figures firing down the passageway. Ed fired instinctively in a blind rage killing every suit in his way. All six were down. Ed fired again at the suits just to make sure. A suit appeared from below. Something clicked in his mind at the last moment he moved and missed even though he couldn't stop from shooting - the suit was Union.

***

"He is not dead Ma'am!" Mickey reported. "But he should be according to Nurse Carter."

Maggie held her head down and rubbed her eyes. Tears needed to come, but this was not the time. In a calm steady voice she asked, "Captain, do you have a recommendation?"

"Yes, Ma'am. But you're not going to like it." Mickey replied.

"I haven't been real fond of anything today. So give me your best shot."

"I cannot shoot a missile because none of the booster bodies left are operable. However, at least two warheads are functional. We are going to strap the two warheads on the bow of *Saipan.* That destroyer will be on us within the hour, I intend to use *Saipan* to ram the destroyer, while you take all of the survivors in your yacht and run."

"I won't be a party to anyone committing suicide!"

"I have no intention of suicide. I plan to bail out. You can pick me up later. You must survive, if for no other reason than the complete psychological advantage gained by failing to kill you."

"It might work since the destroyer is practically blind. He might think that he's accomplishing his mission by colliding with us."

Within minutes anyone not assigned a watch station was pressed into service. The missile warheads were detached and then prepared for operation. It was a grueling task to move the warheads down through the ship then forward to the bow compartment. It took three walkers to maneuver the warhead into place outside the ship. Abe welded massive D rings to the hull while Ed and York used old-fashioned chains and binders to secure the warheads in place.

Meanwhile, all wounded along with food and medical supplies were moved to the little Yacht Crystal. The navigation console was moved back into the yacht along with all logs from Saipan. The main stateroom in *Crystal* had been turned into a sickbay. That's where Maggie found Mike. Ruby was sleeping by Mike exhausted from working on the wounded for hours. All of the other wounded in the compartment also appeared to be asleep. His shirt was off and with his chest and abdomen covered with compression dressings from his armpits down to his waist. Wisps of gray hair on his chest stuck out above the bandages. Several large crimson spots on the dressings indicated leakage of blood. Each arm had an intravenous fluid bag attached. The IV bags were rigged for zero gravity use. Encased in a clear pressure chamber that kept the bag at minimal inch pounds above the patient's blood.

Mike's eyes were open and alert. Those ever-piercing blue eyes glazed out from a drawn pale face. "Good to see you, old girl." His voice was raspy.

Maggie took his hand. "I never could get you to keep your head down."

"Guess not, but I got my share too."

"I know." She bent over and kissed his forehead. "I need you to take it easy and get well now. I can't do this job without you."

"Sure you can. It has always been all you. Don't worry about me, I'll be all right. You have to save these people. I know you can do it."

She patted his hand and pushed off. There was nothing else to be said. Ruby was awake and looking at her. Maggie motioned for her to follow.

Once in the small passageway, Maggie rolled her head towards the after cabin. "Give me your best assessment."

Ruby hesitated. She wanted so desperately to tell her mother's friend that her husband was going to be okay. "It's been touch and go. He's tough but he has lost so much blood and I don't have any more for replacement. What he needs is an operation by a good surgeon and soon. He's bleeding internally."

Maggie held Ruby's by the shoulders. "I know you have done everything possible. I appreciate the honest answer. It confirms what I suspected. Keep him comfortable and let me know if there's any change. I'm going to get us out of here and we will find a doctor soon."

Ruby turned to leave and Maggie went forward. In the main salon she found Mickey, Abe, Ed, and Nathan. They were a tattered group. Ed had a large purple bruise on the side of his face. Nathan was wearing a bandage on his head. Mickey's uniform was ragged and Abe had a broken arm that was bound in a sling.

Nathan looked at her. "How is he?"

"Not good." Maggie sat down.

Nathan continued, "Captain Horton can't handle the ship by himself, so I am going to stay with him."

"No, that's not possible," Maggie was emphatic. She looked hard at Nathan. *The look told him why it was not possible.*

"Then I'll stay," Abe volunteered.

Mickey spoke to Maggie. "Abe here has a family. I swore to get the last of this crew home. Maybe we can rig something so I can run the ship."

Abe snorted. "Under any normal condition that would be possible, but there are just too many broken systems."

"Then I'll stay and help," Ed piped up.

"I don't like it," Abe said. "He doesn't know the systems."

"I agree," Nathan chipped in.

"I don't like any part of this wild plan," Maggie interrupted before anyone else could say anything. "Yet we seem to have run out of options." She looked at Ed, "Are you sure you want to do this?"

Ed took a deep breath while nodding yes. "Someone must stay. Abe here has a bum wing. I may not know the ship, but all Captain Horton needs is a good set of eyes and hands to follow his orders."

"All right, I agree." Maggie had made the decision. She leaned over and kissed the boy on his cheek.

***

There were only twenty-one survivors who would be going with yacht *Crystal*. Maggie was strapped into the pilot's couch with Nathan in the co-pilot's seat. Abe was seated in the engineering and navigation station at the rear of the small cockpit. The after bay doors were open. When he was ready, Mickey would give the word and Maggie would apply full thrust and launch freely out into space.

She had a repeater from the bridge console on the battle-ravaged frigate. The repeater was simply a dummy display device that relayed bridge telemetry to the yacht as long as the yacht stayed connected to the mother ship. Mickey was ready and the destroyer was already within a half a mile of *Saipan.* For two large ships in space that is considered close proximity.

It started. Captain Mickey Horton stopped the main engine on Saipan and applied forward and after thrusters on opposite sides. The frigate shuddered as it flipped over end for end. Half way through the maneuver, he applied the opposing thrusters. Saipan came to a stop with the bow facing the oncoming destroyer. With Saipan's navigation system so badly damaged, Ed was located in a forward turret so he could visually line up on the destroyer.

Mickey's voice came on the line, "*Crystal*, cleared for launch. Launch when ready, good luck."

Maggie keyed her mic, "Launching! Good hunting, Captain Horton." A moment later she advanced the throttle and ignited the yachts engine.

The yacht was thrown clear of the frigate. The after shuttle bay is housed right in between the four big main boosters on the stern of the frigate. As she cleared, she could see one lonely engine on Saipan igniting. She was going one way and *Saipan* with Mickey and Ed was going the other way.

She turned the yacht so she could watch. It was a sickening sight as the once proud ship advanced on the destroyer. It took almost ten minutes for the gap to close. No one in the small cockpit spoke. At the last minute the captain of the destroyer must have realized what was happening because he tried to change course, but it was too late.

The detonation was spectacular. The destroyer was blown in half. The forward third of *Saipan* was vaporized. Maggie shut her eyes for a moment visualizing the hundreds of deaths occurring within the ships.

"Start looking for transponders," she said breaking the silence.

"It's working already," Abe called back immediately. "Negative so far."

Maggie banked around and went back towards the ships. She laid in a course along the track that *Saipan* had followed. For more than thirty minutes, they searched with no luck. Well, she wouldn't give up easily. However, if there was no transponder signal, the chances of finding a lone, suited man in space was slim.

"We have more problems," Abe called out. "I've picked up a ship nearing. Sending the coordinates to your console, Admiral."

"Crap," Nathan responded. "Sergeant Major standby your gun."

"It's too big of a ship to fight," Maggie said. "We'll have to run."

"I've got it," Abe shouted. "A transponder signal."

Maggie was frustrated. If she stopped to pick up the man, they might not get away. If she accelerated now, she might be able to slip away with all of the junk floating around.

Nathan was smiling. He motioned for Maggie to look at the sensors display. "Maggie let's pick up our man. The ship approaching is a Union cruiser." Maggie looked carefully at the display - *he was right!*

****

Chapter 11-3
0930 Sunday 20 April 2228
Fleet Headquarters, Mars
Hospital Compound

Samantha looked up at Arlene. "Bet I look a sight."

"You look fine." Arlene smiled with relief. "What's most important is that you are awake. Any pain?"

"No, not really." Then she added, "I can't feel my feet."

"Well, that's the bad part. The bullet cut your spinal cord in half. They tried to reconnect but there was more than two inches missing. I'm afraid that you are paralyzed."

Samantha turned her head. She did not want her friend to see the tears. "Somehow I knew all ready that it was bad."

"There's no easy way to tell you

something like this. However, I prefer that you hear it from me rather than from someone else. I was hoping that there were other alternatives - some medical solution to the obvious problem. My friend Doctor Nayler ran the tests, but, it's unlikely that you will be a candidate for advanced neuron surgery."

"It's okay. One thing any military officer has to accept is that there is a job related possibility that anyone can become maimed or killed in the line of duty. Only, I didn't anticipate being wounded behind the lines, so to speak. Does anyone have any idea what happened?"

"No, but I have been fending off Silvia Maverick. She wants to talk with you. I told her to come back tomorrow."

Samantha used the bed sheet to wipe her eyes. "I feel okay. I'd like to hear what she has to say."

"All right," Arlene agreed reluctantly.

Before leaving, she looked over the biomedical monitors noting pulse, respiration, brain activity, and blood gas levels. Then she stepped into the hall and motioned for Silvia. Silvia came in flanked by a middle-aged man in a rumpled suit. Silvia was dressed in a one-piece form fitting silver jumpsuit. She was such a thin, tall woman it was really quite flattering. Her close-cropped black hair and dark almost black eyes against her pale skin made a stark contrast. Samantha recognized the man. He had been around doing some investigating.

"Commodore, you may not remember me. We met a few years ago at a fleet reception. I'm sorry to have to bother you at such a time as this, but as you know, it's necessary." Silvia paused indicating the man. "This is Chief Inspector Kohler. Show the nice lady your badge."

The rumpled man fumbled in one pocket then another. For the first time Samantha really looked at him. Sandy red hair around a chubby face. Some place back in his lineage was some Asian influence. It showed around the eyes. His blue-gray eyes were bright and alert. The rumpled exterior was a façade. He didn't miss much. A pot belly jutted over his belt but his shoulders were broad and indicated strength. Finally, he produced the badge. Just a lone badge no fancy case that so many cops flash.

"Sorry, Ma'am," he mumbled. "Just a few questions if you feel like it."

Silvia spoke before Samantha could reply, "Inspector Kohler will be handling the actual case. He has a background investigation and can be cleared to any level security wise. He has been officially assigned to your staff. This was approved by Admiral Watson."

"Okay," Samantha replied. "What happened?"

The little man pulled out a small pocket electronic notepad and referred to it. "You were shot by a sniper shooting two hundred and ten yards from a ventilation duct, using an old-fashioned bullet. We think it was a seven millimeter long gun with a silencer or muffler. The shooter lined the duct and stripped it when he left. No DNA could be found. In fact, the entire hall leading to the duct was thoroughly chemically cleaned recently. A very professional job. I am hoping that you can give me some reason that someone would want to kill you."

"You mean other than the fact that I am the head of intelligence and we are at war?" Samantha pulled her covers up. It was a little chilling to hear the raw facts. "Seems to be very good shooting."

"It was," he responded. He held out a small recorder and showed her that the record mode was selected. "So there is no specific project that has presented a situation where someone might find it to be more advantageous for you to be dead."

"None really comes to mind. However, I'll give it some thought."

"Why were you out in the hall that day? Do you have a habit of being out there about the same time of day?"

"I went out there to meet with Lieutenant Dolores Mako. She was coming to visit. And no, I don't have a habit of being in that particular hall at that time of the day. The only thing regular about my schedule is the irregularity of it. I do try and attend the daily staff briefing at zero seven hundred every morning. I've missed three in the last week alone."

"What was the purpose of the Lieutenant's visit?"

"Mostly to chat as old shipmates. But also to talk about a project that she was working on."

"What kind of a project?"

Samantha balked, "I'm not sure I want to say. It's a highly classified project."

"That's why I came along. You must be forthright with the Inspector."

"I can't make that decision." Samantha was now confident. "It will be up to the Fleet Admiral."

The little man was persistent. "Why is it that a Commodore is running out to greet this lowly Lieutenant? When I was in the service, Lieutenants went to the Commodore."

"Since you need to be satisfied in some way. First, the Lieutenant is very much in a family way and I intended to lead her in past the normal security barriers. Second, this particular Lieutenant is one of the most important assets in the Union. She may be the greatest mathematical mind since Albert Einstein."

"Okay, I'm convinced. She's important to you and your department. Is she working on one of your highly classified project?"

"Yes. In fact she is the project."

Samantha whispered. Her voice was fading, so she eased back down in the bed. "I will try and think about things. Maybe I can remember something that can help. Can we finish this later? I'm getting tired."

"Of course," the Inspector said. "I'll be coming back around."

****

Chapter 11-4
2130 Monday 21 April 2228
Holy Crimbian Palace,
Earth

Ruffus was in a rage. He tipped over the vase by the door and kicked the table. The table however was made of stone, so all he got was a very painful foot. He hopped around clutching the sore foot. Sky Marshal Custus came in, just as Ruffus allowed himself to fall backwards on a pallet of pillows. After all the weeks of getting better, now, he was in pain again.

Ruffus watched as Custus gave the prayers of acknowledgment to himself. Then Custus bowed acknowledging his exalted authority.

"Your late," Ruffus snapped in a high-pitched squeak. "I sent for you over an hour ago."

"I was collecting the latest information so when we talk I would have accurate facts for you." Custus said calmly coming to attention.

He knew he had to calm Ruffus down. In

past rages, Ruffus had been known to slap and knock around some of his women. He on previous occasion had thrown a book at the Secretary of State who had the unpleasant duty of giving bad news. These fits were bad on Ruffus too he had old injuries and a weak heart.

"How can this happen?" Ruffus demanded. "Four humiliating defeats within the last week."

"What do you consider defeats, Your Holiness?"

"First the Union resistance terrorists on the moon got away with prisoners for conversion. We have failed to kill or capture the Union Fleet Admiral even though we knew the exact position. There is a battle group is missing and does not respond. Now I am informed that our grand Armada has been defeated at Eros." Ruffus had to stop to catch his breath.

"Let's put things in perspective." Custus continued calmly. "Military operations are not without setbacks the Prophets own teaching tell us that. The defeat at Eros is unexplainable we should have won. We had more ships, troops, and fighters. I am investigating. It will take time to find out why we did not overwhelm the Union forces. Still, I intend to see if there are any man-made explanations. This may be a test by God to verify our dedication to the task, as the scripture tells us."

Ruffus nodded his head then said in an

almost normal voice, "Continue."

"As far as the terrorists on the moon go, yes, some did get away down tunnels and holes that we did not know even existed. I have relieved the commander that failed us and he has been turned over to the priesthood for cleansing and reassignment. We have found the holes now and I have given the mission of hunting down the Union resistance to the Black Priesthood. So it will just be a matter of time before they are located and eliminated."

While talking Custus had walked over and had filled two glasses with Holy Ale. Ruffus especially liked the drink. He handed one to Ruffus, waited for him to drink first, then took a small sip himself before continuing. "It was a valiant effort to attempt to kill their Fleet Admiral. But if you remember I told you it would be a long shot to get her. At best, it would have only been a psychological advantage. I believe quite possibly we've managed to put the fear of God into her."

"You didn't mention the missing battle group." Ruffus was talking in a more normal voice now. The high-pitched squealing was gone.

"Missing or out of communications range is one thing. Let's not assume they have been defeated in battle. It is a formidable group and it would take more than just one ship to cause them problems. I have instructed all priests to pray for their deliverance."

Ruffus asked, "Do we know anything about the whereabouts of General Weems?" Now that he had settled down, he redirected the conversation back to the real problem.

"No, I have not heard from the General. I have heard from Commander Glennan who is leading the remnants of the group back to Earth. It seems that the commander managed to slip away with about thirty ships. Some of them are heavily damaged. It will be weeks before they return with any real details."

"So what do we do now? Just sit and lick our wounds?"

"We cannot. If the full extent of this defeat were allowed to affect our troops, it would be too demoralizing. We must have a victory. As you are aware, the Second Corps has been training for an invasion of Australia. If our Crimbian Empire is to control the entire Solar System it's important for us to control this entire planet! Australia has been helping the Union forces. I believe the time is right to take Australia and control this entire planet. Such a victory would provide needed prestige and moral to our troops no matter what the true situation is on Eros."

"I agree," Ruffus bubbled with enthusiasm as he took a gulp of the Ale. "I will pray for your success."

"May I take my leave, your Holiness?"

Custus kneeled.

"You are dismissed."

"Should I send in your daughters to give you comfort?"

"Yes. Thank you." Ruffus replied watching Custus as he backed out of the room.

Ruffus thought about the situation. *The men lost on Eros and the moon, and even the crew of the destroyer. They must have lacked pure faith or they would have succeeded. Once his daughters finished comforting him, he would pray to God that those who had failed him would get the punishment or forgiveness that only the love and wrath of God could deliver.*

****

Chapter 11-5
2040 Tuesday 22 April 2228
CE-46 Galileo
Flag Bridge Conference Room
In Eros Sector

Doyle looked around the room. Everyone was here except for the Admiral. He motioned to Jonesy. Jonesy stepped out to get the Admiral. "Joe, are you ready," Doyle asked. As the flag operations officer Major Joe Banks had been compiling a post battle analysis of the battle.

"Yes, sir." Joe fumbled through a stack of document vellums that he had brought.

"Attention on deck!" Jonesy called out. All of the officers in the room stood and came to attention. Lorraine walked to the head of the table.

"Be seated ladies and gentlemen. This meeting is called at the insistence of Commodore Doyle. The simple question is why did we win over such an overwhelming force? Major Banks and Major Markel have conducted a review of logs and events; ours as well as the surviving enemy logs. They have also had access to the debriefings with various prisoners of war. General Ridgeway was gracious enough to loan us a team of his communications specialists to correlate the data bank. Major Banks you have the floor."

As Joe stood and looked around, he picked up placed a pair of glasses on his nose so he could read. "Admiral we've worked with the Fleet Historian to produce a detailed document of this battle." He patted his hand on the large stack in front of him. "The summary is quite simple. The enemy was sick. Everyone here remembers the solar storm just before we attacked. Our enemy didn't have the same respect for the storm. Their fleet crews as well as their troops were suffering from radiation sickness. They failed to provide adequate shelter for everyone. Their senior officers were protected, but many of the troops never made it to shelters. Our enemy defeated themselves."

"How can that be?" Patty Sue Smith asked. "Our troops fought hard for every inch of that rock."

Major Markel stood and picked up a vellum. “If I may, Joe.” He placed the image on the viewer. “The troops who defended the rock and station initially were well. They were in adequate shelters. You can see in the data how their sickness increased on a daily basis. The troops who counterattacked were already sick. They were unable to kill us off even though they had all the advantage. By the time Commodore Doyle attacked the armada, they were only able to send twenty percent to battle stations. There were a lot of unmanned guns.”

****

Chapter 11-6
0915 Wednesday 23 April 2228
Ambulance Shuttle Booming Betty
Enroute Phobos to Fleet Headquarters, Mars

Maggie looked tired and drawn. She was seated in the observation cubicle that allowed her to watch the medics and nurses tending to Mike. He was lying on a stretcher and appeared to be asleep. The surgery onboard the cruiser had gone well and Mike was listed in stable condition. Seated next to her was Admiral Tom Watson. He had come out to Phobos to meet her.

She reached over and patted Tom on the leg. “Thanks for coming up. It helps to have some moral support.”

“It appears that you guys were lucky.”

“We were lucky that Mickey Horton came along.”

“It’s too bad he went down with his ship.

Well, you got the kid back. Cadet Carter is a real fighter - and lucky too."

"I've recommended Mickey Horton for the Medal of Honor and permanent advancement to Captain. Set it up for a ceremony in a couple of weeks." She paused for a moment. "Send Abe James to Officer's Candidate School."

"What do you want to do about young Mr. Carter? I read about the stunt he pulled on that spacewalk. I'm not sure I'd have guts enough to do it."

"Me neither. The kid has more guts than brains." Maggie agreed. "Let's give him a Gold Cross. I don't want to draw too much attention to him by making him a double Medal of Honor winner. Anyway, Mike wants to take care of him."

"All right."

"Let's change the subject. Tell me something to take my mind off my worries about Mike."

"Well, I guess the most important thing to tell you is that Wilson and Doyle have a victory at Eros."

"I saw it on the news. How accurate are the reports? You know the media. They tend to exaggerate."

"Well, apparently they didn't this time. It seems that Doyle took his ships up against a vastly superior force and soundly defeated them in a battle that lasted less than three hours."

“You’re not telling me something.”

Tom reached into his chest pocket and pulled out a rolled vellum. From its condition, he had obviously carried it a couple of days. Maggie’s hands trembled as she read the message.

BEGIN TRANSMISSION

FROM: ADMIRAL LORRAINE WILSON

TO: FLEET ADMIRAL MARGARET O’BRIAN

PERSONAL EYES ONLY

IT IS MY SORROWFUL DUTY TO REPORT YOUR DAUGHTER LUCY O’BRIAN KILLED IN ACTION WHILE ENGAGING THE ENEMY ON 13 APRIL 2228. YOUR DAUGHTER DISPLAYED COURAGE AND DEDICATION TO DUTY IN HER FINAL ACTS. SHE WAS PART OF A FORCE WHICH ATTACKED PAN CRIMBIAN WARSHIP EX-EXPLORER ARMSTRONG II - THE SHIP WAS DESTROYED PROVIDING RELIEF TO THE FORCES UNDER ATTACK BELOW. DETAILS OF EVENTS WILL BE INCLUDED IN MY FINAL MISSION WAR REPORT.

REGRETS

LORRAINE WILSON

ADMIRAL

END TRANSMISSION

Maggie covered her eyes and wept. Tom placed his arm around her shoulder and held her while she cried. Then she stopped and shook off his arm. She looked down at Mike.

"Does Mike know?"

"No."

"Then, I'll tell him later after he wakes up." She rolled the message up and placed it in her pocket. "So what else do you need to tell me?"

"You remember that hell cat Jackie Thomas.?" Maggie nodded yes so Tom plowed ahead. "Well, she took her ship alone up against a squadron of Crimbian destroyers and a dreadnought."

"Oh, that's too bad. I liked her."

"She's hard to kill - she won the battle and captured the dreadnought, with just a single ship. Now Admiral Unger wants her relieved and cashiered. It seems that Jackie failed to follow her orders on multiple occasions."

He reached in his pouch, and pulled out two more messages.

BEGIN TRANSMISSION

FROM: COMMANDER TASK FORCE D

TO: FLEET ADMIRAL – HEADQUARTERS

SUBJ: BATTLE REPORT

TOP SECRET BLUE

AS ORDERED HAVE LOCATED PAN CRIMBIAN TASK FORCE LED BY

DREADNOUGHT BLITER. ENEMY FORCE HAS BEEN DESTROYED. THE DREADNOUGHT AND ONE OTHER DESTROYER CAPTURED. CRUISER ARIAL SUSTAINED SEVERE DAMAGE. SENDING THE DREADNOUGHT TO MARS, IT SHOULD MAKE A GOOD TROPHY.

CAPTAIN THOMAS OF ARIAL IS PRIZE SHIP COMMANDER. RECOMMEND THAT SHE BE RELIEVED OF DUTY UPON ARRIVAL. CHARGES AND SPECIFICATIONS TO FOLLOW BY SEPARATE MESSAGE.

CONTINUING ON MY ASSIGNED MISSION. REVISED ETA EARTH SECTOR 28 JULY.

VERONICA UNGER

ADMIRAL

END TRANSMISSION

Then Maggie read the next message.

BEGIN TRANSMISSION

FROM: COMMANDING OFFICER COMBAT CRUISER ARIAL II - PRIZE BLITER

TO: FLEET ADMIRAL - HEADQUARTERS

SUBJECT: MK21 MISSILES

TOP SECRET BLUE

UNDERWAY FOR MARS WITH DREADNOUGHT BLITER AS PRIZE RENAMED ARIAL II. BATTLE

EXPERIENCE WITH MK 21 MISSILES REPORT. ARIAL CREW MEMBERS UNDER MY ORDER AND AGAINST THE ORDERS OF ADMIRAL UNGER RAN A SERIES OF FIELD TESTS TO PROVE THE FUNCTION OF THE MISSILES. RESULTS APPEAR TO PROVE THAT THE MISSILES WERE NOT SUFFICIENTLY TESTED DEFINITELY NOT READY FOR DEPLOYMENT AND WAR. ATTACHED IS A SERIES OF TESTS AND THE RESULTS. THE MISSILES WITH THE ENCLOSED CHANGES NOW WILL FUNCTION IN BATTLE. HOWEVER, THE MISSILES DO NOT PERFORM TO THE SPECIFICATIONS AS LISTED IN THE CURRENT OPERATING PROCEDURES. PLEASE FORWARD MY CREWS EFFORTS ON TO THE TESTING AND EVALUATION CENTER ON GANYMEDE. I TAKE FULL RESPONSIBILITY FOR THE ALTERING OF THE MISSILES FROM DESIGNATED PARAMETERS. NO MEMBER OF MY CREW SHOULD BE HELD ACCOUNTABLE AS THEY WERE ACTING ON MY DIRECT ORDERS.

JACQUELINE THOMAS

CAPTAIN

END TRANSMISSION

Maggie looked up and smiled, “You sent off the test data to Gorball?”

"Oh, yeah. Got his reply this morning."

BEGIN TRANSMISSION

FROM: MAJOR GORBALL - TECHNICAL WEAPONS ADVISOR

TO: FLEET ADMIRAL - HEADQUARTERS

SUBJECT: MK21 MISSILES

TOP SECRET GREEN

REVIEWED ALL DATA. BASED ON INPUT FROM OTHER FLEET SOURCES AND A VERY BROADMINDED CAPTAIN THOMAS WE HAVE RESOLVED TARGETING AND DETONATOR PROBLEMS WITH MK-21 MISSILES. ALL COMMANDS BEING ADVISED OF CHANGES REQUIRED BY TECHNICAL BULLETIN TODAY. SHOULD BE GOOD HUNTING.

GARY W. GORBALL

MAJOR

END TRANSMISSION

Maggie looked up and spoke in her commanding voice. "We aren't going to court martial any Captain who shows initiative and is as successful as she has been in battle, not to mention solving the missile problems."

"You're going to make Veronica Unger even madder. She is a bad one to have as an enemy."

"The hell with her. She never liked me anyway. I'd rather have her mad at me than Captain Jackie Thomas."

****

Chapter 11-7
2155 Saturday 26 April 2228
Admirals Shuttle
Eros Sector

Jonesy looked out into the void. It seemed to be a fine day. All he had to do was complete this one last trip. They had already delivered the package. Their mission had been simple. Travel out to the incoming Explorer *Thomas Edison* and deliver a pouch to the relieving commanding Admiral. There would be no face-to-face meeting between Admiral Wilson and Admiral Arrow. The Army troops started arriving two days ago. The relief of the Marines was almost complete.

Admiral Wilson wanted to get underway as soon as possible. Once Jonesy arrived back at *Galileo*, Task Force C would be off to Mars. Seated next to him in the co-pilot's seat was Patty Smith. The only other person on board was the young, recently commissioned Second Lieutenant Don Thompson. Don had crawled back into the bunk area and had crashed. Marines were always short on sleep.

Jonesy looked at her. "I think I'll go back and find something to eat. You want a sandwich or something?"

"Sure," Patty replied.

After he was gone, she sat back thinking what a strange man he was. *So big, yet so gentle. So brave, yet so vulnerable.* So when he returned handing her a sandwich in a holder and a cold drink, she had to ask.

"What's the story with you and the Admiral?"

Jonesy coughed and almost choked on his first bite. "What?"

"Are you and the Admiral an item?"

"You're asking me if I sleep with the Admiral?" Jonesy was obviously flustered.

"Yes, I thought it was a simple and straight forward question."

"No. Why would you ask such a question?" Jonesy changed the tone of his voice indicating that he was insulted.

"Because, I want to know if there's any chance of me and you."

"I've always kept any relationship with a female with whom I'm serving on a strictly professional basis."

"I know. Hell, every woman who has served with you knows. Maybe that's why you're so desirable. It's obvious to me that the Admiral cares deeply for you."

The silence was deafening. Both ate without looking at the other. Finally, Jonesy answered. "Patty, I want you to know that I am flattered beyond words by your suggestion. If the circumstances were different, I'd accept without hesitation. I certainly haven't had a better offer in years. But I can't stop being who I am. Now that you broached the subject, I guess I have a soft spot for the Admiral, we went through a lot together. You know we were chained together like animals. That's a bond we share, but there hasn't yet been anything personal between us. And there won't unless she decides different."

"I know you've always been a standup guy. You know there are always rumors, which I've always squelched. On the other hand you know me I'm a very direct person, I had to ask..."

An alarm buzzer on the control console interrupted them. It was on her side so Jonesy asked, "What have you got?"

"A small shuttle running without lights or emissions."

"Any identification?" Jonesy asked.

Patty looked over the display sensors carefully. "It appears to be one of ours. It's a standard exploration shuttle, but it doesn't respond to IFF. Did you know we're off course?"

"No." Jonesy sounded unconcerned. "How far?"

"How far to the target or how far off course?" She asked.

"Now that you bring it up, both would be nice."

Patty replied immediately. "About two

miles off course and it's almost ten miles to the target."

Jonesy had been looking over her shoulder at the display. "Something is wrong. A shuttle that small should have a mother ship. However, some of our larger EX shuttles have very long range and built along the lines of a yacht. It is possible to make an interplanetary flight in one." He pointed to the screen. "See the wobbles. Someone is flying manually and trying to be subtle about moving away from us."

Jonesy applied the breaking rockets and changed course on the fly. He deftly applied thrust to overtake the other ship. For the next forty minutes, they watched as the two shuttles closed.

Jonesy toggled the short-range communications circuit. "This is fleet shuttle GG-1 of *Galileo* to unidentified shuttle. Identify yourself."

The response was immediate. The belly turret started firing. A couple of the energy pulses glanced off, shaking the entire ship. Jonesy depressed his nose cannon and returned fire. If for no other reason, he wanted them to know that the gauntlets were off.

Both Jonesy and Patty were concentrating on the screen when another voice startled them. Don asked, "Just what the hell is going on?"

"We're not sure. We apparently have stumbled across a peculiar ship. Do you mind manning our turret?" Jonesy asked.

"Might as well since you're not going to let me sleep." Don reached up and fastened his helmet in place.

Jonesy felt a little foolish as he pulled up his hood and closed the visor on his suit. It would be very stupid to have holes shot in the hull leaving the pilot breathing vacuum. Patty realized the same and closed up her suit.

Jonesy changed course. This maneuver brought them up on the stern of the other ship. All they could see was engines. That was good it kept the other ship from shooting and he was looking at the most vulnerable part of the shuttle.

Jonesy opened a mic link to Don. "Fire when ready. Concentrate fire on the servos!" Jonesy held his hands over the controls to make adjustments, but the computer in the little ship was good it adjusted as the turret fired into the other ship keeping the velocity and course constant.

A voice came on the general circuit. English was obviously not his native tongue, but he got his message across. "Stop! We yield."

"Maintain course and speed," Jonesy called back. "Open your docking ring. Prepare to be boarded for inspection."

It took him only five minutes to maneuver around and dock with the other shuttle. Jonesy locked the control board to hold the ships in place. "Patty, you have the con!" He pulled a pistol from the rack mounted on the bulkhead at the back of the cockpit.

Don had a Chattergun. He followed Jonesy down to the access hatch. The tube was already pressurized so the hatch opened easily as did the hatch on the other ship. When Jonesy floated in, they got him from both sides. There were four of them. Unfortunately for them they all concentrated firing on Jonesy. Don used his Chattergun to cut them down. Two took head shots which splattered blood into their helmets and the other two took chest shots which left them in convulsions of death.

Don couldn't stop he went forward finding another man he fired again killing him before he realized he was unarmed. He forced himself to slowdown. At the cockpit he halted. Using the butt of the Chattergun he rapped on the bulkhead. "Are you coming out?"

"Yes," the voice called out in accented basic English.

"Your hands had better be empty!"

They were. Don was puzzled he had never seen the uniform the man wore. "Who the hell are you?" he snapped.

"General Weems."

"Okay, General, how many total including yourself onboard?"

"Six."

That accounted for everyone! Don motioned with the Chattergun. "Move out!"

Back they went to the hatch. Patty was already their checking Jonesy. She had cut his suit and had applied a compress to the two wounds to his chest. Don checked Jonesy's suit indications. His suit sensors indicated that he was still alive with pulse and respiration, but it was bad. Blood droplets floated from the dressing and he was unconscious. The other five Pan Crimbians were not so lucky – they were dead. The man was mumbling.

"What are you saying?" Don demanded.

"Prayers for the dead."

"Save your prayers for yourself." Don motioned with the Chattergun to Jonesy. "Bring him along."

"Oh I think that I am safe enough. Your commanding officer will want me alive." The man was arrogant enough for three people.

Patty spoke for the first time. "Don't be so sure. Pick him up carefully, General! This wounded officer is the Commanding Admiral's aide. Carry him real carefully because he is also the Admiral's man. If he dies, she just might gut you herself before she has you spaced."

The color drained from Generals Weems' face.

****

Chapter 11-8
0930 Thursday 3 May 2228
Fleet Hospital,
Mars

Samantha was seated in the patients' lounge on a couch. The sun was shining in through the windows. The room was filled with plants and flowers. On one side was a cage with monkeys. On the other was a cage of tropical birds. The entire setting was designed to be as aesthetically comfortable as possible. She was ever conscious of the mechanical contraption strapped to her legs that allowed her to walk and sit, somewhat in a normal fashion.

Samantha's legs were encased into a power walker. Power walkers were the answer to so many who couldn't walk or move about due to a physical disability. Power walkers were an offshoot of the technology which created armored pressure suits used by Marines and Soldiers in combat. But instead of making someone look like a metallic gorilla, power walkers were strapped on and worn under clothing often allowing the wearer to lead a basically normal life. The one Samantha was wearing went on over her clothing which allowed easy access by the medical specialists to make adjustments. It was a training walker that still required constant adjustment.

Samantha was still recovering from a series of surgeries performed by a doctor trained in cybernetic prosthetics and neuro-surgery. The key component that allowed her to walk almost right away was the installed port into her spinal column above the break. It was a slow painstaking mapping procedure to discover which neurons controlled the functions below the break. As precise and as delicate as these surgeries were they had only mapped about half of the pathways. Once the power walker was plugged in directly to her spine, her body's nerves should be able to remember allowing the walker to do anything that she could do before the injury occurred: dance, run, even jump. Of course, if you couldn't do the tango before, you still couldn't do the tango.

Over the course of the past weeks, she had started to learn to walk again. The walker also allowed her to sit upright again somewhat on a couch. Maggie smiled at Samantha as she entered. There was no hesitation. The two old friends hugged and then held each other's hands.

"You're looking especially beautiful today," Maggie informed her friend.

"Don't try to rub me down. I know that I look like crud. But I'm feeling much better today. In fact, the Doctor says I might get out on limited duty in a couple of days."

"Good, we've been missing a good chief of Intel."

"It's not the job that worries me. I can do that no matter how crippled up I am. My worry now is Rob Doyle."

"The conquering hero returns. Don't worry about that. He won't care about your disability if he really cares for you. A bigger worry is the spotlight that is on him now since the media has adopted him as the greatest officer ever produced by the fleet. You'll have to be careful not to let the spotlight shine on you. No one who runs an intelligence agency can be a media celebrity."

"It's not as if I haven't made the news myself, by getting shot up," Samantha replied.

"That's true but, it's already dyeing down. Maggie said.

"Do you think the notoriety now being focused on Doyle will die down too?"

"I don't believe it will." Maggie said. "I have been asked to prepare a very public hero's welcome for him, and his entire force. Lorraine Wilson and Steve Ridgeway seem to be lost in all the media hype."

Samantha though about it for a moment. "Well it certainly appears to be deserved."

"I agree," Maggie responded. We have a needed a positive public relations shot in the arm for a long time. Tom Watson's victory came at too high a price and Admiral Walker never returned from his victory. So Doyle, Wilson and Ridgeway now become the first to return with an overwhelming victory. Yes, this is the public relations shot in the arm we so badly need."

They were interrupted when the nurse

wheeled Mike in. He was seated in a wheelchair with a blanket covering his legs. Mike, unlike Samantha, had no trouble sitting up. He was healing quickly from the wounds. Oh, he had lost about ten pounds and moved a little slower, but there was no doubt that he was well on the road to recovery. Maggie realized that for the first time, her man was looking his age.

Maggie went over bent down and kissed the Mike.

"Are we early?" Samantha wanted to know.

"No, they're late," Mike responded. "But, it's better this way. It ensures that we are ready."

"Are you sure this should be done this way?"

"I'm sure," Mike replied. "Herb is sure it's the only way."

Just then, the door opened and Inspector Herb Kohler came in. He looked his usual rumpled self. He was eating a doughnut and leaving a trail of crumbs. "Sorry, have I missed anything?"

Mike smiled. "You called this little get together. We're waiting on you."

"Quite so."

The door slid open and Sara walked in. She looked quite elegant in her class 'A' uniform. She saluted as was the Army way. "You sent for me, Madam Fleet Admiral?"

"Yes." Maggie did not return the salute. She pointed to Herb. "This is Inspector Herbert Kohler. You already know everyone else here."

"How do you do?" Sara responded.

Herb pulled out his badge. "Colonel Samuels, this is an official inquiry. We were hoping that you could help in my investigation."

"I'll be glad to be of any assistance. What exactly are you investigating?" Sara showed no emotions or indications that she was concerned.

"I will get to that in due time, however, first things first." Herb coughed and turned his head. At the same time, he pulled out his pocket recorder and energized it. "Sara, I know that you are actually Army Colonel Sara Lynn Samuels because I sneaked a piece of DNA from you bed and did another match at central headquarters. As you well know, all military personnel and first class citizen's DNA are on file." Sara just nodded so the man continued. "What I am trying to figure out is why an army officer would shoot Commodore Norris here and have a secret Pan Crimbian transmitter. The only word that comes to mind is traitor. Oh, by the way that amnesia bit was real cute. It almost worked."

There was a long pause as Sara appeared to gather her wits as she wrestled mentally. When she spoke, it was very matter of fact. "How did you know?"

Herb was smiling, “Actually, I wasn’t a hundred percent sure until just now when you confirmed it. The problem with shooting with old bullets is that you can leave DNA on the projectile. It wasn’t much, but there was a slight trace of DNA that didn’t belong to Commodore Norris. Yours was similar, so when I started digging, I found that Senior Warrant Mike O’Brian over there had already started investigating you, just on a hunch. Once I focused in, it was easy to follow you. You have been very bad. I have you conducting unauthorized transmissions and planting bugs to listen to conversations around headquarters, as well as a whole list of things I found in a hiding place. I’m sure we’ll find other evidence.” He covered his mouth and coughed before going on. “Now Colonel, I must arrest you.”

Sara moved with blinding speed. In an instant, she had a gun in her hand. Everyone was caught flat-footed. “Inspector, you will take out your gun and lay it on the floor.”

“I don’t carry a gun.” He was holding his recorder in one hand and his badge in the other using one thumb he carefully opened his coat to show her his waist.

She turned to the others. “I’ll be leaving. So I guess I’ll just have to do the job myself.” Sara glared at Maggie then at each of the others. “I cannot believe an entire destroyer couldn’t kill an Admiral. Such a simple job...”

Maggie interrupted before anything else could be said. “Excuse me. If we are going to die could you please answer just one question?” Sara looked back at Maggie. “Just one question. Why? Why would you do all this and betray the Union?”

“The Union is nothing,” Sara almost snarled in reply. “The Pan Crimbian Empire is the future of the human race. Only in commitment to God can there be peace. Crimbian is the faith and only with the faith can there be peace. Most of all the faith must be pure.”

Something made a noise. Sara turned her eyes briefly towards the noise. That was all Mike needed. He shot straight. Three energy blasts into her chest. One would have been more than enough to kill. Sara dropped where she stood. Her tunic smoked from the blasts. The air was filled with the nauseous smell of burning flesh.

Mike brought out the gun and tossed the smoking blanket off his lap.

“That was close.” Samantha glanced around. “What was the noise that saved us?”

Herb coughed then clearing his throat said, “I threw my badge into the corner.”

****

"There is no honorable way to kill. No gentle way to destroy. There is nothing good in war, except its ending." *Abraham Lincoln*

Part 12 - Epilogue

Solar Union victories had been painful. Notwithstanding the true followers of the faith went forward with the knowledge in their hearts that the Crimbian faith was true and these setbacks were only tests of faith laid out by God. Those who died in glorious battle would prevail and were already in paradise.

Holy History of Crimbian VIII

Chapter 12-1
1630 Monday 30 June 2228
Fleet Headquarters, Mars
Office of the Fleet Admiral

Maggie looked up from her desk after hearing the light tapping from Warrant Carol C. Mayfield. She stuck her head into the office door. "Ma'am, I have a young man out here in the ready room. He insists on speaking with you. He doesn't have an appointment."

"His name?" Maggie smiled. Carol was one of Mike's aides who was helping out while Mike was recuperating. Mike was still only allowed to work four hours a day in headquarters. Meanwhile, Carol filled in but it just wasn't the same.

"Sorry, he said Corporal Alexander D.

Savage, a lunar Marine. He said to tell you he has a gift from Major Earnest MacLean. He standing in my outer office along with two retired fleet officers, a Captain Ben Papers and his wife Warrant Freda Papers of the *Amelia O'Leary*."

Maggie puzzled - *the only name she recognized was Earney Maclean who was on Luna. Then she recalled the screwy message about a gift.* "Show them in."

"You don't have time. You have a meeting with the operations boss in ten minutes. I tried to send them away, but they took out their dinner and told me they would wait all night and even to next week if necessary. I was hoping that you could just give me a time to tell them to return."

"It's alright. I'll be brief." With that assurance, Carol was gone.

The door opened, a boy with an acne-covered face tentatively came in. "Hi, Ma'am, your grace, Fleet Admiral," he stammered obviously uncomfortable and searching for each word. "I'm Alex Savage. The Major sent me to you."

"Where are the others?" Maggie tried to put the boy at ease with a calm voice.

"They can't know what I have. The Major said only you. Then you would decide who could be told."

"Okay, what have you got?" *It suddenly occurred to her that this kid could be carrying a bomb or some kind of weapon.*

He began ripping out the seams of his jacket and laying pieces of metal and plastic on her desk. “I had to take it apart and just bring it in pieces. Don’t worry. I can put it together again.” Then he took out a shining cylinder, much smaller than the last one she had seen.

Maggie gasped as he sat it down on her desk. She reached and picked it up very carefully. “Do you know what this is?”

“You betch’a. I helped Earney steal it from a Crimbian communications center. No one else knows I have it, except’n Earney. We blew the place; vaporized it with a nuke. You now are the third person who knows we have this. With this we can read every bit of code the Pannies send out.”

“Thank you, Sergeant.” Maggie said. Then she looked him over carefully. He reminded her of Ed Carter. Someone too young to be fighting a war. “How old are you Alex and how did you get here?”

“I’m 16. Major MacLean enlisted me after my folks were killed. He put me on the *Geosearch* with Ben and Freda. We were captured, but got free when a Union privateer ship took over the Crimbian ship. The Crimbian’s called them pirates, but they are loyal to the Union.”

Maggie picked up her comm link. “Carol, cancel my meeting with the Ops boss. Get Captain Kestler up here. Also find Officer Cadet Charles Mako and Lieutenant Dolores Mako.” Maggie picked up the cylinder and placed it in her pocket, while carefully placing vellums on her desk to cover the rest of the pieces. "Also send in Captain and Mrs. Papers."

"Yes, Ma'am," Carol replied.

The door slid open. Ben Papers walked in along with Freda. Maggie looked at the two, "Captain Papers, you have an authorization request from Major MacLean?"

"I did, it was lost. Did the kid bring you something really important? I don't want to know what it is. I just want to know if it is worth the loss of my ship and everyone who sacrificed so this kid could get here."

"Yes, Captain Papers. It's something worth much more than your ship and maybe even more than an explorer and a battalion of marines." She looked at Ben carefully, "Did we serve together?"

"Yes," Said Ben, looking a little uncomfortable.

"Aha, yes I remember." Maggie looked at the man then over at the woman. *She realized the two had had a tough time of it.* "Why don't you two go and see the duty officer. Tell him I said to put you up in one of the VIP suites. Get a second room for the Sergeant here and let my aide know the number. Come around and see me tomorrow and I'll see about finding you another ship."

"Thank you," Freda spoke for the first time.

When they were gone, Alex asked idly, "I know the Major promised them a million bucks. I wonder why they didn't ask for the money?"

Maggie did not reply right away as she pulled out the cylinder. Handling it by the edges, she looked it over carefully, as her thoughts drifted. - I*t was beautiful. Earney MacLean she decided knew how to warm the Fleet Admiral's heart.* Finally, she replied, "Maybe, they are more patriot than pirate."

****

Chapter 12-2
1830 Tuesday 1 July 2228
Capital City,
Mars

The autopilot car swung the car to the curb where Mike had programmed it to. As the car settled down into the resting position, the door opened and Ed slid into the front seat beside Mike. Mike touched the screen and the car was underway sliding back into the city traffic pattern. He keyed in the destination and verified the auto driver computer was engaged. It is such an automatic procedure that neither of the occupants in the car was aware of the thousands of computer function operations that were occurring as the city's computer grid advised the cars computer on course and speed. All of which allowed both occupants to relax and enjoy the ride.

"Where are we going?" Ed was curious.

The old man looked at the youngster in

an appraising way. Ed felt uncomfortable under the stare of the bushy eyebrows. “I know you have courage. You’ve proven that on more than one occasion. I know you have deep anger from the loss of your family and I know you are very intelligent. You have shown the capacity to love. I’ve watched you with Ruby. Now I am going to offer you a once in a lifetime opportunity.”

“I’ve got opportunities. My career in the service and even more education opportunities. I don’t understand what more could you could offer?”

“There is a club for lack of a better word, that I am going to recommend your membership in. It is an organization which requires a lifetime of dedication. You can never tell anyone that you are a member while you live. We don’t advertise our memberships. We operate not necessarily in secret but privately. Ed do you have the honor and dedication to our civilization to become a Knight?”

“I don’t know.” The young man stammered. *Everyone read about the legends of Knights. Many of the most prominent citizens of the Union were Knights. There were no real facts on how one became a Knight it was a mystery of the Union. Now Ed knew, another Knight had to recommend you.*

“That’s a good answer,” Mike replied. “Perhaps if you understand what is required of a Knight, you could answer the question.”

"Okay."

"The function of a Knight is always to do good deeds. You are required to find someone who needs help and help them. The rules that are imposed are that the person must never be told you are a Knight, and they can never tell anyone that you provided help."

"If no one knows then how is the good deed known to the other Knight's?"

"The important thing is that you know. Most good deeds are never known. However, the Council of Knight's has ways of finding out. Enough to know if a Knight is following his or her oath. What's most important is that you know. That knowledge alone must be reward enough." Mike was smiling. He enjoyed the company of this young man. *Ed made him remember back to his youth just understanding for the first time. The same joys he got from his children when they made new discoveries. He remembered his oldest daughter coming up to him and saying 'Daddy something is moving in my chest'. It was one of those small joys of life explaining to her it was her heart beating.*

"Do you remember Admiral Allen Walker? His wife was honored at the same ceremony when you received your Medal of Honor."

"Oh, yes. It was so tragic he won a great battle and was killed. I really felt sorry for his wife. She was a nice lady."

"Allen Walker will be honored again

tonight. He was the epitome of what a Knight of the Union should be. They will list his lifetime of achievements not his service to the Union. Not as a Fleet Officer but his contribution to our civilization as well. His service as a Fleet Officer is just a small part of his life. One of his achievements was when all of the refugees came back from Luna and Freedom settlements. He had the money and position to set up a camp and help a multitude of the people who were desperate. That is the kind of man you want to emulate. He didn't have to come back onto active service and go out again, but he did."

"All right, I've heard enough to understand what it is. I am ready to make the commitment."

"One more thing," Mike added, "The only people who will ever know that you are a Knight are other Knights. We seldom meet. Most of your communications with other Knights will be through correspondence. For the most part, it will be a personal lonely endless quest. Thomas Jefferson called this the Pursuit of Happiness. It was an ancient idea passed down from the Greeks. It was about the way one lives their life. Happiness is the term they used for this lifetime commitment to living a balanced life of goodness. It can only be measured after you die."

"Can I ask who other Knights are?"

"Once you are a Knight, you can look at

the list with the names of other Knights. And yes, Earney MacLean is a Knight, as is the Fleet Admiral. The Fleet Admiral is recommending your membership. I am your sponsor."

While they were talking, the car had left the city and was now crossing open countryside. The sun was setting giving a reddish hue to the entire landscape. Ed settled back and realized that for the first time he felt truly content. Why? Suddenly he realized he had found a new family. He finally was able to let go of the anger of losing his own family. It was up to him to make a new family.

****

Chapter 12-3
1430 Wednesday 2 July 2228
Holy Palace,
Pan Crimbian, Earth

Ruffus was seated on his altar of pillows in the Grand Reception Room of the palace. He was surrounded by daughters attending his every need. Two each held his hands and were doing his nails. Ruffus so liked having a manicure. At the same time, another was bathing his feet while another massaged his neck allowing the tension to flow from his body.

"Sky Marshal Custus to see his majesty," called out a voice.

Ruffus sat up and checked to see if the viewing cameras were on. Little green lights beneath the cameras indicated they were on.

"Daughters, dry me. I must speak with the Sky Marshal."

Towels appeared and were quickly used. His feet were covered and the daughters assumed their royal positions in a circle around him. He glanced to see that they were all in the proper position before continuing, realizing that this was a whole new group since his return from space. Attendants rushed around adjusting the lighting and ensuring everything was in its proper place. Ruffus waited for the signal from the event recording technician, then he spoke in his best grand voice. "Send in Sky Marshal Custus."

Custus entered and the cameras followed him as he walked along the velvet carpet symbolizing the path of righteousness towards the Altar of the Oracle. He was wearing his full dress uniform. Custus kneeled and went through the formal prayers of acknowledgment.

"Sky Marshall what brings you to my presence this night?"

"I bring you news of glory. Glory of Crimbian faith and Pan Crimbian Empire."

"What is this news of glory?"

"The forces of Pan Crimbian fighting in the Holy Cause have won a great victory. Australia has fallen. We now control the entire continent. The last of the Army of Australia forces surrendered this morning after a suffering final defeat at Sydney. With the treaty of capitulation from Argentina now there are no forces on Earth, which are not controlled by Holy Forces or are not allies of Holy Forces. You Ruffus, have done what has never been done before in all history, you have conquered the entire Earth. The Faith is Pure."

****

Chapter 12-4
0630 Thursday 3 July 2228
Phobos Base
Space Dock 3

Admiral Price walked up to the rail and stood next to Maggie. "Good Morning Fleet Admiral." Maggie turned her attention from the scene she was watching. The huge dreadnought was slowly being pulled into the space dock after an hour of removing the battle-damaged cruiser *Arial* from the side of the larger ship.

Maggie smiled at Price. "Did you bring it?"

Admiral Price was the Military aide to the First Citizen and an old friend of Maggie's. He handed her the box and a vellum with the First Citizen's signature. "Everything is taken care of."

"Good, let's go and see Captain Thomas."

Ten minutes later, they were inside the dreadnought. Everything was spacious but stark. There was no luxury built into these Pan Crimbians ships. The first thing Maggie noticed about the strange ship was the foul smell; a musty or moldy smell. Union ships smelled liked clean compressed air not dirty or foul.

They found Captain Thomas strapped into the command couch on the main bridge. A voice called out, “Fleet Admiral on the bridge!” In a no weight condition there was no standing at attention.

Jackie looked up to see the two Admirals. She motioned to the couches next to her, “Welcome aboard Fleet Admiral. Please have a seat.”

Maggie and Bill sat and strapped in. This allowed them to watch the completion of the evolution. They didn’t intend to bother a captain at work trying to dock her ship. Especially during this evolution trying to land a dreadnaught onto an explorer cradle.

The Port Captain was in communications with dozens of yard workers calling out various adjustments. Even though the Port Captain had the conn and control of the ship, the movement of a ship was still the ship Captains ultimate responsibility, a responsibility that could not be delegated to anyone else, not even the Port Captain. She watched Jackie coach the pilot. She was doing a good job. Maggie punched up the console and looked for Jackie’s Patrol report. After a couple of minutes, she had it open for reading. Maggie skimmed quickly through the executive summary to the days of the battle with the dreadnought.

Just as she thought!

Finally, the big ship was settled on the cradle. "Grounded," one of the weary specialist called out. Everyone in the room relaxed.

She turned to the Port Captain, "Thank you for your assistance."

The Port Captain said, "Thank you Captain Thomas for a most interesting experience. I must leave and go outside and ensure the ship is properly gripped into place. Good morning Fleet Admiral."

Maggie just nodded an acknowledgment. "Carry on Captain." With that the old captain departed.

Jackie picked up a handset, "Engineering shut down all reactors. Shift to shore power when ready." She hung up the phone handset and spoke to the Master Chief Helm pilot, "Set ground watch. The control room is yours, Master Chief. Page me if you need me, I must speak with the Fleet Admiral."

Maggie was standing lightly in the low gravity with Bill Price. The two Admirals looked formidable to Jackie. *Time to face the mast.*[13]

Jackie spoke to Maggie, "Ma'am there is a Captain's conference cabin just aft of the bridge."

Maggie motioned for Jackie to lead the

---

[13] Face the Mast or Face the Music - from punishments of the sailing days, when seamen were lashed to a mast and flogged to the musical beat of a drum.

way. Once inside the cabin Jackie, silently offered them comfortable chairs. She pointed to the coffee pot both nodded. The entire cabin was large and spacious more so than Union fleet standards. Doughnuts were sitting in a zero gravity capture basket in the center of the table. Bill Price helped himself while Jackie poured coffee for everyone.

"Captain, do you know why I am here?"

"Yes, Ma'am. You are here to relieve me of my command and order me to the Inspector General for court martial for the loss of my ship."

"No, Captain. I don't punish captains who fight battles and win. I would be drummed out for even a consideration of such actions. You have brought back one of the most significant prizes of this war. The sale of this ship will make you and your crew wealthy."

"I'm confused. You had me slow down my arrival to this certain day. Why?"

"I wanted you to arrive at the same time as the *Galileo* returning with task force C. The First Citizen has ordered public recognition of victories. God knows there have been enough defeats in the past year. You will be decorated with a Gold Cross of Valor for your battle victory and for capturing this important enemy ship. You will lead your crew in a victory parade this afternoon."

"You are joking." Jackie was completely off balance and flabbergasted.

"No joke," Bill Price interjected. "The parade will include the returning heroes from Eros, as well as your crew and some others who have been successful. Remember the Union is a Republic and can only conduct war with the will of the people. The people must see some success and hope for the future. If this war is to end, we must give them some hope. Success is one sure way of giving hope."

Jackie was still a little off balance. "You could've taken me and my crew off the hook and just sent a message. Many of my crew thinks they are going down with me."

"Well, you can assure your crew that they are not and any award recommendations will be approved for you crew. However about you, until a couple of days ago, I wasn't sure what I was going to do with you. Then I decided. But I wanted to talk with you face to face." Maggie trailed off.

"Face to face about what?"

Maggie hesitated. "When you captured this ship. Did you get the crypto decoding room?"

"Not a chance. That was in my detailed transmitted report. The Pan Crimbians who held the crypto room hit the self-destruct rather than allow it to be captured."

"Good. When the reporters arrive and you give them a tour of the ship, be sure the comm center and crypto room is included along with what you just told me about its destruction."

Maggie looked at the other woman's face. She could see the long lines eased with relief. But there was something else. "Captain, you've been going through ships very fast. It seems this is your third within a year."

"Yes, Ma'am. I'm sorry about that."

"The fact is, you are one of my most successful Captains. However at the present time I don't have a ship for you. Would you be willing to do a special job for me?" Jackie started to answer, but Maggie held up her hand. "Hear me out. I'll allow Admiral Unger's charges to publicly stand and you will present your letter of resignation to me. It will appear that you have been rewarded for the capture of the ship but allowed to resign under a cloud."

"Why would I do that? Especially, if I'm not actually going to be charged."

"Because I want someone with real intestinal fortitude to be the captain of a special ship. A ship that will not be commissioned, but it will be crewed by a group that you and I will personally pick for this mission. If captured, you'll probably be called spies and shot, or worse. If you're able to perform this mission, you'll perform a valuable service needed by the Union."

Jackie shook her head. "I see no

advantage for me to disgrace myself and my family."

Maggie motioned to Bill. "Give her the vellum."

EXECUTIVE DIRECTIVE TS-1444-2228

FROM: COMMANDER IN CHIEF SOLAR UNION

TO: CAPTAIN JACQUELYN THOMAS

SUBJECT: COMMISSION OF ASSIGNMENT

CAPTAIN PLEASE ACCEPT THIS VITAL ASSIGNMENT FROM THE FLEET ADMIRAL. THIS DIRECTIVE IS ON FILE AT THE HIGHEST LEVEL TO DOCUMENT THE FACT THAT YOUR RESIGNATION IS A FAÇADE. IN THE EVENT OF THE FLEET ADMIRALS DEATH OR MINE, THIS ORDER IS BEING FILED TO ASSURE YOU OF YOUR RANK IN THE FLEET SERVICE. THERE WILL BE NO BREAK IN YOUR TENURE AND ALL PAY WILL CONTINUE AT THE RANK OF CAPTAIN.

UPON COMPLETION OF THIS ASSIGNMENT, YOU WILL BE RECOMMISSIONED AND GIVEN AN ASSIGNMENT AT THE RESPONSIBILITY LEVEL OF YOUR RANK AND GLORIOUS VICTORIES YOU WILL HAVE ACHIEVED FOR THE UNION.

VERNON QUILTMAN

COMMANDER IN CHIEF

Jackie looked up. "Okay, I agree. Now are you going to tell me what this is all about?"

"The details are unimportant right now," replied Maggie. "Take a week off, then come and see me."

****

Chapter 12-5
1015 Thursday 3 July 2228
CE-46 Galileo
In Orbit around Mars

Mike took his time moving through the various passages on the Explorer. Finally, he located the door marked Sickbay. A young nurse blocked his way, doing what nurses throughout history have done, see to it that their patients are not disturbed.

"May I help you Senior Chief Warrant?"

"Yes, I want to see Chief Warrant Jones."

"I'm afraid that isn't possible. Only one visitor is permitted at a time, he is still listed in serious condition."

"I know he's in serious condition. That's one reason I'm here – we are old shipmates."

"The rules are the rules!" Her voice was becoming shrill.

Mike was exasperated. Most Fleet specialist saw his rank or looked at his ribbons and yielded to his wishes. She was obviously too young to realize. "Young lady you are trying my patience. I'm Senior Warrant O'Brian. It has been years since I have been forced to throw my weight around. If you persist and send me away, I'll be back with the Commanding Admiral. She no doubt will be forced to chew out Commodore Doyle. What do you suppose will be left of you after he tears into the senior medical officer over something so trivial?"

Tears welled up in her eyes. "I'm sorry, but the Commanding Admiral is in with Jonesy now."

"Good!" Mike responded. "Go tell her that she has to come out and see the Fleet Admirals aide, who can't be admitted."

"Please go right in. Stateroom four." She pointed down the hall. "Mr. O'Brian, I did not realize... Sorry."

Mike left chuckling to himself. Every once in a while these youngsters needed a little guidance. She was just the right kind - dedicated, and diligent. He would have not gone to the Admiral, but she didn't have to know that. He knew that he would have gotten faster results by finding the Warrant Nurse.

Mike knocked at the door marked four. It immediately slid open. No wonder only one visitor was permitted at a time. The room had to be the smallest on the entire ship. He would have to be moved before this afternoon. Jonesy took up most of the room lying on the hospital bed bunk. Admiral Lorraine Wilson was seated on a fold-out chair from the bulkhead near the head of the bunk. Mike realized immediately the big man was in real bad shape. He had IV's in each arm and leg along with tubes coming out of each side of his chest. Mike had already read the reports and knew that Jonesy had been shot through both lungs and his liver and spleen had suffered severe damage. The docs had transplanted clone lungs, liver, and a spleen into him.

"Good to see you, Mr. O'Brian," Lorraine greeted him.

"Glad to be aboard, Ma'am. Would have gotten around to seeing you too, but I needed to see this old Marine first." Mike looked at Jonesy. "You look like crap. I heard that you zigged when you should have zagged."

Jonesy smiled and chuckled, then coughed. "I'm not by myself – heard you managed to get bushwhacked too.

"Yeah, but I managed to keep my lungs."

"I also had to get a new liver day before yesterday. The surgeon we have on board is good."

Mike reached under his tunic and removed a packet. "Based on your recommendations, Admiral, the following medals will be awarded today." He handed her a stack of vellums, "More than three hundred high level personal decorations.

Lorraine glanced at the top one. "What's this about a parade?"

"It's a fact. Both the First Citizen and the Fleet Admiral want a big public display." Mike pointed to Jonesy. "Is he going to be able to attend?"

“Not a chance,” Lorraine retorted shaking her head.

“What’s this?” Jonesy chimed in. “I haven’t done anything except get shot to pieces.”

“You certainly did that. In a very precise and military manner, shipmate.” Mike turned to Lorraine. “We should probably tell him.”

“Yes I agree.” Mike looked at Jonesy. “Since you cannot go dirtside yet, our Commander In Chief, the First Citizen himself will be coming here later tonight with a group of reporters. You will be awarded your second Medal of Honor.”

Jonesy coughed. “For what?”

Mike patted his leg. “For leading a suicide mission and killing an Explorer. Hang on, old stick. You have just joined a very rare club. Only nine others have ever become double Medal of Honor winners. Only one is alive today.”

“Who is the other living double Medal of Honor winner?” Lorraine asked.

Jonesy coughed again. “You don’t know Admiral?”

“No.”

“It is him. Mike O’Brian.”

Lorraine flushed with embarrassment. “I think I’d better get to work. We need to get this information to Commodore Doyle and General Ridgeway.” Then another thought occurred to her. "How long will we be here before we get sent out again?"

"Ma'am, I'm not the right person to be telling you this but this task force is over. Commodore Doyle will be reassigned before the week ends. You will be reassigned also."

"Okay, thanks for the info." For the first time today, she was surprised. Somehow she had been under the impression that the team that had been so successful would be kept together. "Well, I had better go. I will be back later Jonesy."

Mike stood aside and let her squeeze out. Once she was gone, Mike sat down on the little folding chair.

Jonesy looked at the older man. "You were a little hard on her."

"Don't worry she'll find out later today what's up. The First Citizen and the Fleet Admiral wants to tell her that Admiral Lorraine Wilson is to become the Supreme Commander for the Lunar Invasion Expeditionary Force. She'll be commanding four other Admirals, each of whom will have a larger task force than you left here with. She'll also be commanding three divisions of Marines and as many Armies as we can give her. Her new flagship is a new super explorer that is being prepared just for this mission. Believe me. There'll be a lot of very senior admirals and generals who will be devastated when they find out."

"That's good, she certainly deserves it.

Was there something else?

"Sure, guess you can tell. I wanted to know about my girl Lucy. No way you could know, but she was special to me. I raised her while her mother commanded a three-year exploration mission."

"She was a good person. I tried to keep her alive."

"You don't have to sugar coat it. I know the girl had problems. I believe she was drinking. I thought a voyage might help. Guess I was wrong."

"Yes, she had problems at first. She had a double shadow of greatness to follow. Her mother was the Fleet Admiral and her father was the most decorated man in the service. You're thinking that you're somehow to blame. She had to be kicked out of the nest. Well, she fell more than once but she got up. She was flying right long before the end. Lucy did her duty as an adult citizen in the service. If anything, she was more afraid of living in your shadow than of death. I recommended her for a gold cross."

****

Chapter 12-6
1815 Thursday 3 July 2228
Capital City
Mars

Jill had spent all day moving from one window to another in the little room she was in. She paced and paced back and forth, trying to make sense of her frustrating situation and her failures. She knew no one on Mars. Ben, Freda, and Alex were somewhere in Fleet headquarters. She had too much pride to even attempt to contact them.

She was been staying in a rundown dive in Old Dome City. After three days of eating and sleeping on credit, the bills were coming due soon. She had no money. Everything she had and who she was, had been lost on Luna. Even the clothes she was wearing were borrowed or given to her by some of the women on the ship.

She tried to get a message to Earney. But, she had been unable to locate any information on Major Earnest MacLean. In fact, all inquiries into military records met with resistance. She had run the gamut of bureaucracy. In typical fashion, she was passed from one department to another and finally back where she started - a complete circle to nowhere.

First, she had suffered at the hands of the Pan Crimbians, now she was being humiliated by her own people. She was angry, frightened and really didn't know where to turn.

A knock on the door brought her back to the present. She opened the door and looked at the portly rumpled man. He held up a badge. "Miss Jillian Parks?"

"Yes," Jill replied. *Wondering how he knew she was here*?

“My name is Inspector Kohler. May I come in and have a few words with you?”

“Sure.” Her heart surged, maybe this was her answer to finding out about Earney.

After the door closed, he started. “Miss Parks, you have been asking all sorts of embarrassing questions concerning a Fleet Officer, one Earnest MacLean. I have been sent by certain authorities to ask you to cease.”

“But I am just trying to find out if he is okay.”

“I know, but officially he is listed as missing in action and has been missing for almost eight months.”

“That’s crazy, I was with him less than four months ago on Luna. As a matter of fact we’re going to get married.”

“You don’t understand. MacLean is not on Luna. He is missing in action with the loss of the frigate Carthage last year. There can be no more talk publicly, especially about him on Luna. It’s important to his safety. You’re safe now. If you’re planning to get married, then what is most important to him is that you are safe. The alternatives are not good.”

“What alternatives? I have my rights as a citizen.”

“Yes, but the state also has a duty. If you persist on this subject, then someone might think you crazy. There is no Writ of Habeas Corpus in a mental hospital.”

“I get the picture, Inspector.” She opened the door. “I believe this conversation is over.”

He hesitated in the door. “Believe me, young lady. I don’t like bullying you. But it’s my job and it’s for the safety of everyone involved.”

“I suppose I’ll have to go back to Luna.”

“Until the war is over, the only transport to Luna will be the military. Whenever they invade.”

He shut the door behind him leaving her in the seedy little room. She wanted to cry, but her captivity had taught her to control. She needed to take a walk. Out into the streets she went just wandering around for hours. Suddenly she came upon tent city which stretched out for miles. These were the orphans and refugees of war. She was drawn to the area by curiosity. Walking among the tents she saw her fellow citizens that had been beaten by the Pan Crimbian invasion forces. These were free people who once were trying to live, raise families, and die with dignity. All that was gone from these people. Now only this mass of fellow citizens struggling to survive was left.

She turned and walked out of the tents. She couldn’t take any more. Backtracking, she found the place she had passed earlier. Inside she could see a man seated and reading a vellum. He looked up after she rang and buzzed her in.

"What can I do for you, young lady?" The man was a Sergeant Major with silver hair. He was obviously too old for active service. He was actually feeble. Anyone who could still get into an Armored Pressure Suit was already there. The old and lame would be left to tend a recruiting station.

"I'm here to enlist."

"Young lady, it's late. Are you sure?"

"I was captured by the Pan Crimbians and tortured. I'm a free citizen of age and healthy asking to exercise my right to fight. I'm determined to return to Luna. It was pointed out to me that the next passage would probably be the Marines landing. I intend to be with the Marines when they land."

"Okay, have a seat. Let's see about making you a Marine!"

***

Back on Luna Earney was crawling in a pipe which was just wide enough to allow him to get through with a pressure suit. Jake was right behind him pulling a sack of supplies. Earney stopped at the intersection and took out his map.

Jake asked, "Are you sure we aren't lost?"

"No. We're okay. We need to go to the right."

Earney led off into the pipe on the right. There was more liquid in the pipe now which made the going slower. Finally, they entered a tank only about six feet high but wide and long. It was half full of a tar-looking liquid.

"So where are we?" Now that they had arrived, Jake wanted to know. Earney had been so mysterious, like a leprechaun with his little joke.

"This is the main sanitary collection tank for Jay City."

"You mean we're standing in crap?"

"That's right." Earney confirmed his conclusion.

"We're going to stink so bad, they're not going to let us back into the cave."

"Probably not! Give me your bag of goodies."

Jake pulled the bag up out of the muck. Earney opened it and took out the explosives. He reached up and placed the first one on the ceiling of the room. Once done, he pressed the arming switch. A light came on and the timer activated indicating a backward countdown. They had two hours to get out.

Earney took out a couple more and indicated to Jake. "I'll put these on this side and you can do over there. This might be a stinky job, but just think about all those Pannies who will be forced to crap in bags and then drag the waste out on the surface. It will take weeks to repair something like this. Jay City will be a real stinky place for a while."

Jake chuckled. Jay City had been a series of Union affluent resorts. It was a sure bet the Pan Crimbian high priesthood had found the luxury suites to their liking. He placed his bombs and followed Earney back down the pipe. It would be worth the effort cleaning his suit to inflict this kind of misery on the enemy. Jake had to admit, Earney had become much more creative in the past weeks. Then a thought occurred to Jake.

"You know, we could increase the effectiveness of this, by pouring something in the water supply to cause backdoor trots."

"That's good thinking," Earney replied. "We'll work on that tomorrow."

Earney moved along thinking. *It would be nice to make the enemy so miserable that by the time the Marines got here, the Pannies should be wanting to leave.*

****

Chapter 12-7
1800 Thursday 4 July 2228
Fleet Admirals Quarters
Mars

Doyle paused by the door before knocking. He looked down at the front of his uniform. Everything looked in place. He took the heavy Medal of Honor from around his neck and slipped it in his pocket. Then he rang the doorbell. The door slid open and Mike motioned him to enter. Doyle expected to see a room full of people, but the room was empty.

"Welcome," Mike grinned. "May I offer you some refreshments? Something to wash out the trail dust from your long voyage."

"Yes, that would be great." Doyle looked around. He felt confused and asked. "Am I here at the proper time? Where is everyone?"

"You are at the proper time. Everyone else was told to be here an hour from now. Since you seem to be unsure what you are drinking, I'll assume bourbon. I have a fine old very traditional sour mash."

"Okay. Are you going to tell me what's going on?"

Mike had gone to the bar and was already pouring out a glass of amber liquid over ice cubes. He handed the glass to Doyle. "In due time." Mike picked up his glass and held it in the toasting position. "Have a sip of courage my friend. Salute."

The two men drank.

Mike put down his glass and pointed to the terrace. "She is out there waiting. Good Luck!" Mike turned and left the room, leaving Doyle standing all alone.

Doyle wasn't sure who was out there but he had to go, if for no other reason than to satisfy his curiosity.

Samantha was seated in the lounge chair, with a blanket over her lap to cover the power walkers. Doyle walked over and kneeled. "I was wondering when there would be a chance to see you." Kissing her lightly on the lips and then hugged her, she responded to his efforts. He leaned back and looked at her. "I see, you set this meeting up. We first met out on this terrace. You didn't have to go to this much trouble."

"I do need to go to this much trouble. I have something to tell you. I wanted to do it right."

"Okay."

"As chief of intelligence it is not appropriate for me to be around you."

"Why?"

"Because you are a national figure and Maggie feels it draws a spotlight on me too. It makes me ineffective in my job."

Doyle stood looking at her. "Are you telling me this because you want to end it between us or are you saying this because you're afraid I'll reject you since you can no longer dance on your own?"

"How did you know? No one was supposed to tell."

"It doesn't matter. You're getting shot is too big of an event to be kept a secret. Not only that, I have my computer keyed with your name. Anything it can find with your name, it downloads. I want to know everything I can about you. I care for you, the person Samantha Norris. Whatever is wrong with your legs can be fixed with technology. I thought after all these years that I'd found a friend and a true companion. Have I?"

Tears were flowing down her cheeks. "I'm not a whole woman anymore. We can probably never have children."

"Is that what this is all about? Forget that. No, don't! If you want kids, we'll find a way. But, you listen. You're a good woman. I'll take you any day as a quarter or even half rather than any others at a hundred percent. Do you want to be Mrs. Samantha Doyle?"

"Yes." Her voice broke.

"Then it's settled." They hugged again. This time with passion.

***

The two were still sitting and holding hands when Mike came out. "The guests have arrived and your presence is requested."

Doyle stood and held her hand as she stood wavering slightly before the gyros kicked in. Doyle held out his arm. She took it. Now she was steady.

Doyle looked at Mike. "I want you to be the first to know. We're going to get married. Do we need the Fleet's permission?"

Mike just grinned shaking his head no. "Tell me something I didn't know. I figured you two would have been married already if you had stuck around." He motioned for the door. "Let's not keep the First Citizen waiting."

Mike led them through the great room into the dining room. The long table was crowded with senior officers and their spouse or escorts. The First Citizen was standing at the head of the table. The applause started and continued for almost five minutes. Doyle was embarrassed. Lorraine Wilson was standing and motioned for him to a chair next to her. When the applause stopped, the First Citizen motioned for everyone to be seated. He remained standing.

"Ladies and Gentlemen, thank you for your recognition of this man. I am sure once he thinks about it, he'll realize that it's not just about him but it about each and every one of us who have made a commitment to keeping the Union safe. By keeping the Union safe, we create the fertile bed for our civilization to grow. There is always the need to nourish the tree of liberty. It's unfortunate that the tree requires the blood of patriots. I request a moment of silence and prayers for the heroes of Eros - those who gave their last measure for us."

Heads were bowed. Some mumbled prayers and others gave the sign of the cross when finished.

The First Citizen continued. "Mr. Doyle, there is one more accolade. Please come up."

Doyle was stunned. What else. He walked up in front of his Commander in Chief.

Mike handed a vellum to the First Citizen. He opened it and read out loud.

"EXECUTIVE PROCLAMATION

FROM: COMMANDER IN CHIEF OF SOLAR UNION

TO: ROBERT M. DOYLE 477-798

YOU ARE HEREBY ADVANCED TO THE RANK OF ADMIRAL. PURSUANT TO QUALIFICATIONS AND PHYSICAL EXAMINATION REQUIREMENTS OF FLEET FLAG OFFICERS.

CONGRATULATIONS.

VERNON QUILTMAN

COMMANDER IN CHIEF AND FIRST CITIZEN"

Maggie took the Admiral's Crest out of her pocket and handed it to Samantha. Samantha removed his Commodore's crest and placed the Admiral's crest on his chest.

Maggie shook his hand. "Fly your flag with pride Admiral. That particular Admirals crest was last worn by Admiral Bull Smith. I thought you would appreciate it."

Doyle only nodded his thanks to Maggie. Admiral Smith was a man who Doyle greatly admired.

The First Citizen shook his hand. "Admiral Doyle will you please say a few words?" With that, the First Citizen sat down.

Doyle just stood there trying to clear his head. Finally, he spoke softly, "I was a poor farm boy who had a dream to go into space and travel around. Then I dreamed of being a ship's captain. To command a ship in space until now was all I ever wanted. Now I want to get married and see the end of this war. Today I've been honored far more than I'm worth. I'm no hero, just a guy doing his job. As the First Citizen so eloquently put it, the real heroes didn't come home. I accept these honors for those true heroes."

THE END

****

Explorer Ships of the Union are named for Famous Explorers and Scientists.

Neil Alden Armstrong (1930-2012)

American astronaut and the first man to ever step on the moon. He was also an aerospace engineer, naval aviator, test pilot, and a university professor. As a boy he took flying lessons and earned his pilot's license on his 16th birthday. He was a Boy Scout who earned the rank of Eagle Scout. He began studying aeronautical engineering at Perdue University on the Navy Holloway plan, which was a path to becoming a Naval Officer. At 18 he entered the Navy flight training program at Pensacola Florida. So by the age of 20 he was a fully qualified Naval Aviator qualified for carrier landings at sea. He served during the Korean War and flew 78 missions. After the Navy and the war he completed his bachelor's degree in aeronautical engineering. He was hired by National Advisory Commission (which later became NASA) and became a test pilot. He flew many experimental, high altitude, and speed rocket planes such as the X-15. He was then selected as an astronaut for the U.S. Gemini and Apollo space program. He was the command pilot for Gemini 8. He was then the Apollo 11 mission commander. On 20 July 1969 he landed the lunar module Eagle on the moon at Tranquility Base, leaving Michael Collins in the command ship above. He and Buzz Aldrin spent a total of two and a half hours on the moon. He was a private man who was called the reluctant hero.

"That's one small step for man, one giant leap for mankind."

Galileo Galilei (1564-1642)

Italian scientist considered among the top 10 intellects of all times. He excelled in all fields of science: Astronomy, Mathematics, Physics, Philosophy, Engineering, and Cosmology. Considered the father of modern science. He used his improved telescope to make the first observations of moons of Jupiter and the rings of Saturn. He studied the landscape of earth's moon in detail. As a scholar he began his studies in medicine but soon became more interested in mathematics. His first discovery was describing the rules of the motions of pendulums. Then as chair of mathematics at several universities, he performed his classic experiments from the tower of Pisa on falling bodies. His Astronomy studies brought him into conflict with the Christian Church's accepted Aristotelian view of the universe which placed the earth at its center. Galileo was brought to trial in Rome in 1633, and convicted of heresy. Under threat of torture he was forced to recant, express sorrow, and curse his errors. Thus at 69 he was isolated in a form of house arrest. He spent the last nine years writing a summary of his motion experiments, which became his final great scientific work. Galileo's final legacy was his push towards the scientific method, of using throughout hypotheses then using experimentation to prove or disprove the theory.

"All truths are easy to understand once they are discovered; the point is to discover them."

Appendix A: Future History

The events in this story take place during the war between the Solar Union Settlements, which inhabit many regions throughout the solar system, and the Empire of Pan Crimbians, the dominant governing influence on Earth in the year 2227. Pan Crimbian is a unification of most of the Earth's population under a single ruler. The government of Pan Crimbian is of a religious nature, rather than a hereditary monarchy. This story takes place in the early months of the Solar War, which began in 2227. To enable the reader to better understand the events, this future history timeline is provided.

Future History Timeline:

1969 - Moon Landing. Mankind first travels to the Moon from planet Earth. The age of space exploration begins.

1990 - First AIDS epidemic begins. It spreads rapidly, and as most of its victims are from the lower classes it is largely ignored and allowed to proliferate.

2001 - War on Terror begins after Muslims attack the United States.

2003 – International Space Station established. It will become the Solar Union Freedom Settlement.

2014 – Beginning of first of many epidemics. Beginning with Ebola

2034 - First Mars Landing – a joint USA /

Japan expedition. Second AIDS epidemic has killed one- fourth of Earth's population.

2035 - Hemorrhagic fever outbreak in Africa kills one-third of its population.

2037 - First lunar settlement established.

2048 – Second expedition to Mars. Gold and uranium are discovered on Mars.

2051 - First Mars settlement established.

2052 – First successful human clone

2052 - World War III. USA, European Union and China vs. Middle Eastern Muslim Empire. Space settlements established by USA, Russia, and Japan become isolated after the war. As the nations which comprise the United Nations fall, social unrest increases, and many areas become desolate. Settlements in space are forced to become self- sufficient or perish.

2053 - Dark Age begins. Disease and radiation bring a series of plagues and disasters.

****

SOLAR DARK AGE 2053 – 2155

The Solar Dark Age is a period of about 100 years of social and economic stagnation on planet Earth. By 2059, two-thirds of Earth's human population is dead. Waves on new epidemic diseased sweeps the planet reducing world population to below one billion. Most major cities fall to ruin. Worldwide communications fail. The Earth's remaining population settles into isolated groups and clusters. Governments turn toward religion as people seek hope within spirituality. The space settlements learn to exist without support from the mother planet, Earth.

****

2135 - The Oracle of began preaching the Crimbian faith.

2139 – The Union of Solar Settlements is established. Initially there were nineteen space settlements, and while the Earth sat idle these first settlements grew. They worked to establish new settlements and soon evolved into a new civilization in space. The Union of Solar Settlements was established to promote commerce and provide common protection.

2141 – Union terraforming of Mars begins. Religious war breaks out on Earth between the new Crimbian religion and Islam - Islam is crushed within a few years. New waves of religious fervor spread across Africa and the Middle East. The priests of Crimbian use cloning and genetics to breed new humans of the faith – they are stronger and more resistant to disease.

2142 – Union Expedition to Jupiter Moons. Civilization begins to return on

Earth.

2143 – Rise of Crimbian religion sweeps across Africa, the Middle East and what was once India. Catholics in Argentina emerge as a dominate world power. Australia, an island continent, tolerates all religions and resists genetic engineering. Areas of the Northern Hemisphere remain mostly uninhabited.

2147 – Union Expedition and Exploration of Uranus.

2151 – Union colonies established on Ganymede and Triton.

2157 – Union Exploration Mission to Pluto.

2159 - Solar Union vs. Argentina War. The Solar Union has a developed a practice of raiding Earth for water, oxygen, animals, and captives. Argentina has built a space fleet and a space station.

2161 - The Solar Union wins the war using newly developed weapons and a superior space fleet to conduct precise weapon deployment in strategic areas. The lunar settlement expands and is able to raid Earth at will now.

2165 – Union Exploration Mission to Mercury.

2167 - Asteroids are explored and settled over a twenty-year period. It is a wild and wooly period of exploration. Minerals, gems and rare elements are discovered in abundance. By 2175 there are hundreds of small settlements on the asteroids.

2176 - Australia fights a brief war with the Catholics of the South American Alliance led by Argentina. The pope in New Rome declares the Australians to be ungodly barbarians. Argentina has built a new space station, and now has a significant military space force, navy, and army. However, Argentina is being economically strangled by Australia, which trades freely with the Solar Union.

2177 - End of the Australian-Argentinean War. Argentina is forced to accept a peace as the war grinds to a stalemate. Although Argentina is the superior force, they cannot defeat Australia which is supported by aid from the Solar Union.

2201 - The South American Alliance goes to war over Luna (Earth's moon). Although the Solar Union has several settlements and bases on the moon, the political powers on Earth demand possession of Luna - they need bases and vital resources.

2203 - The war ends and is settled by an agreement allowing Argentina and other Earthers to establish small outposts and mining bases in certain regions of Luna.

2208 - First exploration mission to the nearest star, Alpha Centuri, departs. They are expected to be gone for forty years and take enough ships and people to establish colonies if conditions warrant.

2214 - Beginning of both Solar and Earth-wide economic collapse. A great depression lasts for three years. Thousands starve on Earth, and commerce in the Solar Union comes to a near standstill. Conditions on Earth are much worse than those in space; for every death in space there are thirty deaths on Earth.

2218 – The forces of Crimbian unite into the Pan Crimbian Federation. The priests of Crimbian exert influence on all aspects of life. The pure of Crimbian prosper and unite under Ruffs, the leader of the Pan Crimbian Federation, as a new wave of religious fervor dominates the populace. The Federation begins a vast military buildup. Between 2219 and 2227 there are continual conflicts between Pan Crimbian Empire and the Solar Union.

2221 - Pan Crimbian Empire builds an orbiting space station (Zooie) almost as large as the Union's Freedom Settlement. Ruffs realizes that in order to effectively deal with the Solar Union's monopoly on space the Pan Crimbian must have a strong space force.

2225 - A series of treaties begins. The Solar Union concedes more and more to keep the peace. The Union resents the Crimbian forces infringement on their territories, while the Crimbian Empire resents the Union's strangling them with unfair trading practices and preventing them from obtaining needed basic resources. Tensions continue to build over a two-year period. As each incident occurs, the strain increases.

2227 - Pan Crimbian Empire strikes and with a sweeping surprise attack conquers Earth's moon Luna and Freedom Settlements.

Appendix B: List of Characters

In order of appearance

1-1 **Earnest K. MacLean (Earney) Major (Bvt.)** - Commanding Luna Resistance Forces

Alexander D. Savage – Sergeant (Acting) - Lunar Resistance Soldier

Von Gibbons - Major Pan Crimbian *

1-2 King Ruffus - Leader of Pan Crimbian & Holy Faith

Alex J. Custus – General - Sky Marshall for Holy Forces

Sara Lynn Samuels – Colonel Solar Army

1-3 **Arnold B. Jones** - Warrant Aide to Admiral Wilson

Lorraine E. Wilson - Admiral CO Task Force C

1-4 **Nathan P. Graham** – General - Commandant of Marines

Michael A. O'Brian - Senior Chief Warrant Officer - Aide de Camp FA

Margaret G. O'Brian - Fleet Admiral Commander Union Fleet

1-5 **Robert M Doyle** - Commodore - Commanding Explorer Galileo Galilei

Samantha F. Norris - Commodore Fleet Chief of Intelligence

Dolores Mako - Lieutenant Mathematician (Instructor Fleet Officer Academy)

Charles R. Mako - Cadet Officer Student – Lieutenant FMF (Bev) (Fleet Intelligence Officer)

1-6 **Jacob (Jake) A. Sutter** - Chief Lunar Exploration Force

Gus B. Collins - Sergeant Major - Lunar Exploration Force *

1-7 **Donald P. Thompson** – Sergeant FMF (Nighthawk) 2nd Marine Division

Sidney C. Markel – Major 2nd Marine Division

1-8 Ben Papers Commander Yacht *Geosearch*

Freda Papers- First Officer Yacht *Geosearch*

Jillian D. Parks (Jill)- Scientist

Dr. Clayton F. Parks - Scientist *

2-1 **Jacqueline (Jackie) P. Thomas**, Captain CO Cruiser *Ariel*

Jane A. Polanski – Major First Officer *Ariel* *

Captain Trevor Porter – Port Captain

2-2 **Thomas Robert Watson** - Admiral Chief of Staff

Corporal Lucy O'Brian – Communications specialists CE *Galileo* *

2-3 Corporal Lewis Brach (Diver) *

Mason Stevens (Falcon) Corporal *

Jessie Trent (Bullfrog) Private *

Private Lena Sampson (Flash) Private *

Private Bond Noble (Wolf) Private *

Private Alvin Duncan (Grit) Private *

Private Festus O'Tool (Acid) Private *

Private Susan Ann Weathers (Wasp) Private *

Private Brent McKnight (Croaker) Private *

Private Jerome Arken (Snowflake) Private *

Private Solemn Carpenter (Pepper) Private *

James A. Travis (Cobra) Gunnery Sergeant

2-4 Steve Ridgeway – Brigadier 2nd Marine Division Commander

David Snicker – Captain Commander Transport *Guardiant*

Bud C. Kadel – Captain First Officer *Galileo*

Isabell Davis – Colonel Commander Marine Detachment *Galileo* *

Joe Banks – Major Flag Operations Office to Admiral Wilson

Patty Sue Smith – Warrant Captain Doyle's Warrant on *Galileo*

2-5 Weams, General Commander Pan

Crimbian Lunar Forces

2-9 Zepherine Chin - Commander *

2-10 Mickey K. Horton - Warrant (Commanding CF *Saipan*) MIA*

Abraham (Abe) C. James - Chief (Engineer CF *Saipan*)

3-1 Corporal Blake Sims - specialists CF *Saipan* *

3-4 Jerome Oakland, First Class Crew CE-*Galileo*

Carry Ann Gilpin - Chief Environmental Tech. Crew CE-*Galileo*

Barbara D. Ryan - Sergeant Weapons Tech Crew CE-*Galileo*

Roy L. Burke - Chief Science specialists Crew CE- *Galileo*

4-1 Samuels A Waters - Lieutenant Weapons Officer CC *Arial*

Russell B. Mahoney - Warrant Bos'n CC *Arial*

Blake D. Greer - Major CC *Arial*

Arnold Kelly -Corporal CC *Arial* *

Sally Martin - Corporal CC *Arial* *

Jolly Carns - Apprentice CC *Arial* *

4-2 Veronica P. Unger - Admiral Commander Task Force D

Juan Gonzales - Admiral of Fleet Construction & Development

4-6 Mrs. Susan Walker

Sister Mary Ann

5-2 George G. Evans – General FMF

5-3 Sub Priest Cessan *

5-4 Dr. Arlene K. Smith – Major MC Union Fleet

Dr. Harold P. Naylor – Captain MC Union Fleet

5-8 Clarence P. Bell - Science Chief CC Arial

6-1 Buck Cardif - Captain *Amelia O'Leary**

Amelia Cardif - 1st Officer *Amelia O'Leary*

7-2 Gary Gorball - Major

Chester Hale – Senior Chief Warrant Officer

7-3 Brigadier General Solas*

7-5 Major Xene

Sergeant Arank

7-7 Grand High Priest Kaler

Minister of Finance Drassic

Secretary of State Millerfred

9-2 Sal York - Sergeant Major FMC Aide to Commandant Fleet Marine Force

10-2 Lloyd Quinton Reynolds - Chief Warrant Aide to Admiral Watson

W. H. Short

10-3 Sub Lieutenant R. T. Zenninki *

Walter Kestler – Captain Intelligence Officer

11-3 Silvia S. Maverick - Commissar of Federal Police

Herbert T. Kohler - Chief Inspector Federal Police

*KOA

Appendix C: Ships of the Union Fleet

All ships of the Fleet are classified either as a combat ship or a support ship.

Combat Ships

Explorer - CE

Mission: Combat flag ship and exploration base ship

Ships Named for: Famous explorers and scientists

Commander Rank: Commodore

Length: 26,400 feet (5 miles)

Diameter: 3,768 feet (0.75 mile)

Number of Decks: 314 to 355

Number of Crew: 2,00 to 6,000

Cruiser - CC

Mission: Heavy battle and exploration support

Ships Named for: Planets, moons, settlements

Commander Rank: Captain

Length: 6,040 feet (1.1 mile)

Diameter: 1,508 (0.25 mile)

Number of Decks: 57 +/-

Number of Crew: 580-600

Frigate - CF

Mission: Battle and light exploration support

Ships Named for: Famous battles and wars

Commander Rank: Captain

Length: 603 feet (0.11 mile)

Diameter: 183 feet

Number of Decks: 8

Number of Crew: 110

Corvette - CV

Mission: Battle support and exploration support

Ships Named for: Famous persons

Commander Rank: Jr. Captain

Length: 480 feet

Diameter: 183 feet

Number of Decks: 11

Number of Crew: 84

Picket - CP

Mission: Battle scouting & exploration search

Ships Named for: Stars and Comets

Commander Rank: Lieutenant or Warrant

Length: 305 feet

Diameter: 118 feet

Number of Decks: 5

Keep the Faith Pure

Number of Crew: 65

Support Ships

Tender - SR

Mission: Ship repair and exploration support

Ships Named for: Elements and Chemicals

Commander Rank: Captain

Length: 21,121 feet (4 miles)

Diameter: 3,050 (0.57 mile)

Number of Decks: 251

Number of Crew: 1,540+

Space Dock - SD

Mission: Ship repair and overhaul

Ships Named for: Renown Persons

Commander Rank: Commodore

Length: 31,680 feet (6 miles)

Diameter: 10,560 (2 miles)

Number of Decks:149 - 152

Number of Crew: 2,300

Transport - ST

Mission: Troop transport, exploration, & hospital

Named for: Places of sanctuary

Commander Rank: Captain

Length: 5,280 feet (1 mile)

Diameter: 1,377 feet (0.25 mile)

Number of Decks: 114

Number of Crew: 520 + @ 8,000 passengers

Cargo - SC

Mission: Large cargo and fleet replenishment

Ships Named for: Bodies of Water or Seas

Commander Rank: Captain

Length: 5,820 feet (1.1 mile)

Diameter: 1,650 feet (0.3 mile)

Number of Decks: 59

Number of Crew: 110

Survey - SS

Mission: Solar mapping and survey

Ships Named for: Birds

Commander Rank: Major or Lieutenant

Length: 690 feet

Diameter: 168 feet

Number of Decks: 9

Number of Crew: 88

Salvage - SV

Mission: Rescue, towing, and salvage

Ships Named for: Events or places of rescue

Commander Rank: Jr. Captain

Length: 720 feet

Diameter: 118 feet

Number of Decks: 5

Number of Crew: 76

Jeep Tug - SJ

Mission: Dock and base support

Ships Named for: Animals

Commander Rank: Warrant or Master Chief

Length: 140 feet

Diameter: 46 feet

Number of Decks: 2

Number of Crew: 18

Appendix D: Union Fleet Ranks

Rank Title Insignia

O-1 Fleet Admiral* Sunburst w/ 5 Planets in orbit

** Only one Fleet Admiral authorized at present*

O-2 Admiral Sunburst w/ 2 Planets in orbit

O-3 Commodore Sunburst

O-4 Captain 4 Planets orbiting around sun

O-5 Major 3 Planets orbiting around sun

O-6 Lieutenant 2 Planets orbiting around sun

O-7 Ensign 1 Planets orbiting around sun

O-8 Cadet Officer 1 empty orbit

Note 1: *All officer insignias and tunics are Gold.*

Note 2: *Jr. Captain is any Rank serving as Commander of a ship.*

W-11 Senior Fleet Warrant 5 Planets in orbit

W-12 Fleet Warrant 3 Planets in orbit

Note 3: *All chief warrant insignias & tunics Silver*

E-13 Fleet Master Chief 2 Planets in orbit

E-14 Fleet Chief 1 Planet in orbit

E-15 Fleet First Class A Planet above

4 stripes

E-16 Fleet Sergeant A Planet above 3 stripes

E-17 Fleet Corporal A Planet above 2 stripes

E-19 Fleet Apprenticed A Planet above 1 stripe

Note 4: *All crew specialist's insignias are red.*

E-20 Fleet Cadet No insignia

Note 5: *Enlisted wear a shirt or tunic indicating specialty color. (See Appendix E)*

Solar Union Army & Marine Ranks

Rank	Title	Insignia
O-1	Commandant/Marshall*	Five Gold stars (circle)
O-2	General	Four Gold Stars
O-3	Brigadier	One Gold Star
O-4	Colonel	Gold Eagle
O-5	Major	Gold Leaf
O-7	First Lieutenant	One Gold Bars
O-9	Second Lieutenant	One Silver Bar
O-10	Cadet Officer	Empty orbit
	NOTE: All officer insignias Gold	
E-11.5	Senior Warrant	3 silver stars
E-11	Chief Warrant	2 silver stars
	NOTE: All chief warrant insignias Silver	
E-13	Sergeant Major	6 stripes (3 up 3 down)
E-14	Gunnery Sergeant	5 stripes (3 up and 2 down)
E-15	Staff Sergeant	4 stripes (3 up and 1 down)
E-16	Sergeant	3 stripes (down)
E-17	Corporal	2 stripes (down)
E-19	Private	1 stripe (down)

NOTE: All enlisted Marine stripes red - Army enlisted stripes green

E-20	Cadet	No stripes

**The Senior General of the Marines is titled Commandant, however the Senior General in The Army is titled Field Marshall of the Armies. Both are of equal rank to the Fleet Admiral in the Armed Forces of the Solar Union. There is only one authorized in each of the services, at this time.*

Appendix E: Union Fleet Uniforms and Specialists Sub-Specialties

All uniforms worn by Fleet Personal are very similar. Dress uniforms all have black or white pants, or black or white skirts for females or Kilts for men. The bottom of most pants tuck into the space boots which are very flexible to allow the person to quickly slide into a space pressure suit. The normal shipboard shirt is a tee shirt of a designated color indicating the specialty of the fleet member. Also permitted underway is a coverall with black legs and appropriate upper part colors. Dress coats are of a tunic style, which close up all the way to the neck and have a one-inch ridged collar. Rank insignias are worn on the left side of the chest, attached by clip, Velcro, or stenciled on. In full dress uniforms ribbons or medals are worn on the right side. Only one medal is worn around the neck on a ribbon 'The Medal of Honor'.

Officer and Command Uniforms

Officers of the Line	Gold Tunics or Shirts
Warrant Officers	Silver Tunics or Shirts
Enlisted Commanders	Technical Color Tunic with Gold Vest
Support Officers (i.e. Medical etc.)	Gold Tunic with Vest indicating Specialty Color

Note: *Admirals wear a gold stripe on trouser legs of dress uniform. Senior Warrants wear a silver stripe on trouser legs.*

Technical Uniform Color Designations:

Enlisted specialists wear a color tunic or shirt indicating their technical specialty.

Operations/Communications	Gray
Science / Exploration	Green
Weapons	Red
Administrative	Blue
Logistics	Yellow
Propulsion Engineering	Orange
Auxiliary Engineering	Violet
Construction	Brown
Medical / Health	White

Officer Occupational Sub-specialties

000	Warfare, Command, & Strategy
001	Astro-navigation / Communications
002	Science, Exploration, & Engineering
003	Weapons Engineering
004	Administrative /Legal
005	Logistics / Fiscal
006	Main Propulsion Engineering
007	Auxiliary Mechanical /Electrical Engineering
008	Space Repair / Construction / Civil Engineering
009	Physicians / Dentists / Physiologists

Chief Warrant Officer Occupational Sub-Specialties

00	Chief Boatswain (Bos'n)	Master Explorer
01	Chief Astro-Navigator	Master Navigator
02	Chief Scientist	Master Scientist
03	Chief Gunner	Master Weaponeer
04	Chief Yeoman	Master Yeoman
05	Chief Purser	Master Logistician
06	Chief Engineer	Master Engineer
07	Chief Machinist	Master Machinist
08	Chief Builder	Master Builder
09	Chief Nurse	Master Nurse

Enlisted Fleet Specialists

Fleet enlisted specialists have a fleet enlisted classification which includes a number and a two-digit letter code which identifies their particular specialty.

1 Operations and Communications Specialists

10	Communications Mate	OC
11	Ships Pilot/ Helm Mate	OH
12	Shuttle Pilot Mate	OP
13	Sensors Mate	OS
14	Intelligence Mate	OI
15	Chart / Astro-Navigation Mate	OA
16	Space Controller Mate	OX
17	Display Operator / Repair Mate	OD
18	Electronic Warfare Mate	OE
19	Satellite Repair /Service Mate	OV

2 Exploration and Science Specialists

2	Mission Specialists Mate	S

0		M
21	Exploration Mate	SE
22	Data Collection Mate	SD
23	Science Laboratory Mate	SL
24	Astronomy Mate	SA
25	Atmosphere Analysis Mate	SX
26	Photographer / Visual Mate	SP
27	Geological Survey Mate	SG
28	Computer Programmer Mate	SC
29	Probe Mate	SP

3. Weapons Specialists

30	Master-At-Arms / Police	WP
31	Fire Control Mate	WF
32	Missile Mate	WM
33	Mine / Bomb Ordinance Mate	WO
34	Explosive Ordnance Disposal	WE
3	Gunnery Mate	W

5		G
36	Strategic Shield Stealth Mate	WS
37	Ultrasonic Weapons Mate	WU
38	Gunsmith Mate	WH
39	Research and Development	WD

4 Administrative Specialists

40	Secretary	AS
41	Yeoman	AY
42	Data Systems Mate	AD
43	(deleted)	
44	Journalists Mate	AJ
45	Personnel Services Mate	AP
46	Legal Clerk	AL
47	Counselor Mate	AC
48	Personal Placement Mate	AX
49	Education Specialist Mate	AE

5. Logistics Specialists

50	Pay Accounting Mate	LA
51	Purchasing Clerk Mate	LP
52	Cook Mate	LC
53	Supply Mate	LS
54	Mail Postal Mate	LM
55	Laundry / Tailor Mate	LL
56	Musician Mate	LX
57	Entertainment Mate	LE
58	Barber / Beautician Mate	LB
59	Unused	

6. Main Propulsion Engineering Specialists

60	Reactor Operator Mate	PR
61	Electronic Mate	PT
62	Electrician Mate	PE
63	Rocket Engine Mate	PX

64	Engineering Laboratory Mate	PL
65	Precision Instrument Mate	PP
66	Solar Energy Cell Mate	PS
67	Ion Engine Mate	PI
68	Mass Drive Mate	PM
69	Research and Development	PD

7. Auxiliary Engineering Specialists

70	Hull Structure Repair Mate	ES
71	Damage Control Repair Mate	ED
72	Hydraulic Systems Mate	EH
73	Environmental Life Support Mate	EE
74	Water Plant Operator Mate	EW
75	Gas Systems Operator Mate	EG
76	Shuttle Repair Mate	ER
77	Launch Bay Mate	EL
78	Sanitary Controls Mate	EC
79	Pressure Suit Repair Mate	EP

8. Construction Repair Specialists

80	Solar Builder Mate	CB
81	Welder Mate	CW
82	Pipe Fitter / Plumber Mate	CP
83	Machinist Mate	CM
84	Tool & Die / Gauge Maker Mate	CG
85	Drafter / Illustrator Mate	CD
86	Optical Mate	CO
87	Solar Construction Mate	CC
88	Heavy Equipment Mate	CH
89	Telephone Interior Communications	CT

9. Medical Hospital Corpsman Specialists

90	Corpsman Nurse Mate	MN
91	Corpsman Emergency Medic Mate	ME
92	Corpsman Surgical Mate	MS
93	Corpsman NIV* Mate	MX
9	Corpsman Lab / Pathology	M

4	Mate	L
9 5	Corpsman Pharmacy Mate	M P
9 6	Preventive Medicine Mate	M E
9 7	Corpsman Dental Mate	M D
9 8	Occupational/Space Health	M O
9 9	Medic Research and Development	M R

*Non-Intrusive Visualization (X-ray, CAT scan, etc.)

ABOUT

W. H. Short

William Harry Short

I graduated from High School during the Vietnam War and enlisted in the Navy immediately upon graduation. I was trained initially as a Hospital Corpsman, but then I trained and qualified to be a first class deep sea diver then as a saturation diver. My medical specialty was diving medicine. For the next 13 years I worked as an independent duty corpsman and saturation diver. Then an opportunity came, and I changed my rate which allowed me to become a master diver.

After completing 20 years I retired as a Master Chief and a Saturation Master Diver – BMCM(MDV)(SS)(SW). While in the Navy I managed to complete college - B.S. and an M.S. I taught school for a year in Los Angles after retiring from the Navy. Worked for a major corporation SAIC for over 20 years. Taught diving and hyperbaric medicine at the College of Oceaneering which became part of National University. Then served as the Academic Dean.

I started writing in the Navy, mostly by accident - when no one else would. That led to more and more involved publications such as ships' information books, engineering specifications, technical manuals, diving safety manuals, and then little stories about the Navy. I also have written various educational support documents, such as:

curriculums, lesson plans, study guides, self-studies, etc.

Now I write novels full time. I have published eight novels, have five projects in the works; coming soon. Also, I have a list of at least twenty-five undeveloped good ideas. I always have been partial to fiction; westerns (especially historical novels), science fiction (not horror or fantasy) but futuristic themes such as space travel, and mysteries. I would like to write a non-fiction text on American history.

I use life experiences with which to blend into a story. I have been a deep-sea diver, truck driver, cook, submariner, combat veteran, health care professional, merchant seaman, ships mate, husband, father, and grandfather. I have traveled extensively around the world and have been on every continent except Antarctica.

Currently living in Fort Pierce, Florida with my wife Lorraine of over 49 years. We have 2 daughters and 4 grandchildren.

If you enjoyed this book please feel free to go on amazon.com and give a recommendation for other readers.

Other books by W. H. Short:

Non-Fiction - *Diving Dictionary*

Fiction – *'Two Weeks', 'High Ground', 'Web of Time', 'Apache Kid', 'The Nanny', 'Keep the Union Safe', 'Doc', and 'Pig Boat'.*

All available at

www.ashortnovel.com

or on amazon.com. in book or electronic kindle format.

This book is the second of three.

The previous book in this series is:

'Keep the Union Safe'.

The next book in this series is:

W. H. Short

'Keep the Peace'.

www.ingramcontent.com/pod-product-compliance
Lightning Source LLC
Chambersburg PA
CBHW052339020726
47503CB00001B/34